YUKIKAZE

CHŌHEI KAMBAYASHI

YUKIKAZE

雪風

CHŌHEI KAMBAYASHI

HAIKA
SORU

SAN FRANCISCO

YUKIKAZE

© 2002 Chōhei Kambayashi
Originally published in Japan by Hayakawa Publishing, Inc.
All rights reserved.

Cover illustration by Shoji Hasegawa
English translation © 2009 VIZ Media, LLC

HAIKASORU
Published by
VIZ Media, LLC
295 Bay Street
San Francisco, CA 94133

www.haikasoru.com

Kambayashi, Chohei, 1953-
 [Yukikaze. English]
 Yukikaze / Chohei Kambayashi ; translated by Neil Nadelman.
   p. cm.
 ISBN 978-1-4215-3255-4
 I. Title.
 PL855.A513Y8513 2010
 895.6'36--dc22   2009038793

Printed in the U.S.A.
First Printing, January 2010

CONTENTS

FOREWORD

From "The FAF and the Special Air Force"
in *The Invader*, by Lynn Jackson (15th edition)

AN OBSERVER LOOKING at historical maps of the world would soon note that in nearly every age places free from conflict are the exception, not the rule. Even today, areas of strife paint the map red, staining it with blood spilled in confrontation. The history of mankind is a record of warfare. Humans have fought against other humans and even against nature itself. This remains unchanged, the same now as it was then.

However, when comparing the current world map to the maps of the past, our theoretical observer would be able to see one red mark in the Antarctic indicating a site possessing far greater significance than any battlefield. Since it's such a small mark it's easy to overlook, and in point of fact most people these days seem to have forgotten about it. However, it is there. The site is at a point on the Ross Ice Shelf six hundred miles from Earth's south pole, at approximately longitude 170° west, and is barely a third of a mile in diameter.

This is the hyperspace corridor that we know as the "Passageway," the portal that the aliens called the "JAM" used in their attempted invasion of Earth. The Passageway looks like a gigantic spindle, with a maximum diameter of just under one and a quarter miles and a height of over six, its lower end seemingly driven right into the ice shelf. When conditions are right you can see it with the naked eye, an impossibly huge cloud of mist that resembles nothing so much as an enormous missile shot into the ground from the heavens.

It's not clear exactly how long the Passageway has been there. The human race first learned of its existence thirty years ago, when the JAM came swarming out of it to launch their first strike. Later, during our counterattack, we traveled back through the Passageway, and when the Earth Defense Force's reconnaissance units emerged on the other side they discovered a hitherto unknown world. Behind them towered the huge white cloud that pierced our world. Around them spread dense forests. To this day the planet Faery has hid its many mysteries well; we have made little progress in learning about its geography or ecosystem, or even which star system it is in.

If, say, a laser were to be fired through the Passageway from Earth, the beam would pass through cleanly, stretching into Faery's airspace as though fired from within the Passageway. The mist itself is not the Passageway but rather encloses a separate space that exists within it. It may be the result of some function of the Passageway. Or perhaps it's an illusion of sorts. The JAM, however, are not an illusion. Mankind has fought them. It fights them even now. The only difference is that the battlefield has moved from Earth to the planet Faery. The threat of the JAM is still there.

The Earth Defense Force's main combat body on the planet is the Faery Air Force, referred to more commonly as the "FAF." The FAF's units are arrayed in a roughly even distribution around the Faery terminus of the Passageway and are organized into six enormous bases: Sylvan, Brownie, Troll, Siren, Valkia, and Faery, with Faery Base acting as the general headquarters over all. As the key base there, it is by far the largest in scale.

At the current time the FAF's most powerful fighter plane is a twin-engine, all-condition tactical fighter known as the "Sylphid." It is a high-performance machine boasting advanced electronic armaments and engines that possess a multitude of improvement modifications to optimize them for the skies of

Faery. There are not that many Sylphids, owing to their high cost, but the FAF has made great advances in their production processes and is now building more of them.

Of the few original Sylphids produced, thirteen of them have been modified for tactical reconnaissance. These thirteen planes have been equipped with onboard computers that are even more highly advanced than the ones used in the ordinary fighters. This variant of Sylphid is known as the "Super Sylph," and while it looks like the other Sylphids it is a completely different beast. In essence, it's a supercomputer with wings and high-output engines.

These thirteen tactical electronic warfare and reconnaissance Sylphids have been assigned to the 5th Squadron of the FAF's Special Air Force. When you look at the official list of the FAF's corps, divisions, and units, the 5th Squadron seems to just be one unit of an airwing attached to the Tactical Combat Group of Faery Base. In reality, however, it has its own independent headquarters and exists as a corps of its own. Now, when one mentions the Special Air Force, one is in fact referring specifically to the 5th Squadron. Its formal unit designation is SAF-V; however, this is really used only in official documents. Within the Faery Air Force, it is commonly called just "the SAF."

When the FAF was formed, the SAF wasn't regarded as a particularly vital unit. However, the staff officers in the FAF command had to admit the need for more advanced and accurate tactical combat intelligence. Thus it was not by accident that the SAF, which was charged with overseeing the collection of all frontline electronic intelligence, was given these top-of-the-line Sylphids. Indeed, their existence is vital. High-velocity computers with the most advanced processing capacities are now essential to the war against the JAM: without these computers, we wouldn't be able to fight them. The central computers aboard the Super Sylphs that collect combat activity data are extremely powerful: no other fighter plane has such advanced, real-time data analysis capabilities. These onboard computers are directly interfaced with the strategic and tactical computers protected deep under Faery Base in the SAF's mission control room. In that respect it would be safe to say that the fighters are moving components of a larger, fixed supercomputer.

The SAF's digital technology is the most advanced of all the FAF combat units. And the single, overriding order of the unit is: come back alive, at any cost. The SAF's fighters greedily collect every scrap of data on the front line, record it into a combat intelligence file, and then return to base. Easily disrupted wireless transmission of the data is used only in emergencies.

The thirteen Super Sylphs attached to the unit are never launched together at the same time. Always just one, or at the very most two, sortie to follow the other aircraft. And even if their fellow fighters are being decimated, they can offer no support; they must simply collect the combat intelligence and return to base. To see this duty through, the Super Sylph is equipped with external fuel tanks and an early warning radar system as good as a reconnaissance aircraft's, all to protect itself and the data files it carries. And for that one purpose, it also carries powerful weaponry.

Given the psychological strain of having to watch their comrades die while still remaining emotionally disengaged, the pilots who perform this duty need hearts as cold as a computer. The pilots of the SAF evidently take a certain satisfaction in this requirement, and individuals with "special" personalities outside the range of normal human standards are selected for this duty. These men put more faith in their machines than in other people and can fly their planes with perfect skill. In a way, they are yet one more combat computer, but organic in nature, loaded aboard the Sylphids to carry out a heartless duty.

These soldiers are of various nationalities and backgrounds. We do not know much about them, as the FAF will not release to the public the personal data files that record their pasts. What we do know is that what's necessary to the SAF is not that these men and women have past combat experience but rather that they be machines that are, through some accident of fate, in human form.

The current war with the JAM demands such individuals. And lately, I've begun to think that it was this—the creation of inhuman humans—that may have been the JAM's primary objective. Even if it isn't, if these are the characteristics and abilities needed by the SAF to fight the JAM, I imagine we will be seeing more and more of this kind of soldier as the war with the JAM drags on. And that in itself is a threat to the human race.

THE JAM ARE no longer on Earth. Their invasion has been held at bay on the planet Faery, on the other side of the Passageway. The Passageway is so small and the war on Faery so distant and removed from day-to-day life that the JAM threat has been almost forgotten in the current international situation. People nowadays regard the war between the FAF and the JAM as they do the fairy-tale battles in children's picture books. But Earth is still being targeted by the JAM. The threat has not vanished. The JAM may be developing plans for a second major invasion. Or perhaps they have prepared an indirect strategy that is unfolding at this very moment.

The true nature of the alien JAM remains a mystery to us. We don't understand how they think, and by the time we finally figure it out, it may be too late. We cannot forget about them. The fight against them is nothing like previous wars between humans. They are a reality that threatens all of mankind.

I

THE SKIES WHERE
FAIRIES DANCE

He had loved many things in his life and had been betrayed by most of them. Now, they only fed his hatred. When the woman he loved finally left him too, he was utterly alone. Now, only one thing gave his heart strength. A delicate, unspeaking machine that would never, ever betray him. A soaring fairy. A Sylphid. Yukikaze.

TWENTY-FOUR ASSAULT fighter planes in combat formation punched their way through the skies toward an enemy base. They were units attached to the Faery Air Force's Tactical Frontline Base TAB-16, 1666th Tactical Combat Group, 666th Tactical Fighter Squadron. Beneath them, a brilliant white desert drew near.

It was a dry, desolate region. Rain clouds couldn't make it across the bordering mountain range, and even what moisture the air could retain was greedily absorbed by the immense forests and countless forest creatures inhabiting the skirts of the mountains. As a result, the winds blowing through the forests emerged parched and dry. But for a very short time each spring, the vast amount of water released by the snowmelt on the mountains was more than even the forest could drink, and it seeped into the desert environs via underground rivers.

It was spring, and from the sky one could see veins of water soaking into the sands. The edge of the desert was stained a light purple by the stubby, rugged plants that were now sprouting there. The new buds, glossy and metallic, sparkled brightly with reflected sunlight. Since the vegetation further into the desert grew more slowly than that toward the edge, the boundary between the desert interior and this purplish grassland was demarcated by a glittering line formed by the young plants. The entire effect suggested a ghostly field of purple flame advancing across the sugar-white sands.

Hidden in the purple grassland were the enemy interceptors. When the 666th fighters' early warning systems detected the enemy aircraft the strike leader barked out his commands.

"Small JAM interceptors. The vertical-launch types are taking off. These guys are decoys. Alpha, Bravo, Charlie, take them. Everyone else, climb now! Combat climb!"

From the grass rose the black JAM fighters. Three of them, four, then five, their boosters spitting out long tails of flame. The planes of the 666th TFS split into two flights, one going into a power dive while the other began to climb at high speed. From above them, a swarm of JAM interceptors dove into their attack.

At the moment that the black JAM aircraft and the gray fighters of the 666th closed in battle, a formation of strike bombers from Faery Base's Tactical Combat Group penetrated the JAM defense line, flying on the deck at supersonic speed. The camouflaged buildings of the JAM supply base could not be visually distinguished from the sand dunes they squatted in, but they couldn't escape the passive sensors of the planes' ground-attack systems.

Just before reaching the base the bombers climbed sharply, their objectives locked on in their targeting systems. With the data now acquired and fed to their air-to-ground missiles, the bombers commenced another ultra-low altitude attack run. As soon as they were within range they released their missiles and withdrew, with the tactical fighters providing cover.

The battle was over. The 666th retook their formation and streaked away from the desert. There were four empty spaces in the formation now, four planes that were not coming back. The 666th strike leader did not know how his subordinates had fought or how they died. Their battle had taken place out of his sight.

However, it had not gone unwitnessed. There was one tactical combat and surveillance aircraft whose job it was to monitor the entire battle without engaging in it: Special Air Force Unit 3, attached to Faery Base. The model of plane was a Sylphid, its name, Yukikaze.

The strike leader didn't know what was in Yukikaze's combat data file, but he knew it had recorded the particulars of the battle fought by the planes of the 666th TFS that had fallen to the JAM.

None of the pilots had managed to eject. Four pilots and their beloved aircraft had been lost, scattered across the skies of Faery. Yukikaze's pilot, Second Lieutenant Rei Fukai, conveyed this information to the squadron with no more emotion in his voice than if he were reading a string of numbers.

"No survivors of downed planes. This is Yukikaze. Mission complete. Returning to base."

The strike leader watched silently as the combat surveillance fighter flew off over the 666th formation after delivering the news of his subordinates' deaths. Yukikaze glittered in the light, then ignited its afterburners and climbed quickly, vanishing into the higher altitudes of the sky where night was drawing near. "Goddamned angel of death," he muttered to himself.

Yukikaze's pilot had stood by silently as the other pilots died, keeping well away from the combat airspace and not actively supporting any of the other planes. He offered no help and issued no warnings. Those were the tasks of the tactical control unit, not his. Don't engage, just gather information and get it back to base, no matter what. Those were his orders. The 666th leader knew this full well, and yet he still couldn't help but wonder: if that powerful, high-performance aircraft had joined in the battle, would his subordinates still be alive? He also wondered about the man who piloted that plane. *Anyone who can just sit by and calmly watch his comrades getting killed isn't human,* he thought. The mysterious pilot always just watched and then flew back home, like a boomerang that never hit its target.

"Useless bastard," the 666th leader growled, then issued the order to return to TAB-16. As the squadron made its way back no one exchanged a word.

YUKIKAZE FLEW TOWARD Faery Base, supercruising at an altitude of 98,000 feet. It flew alone.

Second Lieutenant Rei Fukai looked out of the cockpit at the dark blue sky spread out around him. Night was coming on and he could see the first stars. Below him, the planet Faery was ablaze with twilight colors. Soon it would match the color of the sky. Faery's binary suns glowed crimson above the horizon, their mutual gravitational attraction pulling them into flattened elliptical shapes. A jet of dark red gas could clearly be seen spouting out of one of them. It arced up to the sky's zenith, looking for all the world like the Milky Way, but instead of a pearly white it was a red suggestive of the color of blood. This enormous whirlpool of erupting gas formed what looked like a bloodstained path, and so it had been named the "Bloody Road."

Rei set the cockpit illumination to its lowest level and lifted his gaze from the instrumentation. Nothing was out of the ordinary. It was quiet. He thought back to the battle just fought by the 666th TFS.

"Delta 4, engage. Break right. Right. Starboard."

"This is Delta 4, I can't see them."

"They've spiked you! Look out!"

"Where's the JAM?! I can't see it on my radar!"

Delta 4 had broken into a hard-right diving turn but couldn't shake the JAM fighter.

A pilot who couldn't control his plane perfectly was a dead man. To Rei, that was the natural order of things. Emotions had no place in battle. A fighter plane feels nothing, and a pilot is a part of the plane. Therefore, a pilot who couldn't set aside his emotions and become one with his plane was no warrior. And with someone like that piloting it, even a high-performance fighter would be no match for the enemy. And then that fighter would be—

Yukikaze's wide-area radar warning receiver chimed an alert.

"What's up?" Rei asked his backseater, the electronic warfare officer. "Verify that."

"Not sure," the other man replied. "The passive warning

system's activated, but I can't track the location. It could be a bogey."

"A bogey?" asked Rei. "Then… It's gotta be a JAM. Find it." Saying that, he switched on the fire control system and set the radar to long-range, moving target auto-search mode. The target was entering radar range.

"Target sighted," the EWO called out. "It's small. A fighter. Pretty fast. Speed is two-point-nine and he's nose-on. We should merge in approximately two minutes."

Rei checked the moving target indicator. Was the other craft a hostile? A friendly? But the MTI's display simply showed it as **UNKNOWN.**

"What is it?" Rei asked.

"Negative on the IFF." If there was no response on the Identification, Friend or Foe system, then…

"It's a hostile," said Rei.

He entered the unknown craft into his tactical computer as an enemy. The system automatically adjusted the radar search pattern, frequency, power output, and pulse width to their optimal efficiency and tracked the target.

"Hey, Boss?" said the EWO. "We should confirm this first. It might be a friendly. Maybe their IFF's off-line. I doubt any JAM would be flying around here."

The unknown plane was closing fast, its course unwavering, on a straight line for Yukikaze. *Like a giant bullet*, thought Rei.

"Lieutenant, take evasive action."

In response to the rapidly approaching target, the tactical computer switched the radar mode to super search and automatically locked on to the target.

"Okay, let's reconfirm this. What is that thing? Contact them on the emergency channel."

"I'm trying, but there's no response. Looks like their communications equipment is out."

Yukikaze turned ninety degrees and dived. The unknown plane climbed rapidly, opening from them. However, Rei could still easily track it: Yukikaze was equipped with a powerful, omni-directional pulse Doppler radar that could accurately detect the target and display its location, velocity, and acceleration data on the MTI.

The target banked steeply and began to dive toward Yukikaze at high speed.

"He's a hostile," said Rei. "I'm engaging."

"It's not a JAM!"

"How do you know that?"

As Yukikaze pulled a sudden high-G evasive turn, from his seat in the rear the EWO caught sight of the unknown craft nipping at their heels. It was about half a mile away, a large fighter plane glittering in the light of the setting suns. Via the digital camera in their tactical reconnaissance pod he could make out the distinctive, sharply pointed twin vertical stabilizers on its back.

"You see that, Lieutenant Fukai?" he called out over the com. "That's a Sylph. A Sylphid."

"A Sylph? Who's it attached to?"

"Unknown."

Rei loosened his turn radius and craned his neck back to look in the direction his partner indicated. The other craft was closing on them. It was definitely the same model of plane as Yukikaze. It was now initiating a high-G turn to try and come around to their twelve o'clock. Rei rechecked the IFF. **UNKNOWN** was Yukikaze's reply. Then, detecting the waves of enemy targeting radar, it signaled that the unknown plane was preparing to attack.

Rei set the master arm switch to ARM. The stores control panel displayed his onboard armaments. **RDY GUN, RDY AAM III-4**. Their antiaircraft gun and four short-range air-to-air missiles. He had no long-range missiles to fire.

"I'm shooting it down," said Rei as he hit the dogfight switch.

"Stop! It's not an enemy! That's a Sylph!"

Before his EWO could finish speaking, Rei banked Yukikaze

steeply, then burned into a combat climb to face his target, performing a 180 degree head-on snap-up as he prepared to attack. The radar switched to boresight mode. He squeezed the trigger. The antiaircraft cannon fired a burst. No hit. The unknown plane had evaded him. He turned again, maneuvered to about half a mile behind it and attacked from the rear. The remaining ammo indicator now read zero. Still no hits.

"Have you lost you mind, Lieutenant Fukai?!"

The unknown dived to the right, with Yukikaze in pursuit. It went into a six-G turn to try and come around to Yukikaze's rear, but Rei pulled six-and-one-half Gs at the maximum angle of attack and closed to a range of less than a quarter mile.

He now could see the unknown clearly with his own eyes. It was a Sylphid. But he didn't abort his attack. His IFF couldn't determine if the unknown aircraft was a friendly or not, and as far as Rei was concerned, if it wasn't a friendly, it was a hostile. Yukikaze's central computer wasn't canceling its warning, and the unknown was still preparing to attack. If he had hesitated while wondering if it was friendly or not, Yukikaze would already have been shot down. Although his eyes told him that the other plane was an FAF fighter, it had to be a JAM. He was certain of this. It was a formidable enemy too, as fast and maneuverable as Yukikaze.

Rei pressed the missile release button. There was no launch. The fire control system readout on his head-up display was warning him that the target was too close. The FCS had calculated the relative velocities of the unknown aircraft and Yukikaze, and had used those figures to determine the minimum safety range for the short-range missiles. It had come up with a value of 1,400 feet; firing a missile any closer than that would endanger the plane that launched it.

Rei pushed the missile release button again and held it down, commanding the central computer to ignore the FCS's warning and execute an emergency attack. If he missed this chance, they could be killed in the next instant. The central computer issued the order to attack, and the subordinate tactical computer then overrode the FCS and cleared the minimum mode from the missile seeker's armament control. In that instant, the missile was launched from Yukikaze's belly.

The range was less than 1,200 feet. Yukikaze withdrew quickly, but the unknown executed a sudden Split S maneuver and moved in on a collision course with Yukikaze, as though intending to lead the missile back toward it. The missile banked steeply, thrusting toward the unknown, and barely slipped in on its right.

Yukikaze was now less than 700 feet away. The FCS had been transmitting guidance data to the missile, but sensing the new danger it cancelled the guidance control. The cut-off of guidance data from Yukikaze and the change in the Doppler frequency should have locked up the missile's detonator. A comparison of the Doppler shift of Yukikaze's radar pulse to the pulse reflected back from the target would cause the missile to detect that it was at the minimum Doppler gate when it was at its closest distance to the target, resulting in a detonation system abort. However, its optical sensor fuse still detected the target and activated the thermal battery, which then issued its signal.

The missile detonated. Barely three seconds had passed from its initial launch. The explosion blew apart the right main wing of the unknown plane. Fragments rocketed in every direction.

A piece of the missile's shrapnel hit Yukikaze. It happened in an instant, penetrating the canopy and striking Rei directly in the forehead, smashing into his helmet visor. The pain was intense, and he let out a groan.

"Lieutenant, both engines are out! Flight control's messed up, too."

Yukikaze rolled lazily and began to go down, spinning.

Rei put his hand to the wound, staining his flight glove with blood. If the explosion had happened any closer, the shrapnel probably would have punched its way into his head and torn it off. He felt no fear, though. There was no time for fear. Yukikaze was falling.

"We have to punch out!"

"Wait… I can't leave Yukikaze."

The blood was streaming from him now. The right side of his head and his right shoulder ached.

"The engines are gone. It's no use!"

"Don't panic. There's no way Yukikaze's going to crash."

"Lieutenant!"

"The turbines are spinning. I can airstart the engines."

"It's too risky to waste time trying for a restart!"

Yukikaze was now roughly level, and the EWO wasn't going to let this chance slip away. He made sure the command lever was set to eject only the rear seat and then quickly yanked it. The canopy blew off the plane, followed by the rear ejection seat. The shock of it sent Yukikaze back into a tailspin.

Rei checked his altitude. The cold stabbed at him, the wind howling in his ears. He still had enough altitude to try for an airstart. The engine burner pressure was low. He tried the auto-restart switch, but there was no response. The low-voltage generator wasn't giving him enough electrical power. There wasn't enough time to activate the jet fuel starter, and he feared that using the secondary power unit would kill his computer systems completely.

The right engine was now burning. Fuel transfer to it was automatically cut off. Rei checked the turbine revs indicator, then pushed Yukikaze into a dive. She eagerly nosed down, as though intending to fly straight into the ground.

The increased airflow spun the turbine blades faster, and the generator circuits came back to life. Rei hit the airstart button. The engine ignition system activated and the ignition exciter spark plug flared. The airstart lamp was now lit. Yukikaze plummeted. The left engine came back to life. The turbine intake temperature rose. The revolutions increased. Cutting off the ignition operation, Rei gripped the side stick. Yukikaze climbed quickly, still spinning. He focused all his attention on the side stick, executing a sudden roll to the opposite side to arrest the spin.

The flight control's failed, he thought. He worked the stick cautiously. They were no longer rolling, but now Yukikaze was beginning to fall backwards. He nudged the plane into a gentle roll to try and level it. Suddenly, Yukikaze began rising quickly, bucking like a wild horse. Rei was feeling tired now. There was no time to check the gauges to determine exactly what was out of order. Without the canopy's protection the cockpit was freezing, and the wind pressure kept him from seeing clearly. His arm was numb. Yukikaze began to buck harder.

A signal indicated a fault in the flight computer system. Of the five high-velocity parallel processing computers that analyzed his flight data, three were now completely off-line. Of the two remaining, one wasn't working properly, and it was unclear which of them had the fault. Because the calculations they came up with didn't agree, the central computer had cut off the entire flight computer system. It entered the signal for control of the wings via the direct control assembly.

Rei saw this at the top of his display, and the cause of Yukikaze's wild flight suddenly became clear to him. He loosened his grip on the stick and switched on the autopilot. Yukikaze's violent shuddering immediately ceased.

Rei himself had been the cause of Yukikaze's strange behavior. The injury he had sustained had left him with almost no sensation in his right arm. Yukikaze had been just faithfully following the input from the side stick even though Rei was exerting much more force on it than he should have been. The stick was pressure sensitive: every control surface on it responded to the way the pilot changed the grip of his right hand. The stick itself was immobile—there was no need for motion since it was pressure sensitive—and so under the correct conditions it could execute a pilot's will with lightning speed. Now, the lack of sensation and the pain of his injured arm had caused Rei to accidentally send it the wrong instructions.

He adjusted the altitude on the autopilot, inputting a ground-relative setting of 1,100 feet. Yukikaze began to descend, her radar altimeter monitoring the distance. By the time the pressure altimeter read 4,000 feet above sea level, the fighter was flying roughly level. They were over an area of low mountains, and as Yukikaze flew she followed the soft vertical undulations of the landscape. Rei set the radar to real beam ground mapping mode and activated the forward surveillance system.

"Let's go home, Yukikaze."

The data for their return course had been lost. With his EWO gone, Rei had to work out his plane's position himself with the help of the central computer. The navigation computer linked up with high-altitude support satellites, and the central computer used the data to calculate their current position. He flipped the auto-maneuver switch to ON and the tactical computer initiated guidance, with Faery Base as the objective.

Yukikaze was now locked in enemy auto-search, a mode where in the event of enemy contact she would automatically attack any opponents, fly to a position above the objective, and then bomb it. Fortunately, since she wasn't carrying any bombs at the moment, there was no danger of inadvertently bombing the base.

Rei could have flown back to base via autopilot alone, but if they met any other enemies on the way he wouldn't have the strength to fight them. Sticky, clotted blood had already dried his right eye shut, and the wind pressure was keeping him from opening his left eye all the way. His helmet visor was too damaged from the impact to deploy. So he input the target data into his tactical computer—he could do that using just his left fingertip—and sat back in his seat.

Tactical operations were easier than inputting coordinates into an autopilot. Rei was a warrior, not a navigator. He set the head-up display to its brightest level. Normally, it would be set to its lowest level for nighttime combat, to allow his eyes to adjust to the darkness, but right now he needed it that bright just to be able to see it. The steering cue marker above the HUD showed a straight line toward Faery Base.

Subsonic speed. Flying on one engine. Bleeding heavily. It took him barely thirty minutes to reach the skies over the base, but he was half unconscious by that point. He heard Yukikaze signal to him that they were over the target as though from a great distance.

"B-3, report. Say your status."

"Mayday… Can you read me? I'm in bombing mode… Is this Faery Base?"

"Affirmative. How long are you planning to circle over us?"

"I'm bringing her down now. Emergency landing. I'm wounded. Can't see clearly."

"Can you still land?"

"I'm bringing Yukikaze down in one piece, even if it kills me. I'm coming down. Give me ALS guidance."

Auto-maneuver switch, OFF. Auto-landing system, activated. Auto-throttle control and direct lift control, activated. Yukikaze went into final approach. Gear down and locked.

The suns had set, and Rei knew that Faery Base had to be brightly lit, but he couldn't see it. He tasted blood. *Like a Bloody Mary*, he thought. A little salty. He felt drunk, his mind fading in and out.

Touchdown. Auto-brake. Speed brakes extended to full. *Better landing than I can do,* Rei thought, just before he lost consciousness completely, breathing in the night scents of Faery.

A SKY FAIRY, a sylph, was flying. It soared on glittering, translucent wings, scattering golden particles of light as it went, flaxen hair fluttering behind it. White skin, almond-shaped silver eyes, red lips engraved with an odd smile. Gently curving breasts without nipples, taut thighs, long, slender legs.

A sylph, a fairy of the wind. It flew freely through the skies, rising upon gentle breezes, churning up fierce gales.

The sylph bent both knees at right angles, its lower legs quickly tapering off to knifelike vertical points. It reached its arms back and grasped its wings, which angled back and turned opaque. Its head elongated and darkened to gray.

Large thrust engines ignited. A Sylphid. Twin vertical stabilizers. Clipped delta wings. Underneath the canopy sill was its name. Small, written in kanji characters. Yukikaze.

It flew at supersonic speed, its shock wave mowing down the forests of Faery.

It was Yukikaze. Rei was watching Yukikaze fly. He was in the cockpit. But then, who was he now watching this? Yukikaze turned and approached him. Rei looked at the cockpit. There was nobody in it.

Yukikaze flew away faster than the speed of sound and vanished into the empty sky.

Yukikaze. Yukikaze, where are you going? Are you deserting me?

"YUKIKAZE..."

"Are you awake?"

Rei opened his eyes. He was covered in sweat. The pain of reality. A bandage was wound around his head. From his right eye, he saw only blackness.

"My eye... My right eye!"

"Calm down."

The Faery Base military doctor held down Rei's shoulders as he tried to get up.

"It's not that bad a wound, but it's a miracle you didn't lose your sight in that eye. Some fragments of your helmet visor were embedded in your right temple. If it'd been a little worse, you probably never would have flown again. You're a lucky man."

"What about Yukikaze? How damaged is she?"

"Your beloved plane? Well, I don't treat fighters, so I wouldn't know about that. Just get some rest, and then you can get out of bed and go check yourself. The vice-commander of the SAF is calling for you, by the way. She wants you to report to her."

"General Cooley? That old bitch. If I was dead, she'd probably have me dug up out of my grave to report to her."

"They're thinking of court-martialing you."

"For what?"

"Were you on drugs?"

"Of course not. You can't fly when you're fucked up."

The doctor gave him a look full of doubt, and then shrugged.

"Well, you were sent to Faery because you're guilty of something. But I'm not going to pass judgment on you. Just keep quiet and do what you're told, and in two or three years your tour of duty will be up. If you want to get back to Earth faster, don't go causing trouble."

"Look. First of all, to me Earth's just a big ball of water filled with a lot of bitter memories. Second, what do you mean if I want to get back sooner I should keep quiet? You saying I should just shut up and let the JAM kill me? Screw that. You either kill or get killed out there."

Now the doctor's expression shifted to one of active disdain.

"Is that how you lived back on Earth?"

"My past is none of your goddamned business."

"I figure a normal person would want to get away from the battlefield as soon as possible. But there seem to be more and more of your kind lately. The soldiers of the Special Air Force really are 'special,' aren't they? Have you ever read *The Invader*, by Lynn Jackson? She predicted an increase in the number of people like you. That there'd be a problem once there weren't enough wars waged on Earth. She also talks about how the nations all disagreed on how to control the Passageway. So the countries that weren't military superpowers on Earth passed the Space Heavenly Body Treaty to try and prevent the superpowers from monopolizing control of it."

"'The Space Heavenly Body Treaty'? Is there even such a thing?"

"It was around long before we ever discovered Faery. 'The general principles limiting national activities regarding the exploration and exploitation of the Moon and any other heavenly bodies comprising space.' In the end, the United Nations established the Earth Defense Force as an independent entity, which led to the establishment of the Faery Air Force. Members don't advocate any one-sided ideologies and it has none. It just requires you to be human. The FAF is now a truly supranational group. Its reputation is good, but the truth is that the quality of its members has been gradually dropping as nations use it as a dumping ground to get rid of their criminals and malcontents. The FAF is like humanity's garbage dump. A prison annex. I figured it out before that you weren't just a normal criminal. I can tell just by looking at you. That there must be some other reason why you're such a coldhearted, inhuman killer. You're like a machine."

Rei had begun to tune out during the doctor's lecture, distracted by the throbbing pain in his head, but a surge of irritation brought him back.

"You're the same, aren't you? You were sent to Faery too."

"I chose to come here for research. I'm not like you. I didn't choose to join the FAF because I'd committed a crime and didn't want to go to prison. Let me ask you: you were trained to be a fighter pilot using conditioned response through a direct neural interface, weren't you?"

"Yeah."

"I wish I could have seen what your personality data was like before they did it. I'd like to know if your current personality was caused by the training destroying your previous one or not."

Anger was now burning in the pit of Rei's stomach.

"And what would you do if you knew? Claim that I'm inhuman? Humanity has nothing to do with fighting the JAM, because *they're* not human."

"That's true. But I wasn't saying it was a question of one's humanity."

"Didn't you go through the training, too?"

"No. I don't fly a fighter."

"But you're a lot like me, aren't you? You only value what you're interested in and couldn't care less about anything else. This isn't some aftereffect of my training. I haven't changed at all. I hate anything that can't do the job, whether it's a human or a machine. And I've had enough of you. Let me see my data from the medical computer. My chart. I'll let the computer decide if I can leave or not. I'm done with you. Get out. You're pissing me off."

Rei got up off the bed and undid the bandage around his head. He touched the wound. Just as the doctor had said, it didn't seem very deep. He tried to open his right eye, then squeezed it shut when the bright light hit it. The wound opened up and began oozing blood. The doctor left the room without a word. Rei did not rewind the bandage and instead just pressed the wadded-up mass to the wound.

A nurse arrived and made a fuss over his undone bandage. As she was getting ready to rewind it, Rei brushed her off and demanded that she just put an adhesive over the wound. She did what he told her to do.

PEOPLE WERE ALWAYS asking him, "What were you thinking?" or "Why did you do that?" And that was what the uniformed military court-martial judge asked him too.

"Why did you shoot down an ally aircraft, Lieutenant Fukai?"

"It was a JAM."

"Your gun camera took pictures of a Sylphid."

"It was a JAM. It wasn't responding to me. The IFF read it as an unknown, and I made a decision."

"Yukikaze's transponder was working properly," said General Cooley, who was acting as his defense. "No abnormality in its function was found."

"The other plane's IFF or communications equipment may have been nonfunctional," said the judge.

"If I hadn't attacked it, I would have died," replied Rei shortly. "It may not have been identified as a hostile, but it wasn't a friendly either. And that makes it an enemy."

"But it was clearly a Sylphid. Don't you trust your own eyes, Lieutenant Fukai? You made visual contact with that Sylph, didn't you?"

"The way that you trust your own eyes is the way that I trust the warnings Yukikaze gives me. That's exactly why I've managed to stay alive so far."

"I have a request to make as defense counsel," said General Cooley, pushing the powerful glasses she wore for nearsightedness up with her index finger as she spoke. "I'd like to find out which unit the plane in question was attached to."

"That's right," Rei said, nodding. "I don't recall seeing any unit insignia or personal marks on it. At the very least, it wasn't a fighter from Boomerang Squadron."

"It may have been a unit with the Aerospace Defense or Defense Reconnaissance air groups."

"A strategic recon Sylph would have had a ramjet booster attached for greater speed, and it would've been flying angels above me, at 140,000 feet at least. And it wouldn't have attacked me either."

"You were attacked?"

Rei pointed at the dressing on his forehead. "This is a combat injury."

"Caused by Yukikaze's own missile, I believe."

"If I hadn't fired, I would have been shot down. Wait a minute, what about my EWO? The second lieutenant who was assigned to me. Why don't you ask him?"

"He's dead," answered the judge after a brief pause. "Killed by one of the native reptiles."

"I warned him. If I hadn't gotten the engines restarted, I would have ended up just the same."

"It looks like his parachute got fouled in a tree and he was attacked from below during the search and rescue..." The judge trailed off, then resumed. "I recognize the validity of the defense counsel's request. We'll adjourn for today. Lieutenant Fukai is restricted from operational activities and confined to quarters."

There was no stockade on Faery. Anyone guilty of a crime that didn't rate the death penalty was shipped back to Earth for imprisonment.

The punishment for a second offense varied according to the individual's national origin, but if you were lucky you'd have only attempted escape added to the original criminal sentence. If you were unlucky, you'd face the death penalty with no chance for appeal. Rei wondered what Japan's policy was, then took a deep breath; thinking about his homeland brought with it the usual associated irritation.

As he exited the temporary preliminary courtroom—which most of the time was known as Tactical Combat Group Conference Room #7—Rei was stopped by General Cooley.

"Do you want to smash my face in right now, First Lieutenant?" she asked in a chiding tone of voice.

"I must be going deaf," he replied. "Did you just say 'first lieutenant'?"

"I did—but on the assumption that you're innocent. However, I am glad that you made it back here in one piece."

I'm not surprised the general's glad, Rei thought. The Sylphid was an extremely expensive piece of FAF property.

"What're you going to do with me while we wait for the preliminary court to hand down its verdict? Probably confine me to quarters, right?"

"You are ordered to assist Major Booker."

"Be Jack's aide? I expected some kind of ground duty, but aren't I restricted from all operational activities?"

"There's something the major has to take care of that's been driving him crazy, and it has nothing to do with the war against the JAM. You'll get the details when you see him. That is all. Any questions?"

"None." They saluted.

BEFORE GOING TO see Major James Booker, the only man whom Rei could call a friend, he went back to the air force hospital to get his bandage changed. Although the SAF had its own medical facilities, Rei had been taken to the main base hospital for his treatment. After receiving confirmation from the computer there that his injury wasn't getting worse, he headed to 5th Squadron's quarters.

Faery Base was underground.

The base was the general headquarters for all the forces on the planet, and the importance of its role was reflected in its massive size. Buildings containing the residences that countless people returned to at night as well as military operational facilities had been constructed within an absurdly large underground cavern. Walking its streets, one would perceive no difference between Faery Base and an aboveground city on Earth: the sky seen between the gaps in the buildings was always bright and clear. Most of the time, the inhabitants would forget that the sky they were looking at was artificial. But occasionally showers of groundwater would rain down from this clear sky, and they would look up and think how strange it was for there to be rain when the sky was blue, and then be reminded that it wasn't a real sky they were looking at after all.

Boomerang Squadron was located at a bit of a remove from the base's center. The other squadrons had been given generous arrangements in consideration of their need to scramble quickly, but the Super Sylphs were boxed in a cramped hangar that resembled the below-decks of an aircraft carrier. The hangar was where Rei was headed now. He'd heard from the general that Yukikaze was being brought back from the factory and that he'd be able to see her there if he was lucky.

The sight of ten Super Sylphs arranged with their noses all in a row was something to behold. The ceiling was low—just under twenty-five feet high, leaving barely a yard of clearance between it and the Sylphs' vertical stabilizers—which made the hangar feel even more cramped. And although it was nearly 1,000 feet long, it could house only sixteen planes with a space of barely ten feet between their wingtips.

The Super Sylph was a giant among fairies.

The hangar's top floor was for maintenance and launch preparation. As long as the damage wasn't too severe, a plane would receive its repairs up there, and most of the parts had been designed to be interchangeable between units. However, it wasn't enough for Yukikaze this time; she'd had to be taken to the air force factory, a facility that had the capacity to produce entirely new planes.

Yukikaze had already been returned to the spot reserved for Unit 3. As luck would have it, Major Booker was there too. He was seated in Yukikaze's cockpit inspecting her electronics, holding in one hand a thick sheaf of paper that looked to be a maintenance report. Rei walked around the plane, side-stepped a fat external power cable hanging from the fuselage's underbelly, then crossed under to the left side and climbed the boarding ladder. Hanging on to a grip with his right hand, Rei raised his left in a salute.

"First Lieutenant Fukai, reporting for duty as your aide, Major Booker. Hey, Jack."

"You all right, Rei—wait, did you say first lieutenant? Congrats on that."

Booker told Rei to wait for him down below. He didn't take long to complete his inspection of Yukikaze, only another fifteen minutes or so, then came down and handed the paperwork to Rei. It was a written report detailing every aspect of the repair, servicing, and refitting of the plane. The major folded up the boarding ladder and stowed it in the fuselage, then detached the comm headset and replaced it in a storage compartment in the floor.

"She may look the same, but she's been made even better. The airborne weapons control set, the gun control unit, the central air data computer, the digital data link, the standby compass, et cetera, et cetera, et cetera. We're doing a power test tomorrow, and no, you can't do it. I'd be shot if I let you. I practically feel like I'm standing in front of the wall right now."

"Sorry if I caused you trouble."

"That's not what I meant."

Major Booker frowned, which briefly made the scar that lined his cheek more prominent. There was a certain air of menace to him. It was rumored he'd murdered someone back on Earth and had been sent to Faery for it, but nobody had ever dared ask him about it to his face.

Rei knew the major better than anyone else, so he knew that the man was full of surprises. For example, Booker knew even more about Japan than Rei did. The expertly painted calligraphy below the cockpit that spelled out "Yukikaze" in kanji characters had been the work of the major's brush. It was so artistically stylized that even Rei had trouble reading them, but it was beautiful. And Rei also knew that Booker's past was the opposite of what his face implied. After his initial tour of duty ended he had continued to serve by choice and had been on Faery for a long time now. He'd once been a fighter pilot but was now mainly in charge of aircraft maintenance and duty scheduling. Since pissing him off could result in losing leave time, Rei had initially kept a respectful distance from him.

Then one day, out of the blue, this strange major asked him if he believed in God. Rei wasn't sure if it was a joke, or a test, or if he was just being hazed. When he decided to do the most prudent thing and stay silent, he got punched. There was an unwritten rule acknowledged by everyone in the FAF that ignoring rank was acceptable once you were back on the ground, so the major probably would have let it pass if Rei had punched him back. But Rei hadn't done that. He didn't turn the other cheek either, but simply licked the blood away and went back to reading the equipment inspection chart he had been studying. "I see," said the major. "You're like me, then." Rei had hung out with him ever since.

"You said you were my new aide? Dammit, if you don't learn to get along with the guys at the top, you're gonna make trouble for us poor sods down below. Did Old Lady Cooley tell you anything about this job? Never mind, let's head upstairs. We can talk once we're up there."

The two men rode a small, human-use elevator to the upper floors and entered the squadron's private briefing room, the most notable feature of which was a broad expanse of window that looked out over the maintenance bay. No sorties were scheduled, so nobody was in it. It was a narrow room, but with a high ceiling and an open layout designed for a good field of vision. There was a lounge nearby that was nicer and also had a higher than usual ceiling, but the soldiers of Boomerang Squadron preferred this unassuming room. They treated it as their own, and various personal belongings and hobby items were left scattered around it: books on philosophy, trashy magazines, an abstract painting sitting on an easel, a box full of electronic parts, even a basket full of knitting. Major Booker picked up a curved piece of wood that was leaning against the wall and stroked it idly as he sat down.

"So...first lieutenant?"

"It's not decided yet," Rei replied as he placed a paper cup under the spout of the coffee maker. "Anyway, it's not that big of a deal."

There weren't any enlisted soldiers on all of Faery: all personnel were commissioned officers. Once they had completed their training on Earth and were deployed to Faery for active duty, they were given the rank of second lieutenant. It may have been a ploy designed to improve the reputation of the FAF on the outside, but the result had been the historically unprecedented creation of an army consisting entirely of officers and not a single rank-and-file soldier. Fully half of them were second lieutenants. Effectively they played the same role as enlisted soldiers, but they had the power of numbers behind them, and it was from this that the dynamic arose for people to treat each other equally when they were on the ground. (Combat time, however, was a separate matter.) It was a convenient system, and there wasn't a person on Faery who opposed it.

This system applied to everyone, from the command staff on down to the girls working the streets in the red-light districts. Prostitution had been decriminalized on Faery, and so the women had volunteered to come there and work for the military. Like any other segment of the armed forces, they had their own fixed hierarchy of ranks and pay grades. They didn't wear uniforms and of course bore no insignia on their dresses, but you could generally tell who was higher ranked by the amount of makeup on their faces: the older and more accomplished they were, the less they wore. The women also possessed a strong sense of professional pride.

If one didn't want to use the services of the military prostitutes there were plenty of other potential partners for romance, since there were about an equal number of women as men in the uniformed ranks. But "romance" perhaps was not the best term to describe these relationships, and the women were a tough lot. At least once a year a man would be shot in the name of "legitimate self-defense."

"Anyway," Major Booker continued, "the salary bump is nice. Back when I first got here, I couldn't even afford to get drunk after the alimony payments to my ex."

Rei thought the major's wife might be Japanese but kept that speculation to himself.

"Here," Rei said, setting down a cup of coffee. "You finished making the perfect boomerang there?"

"Thanks. No. And perfection isn't necessarily something to be desired. This scar on my cheek is proof of that... Anyway, it doesn't matter. The truth is, General Cooley drew the short straw in all this."

The major put down the three-foot-long boomerang and sipped at his coffee.

"The first woman I banged when I came to Faery," Rei said as he seated himself in a chair opposite, "was just like the general. She was a captain. She'd knock me down whenever I'd salute her. It was pathetic."

"*Heh…*That's what's called being young."

"Young, huh? So what did you mean before about her drawing the short straw?"

"You hate having to line up, don't you?"

"Huh?"

"I hear there's some big-shot general from the Japanese air force coming to inspect us."

"So?"

"So there's your problem."

"You mean…" Rei tried to imagine the squadron members assembling for review and guessed what the problem was. "You want me to be in an honor guard? Me? The boomerang soldier who fell from the sky? Should I present a boomerang over my shoulder, too? You gotta be kidding."

"Every other squadron had pretty much the same reaction. So we had a lottery and General Lydia Cooley, deputy commander of the SAF, drew the lucky winner. And since the 5th hasn't made an appearance at one of these things before, we got handed the collection plate."

"I don't want to do it."

"That's what everyone else said. It's a mutiny. I don't know what else to do. That wrinkled old hag told me to take care of it. Do you want to get me killed?"

"It's not my fault we don't have a formal honor guard."

"That negative attitude isn't going to get us anywhere. Come on, can't you give me some useful advice on this?"

"How 'bout you stand out there by yourself, Major?" said

Rei as he refilled his coffee cup. "I don't think they'd shoot you for that."

"A drop, a raindrop, a mote," said the major. "Zero. That's the meaning of your name, Rei."

"Look, I was born trouble," Rei replied without turning around, still standing in front of the coffee maker. "My parents split up right after I was born, and I was raised in a home along with plenty of other kids like me. But the truth is, I was happy back then."

"Sounds depressing. What time is it?"

"Coming up on 1900 hours. Wanna check things out up top, Jack?"

"Sure," said the major. "I'll allow it."

The two men left the briefing room and headed for a huge elevator bank on the opposite side of the hangar. They walked in silence. The major carried his boomerang.

Elevator Three, the closest one, was 300 feet away, around a tractor and a maintenance ramp. There were no elevators to the surface just for people here. Rei grabbed a remote control box hanging on the wall and inserted his ID card into the top to activate it as they stepped onto the elevator floor.

"Shall we go?" said the major.

The hundred-by-seventy-foot wide platform began to rise. As they ascended Rei kept his head tilted back, looking up the shaft. He'd always found the pattern made by the rings of light panels encircling it beautiful. The platform paused briefly as they waited for an isolation bulkhead above them to open. There were three of these bulkheads between them and the surface, each ensuring that its respective level was kept airtight. The elevator's power source switched over at these points too; in the event of a failure, power drawn from the previous level would act as a backup system. Between each level there were also emergency bulkheads, each with their own independent power systems, which protected against fire, bombing, and contamination. At the last level, there was also a thick concrete blast wall that merged organically with the deck.

Once the platform stopped moving, the two men exited through an enormous square opening in the wall and were then on the planet's surface. They were in the receiving hangar, although it was more of a shade port than an actual hangar. Bright sunlight streamed down. The generator vehicles, emergency power support units, and fire trucks stood silent.

The two of them did not walk out onto the runway but exited through the rear instead. The grassland outside was pale green. Facing them only about a quarter mile away was the edge of the primeval forest. Rei had heard that Faery didn't have a formal land army because the forest was just too nasty. *I can believe it*, he thought.

With a thunderous roar, three interceptors took off in formation for an air patrol mission. The lieutenant and the major walked until they were clear of the shadow cast by the building's enormous roof, then sat down on the grass. Faery's version of grass was soft and pliant, and did not prickle at all. The blades were a blueish green, with deep blue streaks in the center. When cut, it smelled like irises.

"The wind's delicious," Rei said, taking a deep breath. "Nothing like the filtered air below."

"I like it out here in midday because you can't see the Bloody Road. I can't relax when that thing's there to weird me out."

"That's something I wouldn't expect you to say."

Major Booker drew the large combat knife he carried at his hip from its sheath, studied the trailing edge of the boomerang in his hand, and began cautiously shaving it. "Human instinct," he said without stopping his whittling. "Not accurate, but very rarely wrong."

Rei urged him to try the boomerang out. Blowing the wood shavings off, the major stood up and threw it with a practiced hand. It sailed into the clear, nearly cloudless afternoon sky, making a faint whirring sound as it cut through the air.

"It's not coming back." The boomerang traced a large circular path and then fell about fifty feet away from them. "Was it because of the wind?"

"This doesn't even count as a wind," said the major as he went to retrieve the boomerang. "I made one that always came back, no matter the wind conditions or how badly it flew."

He sat back down and took his knife to the wood again while Rei sprawled out at his side, looking up at the sky.

"Did it break?"

"What?"

"That perfect boomerang. The one you said you made."

"I broke it. Actually, I didn't make it to begin with. A computer did. I fed it the requirements and it executed thousands of simulations in a virtual airspace before spitting out the wing shape data. Then I input the data into a digitally controlled tooling machine and manufactured it. That was Unit 1."

"I take it from your tone that it didn't work."

"The virtual airspace in the computer wasn't a close enough model to real airspace. Next, I got the idea of putting an accelerometer into the wing and then fed that data into the computer. It could do variable pitch and all sorts of things. The one I fitted with a leading edge flap control was the best. That was Unit 2."

"And what about Unit 3?" asked Rei as he spit out a bitter stalk of grass he'd been chewing. "Was that one perfect?"

The major stopped whittling and pointed his knife at the scar on his cheek. "This was the result. The wound that sent me to Faery. Ruined my good looks too."

"I didn't know that," Rei said, raising himself up on his elbows and peering at the major's cheek. "You got that scar from a boomerang?"

"It was fast. It pitched back at me from an angle I didn't expect, and I couldn't dodge it. Even though it had enough load resistance to give me a nasty clip, it still flew past me, made another turn, and came back again. I barely managed to catch it. I'd designed it to come back in a way that would make it easy to catch, but how it actually flew… It made that decision itself, based on the conditions at that moment. I never wanted to throw it again after that."

"Did you put a rocket motor on it or something?"

"No. In the end, it was just a boomerang. But I'd installed a super-layered, single-chip artificial intelligence LSI into it. Since I could never get the feedback control to work, it was necessary to give it a control method to let it look ahead."

"Predictive control, you mean?"

"Yeah. I threw the prototype boomerang again and again. Each time, the LSI would judge the conditions, master them, search for the causes of failure, and gradually learn to accurately predict them and respond instantly. Since the learning function was coded into the circuitry of the AI unit's hardware, I didn't even have to teach it the basic process. I just ordered it to use all the data from its sensors to adjust its flight path so that it would return to the launch point. That's it. I flew it for six months and eventually lost the ability to predict how it would fly. Just when I was thinking that it was getting kind of dangerous, wham! I got three stitches from it. The doctor was clumsy and it hurt like hell. I thought about suing the wanker for malpractice, but he's a doctor in the SAF. And since I'm technically his CO, I'd have to sue myself too."

Booker re-sheathed the knife and stretched. He got up, brushed bits of grass off his fatigues, and threw the boomerang. It flew level and then climbed steeply from about sixty feet away, tracing a large arc.

"That's the real thing," the major said. "Machines are too stiff to fly naturally." The wooden boomerang flew gracefully and landed lightly. "That's why I can't stand them."

"Is that a warning, or are you being ironic?" Rei asked. He had a hard time taking that statement seriously from a man whose livelihood was building and operating advanced mechatronics.

"Take it however you want," the major answered in his usual offhand manner. "My likes and dislikes have nothing to do with you."

Rei was about to answer him, but figured that was a reasonable thing to say and so just watched silently as Booker retrieved the boomerang. As he was about to lie back down on the ground, the remote in his breast pocket chirped.

"This is Lieutenant Fukai. We're busy with Unit 3."

The voice on the other end asked if he knew where Major Booker was. General Cooley was looking for him.

"Major," he called. "Grandma Wrinkles wants you."

Booker shrugged.

"Is it too much to hope that it's news the Japanese commandant dropped dead?"

"They say the review schedule's been finalized and that she wants to give it to you."

"I won't die alone. Let's be chums and line up in front of the wall together. We'll take everyone here with us."

As the two of them rode down on the absurdly oversized elevator, Rei wondered about the major's extraordinary dislike of machines. He was struggling to understand it. It wasn't a matter of how safe or dangerous they were, or how high they let you fly or didn't; it was a visceral aversion that Booker had somehow developed. As he turned this over in his mind, a vision of the honor guard standing stiff as toy soldiers suddenly came to him.

"Say, Jack..." After hesitating a moment, Rei voiced his thoughts. "What if we built some dolls?"

Booker stopped the irritated tapping of the boomerang against his shoulder and tilted his head.

"Androids," Rei explained. "Or robots, I mean. We can have them line up and salute. I doubt we'd even need AI units for them. The commandant is nearsighted, right? So if we get the faces and skin texture down there's no way he'd be able to tell from that distance. It'd work great, since he's the only one that would get anywhere near them anyway."

"Aw, kid, don't be crazy."

"I bet you'd do it if it was your idea."

"I'd have to be the one to call up the general and present that insane proposal. You think she'd say yes?" Booker flipped the boomerang over and continued. "Still… The idea's worth considering. It is absurd, but I think I know a way to make it work."

He turned to face Rei and adopted a pompous tone. "I hereby order you to make the proposal to the general and persuade her to do it."

"Screw that," Rei replied. "I'm no good with Super Granny."

"I'll have you court-martialed for disobeying the orders of a superior officer, for mutiny, treason, and going AWOL."

"Oh, get real. When did going AWOL come into this?"

"Add insulting a superior officer. Think about it, Rei. Which would you rather do: try to persuade 120 squadron members or one woman?"

"The woman would be harder."

They had reached the maintenance level. Rei replaced the remote control on the wall.

"There are women in the squadron, too. Look, you came up with the idea. I'm busy," Booker said, walking quickly.

"You seriously want to do this?"

"I'll check how feasible it is back in my office. Go see the general in my place. It's just your good luck that I was ordered to be in charge here. Remember, you and I are coons from the same hole."

"You mean badgers."

"Oh, is that a real expression? Maybe rats would be better…"

Rei had lost. He'd bought himself a mess of trouble that he didn't need. Feeling depressed, he headed for the SAF's command level.

IN THE END, it was the selfish intransigence of the squadron's human members that propelled the machine-hating Major Booker into the task of building their mechanized replacements. The members of the other squadrons behaved similarly, but the ones in Boomerang took it to a new level. Although it was hardly surprising they did so. Using data on childhood backgrounds, environmental histories, and a variety of other personal profile statistics, the FAF command computers had broken everyone down into several personality types and then compiled a group that had the lowest scores on the sociability and cooperation indices. The result was the 5th Squadron of the SAF. It was General Cooley who had put it together.

The task of greeting VIP visitors should have been regarded as an honor, but the soldiers of Boomerang Squadron regarded it as an insult. Mainly because none of them thought of their visitors as honored guests. And so the consensus reaction was to show no courtesy at all. This didn't arise from any group discussion, but merely from one person telling another that they didn't want to do it, and the other person agreeing, and then telling another person, until by the end of the process it had become the general sentiment.

Of course, Major Booker was a soldier in Boomerang Squadron as well, but his position and personality were different from those of the other members. He didn't want to be demoted, whereas the vast majority of the rest couldn't be busted any lower than they already were. Booker no longer held the bold, some might say nihilistic, worldview of those who lived constantly in the shadow of the fact that they might not return from their next sortie. He was a victor who had survived his environment. You needed to appreciate reality in order to win and live to see another day. If he had to put it into words, he would say that he was a man who knew what fear was.

Rei understood the major's position, but he now realized that there was a slight, or possibly significant, difference in how they saw things. In the end, Rei couldn't quite completely understand

Booker's mentality. Rei was a soldier. And in any case, he wasn't nearly the veteran that the major was.

Despite everything, Rei was able to successfully make his difficult case to General Cooley. Booker greeted the news with a handshake and a "Great job," saying that she never would have gone for it had he been the one presenting the proposal. He said it was Rei's "youthful zeal" that had convinced her, and while their moods were buoyed they set about analyzing how to turn their abstract idea into an actual success.

Naturally, the general's condition for going along with the plan was that the dolls had to be well made. She had even told him that if the robots exceeded standards they would be used for honor guard duty from now on. The whole thing had quickly grown bigger and hairier than Rei had thought it would. "Leave it to me," said Major Booker, spreading out his concept sketches. "No worries." The project was already out of Rei's hands. It may have been his idea originally, but he had the sense that it was growing into an enormous monster that he couldn't control. They had two weeks to get it done.

General Cooley talked the polymer materials branch of the Systems Corps into promising to produce some synthetic skin on short notice. She even arranged to set up a direct data link between the air force factory production system and the computer in Booker's workroom, which allowed him to use the CAD/CAM system remotely. Using just the computer's graphical display and keyboard and a light pen, he could immediately direct parts to be made. Noting Booker's skill as he worked, Rei once again wondered why he had broken his perfect boomerang. To be honest, the major seemed to be enjoying using the computer. Enjoying it a lot more than shaving down wood with a knife.

In the meantime, Rei acted as the pipeline between General Cooley and Major Booker, riding the automated monorail to the military manufacturing plant on errands, being the punching bag for the bitching from the plant team, and helping to put the prototype together. He thought he would die of boredom.

He wanted to be back in the air with Yukikaze as soon as possible. Each time he saw the general he would ask her when the next hearing would be.

"It seems they've been frustrated by the fact that they haven't been able to find any evidence to support their position. You may as well consider yourself a full lieutenant now. Congratulations, Lieutenant," she had said.

Every time after that when he tried to get a more concrete answer out of her, she'd duck the question. Rei suspected she was working secretly with the authorities of their huge organization to destroy the evidence. The chances of that were slight, but if it were true it would be convenient for Rei.

The frame of the prototype doll was completed five days before the commandant of the Japanese air force was due to arrive. Rei went to report this to the general. Walking into the SAF deputy commander's spacious office, Rei saw a severed head sitting on the large desk and blanched in disgust. He knew it was a doll's head, but it looked very lifelike. On top of that, it had the face of his former electronic warfare officer, the one who had got himself killed.

"That's the height of bad taste, General."

"Yes, Your Excellency. It's an honor, sir," said the head. "Yes, Your Excellency. It's an honor, sir."

The general unfolded her hands and pressed the nape of the doll's neck to silence it.

"I'm making our honored dead into our honor guard. Don't question my decision."

"The body frames have some slight defects. I thought you'd want to know," Rei said, still standing. "We'd planned to use stronger materials but ended up having to use cheaper ones."

"It can't be helped. For this batch, getting them ready in time has to take priority. Get them on the production line as soon as you can."

"Roger that."

"Wait. We'll be receiving the preliminary hearing's decision the day after tomorrow. I think you're going to be all right."

"If they're saying that wasn't a Sylph I shot down, then what—"

"If it wasn't a Sylph, it was a bitch. It had to be a JAM. We'll have a short meeting about it tomorrow. Dismissed."

THE MILITARY JUDGE pronounced Rei clear of charges in the same conference room that the preliminary hearing had been held in.

"We have found no physical evidence of misconduct by the accused."

"I'm innocent," Rei said, standing. "I want that made clear. The site where that plane was shot down must be in the combat record. If you'd investigated the wreckage I'm sure you would've discovered that it was a JAM unit. So what are you playing at?"

"If you are making any accusations against this court, we are more than ready to address them."

"We have no objections," General Cooley said smoothly, rising to get Rei under control. "The lieutenant is currently in an emotionally unstable state."

"Lieutenant Fukai, if you would please sign here of your own will and volition, we can end these proceedings."

Although he wasn't satisfied, Rei decided he'd rather not deal with any more of this annoying bullshit and signed the document they handed him.

"Court is adjourned," the judge declared.

The general told him to come to her office, wherein she proceeded to chew him out for his behavior.

"I told you to say as little as possible, and you go and say that to them?!" She paused in mid-rant. "Coffee?"

"No, thanks."

"I did tell you that, didn't I?"

"But, General, why didn't they make an onsite inspection?

It's not that far away. If they found a piece, just one piece of that plane, it'd prove that I was innocent—"

"Shut up at once," the general said in a tone of voice that was low but oddly charged with emotion. "It doesn't concern you, Lieutenant Fukai. As of today, you are a first lieutenant. You may go now and resume your current duties. Any questions?"

"None," he replied, and saluted.

WITH ONE DAY to go until the big show, they had completed 326 dolls. The birth of ghost soldiers, all in uniform. The robots had been brought from the factory to the maintenance floor for a test run. Major Booker attached a wireless mike to his breast to transmit his commands.

The Boomerang Squadron stood, or slouched, inside the glassed-in briefing room. Most of them regarded this strange corps without any expression, although some wore faint smiles. Rei walked along the standing ranks of the dolls, pushing the main power switch on the nape of their necks, and couldn't help shuddering at the coldness of their skin as he did so.

"Salute!" the major ordered. The dolls obeyed.

This was met with applause, laughter, and catcalls.

"Controlling these guys is kinda hard… Column, right! Forward, march! Boomerang Squadron, how about showing some gratitude for our replacements?"

The dolls were taken up on the huge elevator to the surface, where they were bathed in sunlight for the first time.

Rei came along as well. The dolls marched out toward the side of the receiving hangar at the base of the runway. And then one fell. Its arms and legs continued their marching motion even after it had fallen. The dolls coming up behind it began to fall as well.

"No, no, no! Shit! All units, halt!"

Upon the major's order, the chaos instantly ceased. Booker sighed and then sat down on a toolbox.

"Looks like we'll have to cancel the march."

Rei, who had watched all this without a word, let out a sigh as painful as the major's.

"This world really is incomprehensible."

"Did you say something?"

Rei shrugged his shoulders as he leaned against a power supply truck.

"I'm talking about the hearing. I just don't get the general's attitude. And I don't get why she's on my ass all the time."

"It may not have been a Sylph or a JAM. I saw the pictures taken by your gun camera too, and although it looked like a Sylph, I can't say for sure if it was one or not."

"What do you mean?" asked Rei, still brooding.

"It's possible it could have been a trespasser from Earth. A unit that entered the Passageway in violation of international law."

"Why would they do that? What could they possibly be after in this place?"

"Look at this green land, this sweet air. If an Earth nation sent a spy plane, they couldn't exactly complain about it being shot down. If it became public knowledge they'd have to face international censure. On the other hand, Faery isn't a sovereign state, so if we make noise about shooting down a plane from Earth it would cause big trouble for us as well. We don't know what the truth is. It probably was the JAM. You should just forget about it."

"I don't understand at all."

"Don't worry about it. Gimme a hand here. We need to get these dummies back up again."

"Sure. The thing is, this scar on my forehead from shooting down that unknown hasn't gone away. And my partner is dead."

"How about this scar on my cheek? And everyone has to die sometime."

THE FAF METEOROLOGICAL Corps had forecast that the weather would worsen soon but should hold out for the ceremony. The guest of honor came through the Passageway and arrived at Faery Base. The sudden change of environment was probably hard on his old body, but the commandant was known for his love of pomp and circumstance and wasn't about to let it get the better of him.

Since Rei and Major Booker were in charge of preparations for the ceremony, they excused themselves from attendance and headed for the grassy field by the receiving hangar on the surface. Rei brought a portable broadcast monitor with him while Booker carried his hobby boomerang. The grass was soft and the air was warm. If you excused the lack of a blue sky, it was as perfect holiday weather as you could ask for. After dozing off for a bit, Rei was awakened by the major.

"What?"

"It's about to start. Turn on the monitor."

"What…? Oh!" Rei sat up.

The ceremony was apparently being held in the plaza near the control tower, far away from the field they were sitting in. The runway was huge. As they turned on the monitor, a recording of a military band playing the FAF march blared from it.

"Looks like a long opening act has just finished. Okay then, now the review is starting."

The commandant of the Japanese air force walked out to the ghost troops, accompanied by a single Faery Air Force commissioned officer. He was a bantam of a man, walking with his chest puffed out, but did possess a certain dignity.

"Okay, if this works, it all will have been worth it."

"Jack, that officer…"

"Who else would do it? It's the least she could do. It's her responsibility, after all."

They heard voices now.

"You're doing a fine job," said the commandant to one of the dolls.

"Yes, Your Excellency. It's an honor, sir," replied the soldier.

"So, where are you from?"

"Yes, Your Excellency. It's an honor, sir."

White text was crawling along the bottom of the screen now.

> This is a message from Faery Air Force TV service, with an explanation from Boomerang Squadron. These dolls can only say "Yes, Your Excellency. It's an honor, sir." This is a message from the Faery Air Force TV service...

"Who the hell did that?!" yelled Major Booker, leaning forward. But he soon relaxed. "Oh, well. Not my problem."

They cut to a close-up of the commandant's grave face.

"Truly remarkable!" he said. "Not a quiver from them!"

This prompted a laugh from the major.

"Present arms!" General Cooley called out.

The robot soldiers raised their rifles and presented them. At which point there was a motion in the rear. The view switched to a wide shot. Both arms, still tightly holding a rifle, had fallen off of a doll.

> It looks like one of them was imperfectly adjusted. Fortunately, it wasn't in the front row. This is the FAF TV service...

"Damn right it's lucky," said Rei.

Major Booker snorted a laugh.

"What's that, General?" asked the visitor.

"Sir? Oh, that's one of our Sylphids, which we're quite proud of," said General Cooley nonchalantly as she led the commandant away from the dolls. There was the sound of aircraft overhead. Rei looked up at the sky to see five drones flying by in a 5-Card formation.

Please enjoy this high-quality flight by our target
training drones. They feature a turbo-prop power
source with variable-pitch propellers. Naturally, they
are all radio-controlled. This is the FAF TV service...

With a completely straight face, General Cooley began to
describe the various abilities of the real Sylphid to their guest.

"Hm, mm, mm!" he said. "I'd like a few of those planes for
my air force, too!"

The formation executed a perfect 5-Card loop.

Major Booker burst out laughing.

"Why...Why aren't you laughing, Rei? Look, even the general's smiling!"

"It's not funny."

"You need more calcium in your diet."

"Would you just stop?!"

Rei suddenly snatched the boomerang from the major's hands
and stood up. Booker reflexively scrambled into a crouch, his
knife out at the ready. But after a split second he shook his head,
looking embarrassed. He lowered the knife and straightened
up, stretching out his back.

The boomerang shook in Rei's hand. He was enraged.

"A boomerang is a weapon! It doesn't need to come back!"

He threw it at the monitor. It bounced off without breaking
the screen. He sat down hard, arms clasping his knees as his
whole body trembled.

"Rei..."

"I feel like I'm as blind as that commandant. I mean, what
the hell are the JAM? We hit them and hit them and they still
keep coming... Why don't they just finish us off? What are we
even doing here? Why are we..."

"You'll have plenty of time to think about that," Major Booker
said as he picked up the boomerang and lovingly brushed it
off. "As long as you stay alive."

"I've been on leave too long," said Rei. "Way too long..."

REI RETURNED TO regular duty early the next morning. He entered the squadron briefing room wearing his flight suit. Prior to getting the details of the mission operation, he skimmed the general outline. Mission number, conditions for returning to base, Yukikaze's duties, comm frequency and channel, call sign, nav support, weather and visibility, onboard armaments...

Once the meeting was over, it was time to complete the preflight preparations on Yukikaze. Wearing his G-suit and accompanied by his new EWO, he inspected Yukikaze's fuselage. They boarded and checked the ejection seats and the interior systems, then went down the rest of the seemingly endless checklist.

After ascending the elevator to the surface they carried out the final check of authority. Canopy, down. Engine master switch, ON. Engine start. The engine revs climbed. Throttle open. Ignition. More checks to do as they idled. Adjustments made. Outside, it was raining.

"Good luck." Major Booker disconnected the comm jack from the plane's fuselage.

Parking break, off. Rei taxied out onto the runway. As he released the brake, he pressed down on the foot throttle. In an instant, the engines hit MAX afterburner and Yukikaze shot forward like a bullet. Nozzles, full open. Takeoff. Up above was clear, as always. The Bloody Road was bleached of color by the dawn light as Yukikaze rendezvoused with 1st Squadron.

When the AWACS plane informed them of the enemy fighter position, 1st Squadron lit their afterburners and streaked off after their quarry. Yukikaze flew in a large circle at the edge of the combat airspace.

"Enemy units," the EWO warned. "Bearing ten o'clock. Low altitude, high speed and closing."

Rei set the radar to downlook mode and searched for them. There were eight blips on the display. A formation of eight planes. The computer scrolled out the enemy target data: speed, altitude, acceleration, approach vector, threat level—

"They don't have any long-range missiles," said Rei.

"Should we attack?"

"Prepare for air-to-air combat."

The EWO looked for signs of any electronic countermeasures or any counter-ECM activity while Rei checked the stores control panel. **RDY GUN, RDY AAMIII-4, RDY AAMV-4, RDY AAMVII-6.** All antiaircraft ordnance was loaded.

"Enemy units are starting to climb," came the word from the backseat.

An H-shaped mark appeared on the HUD. "Type-1s in firing range. Bandits number eight, range two-five-zero, head-on and closing."

The pulse Doppler radar acquired the fast-moving JAM. Rei looked outside. The planes weren't in visual range yet. He pushed the missile release button on the side stick, signaling the fire control computer that it was free to attack. The FCC made its judgment and released all six long-range missiles at once. A vibration shuddered through the airframe, and then thin vapor trails stretched out toward the enemy Rei could not see. *A fairy can see them though*, he thought suddenly.

The numbers on the HUD were rapidly running down. Missiles would arrive in…three…two…one…zero.

"Direct hits: four. Unclear: two. Three enemy units closing at high speed. They're breaking into two groups and preparing to attack."

Sensing the radar waves of enemy missile guidance, the warning receiver trilled an alert. Yukikaze jettisoned its external fuel tanks.

II

NEVER QUESTION
THE VALUE OF A KNIGHT

He didn't believe Earth was something worth risking his life to protect. When others, especially those who felt passionate about its defense, would discover this, they would usually accuse him of possessing exactly the kind of negative attitude that would lead to the planet's destruction. To which he would simply reply, "So what?"

EARTH HAD BEEN fighting the JAM for thirty long years. Rei Fukai couldn't imagine a reality without them. The war had already begun by the time he was born, and he had been raised in a world where the existence of the Earth Defense Force was a mundane fact of life. So much so, in fact, that back then he never seriously thought about the war itself, nor wondered about its origins or its significance. Since the battle was being fought not on Earth, but on the planet Faery, the staging ground for the JAM's attempted invasion, and since the JAM's military might was not far superior to that of humanity's, it hadn't affected his day-to-day life in any significant manner. And so he'd had no reason to consider it.

Now, Rei was a soldier. He had passed through the enormous, white, spindle-shaped cloud at the South Pole that enveloped the hyperspace corridor connecting Earth to Faery and had arrived at the front lines of battle. But despite this, despite having experienced the war with the JAM firsthand, and despite having access to reams of uncensored information about it, the news reports he'd see piped back from Earth somehow still didn't seem real to him.

The JAM existed; therefore, they were at war with the JAM. He had never once asked himself about the necessity of the fight. The enemy didn't allow the luxury of such questions.

Upon returning from a mission and going off duty, Rei would usually go by himself to a bar in the red-light district and drink. He spoke to nobody and nobody spoke to him. He would silently tilt his glass of beer and think about the next mission and about Yukikaze. No one had ever asked him why he fought. He fought because the enemy was there. Even if the question went unasked, that was the answer. But one day Rei met a man who said that that wasn't the answer. A man who said, "What we need to fight the JAM isn't humans. It's machines."

"HUMANS AREN'T NECESSARY," said the man next to him. Rei had been standing alone at the bar, drinking a dark beer. The place was packed with off-duty officers.

"Right?" the man continued, looking for agreement. "You're a fighter pilot, aren't you? You've got that look to you."

"Tactical Air Group, Faery Base Tactical Airwing, Special Air Force 5th Squadron."

"A Super Sylph driver, huh? A member of the famed Boomerang Squadron. Those are some top-of-the-line planes you boys have there."

The man introduced himself as Colonel Karl Guneau from the Systems Corps' Technology Development Center. He held out his hand, then withdrew it after a few moments when Rei made no move to take it.

"I see Boomerang pilots are as sociable as the rumors say," Colonel Guneau laughed. "I guess you win, Lieutenant…?"

"Rei Fukai."

"Lieutenant Fukai, what I'm referring to is the Flip Knight, a new air-superiority dogfight RPV—a remotely piloted vehicle—that my team has developed. As advanced as it is, even the SAF's Super Sylph can never achieve its full potential as long as it's carrying a human pilot who's as fragile as an egg. A Sylph could never beat a Knight."

"Meaning your Knights would kill our queens?"

"Well, I was just thinking how I'd like to take it up for an operations flight test… It could be quite something." The colonel held a glass in his left hand and gestured with the cigar in his right as he cheerfully went on. "Maybe you'd be interested?"

"The Systems Corps has its own flight test center. If that's not enough for you, you can try and get the Tactical Air Group's training wing to cooperate. The 5th is a combat fighter squadron. It would make no sense for us to be involved."

"It makes perfect sense," said the colonel with a smile. "The knight has thrown down his glove. It's a challenge to duel."

Rei drained his beer mug and then, ignoring the colonel, left the bar. Guneau's loud laughter followed him out into the busy street.

The residential and pleasure districts of Faery Base sprawled across the bottom of the vast underground space that contained them. They constituted a small city unto themselves, one that offered everything its inhabitants might want, from bars to banks to houses of worship of every denomination. A city where one could turn a corner and find oneself in what appeared to be an entirely foreign culture.

Rei did not avail himself of anything the city had to offer, and instead climbed into a small common-use electric vehicle and returned to his quarters in the TCG 1666th barracks #303. The tumult of the city did not reach him here. *A duel*, he thought. *Ridiculous*.

WHEN REI AWOKE the next morning, he'd forgotten all about the colonel. He wasn't scheduled for any sorties and the thought of a solid day of nothing but deskwork had put him in a bad mood.

Exiting the barracks, he headed in the opposite direction from the city center, toward the rocky cavern walls at its periphery. He soon entered a tunnel that opened up into a large hall 1,000 feet further in. The combat base was a solid underground maze. The path cut left, then right, rose and descended. Rei boarded an elevator in a junction hall, got off, and walked through a gradually narrowing corridor—presenting his ID to the guards at the entrance to each block—until he finally reached his room in Boomerang Squadron's offices. The whole procedure was vaguely irritating. Once he fed his ID card into a terminal of the personnel management system and confirmed he had arrived for work, he was in the clear.

Deskwork was tedious, but neglecting it could get him disqualified from flight time. Sitting down at his desk, Rei wondered what he'd do if they ever took his beloved Yukikaze away from him. Thinking about soaring through the sky was the one thing that made the mind-numbing paperwork bearable.

"What's the point of these sortie reports, anyway?" he groused to himself. Then he abruptly stopped jabbing at the keyboard, flashing back to Colonel Guneau's statement about humans being unnecessary. He wondered if Yukikaze considered him unnecessary, then immediately rejected the notion. Yukikaze was the one thing that Rei trusted, and he didn't want to even entertain the possibility that she could betray him. It might have been absurd to think that she wouldn't abandon him just because he needed her, but that was what he chose to believe.

He quickly finished up the multitude of reports and went to see his plane. Checking the airframe was a routine daily task, yet he found it anything but tedious.

The underground hangar was quiet. Units 5 and 7 were out. Rei began his inspection of Unit 3's airframe, starting on the forward left side and moving aft. He circled back to the nose from the right side, checking the exterior for oil leaks and surface damage. There were over a hundred items on the inspection checklist, and although some of them were not mandatory on a daily basis, Rei checked them all.

Once the visual inspection was done, he climbed into the cockpit to perform the onboard tests. Thick cables dangled from Yukikaze's underside, connecting her to the external power supply and the SAF computers. He set the master test selector to onboard test mode. Then, after confirming that the throttle was disengaged and the master arm switch was set to SAFE, he initiated the programmable electronics self-test and began ticking off the items on the checklist. As test signals were sent to all of the avionics and navigation sensors, simulation checks were run on the air inlet control programmer, the automatic flight control set, the central air data computer, the throttle control auto-mode, and a host of other systems.

After that, there were the communications systems to check, the fuel transfer control system, the operations of all the displays, the cockpit opening and closing function... And by that point, it seemed almost a half-measure to not simply go ahead and run the engines, too. Still, it couldn't be helped. Rei climbed down from Yukikaze, feeling like he was being separated from his lover.

"Figured you'd be here, Rei." Major James Booker's voice echoed through the hangar. "So, what was so important that you had to consult Yukikaze after leaving the office without permission?"

Rei had forgot to log his airframe inspection into the personnel control system that Major Booker used to manage Boomerang Squadron. He was Rei's friend, but they were on duty and Booker had not come down there on personal business. The major's tone indicated he was in full superior officer mode.

"What's my punishment, Major?"

"You've got a lot of nerve talking like that after what you pulled."

"What's up? Something happen, Jack?"

The major told Rei to come with him. Rei did as he was told and followed his CO out of the hangar.

"Jesus, Rei. Don't I have enough to do around here without you dumping this crap on my plate, too?"

"What're you talking about?"

"This thing with Colonel Guneau. And yes, I know it's not your fault. I know that without even asking. A Boomerang pilot would never go looking for a fight like this. And you in particular. You meet flattery with a blank look, insults with indifference, tears with a cold heart, and threats with a cool head. You'd just say 'Not my problem' and leave it at that. But

General Cooley isn't a Boomerang pilot."

"You mean Colonel Guneau talked Super Granny into it?"

"He said it would be 'the perfect test of aerial combat technique.' He came to see me, too. That bloke's a smooth talker. Seemed more like a salesman than an engineer. Anyway, as much as I'd like to tell the higher-ups to back off, I'm being forced to do this. And you're the pilot who's going to handle it for me."

"I don't want to have anything to do with this flight test."

"And I don't want to completely cock up the sortie schedule I've already put together. This is classified, but…there's a big attack operation coming down. Believe me, I have no desire to be playing these games right before that."

As he walked shoulder to shoulder with the major, Rei realized that the rumors he'd heard were true: they were probably going to hit the JAM's largest forward base. In fact, it had practically been an open secret, so if the JAM had any spies in here, they probably already knew about it.

"We'll be launching all of our squadron's planes for that operation," the major said as he opened his office door and stepped inside. "I finally get a schedule drawn up for the overhaul rotation for all our planes, and they hit me with this operations flight test. Now it's all gone to hell."

"So just refuse," said Rei as he closed the door.

"Why don't you go to the general's office and refuse for me?" Booker gathered up a sheaf of papers from his desktop and handed it to Rei. "You can hit her with these."

It was an operations manual for the Flip Knight system.

"I don't think that would persuade her."

As far as Rei was concerned, fighting a mechanical knight was a whole lot more appealing than having General Cooley snarling at him.

Major Booker kept Rei standing as he leaned on his desk and told him about the Flip Knight system.

"Listen carefully, Rei."

The Flip Knights were small, unmanned fighter planes designed for dogfighting. They were to be loaded onto a carrier plane and launched in midair after arriving at the battle zone. They would then fight under the command of the carrier's control staff.

"People operate them from the carrier?" asked Rei. "So much for humans not being necessary."

"No, the RPVs have the ability to fight completely on automatic. The problem is the armament."

The major indicated a schematic of a metal cylinder that was about 300 mm long and 40 mm in diameter.

"This is an energy charge for a laser gun. One of these is capable of generating a beam of 0.7 second's duration. The Knight is equipped with a high-powered laser cannon which is practically unaffected by weather conditions."

According to the data in the manual, the barrel of the gun could move 1.95 degrees in any direction, the major explained as he gestured at the document. When a target entered a hundred-foot circle within a three hundred-foot radius in front of the fighter, the gun barrel would be slaved to the targeting radar to keep it constantly centered.

The major said that he had read the research thoroughly. "I think the accuracy rate for this thing is nearly a hundred percent. That's because it doesn't fire physical ordnance that can be put off course. Once it locks on to you, unless you get out of its firing range you're almost surely a goner. You can't outrun a beam of light. Besides that, the Knight has a much tighter turn radius than a Sylph. A Super Sylph is an incredible dogfighter, but the original Sylphid was an all-weather interceptor. Basically, it was designed to take a shot and then get the hell out of there. In a straight-on fight with a Flip Knight, a Super Sylph has no chance..."

Booker sighed. "I have to rework the squadron's schedule. It's a big job, and there's no room for any mistakes. A miscalculation could get one of our soldiers killed."

"We'll do our best. It should be enough."

"Anyway, I'll let you know when the details of the flight test plan are ready. Since we have a major operation coming up, they probably won't be able to put together anything large-scale, but General Cooley has made it a formal order, so it's definitely going to happen. Get ready."

They saluted each other roughly.

REI READ THE Flip Knight manual carefully. Afterward he was even more confused about the point of having aerial combat training between a Sylph and the Knight. It made about as much sense as pitting a sprinter against a marathon runner.

To beat the Knight, he'd have to avoid a close-in dogfight. His best bet would be to fire all six of his long-range missiles and immediately withdraw so that the Knight's main opponent would be the swarm of missiles, not him. Meanwhile, his main opponent would be the carrier plane. Without combat data support from the carrier, even if the Knight could fight autonomously it would be no match for the Sylph. The Super Sylph was unparalleled when it came to electronic indexing of enemy capabilities. The Knight would be so busy trying to dodge those missiles that it wouldn't be able to attack the Sylph. This fight was shaping up to be a proxy one: the Knight versus the Sylph's missiles and the Sylph versus the Knight's controllers.

In the end, Rei decided that the Flip Knight was the equivalent of the antiaircraft machine guns mounted on old heavy bombers, albeit a technologically advanced equivalent with fixed wings and a high degree of maneuverability. It was the command and control capabilities of the carrier plane that determined the Flip Knight's value. Flying autonomously, separated from those systems, the Knight's abilities were merely theoretical.

A good weapon may confer an absolute advantage, but an

advantage does not necessarily ensure a victory. Just as in the old saying that a treasure unused went to waste, it was up to the individual to decide how and when to best utilize a weapon. That was why humans were necessary in battle.

"But why is that?" Rei muttered to himself. It was such an obvious thing that he'd never thought about it before. Why did people fight? Maybe humans should just leave it to the machines. In nearly every field of endeavor, perfect automation was theoretically possible. So why, exactly, were humans required to stay in the mix?

It wasn't as though Rei had a personal creed that required people to be superior to machines. The revulsion he felt at hearing Colonel Guneau's statement that humans weren't necessary came from how it seemed to negate his relationship with Yukikaze, but it didn't go beyond that personal reaction. Rei didn't think that humanity would ever abandon Faery, no matter how good the machines got.

"Humans are necessary in battle."

Rei said it aloud, testing the sound of the words. Why? Why did he think that?

Maybe, he thought, *it's to secure the budget. Nobody cries when a machine is broken, but dead bodies are a silent appeal to Earth to counter the JAM threat.*

You couldn't say that the Faery Air Force's budget was adequate, but then that was the nature of budgets, wasn't it? They weren't infinite, and where there were limited resources there were naturally a lot of people arguing forcefully about what constituted a necessity. That was why they needed to be persuasive. One flag-draped coffin sent back by the FAF spoke more eloquently of how terrible the JAM were than any list of necessary expenditures spat out by a computer.

Is that why people are needed? Rei thought. *So then did I come here just to become a corpse?* The more he worried at the concept, the more that conclusion seemed to be inevitable. Starting to feel like he was slowly throttling himself, he shook his head and drove the ominous thought away. He took a deep breath, feeling foolish for even having considered such a thing.

The oppressive feeling stayed with him into the late afternoon, which was when General Cooley called for him. He found his EWO already seated in the SAF deputy commander's office when he arrived. He was a dependable partner aboard Yukikaze but a cold, blunt man on the ground. *The same as me*, Rei thought. He looked at Second Lieutenant Burgadish, a man who was like a part of him, and had a sudden sinking feeling. *A living corpse.* That odd thought took hold of him and wouldn't let go. They were living corpses preserved in an illusion of life.

General Cooley launched into a rambling explanation of the flight test to be conducted with the Flip Knight. Rei mostly ignored her. The general continued feverishly. "Think of the honor," she said. "The fact that Boomerang Squadron has been chosen for this task is in recognition of our being the strongest unit in the FAF."

Rei was bored. Realizing this, the general seemed to wake from her trance and stopped talking.

"What is the point of this?" Rei asked.

"The point?" The general pushed her glasses up with her index finger. "Lieutenant Fukai, what exactly are you asking?"

"If this is a test of our combat technique, then let me load Yukikaze with live antiaircraft ordnance. The Knight's unmanned. There shouldn't be any problem with that."

"Don't be absurd."

"What that tells me is that the point of this is to satisfy Colonel Guneau's ego. We're meant to be the sacrifices in his little game." Nothing but pawns for the man who saw people as unnecessary. "This whole thing is stupid."

"I fail to see a reason for this type of reaction on your part."

"I'm saying that it's bullshit."

"Lieutenant, it doesn't matter whether you win or lose. It won't be an issue."

"That doesn't make me like it."

"Like it or not, it's an order. Just pretend that you're fighting the JAM."

"We fight the JAM for real. And when you say to a Boomerang pilot who's recently come back from a mission after barely escaping with his life, 'Hey, come on, let's practice,' what he hears is that you just insulted him."

"This is going to be a real battle," the laconic Lieutenant Burgadish said in a clipped tone. "So I don't mind."

Rei understood what he meant. The lieutenant was saying that anyone who wasn't on their side was an enemy. Be it a hypothetical enemy or an unknown one, the single necessity was to get back home without getting killed.

General Cooley, however, let out a deep sigh, clearly not understanding what the problem was. She waved her hand at them to leave.

"I'll give Major Booker the details. You will abide by these commands, readily and immediately. That is all. Dismissed."

MAJOR BOOKER MET them in his office with a tired look on his face. He seemed harried.

"They've decided to initiate the big op in five days," he told them. "The mission code is FTJ83. It's going to be the largest one we've had in years, involving all our forces... What'd you come here for again?"

"The duel," said Rei.

"Right," the major replied. He picked up two copies of a booklet from among the papers scattered on top of his desk and handed them to Rei and Burgadish. "Let's get out of here. I'll explain in the briefing room."

They filed into the high-ceilinged chamber. Rei and Burgadish sat with their backs to the panoramic glassed-in view of the maintenance bay, facing the flat-panel display that took up the entire opposite wall. The major punched up a map of Faery.

"The combat flight test will be tomorrow. You'll take off at 0900 hours and are scheduled to return at 1156."

"We'll be in the air for nearly three hours?"

"We got a complaint from the Aerospace Defense Corps. They said they didn't want us doing this damn fool stunt inside our air defense ID zone. It's a pain in the arse, but since I'm assuming you'd rather avoid the possibility of getting toasted by friendly fire, it can't be helped. That's why we have to go all the way out here." The major pointed to the map. "Sugar Desert."

"That's out in D-zone, isn't it? What about the training areas closer in?"

"They've been closed because of Operation FTJ83. Right now, all airspace is classified as combat airspace. The early warning satellites launched by the ADC were all shot down recently, which has them in a sweat. Now they've got AWACS planes buzzing around all over the place. This is a hell of a time to be doing training flights."

Centered on the Passageway connecting them with Earth was the Absolute Defense Line, which extended to a radius of 125 miles around it. If the JAM broke through the line, they would pour through the Passageway and onto Earth itself. The six giant bases of the FAF were arrayed around the Passageway along this line. Other defense lines had been established further out, at distances of 350, 750, and 1,200 miles from the Passageway, and were known respectively as "A-line," "B-line," and the "Early Warning Line." The area between the Absolute Defense Line and A-line was known as "A-zone," with the B- and C-zones following out. D-zone lay beyond the outermost defense line. The FAF did not have absolute control of the airspace out there, but since it wasn't JAM airspace either, it was tentatively considered to be neutral territory. Of course, the zones were entirely of human invention and so were not recognized by the JAM or by Faery's primitive life-forms.

Major Booker brought an aerial photograph up on the display. It was dazzlingly white. Casting a large black shadow on the pure white sand was a 9,000–foot tall mountain that most of the pilots affectionately referred to as "Sugar Rock," since it looked more like an enormous piece of rock candy abandoned in the sugary sand than a mountain. There were no other peaks around it, and it rose up so unexpectedly that it made for an excellent landmark.

"You'll fly straight out to here, engage in a mock air battle for three minutes, and then return. On your way there and back, you'll be flying a combat air patrol. If you encounter the JAM, you will intercept and engage. In that event, the nearest front line bases are TAB-13, 15, and 16. We'll also have an in-air refueling tanker on the rear line as backup. If you encounter the JAM while outbound, the flight test will be cancelled."

Rei looked at his onboard stores list.

"I'll be flying with heavy equipment. Quick maneuvers are going to be impossible. That'll put me at a disadvantage against the Knight."

"You picked this fight. Can't give it back now. You've been authorized to use live gun ammo, by the way."

"What?"

"Colonel Guneau's full of confidence about this. He said we can try whatever we wanted. The Knight won't be firing at you, so don't worry about that."

"I'd never be able to beat it if I got within cannon range. I can practically see him laughing at us right now."

"Are we done here?" asked Lieutenant Burgadish.

"Yeah," answered the major. "Memorize that schedule. Dismissed."

Rei watched his partner quickly leave the room.

"Want some coffee?" Booker asked as he killed the display and moved over to the table. "I'm tired."

"It's like he's wearing a mask…"

"Who, Burgadish? Hmm… He's like the poster boy for Boomerang Squadron. What I find interesting is that you may be losing what it takes to be a Boomerang pilot, Rei. You gonna break up with Yukikaze and become my assistant?"

"I have no interest in breaking up with her," he answered, and then quickly changed the subject. "Active homing missiles would be effective, even against ECM. And I can also use them as decoys to break my opponent's weapons lock."

The major set a cup under the coffee maker's spout.

"Only your gun's going to have live ammo. If you can't live fire your missiles, why not pop off chaff and flares instead?"

"That may not be very effective against the Knight. Aside from radar it uses video cameras and pattern recognition software for targeting. Even if I goof its radar with chaff and jamming waves, it could still visually tag me with its targeting reticule and get me that way."

Booker slurped at his coffee. "How about you carry smoke-screen shells, too? Any particular color you'd like? I can even get you rainbow-colored ones."

"This whole thing's just making me depressed."

"So...blue, then?"

"I wonder just what sort of dogfight the Flip Knight is going to give me."

"Do it and find out," answered the major.

YUKIKAZE TOOK OFF the next day at the appointed time. She was accompanied by a large AWACS plane that had been temporarily fitted out as a combat training control unit. During the training, the control plane's combat data section would be on Yukikaze's side; the Flip Knight would be challenging the Super Sylph without any support from it. The control plane would synthesize the tactical data of the Knight, its carrier plane, and Yukikaze, and then automatically render an instant verdict of which plane won or lost.

Yukikaze flew at high altitude at a fuel-conserving cruising speed toward Sugar Rock. Rei didn't care anymore about the purpose or rationale behind this flight test. The troubles and expectations of the world below were left outside the cockpit. In the skies of Faery, all that mattered was the simple principle of kill or be killed. Anyone who allowed himself to be distracted by questions about why he was fighting or why the JAM were here would be killed by his opponent in short order and never make it back alive.

The winners were the ones who made it back.

Rei looked up at the deep blue sky above him. What more was there to think about than that?

Above the thin atmosphere hung the flattened ellipses of the binary suns. The Bloody Road that spilled out from them painted a crimson swath across the sky. A little higher up and he could see it, even in daylight: an enormous whirlpool, like a red Milky Way. Maybe if Faery didn't have twin suns and there were no Bloody Road and the sky looked the same as it did on Earth, then maybe he would be able to look at things more rationally. This world was too illusory, so exceedingly unreal with its bizarre sights. It was like a dream, or an amusement park, or something out of a fairy tale. It seemed more so at night, as if the very air itself contained a hallucinatory power.

They were approaching the training area. Making a tactical guidance call, Yukikaze headed toward the target point using the comm line and tactical data link it established with the control plane. The control plane remained inside of C-zone and would continue to direct them from approximately fifty miles to the rear.

Lieutenant Burgadish had already picked up their opponent's radar emissions on the passive detectors. Yukikaze's central computer automatically input the data into its file and compared the radar waves' frequency and special characteristics to data on known types it had stored. The onboard computer classified the radar signature as UNKNOWN, but just then a call came from the control plane: "B-3, tactical control signals for the Flip Knight system detected."

Their passive detectors could not pinpoint an exact target

location, so the control plane fed them the necessary data. Lieutenant Burgadish confirmed the position of the Flip Knight's carrier plane on Yukikaze's radar display. It was about 130 miles out and closing. While Yukikaze's radar was better than that of most fighter planes, it could not compare to the giant radome of the AWACS plane.

"The carrier's taking its sweet time flying to our rear," Burgadish said over the comm in his usual bored tone. "The Knights should be launching soon."

"B-3," called the control plane. "K-I, K-II, K-III, closing rapidly on your position."

"What?" said Rei. "Lieutenant, confirm."

The fire control radar Rei was operating had acquired the target and was tracking it, but it could only detect on a very narrow range.

"Can't confirm... I see them now. Behind us, closing fast."

A target symbol appeared on the multi-function display near Rei's knee.

"Why didn't the control plane give us an intercept course faster? Are they trying to kill us?"

"The point of this exercise is to simulate an actual assault. Okay, let's do this."

Rei sent them into a loose roll down toward the pure white sand, then pulled hard up and about. Out of the corner of his eye he caught the glitter of the Knights climbing up at them. He set the radar mode to super search, flicked the master arm switch to ARM, and pushed Yukikaze into a power dive toward the odd mountain rearing up out of the sugary sands before them. Trying to shake off the pursuing Knights, he used the velocity gained from the dive to whip around Sugar Rock, flying in its shadow with wings parallel to the mountain's face.

He had anticipated that the Knights would break formation at this point. Most likely, one plane would stay high while the other two would split up to fly around either side of the mountain. He was hoping dearly that they would, because unless he split them up, he'd have no chance of beating them.

About three-quarters of the way around Sugar Rock, the fire control radar picked up Knight-II ahead, almost dead abreast of them, and locked on immediately. Range zero-point-eight. Rei set the dogfight switch to ON, and the head-up display automatically switched to gun mode.

The Knight was small and hard to see, but the target designator reticule on the HUD framed the plane and showed him its position. However, Knight-II evaded him before he achieved optimal firing position. Not three seconds had passed since the radar lock.

Rei banked Yukikaze hard at full thrust and pursued Knight-II. He got back into targeting position, and as soon as they were within firing range he squeezed the trigger. The number readout on the HUD that showed the rounds remaining in his cannon rapidly began counting backwards. No hit.

"Evasive, right!" Burgadish called out.

Rei reflexively aborted his attack and went into a high-G turn. Knight-I was savagely charging up at them from below: Knight-II had been a decoy.

As they accelerated and slipped over the peak of Sugar Rock, diving starboard, Knight-III came at them nose-on. They merged before he could even pull the trigger. Knight-III made a sharp turn and was on his six in an instant.

"Okay, B-3, that's it. RTB."

"Roger."

"B-3," Colonel Guneau's voice cut in. "How does it feel to get killed twice, Lieutenant Fukai?"

He hadn't been killed, though. He was still flying. He was still alive, so he hadn't lost. That was the single essential truth of these skies.

"MK-1, Colonel," Rei replied. "Looks like this flight test turned out just the way you planned it. Satisfied?"

"Very satisfied. The Knight really is brilliant. It exhibited even better combat decision capacities than I had expected."

"Was that attack conducted in full automatic mode?"

"It was." Colonel Guneau sounded very pleased with himself. "Are you starting to accept the truth now?"

Rei was silent. The fact he couldn't object irritated the hell out of him. It wasn't so much the result of this flight test that pissed him off as it was the colonel's attitude. The outcome of the flight might have been different if the initial parameters they set up for him had been changed, but Colonel Guneau just now had all but admitted that the outcome was a foregone conclusion, one that had been fixed in the planning stages. Rei recalled how frustrated he felt when he couldn't adequately put into words his thoughts that, no matter how advanced machines became, people would still be needed.

He didn't want to believe that he was here only to become a corpse, because that line of thought inevitably led to the colonel's conclusion.

"I know how hard this must be for you," the colonel said, "but a loss is a loss. Just accept it."

"Colonel Guneau," Rei asked. "Do you have any real combat experience? Any actual flight time in a fighter?"

"No."

Then you don't know shit about how I feel, Rei thought. Colonel Guneau didn't fight. He didn't understand the mentality of a soldier. Rei wondered what Major Booker would have to say about it and was struck by the realization that, as a former fighter pilot, the major *would* understand his feelings.

As he climbed higher to fly his CAP on the way back to the base, Rei thought about nothing. Lieutenant Burgadish didn't say a word about the flight test, either. Rei didn't ask his partner what he thought about the colonel. He could pretty much imagine the response. "What the colonel thinks has nothing to do with us," or something to that effect.

With their quiet patrol over—they didn't encounter the JAM that day—Yukikaze came in for landing. As they descended to the maintenance bay on the elevator, Rei's tension dissipated somewhat. But the fact that he hadn't managed to shoot down even one Knight, that in the end he hadn't beaten Colonel Guneau, left him agitated.

Major Booker was waiting for them in the maintenance bay, with his usual "How'd it go?" greeting to his returning soldiers. Rei gave the same reply he always did: "We're still alive."

"How was the Knight?" the major asked as he followed them to the locker room. "Tough as we thought?"

"We didn't win, but we didn't lose either."

"Hm," said the major, nodding. He knew how Rei felt. "I want a full flight test report from you. We can use the data to improve the Super Sylph's performance. Later, then."

"Humans are necessary in battle," Rei suddenly said. "But why?"

The major halted mid-step and turned around.

"Because wars are started by humans, which means we can't very well leave it to machines to fight them."

That's it, Rei thought. When you put it that way, it was a simple enough reason. Booker gave him a searching look for a moment and then left the room.

Rei checked the schedule board on the wall. FTJ83 had been entered, commencing in four days. Normally, underneath the mission number would be written the numbers of the planes assigned to sortie and the crew names, but the column under FTJ83 was blank except for the words "All units to sortie."

He couldn't keep dwelling on Colonel Guneau. Rei changed his clothes and left the locker room. He'd already put the Flip Knight system out of his mind. *Once it's perfected, it'll be the JAM's problem, not mine,* he thought. The test was over.

REI HAD THOUGHT that was the last he'd have to deal with Colonel Guneau. The next day, with FTJ83 just three days away, all the members of 5th Squadron had been assembled to hear the mission brief from General Cooley. Afterward, he was summoned by Major Booker to receive an unexpected order: he was to fly backup for Guneau.

Seeing Rei enter his office, Booker stood up and walked around his desk, brandishing a piece of paper at him. "Look at this," he said. "It's Colonel Guneau again."

"Does he want a rematch?"

"No, this time it'll be real combat. FTJ83. They're sending the Flip Knight out for air defense. It looks like the good colonel's going to be celebrating by flying in the carrier plane personally. That's where you come in." Booker flicked the paper with his finger. "Yukikaze has been tasked to provide guidance support. The orders came in from above, although you'll never guess who they're from."

"Not General Cooley?"

"Try General Jenner, commander of the Tactical Air Force."

"Okay, what's going on?"

"Officially, the story is that the TAF has volunteered to provide Colonel Guneau with backup. For instance, if the Knight flies too far from the carrier and gets lost, Yukikaze would guide it home or possibly even guide it to its target. The Knight can fight autonomously, but it's still limited in its ability to search for an enemy."

"But why Yukikaze?"

"The TAF's real intention is to make the Knight system its own, with this temporary utilization as a fig leaf. Basically, this is a demonstration to get funding for it. If they get hard proof that the system can be used well tactically, they may form a new unit combining Sylphs and Knights. It looks like the TAF and the Systems Corps came up with this scheme beforehand. Yukikaze was chosen on Colonel Guneau's recommendation."

"I don't believe this… And I have to do this on top of my regular duty? It's gonna be a royal fucking pain."

"I agree completely. But now we have to get Yukikaze fitted with the Knight's tactical guidance system ASAP. We can do it in time, but getting the system mounted, tested, and adjusted properly is going to take a lot of work. We can't just slap it on and make it look pretty. If it doesn't work to spec, it'll be dangerous. We're going to be working on this from now through tomorrow, and it's already giving me a headache."

The major returned to his desk, picked up the control set manual for the Knight, and handed it to Rei.

"We've already begun the preparations. If you want to see for yourself, head down to the maintenance bay. You need to read this in case you're given guidance authority."

Rei flipped through the manual, then shrugged. "If that happened then I'd have the Knight operate on full auto. It'd do a better job than me."

"I'll leave that decision to you. I'll officially brief you on the mission conduct tomorrow."

ALTHOUGH ALL UNITS were flying out, the squadrons were going to be launched on a staggered schedule. Because the scope of FTJ83 was so enormous, the operation had been broken into nine phases. The planes of Boomerang Squadron were assigned to launch in the different phases in accordance with the master battle plan. Each plane would take off on its own, rendezvous with the strike unit it was attached to, then gather battle progress data from the front lines and return to base. That would be the extent of Boomerang Squadron's duty.

To say that coordinating all of this was keeping Major Booker busy would be an understatement. Unlike all the other fighter squadrons, which would operate according to one set of orders, he had to devise and transmit flight plans for all thirteen individual units in his squadron. This involved the takeoff times, the mission action outlines of the squadrons they were attached to, the return flight courses, the in-air refueling points, emergency support conditions, and a myriad of other elements. On top of that, a normal mission would usually require the launch of just two planes, but in FTJ83 all of them were going out. Add in Colonel Guneau and his Knight system, and the whole thing was enough of a mess to drive Major Booker to tears. Enough so that even Rei felt sorry for him.

"Thanks for all your hard work, Major." Rei saluted.

"You know, that's the first time I've ever heard a Boomerang pilot thank me for anything. Rei, if you really feel that way, break up with Yukikaze and come work with me in control."

"Can't do that," Rei said as he lowered his hand. "Yukikaze would never leave me."

"You can't kiss a machine," said the major. "If she ever makes like she's going to crash and kiss the ground, you make sure you leave her in an instant. Understand?"

"Don't worry. I'll always make it back alive. That's your one standing order, isn't it?"

The paramount directive of Boomerang Squadron: Even if you have to watch your comrades die, make it back alive. If asked, none of its members would say that they considered this a heartless duty. To them, even entertaining the question would be a pointless waste of time. Those were the kind of soldiers who made up Boomerang Squadron.

Rei saluted once more, then left Major Booker's office. He went to see Yukikaze and get a detailed explanation of what was being done from the crew chief. Enveloped in the tense atmosphere of the maintenance bay, Yukikaze was almost intoxicatingly appealing.

FTJ83. THE ENORMOUS operation commenced at 1100 hours with the destruction of the JAM's strategic reconnaissance satellites. Simultaneously, ballistic missiles were launched from strategic bases while frontline division bases launched anti-radar cruise missiles. Most of the missiles were shot down, but during the barrage the strike units were able to successfully penetrate the targeted JAM sphere of influence. They achieved air mastery through overwhelming force, destroyed the JAM's surface installations, and neutralized the enemy's counterstrike capabilities. Cruise bombers then dropped a devastating amount of ordnance on the central objective.

And thus was the JAM's largest frontline base destroyed—or at least, that was how Rei heard it from inside Yukikaze. *Well, now it begins*, he thought, but he doubted that the JAM had really been hit fatally. Part of their forces could have been hiding deep underground, and anyway, this wasn't the only base the JAM had. There would be payback.

Rei was flying a CAP armed with twelve medium-range missiles and four short-range missiles. He was holding at a high altitude in C-zone near Sugar Rock, looping in a figure-eight pattern. There were three squadrons of ADAG interceptors nearby, flying at a slightly lower altitude than Yukikaze, all fifteen planes maintaining plenty of space between them. The Flip Knight and Unit MK-1, the carrier plane Colonel Guneau was on, were positioned fifty miles to the rear along with the airborne control plane AC-4.

It was unusual for Yukikaze, a plane attached to the Tactical Air Force, to be operating with an Aerospace Defense Corps unit. But then, according to the letter of their mission, Boomerang fighters were supposed to operate with any squadron, so Rei didn't particularly feel one way or the other about it. It was just that this was the first operation where he'd had enough time to wonder when and how the enemy would come at them, or even whether they would come at all, and he found the suspense painful.

The dense forest was spread out below him. The dry air blowing in from the nearby desert gave the atmosphere a crystalline quality, and even from this distance the true hues of the vegetation—not the expected dark greens, but rather pale blues—were faithfully conveyed to his eyes. The forest ended abruptly before the ocean of pure white sand. The contrast was beautiful. Sugar Rock glittered in the sun. Looking down on the forest side, Rei could see a sea of clouds mounting up in the distance, with storms likely blowing beneath them.

The area was mountainous, although the heights were less like mountains than like enormous geological waves that rose and fell 9,000 feet. Seen from this high up, the ranges really did look like waves. Since the dominant plant species on the mountainsides varied between the heights and lowlands, you could roughly estimate the altitude from the color of the vegetation. It grew more and more purple the higher you got. Faery Base was beyond the horizon, past those waves. Beyond it was the Passageway, and beyond the Passageway, Earth.

What a boring-ass mission, Rei thought, stifling a yawn.

"Is it time to go home yet, Lieutenant?" Rei asked his EWO.

"Still…sixty-three minutes to go."

They flew on silently for thirty more minutes, not even talking during the in-air refueling. Just as Rei was wondering if the JAM would ever show up, a call came from the control plane.

"All units, attention. This is AC-4. We've picked up the JAM. Map point D31-49, flying on the deck. Multiple contacts, speed of zero-point-nine and closing. They look like cruise missiles, three large groups. All units, prepare to intercept. Commence intercept."

The interceptors rolled in, automatically guided by AC-4 into their dive. Yukikaze followed after them.

"Targets confirmed," Lieutenant Burgadish said over the intercom. "Range of one-five-zero. At current speed, they should pass just under us in two minutes. Picking up scrambles from TAB-15 and 16."

"What vector did they come in from? What about the Flip Knights?"

"Still haven't launched," answered Burgadish. "Three groups targeted, each group approximately forty units. Total of 120, closing range."

"B-3, this is MK-1," called out Colonel Guneau's voice. "We'll draw them off."

It was rare for the Systems Corps to be participating in actual combat. The colonel's confident voice now gave Rei a different impression than it had during the flight test. Back then it had seemed to him merely unpleasant; now, it had the tone of childish boasting. *This is dangerous,* Rei thought.

"MK-1, launch the Knights at once, then withdraw the carrier plane."

The colonel asked why, probably suspicious of Rei's reasons for requesting guidance authorization for the Knights.

"Lieutenant, one group of targets has begun to climb rapidly," Burgadish warned. "Range nine-zero."

"Colonel Guneau, this isn't a flight test. The JAM are headed for the carrier plane too. You think they're just going to turn off or pass by you?"

"I don't take orders from you."

The enemy was drawing closer, and Rei dismissed the colonel from his thoughts.

The JAM penetrated the Early Warning Line.

Yukikaze's central computer automatically began gathering data. The positions of the JAM, the positions of the interceptors, tactical guidance data from the airborne control plane, the comm chatter between each plane, interception results: the computer voraciously sucked in all of it. If it noticed any data overlooked by the control plane that could be deemed a possible threat, Lieutenant Burgadish would inform the control plane or the interceptors, but they'd take no further support action beyond that. They would simply watch over the scene. The missiles Yukikaze carried were for her own defense, not for any sort of proactive attack. The interceptors could withdraw from the combat zone at full speed after releasing their missiles, but Yukikaze didn't have that option. It hadn't a single missile to spare to defend the other planes.

Burgadish's analysis showed that the vanguard within the three clusters of JAM aircraft appeared to be anti-interceptor assault units.

"They're all giving off the same radar emissions and are all the same size. Can't ID them, though… The main force is to the rear, surrounded by escort units, possibly dummy planes. Their target points are our frontline bases, Faery Base, and if they break through, they might even try diving into Earth itself."

"They're unmanned?"

"Considering we don't actually know what the JAM really look like, I can't say for sure. But they may be autonomously functioning units, like the Flip Knight."

No human had ever made direct contact with the JAM, and so nobody knew exactly what sort of life-form they were. A strange thought suddenly crossed Rei's mind: Maybe they weren't living creatures at all. Maybe they were something that defied all human comprehension.

"Lieutenant, two bandits, closing fast. Range three-zero, bearing 1-6-R."

"Engaging."

Medium-range air-to-air missiles set to attack mode. Auto intercept system, activated. The intercept computer automatically acquired the two approaching targets. After releasing two missiles simultaneously, Yukikaze rolled away from them.

Switching the throttle control to auto mode, the computer opened up the throttles to MAX. Analyzing the situation, it calculated the optimal withdrawal course, then automatically cancelled the intercept system as the threats were terminated.

"Main enemy force passing directly below us…Flip Knights, launching!"

Gun mode didn't activate the auto intercept system, and Rei wondered whether he would have been able to beat the Knights if he'd used it. Maybe, but in a way, it would have only confirmed the colonel's theory. There was no time to think about it now. He pursued the moving battle line of the JAM invasion. The Knight's carrier plane retreated before them.

The JAM had lost close to a third of their number at the Early Warning Line, but the main formation penetrated C-zone unscathed. Command and control passed from AC-4 to AC-3. Faery Base's intercept control computer was probably working at full capacity.

Yukikaze was flying at high altitude, looking down on the targets from 98,000 feet, using its powerful pulse Doppler radar to monitor the JAM flying ahead and below at a line-of-sight distance of thirty-five miles. Rei maintained this distance as they flew. The JAM were on a straight-line course for Faery Base. The invasion was on.

The multidisplay was lit up like a Christmas tree. The interceptors launched by the frontline division bases were fighting hard. The JAM reassumed their V-shaped battle formation, with the main force splitting into smaller formations on the left and right. They seemed to be headed for frontline bases TAB-15 and 16. Rei adjusted his own course to starboard. MK-1, the Flip Knight's carrier plane, was on course for TAB-15, the JAM's main objective.

"Enemy, increasing speed," said Lieutenant Burgadish. "Speed of one-point-seven. Just under four minutes out from TAB-15."

"B-3 to MK-1. Withdraw."

On the display, the JAM were quickly closing in on MK-1. Five Flip Knights prepared to intercept them. The symbols on the display were so close together now that they were almost merged. But Rei decided that it was all right. The JAM were slipping past the carrier plane a mile to its side—

"EMP, confirmed! Nuclear detonation!" Burgadish shouted. "Looks like the Knights destroyed a JAM missile in the middle of the formation."

A warning tone sounded and a readout suddenly appeared on the stores control panel. RDY FK I II V.

"The carrier plane's gone. I estimate that nuke was in the fifty kiloton range. Eight targets now closing on TAB-15."

"MK-1. Colonel." There was no reply. "MK-1, this is B-3. AC-3, respond."

"This is AC-3. MK-1 has been destroyed. B-3, provide guidance for K-I, II, and V. K-III and IV have been shot down."

"How much longer can the Knights stay in the air?"

"About three-zero more minutes. Indicating attack targets. B-3, don't get too close to the JAM."

"B-3, roger."

Rei flipped the Knight guidance switch on the stores control panel, establishing a command link between Yukikaze and the Knights independent of the other planes. He pushed the missile release button and Yukikaze's fire control system sent the Knights toward the targets indicated by the control plane.

There were eight large JAM aircraft flying in formations of two, three, and three. They kept at a distance of about three miles from each other, never drawing any closer, and from this Burgadish reckoned the one unit in the center was carrying a nuclear missile.

"They're maintaining a space cushion so that they aren't all destroyed in case that missile detonates."

The three Flip Knights were nipping at the heels of one of the three-ship JAM formations. The JAM fighters quickly detected the pursuit and the two groups of planes began to maneuver.

Rei flicked the dogfight switch to OFF with the tip of his finger, transferring the Knights' gun control from Yukikaze to the individual units so that they could attack on their own judgment. Since the control protocol was hastily installed temporary logic, he couldn't give them advance guidance control. Rei left it to the Knights themselves.

The data transmitted by the Knights was projected onto the HUD as he watched. The three enemy craft were coming into the Knights' firing range when one of the JAM pulled a snap turn and rushed at Knight-I to attack. Knight-II provided cover, crossing Knight-I's flight path, and a firing cue appeared on the HUD as Knight-II opened up with its laser cannon, annihilating the JAM fighter. Knight-I continued straight along the clear path that had been opened up for it, with Knight-II now to its rear, providing backup.

The other two JAM moved into a fighting wing formation, closing on their target at supersonic speed. Now that it had become apparent that they'd most likely lose in a dogfight, the JAM to the rear seemed to be sacrificing themselves to shield the nuclear missile carrier that was now in the lead, and worse still, accelerating.

Knight-V charged forward and began firing its laser at the fighters as soon as they were in range. A hit.

Having lost its escorts, the last JAM flew on, staying just outside of firing range. They were now barely six minutes from the target point.

This was all happening too far away to be seen by his naked eye, so Rei watched it on his HUD and on the multidisplay below. *Humans aren't necessary, huh?* he thought bitterly. Colonel Guneau had died in battle precisely because humans were necessary to the fight. Rei could feel it in his skin, as though he'd been struck. *That's right,* he thought. *I'm the one who's fighting here.* It wasn't the JAM versus Earth machines: it was the JAM versus people, just as Major Booker had said. It was just so obvious, but… Watching the movements of the JAM and the Knights on the displays was more than enough to cause his misgivings to well up. He was beset by a powerful feeling of alienation, as though his mechanical allies were fighting of their own accord.

Maybe they are, Rei thought as a shudder traveled down his spine. Perhaps it wasn't such an obvious truth that people were necessary to the fight. The JAM were aliens. It wouldn't be so incredible for them to believe that it was machines, not humans, that ruled Earth.

Humanity believed that the JAM had arbitrarily attacked them, but perhaps Earth's machines had accepted the JAM's declaration of war. If that were true, then humans had no reason to be in this war. If that were true, then the JAM and Earth's machines might regard this as *their* fight, one that humans had no place in.

Rei gave his head a quick shake, as though to drive the thought from his mind. *That's crazy.*

"Targets increasing velocity. Speed now three-zero... The Knights can't catch up to them."

Before Burgadish had even finished speaking, Rei had keyed the dogfight switch to ON and pulled the trigger. Knight-I and V, nearest to the targeted JAM, fired their lasers. There was a long delay from Knight-II, or rather, it seemed like a long delay but was not even five seconds. Target detonation. Knight-I and V couldn't avoid being caught in the heart of the nuclear blast. However, Knight-II quickly changed course and fled. Almost as though it were alive.

"B-3," came the call from the control plane. "Send K-II to the target indicated. What's wrong, B-3? You want the Knight to get lost?"

Rei came to himself again. He released his finger from the trigger. The stores control panel read **RDY FK II.**

Knight-I and V had disappeared. Flipping the dogfight switch to OFF, he guided Knight-II to its next target.

"Come back alive," Rei murmured. *At the very least, don't get killed.* He could sort all this out later. He'd have plenty of time. As long as he kept himself alive.

III

MYSTERIOUS BATTLE ZONE

The JAM were targeting Yukikaze. She was fighting them to the utmost limits of her abilities. He could not perceive the fierce battle being waged between them, yet he knew the enemy was there. She was warning him: They're here.

THE MAN CAME bearing nationalism. After touring several sectors of Faery Base, his pale blue eyes protected behind a pair of Ray-Ban Aviators, he announced that he wanted to learn more about the mindset of the soldiers who fought the JAM.

Although he had a press pass issued by the United Nations Earth Defense Force GHQ, Faery Base's authorities didn't want him there, which they made clear in the way they treated him. They carefully questioned him to make sure the purpose of his investigation was not simply to reinforce his own preconceptions and warned him not to write an article that would be slanted in favor of a specific country.

"And just what is that supposed to mean?" American freelance journalist, military critic, lobbyist, and writer Andy Lander asked with an irritated air. "Are you suggesting that I'd intentionally write a biased article?"

"Not at all," answered Colonel Roland of the base's Office of Public Affairs. "I'm just asking you to recognize the fact that this is a war between all of humanity and an alien race. As to how you do your job—"

"Yes, of course I realize that. But I think that approach is a little too vague. I want to ask the soldiers about what tangible things they're fighting for here on the front lines of Faery, not about some abstract sense of duty."

"Our mission is to defend Earth. What's so abstract about that? The only reason we're here is to keep the people of Earth from being attacked."

"I'd still like to try and conduct a deeper analysis than that."

"Then why don't I save you the trouble?" Colonel Roland responded with an irritated look on his face. "Here's what we're

fighting for: self-preservation. In combat, that's all that matters."
His expression suddenly softened. "A perfect answer, don't you
think? A solid answer. It's not as if anyone here actually wants
this war."

"Would anyone be that crazy?"

"There are plenty of people back on Earth who might be. A
lot of individuals and organizations are making huge profits
from it."

In the end, Lander never heard anyone in the FAF say that
they were fighting for their homeland. And he had certainly
never anticipated witnessing a scenario in which Russians
were fighting using American-made weapons, or even more
shocking, vice versa.

Although the materials for the majority of the fighter systems
the FAF was equipped with came from Earth, the designs were
entirely their own. Lander tried to gather information on the
research and development teams but was given no details: each
time, his inquiry was blocked for "security reasons." Finally,
in a fit of pique, he declared that he thought it was a misuse
of funding for the FAF to be developing fighters on its own
without passing that technology back to Earth. He demanded
to know what sort of fighters were being developed and was
determined to see one for himself. Then he formally requested
the opportunity to go up in one. He had never flown in anything
aside from passenger jets, but he was an intrepid individual
and in good physical health. He was a man who had traveled
the world, after all.

The FAF authorities, partially to rid themselves of what
was becoming a significant annoyance, granted him immediate approval. Colonel Roland told Lander that he hoped he'd
appreciate being able to personally evaluate the sort of high-
performance equipment being used to protect Earth. Lander
was given a physical exam and some simple anti-G training,
and then signed a waiver stating that the air force could not
be held responsible if anything happened to him.

"So," Lander asked, "what sort of plane do I get to ride in?"

"A Sylphid," said Colonel Roland.

"Huh," Lander responded with a faint smile. "That's a pretty girly sounding name." He adjusted his sunglasses and brushed back his hair, which he had dyed black from its natural blond. Blond hair, Lander believed, looked too effeminate.

"ANDY LANDER? NEVER heard of him"

Rei paused while eating his lunch and looked at Major Booker, who was seated across from him. Rei had lost at cards the night before and as a penalty had to buy lunch, but the major's tray was a modest affair, with just a ham sandwich and a Coke.

"Has he ever even flown before? Why do I have to have this joker in my backseat?"

"Are you going to make me spell it out for you?" said Booker, miserably gnawing on his sandwich. "Orders. As in General Cooley's. And more importantly, it's the central computer's orders too. It went through the personnel files and came up with a list of possible candidates for this duty. Oddly enough, they were all in Boomerang Squadron. Well, I suppose it was an obvious result given the kind of man Lander is."

The major laid a printout of a current affairs magazine article down in front of Rei. Rei picked it up and skimmed it; it was a diatribe about the United States not using American-made goods anymore. He checked the date on the bottom of the page. The article had been written just six months ago. He wouldn't have been surprised if the dateline had been decades before that.

"He's like a relic from the last century. An ideological throwback."

"Well, he's not alone. Considering how tense the current international situation is, the fact that a transnational organization like the FAF even exists is practically a miracle. It's too dangerous to let him wander around here for very long because he can use the material he gathers to stir up all sorts of prejudices back on Earth. So where do you quarantine an ultra-nationalist prick on a fact-finding mission? Say, oh, a squadron isolated from the rest of the normal combat units. Get it now?"

"Shit. I'm getting tired of being the 'special' in 'Special Air Force'..."

Rei was already short-tempered because for nearly a week he had been undergoing a battery of psychological analysis tests conducted by a Dr. Halévy of the Air Force Combat Psychology Research Center. Halévy was supposed to be the leading man in the field of combat psychology, but to Rei it was a pretty pointless distinction. When Rei commented how ironic it was that the doctor spent his days talking about air combat theory while remaining perfectly safe underground, Halévy folded his hands and looked grave. "Lieutenant Fukai," he intoned, "I'm fighting, too." *I'd like to see you fight off a missile with theory,* Rei thought sourly. On the battlefield, theory and abstract analysis were useless. Why couldn't anyone not on the front line understand that?

He shook his head and went back to eating his lunch of fried rice and meat loaf.

"Go to General Cooley. Your preflight briefing is at 1440." The major got up from his chair.

"Yes, sir. This isn't because I lost at poker, is it?"

Booker gave him a look. "And no matter what Lander asks you, you keep quiet. This is just a simple sightseeing flight."

Rei shrugged. Then something occurred to him. "Hey, Jack? Are those sunglasses Ray-Bans?"

Booker picked up his tray. "Nope. Nikons." Then, a smile playing across his lips, he left the cafeteria.

AFTER A SHORT briefing, Rei boarded Yukikaze. He continued performing the preflight checks on the elevator up from the underground hangar and felt himself calming a little. Having to give a biased journalist from Earth his own personal little flight tour stuck in his craw, but he knew he'd feel better once they were in the air.

After he emerged onto the planet's surface, a car approached from the side of the shade port and pulled alongside Yukikaze. General Cooley and a man got out. Andy Lander. Lander jovially waved at him. Rei answered with a slight nod. *What did this guy come here to investigate?* he wondered. Just going by Lander's looks, Rei guessed he was after material to argue that Earth had to be protected with American-made weapons or something.

Lander was built like a wrestler; the flight suit he wore was ill-fitting and did not favor him at all. Major Booker deftly inspected Lander's suit, then helped him aboard Yukikaze, fastening his shoulder harness and connecting his anti-G hoses.

Engine start. First the right, then the left.

"Take it away, Captain," said Lander.

"We've got ideal weather for a sightseeing flight," replied Rei.

Emergency generator test. Data link power display control power, on. Head-up display, activated. Flight control check via the indicators. Display, flight computer, check.

Once the check of authority was complete, they taxied onto the runway. The wind was strong, so Rei set the canopy control to BOOST. It lowered hydraulically and locked.

He called the tower for clearance to take off. Clearance granted. Throttle to military power. They began to climb. Rotation. Landing gear up. Flaps up. Hydraulic system set to flight mode, cutting the hydraulic supply from the landing gear and non-flight steering system. Reconfirm flight instruments. All systems normal.

Informing Lander that they would be climbing quickly, he moved the throttle to MAX. The afterburners kicked in and the thrust increased dramatically. Armed with just four short-range missiles and a gun, unencumbered by additional tanks or equipment, the agile Sylph could climb nearly vertically. Still, he shouldn't overdo it. Lander groaned. With a sigh, Rei brought them back to level flight. He performed a loose turn onto their flight path, a square of about 150 miles per side that would bring them back to their starting point.

"I heard that Faery's sun is a binary star," Lander said as he operated a camcorder, "but I can only see one. Just the main star. Wait, I see it. The companion star is that shadow, right?"

"You've got good eyes."

"The camera's digital viewfinder is picking it up. Can you fly steady like this for a bit without any maneuvering, please?"

Rei didn't mind that Lander said this with the tone of a hunter ordering his guide. He couldn't bring himself to be irritated by someone who he didn't care if he lived or died.

It was quiet for a while.

Then, perhaps bored with shooting his video, Lander began asking all sorts of questions. Where was Rei from? Had he been on Faery long? What did he plan to do when he returned to his native country?

Rei gave suitable, innocuous answers, but when Lander asked him, "Why do you fly?" he was stumped.

"To kill the JAM," he said finally, after buying some time with the excuse that he had to confirm their heading.

"That's just the result of your actions, not the cause," Lander replied. And with that, he'd crudely and unknowingly cut to the heart of the doubt that had been tormenting Rei. Rei tried to ignore him, but Lander continued, unheeding. "You must have a more concrete reason for fighting than that. For Earth, for your country, for your lover, for money, to get back alive, and so on. What are you thinking of when you're in combat?"

At least that question was simple to answer.

"Nothing," Rei said. "I don't think about anything. I'm blank. Here, I'll give you a taste of what it's like."

He gripped the side stick, cutting off the autopilot, and did some subtle footwork. Yukikaze snapped into a turn, executing a series of continuous barrel rolls. Returning to level flight, he performed a four-point roll in the other direction. They rose up vertical to the horizon, then were completely inverted, then vertical again, and finally back to normal. A steep climb that led into a loop. He performed several small, high-G loops, drawing Q-shapes in the sky. He pulled them into one final steep turn, and then they were back on course.

"How'd that feel, sir?" Rei asked.

There was a pause before Lander answered. "A man always has to be ready for surprise attacks. I was careless. Even though I half-anticipated it."

"What's that supposed to mean?"

Lander kept his mouth shut, and Rei was relieved to have been freed from his annoying questions. Now he and Yukikaze could become one in the silence. *Maybe that's the reason I fly,* he thought.

The clear sky was dazzling and lonely. A three-ship formation, most likely flying a CAP, overflew Yukikaze high above. From this distance the planes almost seemed translucent, like they were made of glass.

As he stared at the beautiful sight, a warning tone brought him back. The passive airspace radar was getting a reaction. He output the data onto the multidisplay and frowned, unable to comprehend what he was seeing. The radar was showing an enormous wall about fifty miles ahead of them. It was like a tsunami. Rei lifted his head and looked out of the cockpit, but all he could see was the quiet scene of Faery's primeval forest and the sky.

He couldn't confirm the existence of the wall with the standard radar system either. It reflected no electromagnetic radiation. What the hell was this?

The passive airspace radar was a detection system that had been developed to counter the various methods JAM fighters used to mask themselves while attacking. Because it utilized a type of cryogenically cooled visual sensor with an ultra-high receptivity, it had been nicknamed "Frozen Eye." No matter how an enemy craft might hide itself electromagnetically or optically, as long as it displaced air it could be detected. The system gave the SAF pilots an ability to find and kill the enemy that was so accurate it seemed almost instinctive. And now that same system was telling Rei that something monstrous was before him.

Was it a JAM force? It seemed way too big to be that. It was almost like a massive disturbance of the airspace. The bright horizontal line on the display was drawing closer fast.

The AVOID cue appeared on his HUD. If he did nothing, Yukikaze would automatically maneuver to evade the obstacle when they got too close to it. But Rei didn't wait for that. He pulled the plane back into a high-G Immelman loop, reversing their direction.

The line on the display bowed inward, seeming to wrap around Yukikaze. Rei didn't know what was going on, but he understood that they'd fallen into some sort of trap. The line on the display was now closing into a circle. Aiming for the rapidly disappearing gap, Yukikaze accelerated.

She didn't make it. The circle closed and its diameter began to quickly contract. It fell inward upon Yukikaze, as though intent on swallowing her.

"Brace for impact!" Rei yelled automatically, although the scene outside the cockpit still betrayed nothing out of the ordinary.

The impact, when it came, was like flying into a wall of iron. His ears were ringing. He couldn't see. A gray haze was obscuring his vision. *Must have messed up my eyes,* he thought, disoriented from the shock.

He reflexively checked his instruments. Both engines had stalled. The turbine intake temperature read 560°C, only a little below normal. The auto-restart system should have activated after ten seconds, but it didn't. Rei pushed the airstart button. No response. Had he accidentally pulled the throttle back during the impact? No, he hadn't. Then had the engines themselves been damaged? He checked the tachometer. It was dropping precipitously. If it fell to 8 percent RPM, the engines wouldn't be able to supply power or hydraulic pressure. He had to raise his airspeed and force the turbines to spin faster.

Confirm rate of descent and airspeed. Confirm sufficient altitude. Canopy defogger switch, ON. He thought maybe the canopy had become clouded, but as they fell, the haze cleared a bit. The sky had been cloudless just moments before. *What the hell is going on here?* Rei wondered.

A strange panorama spread out before his eyes. The world looked colorless, like a black-and-white photo. The terrain swirled below them as though it were the surface of Jupiter. He could see parts that looked like trees, and others that looked like deserts or the ocean. *Where the hell are we?*

Lander was stirring in the backseat. "What... We were just flying, weren't we, Lieutenant?" He had apparently lost consciousness. "My ears... They hurt."

"It's Flier's Ear."

"What?"

"Otitic barotrauma. Inner ear damage caused by a sudden change in air pressure."

"You did that on purpose! Why—" Lander suddenly paused. "Hey, am I wrong, or are the engines stopped?"

"I can't restart them."

"Why not?"

"I don't have time to figure that out."

Rei began searching for terrain that would allow for an emergency landing. He switched the radar to ground mode, real beam ground mapping, but the only thing that came on the display was a strangely fixed image. It looked like the transmitter was off-line.

Then, out of the corner of his eye, he spotted something that looked manmade. He banked into a slow turn to get a better look. It was a long and narrow construction without any crosscuts. A runway. It had to be. Even if it wasn't, he was going to use it as one, because otherwise he would have to abandon Yukikaze, and he didn't want to even think about that.

All he could get over the comm system was static. He set the radar altimeter but didn't think he could trust it. If these weren't the skies of Faery, he couldn't be sure of his barometric altimeter, either.

"Mister Lander, do you think you can measure our altitude with that video camera's range finder?"

"Huh?"

"Quickly."

"No good, it's broken. Wait a minute, I've got some digital binoculars with me. Let me try it with those."

Rei inverted Yukikaze.

"Measure in a straight line below us."

Their rate of descent was increasing. That was the only data he could determine for sure. Rei didn't know what the linear proportion was between his barometric altimeter and his actual change in altitude, but he could combine them with Lander's reading for a rough estimate and then reset his altimeter.

He was over the flat expanse that looked like a runway. He executed a wide turn, correcting his attitude, and once again put them on the virtual approach line.

"We're landing."

Gear down. Air brakes opened slightly to regulate their speed. Forty-degree bank angle as they turned and descended. While describing a semicircle, Yukikaze's altitude dropped by a sixth, then a quarter, then to half of what it was. Their altitude was now 2,300 feet. He had a good line of sight now.

Final approach. Flaps down. Pitch regulated. Glide slope, three degrees. Rate of descent, eighty-five feet per minute. A little high. Yukikaze's nose floated up due to the ground effect, which felt a little weaker than normal. Touchdown.

The ground rushing by them at 115 mph was a grayish light brown. Rei stomped on the toe brake, nervous that they might hit a rock and cripple themselves. They were approaching the edge of the runway.

When they finally came to a stop Rei was surprised to see that there was still plenty of runway left. He must have underestimated its size from the air. He was relieved that their landing had still been successful, despite his misjudgment.

They were surrounded by what seemed to be a forest the color of seaweed. So who had cut this runway out of it? He couldn't see any hangar facilities. Maybe it was for super heavyweight planes to land and take off from. If so, the enormous size of the runway implied that these phantom planes would be similarly huge. Since there was only one runway, did that mean there was little wind here, or that the wind direction didn't vary? Maybe they used both the length and width of the wide surface? Or maybe this wasn't a runway at all...

"This is a major scoop!" Lander exclaimed. "Who'd believe there was someplace like this on Faery?"

"I don't think this is Faery."

"Very funny. You don't have to hide it. It's possible you didn't even know about it. I'll bet it's a top-secret area."

Arguing with Lander wasn't going to improve their situation, so Rei dropped it and began testing the electronics.

The master caution light was lit, but aside from that, the other system failure warning indicators remained off. The built-in test system itself was also malfunctioning. Most of the high-level electrical systems were off-line. The multiply protected flight control system was barely operational. Luckily, it had still worked well enough to allow him to land the plane; if it had failed too, he wouldn't have been able to maintain controlled flight for even an instant.

He switched the jet fuel starter to ON and pulled the starter handle. It worked.

The connection to the starboard engine's hydraulic accumulator was intact, and the turbines slowly began to spin. Once the engine got past 8 percent RPM, fuel would flow into it and the autoignition would spark... Negative ignition. Rei killed the JFS.

The fuel wasn't flowing. There were no abnormalities detected in the fuel boost pump, and even if the emergency boost pump had been destroyed, it would still be possible to do fuel transfer via gravity. But if the electronic engine controller was keeping the fuel shut-off valve closed, then—

"Why don't we get out and look around?" said Lander.

Rei sighed and checked the altimeter and external thermometer. Even taking Lander's measurement error into account, the atmospheric pressure altitude variance showed that it wasn't all that different from Faery's. The temperature was 13°C.

Steeling himself, Rei moved the canopy control to OPEN. Lander loosened his harness on his own and climbed out of the cockpit onto the boarding step on the right side of the plane.

"Lieutenant, can you extend the ladder?"

Rei shook his head. The boarding ladder could be extended from the plane only by operating the control handle in the ladder door.

Lander bent down, took hold of the handgrip, and swung himself down to the ground.

Rei stayed aboard Yukikaze, searching in vain for the cause of the problem. He had twenty minutes of electricity left from the auxiliary power unit. He couldn't make contact with the base, either. The twenty minutes were soon up.

Yukikaze fell silent.

In this situation, he needed to start the JFS since its generator system provided power to the self-ignition system and to Yukikaze's vital electrical systems. The central computer's backup power supply was working normally, so at least he wouldn't have to worry about that for another twenty-four hours.

But he couldn't get the JFS to turn over. Lander was gone. Rei scanned their surroundings and saw him at a distance. He was apparently digging a hole in the ground, looking like a child playing by himself.

Rei got down from the plane and inspected the fuselage. He couldn't see any obvious abnormalities on the outside. Since he had no tools, any problems deeper than that were beyond his ability to fix.

The air pressure here was considerably lower. If this were Faery, he'd estimate their altitude to be around 6,000 feet. But he just couldn't see how this place could be only a few hundred miles from Faery Base.

There was no wind. It was quiet.

The sky overhead was cloudy, but it wasn't dark. The clouds looked white. The gray ground beneath them formed a vast, level plane covered with a blackish green haze. *If I could get the engines started,* Rei thought bitterly, *I could fly above it and see what sort of place this is.* Perhaps they'd stumbled upon some unexplored part of Faery. Was this a JAM base? Or maybe this wasn't Faery at all but the JAM's home world. He instantly dismissed the thought. If that were the case, he probably would have been shot down long ago.

Rei recalled the image picked up by the Frozen Eye. It looked like a wall, a bright line that pushed relentlessly forward as though aiming for Yukikaze. He didn't think it was a natural phenomenon. It looked like they'd been caught by some mechanism that could selectively transport objects through space. But Rei couldn't even make a guess as to what intelligence was operating it or who had brought them to this place. Maybe it was the result of some as-yet unknown natural phenomenon. If this were a JAM trap, wouldn't they have done something by now?

Rei sat down on Yukikaze's front wheel and sighed. Lander had returned. There was no hint of concern on his face. Rei couldn't decide if this intrepidness was a personality attribute or whether the man was just stupid. Maybe a little bit of both. To Lander, Faery itself was an unknown dimension. Perhaps, from his point of view, their bizarre surroundings—which were completely alien to Rei—were merely an extension of an already strange world. And Lander obviously saw himself as a man who would never be beaten, who couldn't be defeated, even in death. Rei could just imagine the upbringing, environment, and family history that had made him this way. He probably believed that he was carrying on the pioneer spirit of his forebears.

"Well, why don't we go and have a look?"

"At what?"

"I won't let you stop me."

"I have no idea what you're talking about."

"Have a look through these, Lieutenant." Lander patted the binoculars hanging from his neck. "There's a cornfield just over yonder."

"A field?"

"A big yellow one. This is a major discovery, you know."

At the mention of corn, Rei realized how hungry he was. He checked his chronometer. It would have been early evening on Faery. Lander had no objections to holding off on his exploration for a meal, so Rei climbed Yukikaze's ladder and retrieved some emergency rations from his survival kit along with a thermos of coffee he had stowed away.

The emergency rats were vacuum-packed crackers with jelly. Lander disappointedly asked if that was supposed to be a full meal as he took them.

"No," Rei replied. "Technically, one-third of the B-type is intended to be a full meal." He read from the package: 1 MEAL CONSISTS OF 1 PACK CRACKER (A-TYPE) AND 1/3 PACK JELLY (B-TYPE).

"Got it?"

"Yeah," Lander replied. "So, these crackers..." He sat down on the main wheel and scrutinized them. "I wonder what kind of wheat they're made out of."

"Who knows?"

The jelly was a fluorescent orange and tasted vaguely like apricot. Rei made a face. It was pretty bad.

"I'll bet it's grown here," Lander said as he stretched out his arms. "In complete secrecy."

"This isn't Faery. The suns should have set by now, but it's still light."

The FAF's clocks were all set to Greenwich Mean Time. Since the base was underground and the fighting didn't depend on it being day or night, there was no need to synchronize with Faery's rotation. So it wasn't unusual for noon in the base to be during night on the surface. The flight plan called for them to return when the sun was setting, yet there was no indication that it was getting dark.

"If that's true, it makes me even more suspicious."

"About what?"

Lander chomped on his cracker, as though satisfied he had come to a conclusion about the origin of the wheat in it. "The FAF buys its food from Earth, right?"

"I know that much," Rei answered. "Our supplies go through the UN food management program."

"You know why that is, Lieutenant? It's to prevent the FAF from becoming independent. To prevent the greatest military power there is from standing on its own. That's why it's forbidden for it to engage in food production."

"Huh," said Rei. This was the first he'd heard of it. "They have restrictions like that? I never knew. So, you're thinking this is some secret Faery food production base that's been hidden behind an extra-dimensional wall?"

Lander nodded, either ignoring or not picking up on the sarcasm, and continued to expostulate on his crazy idea. "The FAF has begun to amass money, presumably for industrial use. Now, where there's money, you've got Jews. And then there's the Chinese. China's apparently been shipping its surplus labor to work on Faery. To make money for the state, of course. But the FAF authorities—"

"That's the biggest load of bullshit I've ever heard," Rei said as he balled up the foil wrapper and tossed it away. "You seriously think the FAF is planning to invade Earth?"

"Can you deny it?"

Rei studied Lander's face for a good ten seconds. "Are you kidding me?" he finally said.

Lander serenely took a sip of the coffee.

"What could we possibly do with only air power?" Rei asked as he got up off the landing gear. He walked back toward Lander and took the thermos from him. "Yeah, we may have the most powerful air force, but we wouldn't be able to achieve anything on Earth without ground forces."

"The fact that the FAF has no regular soldiers is important," Lander replied. "You're all officers, right? What that means is that you already have the capability to command thousands of regular soldiers. And soldiers don't necessarily have to be human, you know. They could be robots. Which the FAF has the capacity to manufacture."

"Our enemy is the JAM. And in case you forgot, they're your enemy too."

"I suppose," Lander answered reluctantly. "The JAM… Maybe the JAM gave up trying to invade Earth a long time ago, Lieutenant."

Rei was already well past irritated, and the absurdity of this argument was starting to push him over the edge into genuinely pissed off.

"Listen. Every day I risk my life fighting the JAM. Just what the hell do you think I am?"

"You're a soldier," Lander replied. "Risking your life is part of your job. That's why I asked you earlier what you were fighting for. If you don't actually know the answer to that, well, that would be pretty tragic."

"Are you saying the Earth would be protected even if the FAF were done away with?"

"I am."

Lander told Rei that he had come to Faery to confirm that theory. In his view, the FAF was a modern-day foreign legion consisting of a mishmash of ill-bred traitors who had no place back in their homelands outside of prison. And the thought that Earth was being defended by this group did not sit well with him. Lander believed that Earth must be defended by the most advanced nations possessing the greatest power.

"If the JAM's military power increases," Rei ground out, "you'll find out real quick just how bad that idea is."

"I disagree," Lander answered. "I think we could handle the JAM just fine. If necessary, we can have our regular forces stand against them."

Rei found Lander's absolute certainty unsettling, but at the same time had the strange feeling that he was some sort of a heretic for thinking so. He recalled the words of the historian Lynn Jackson, who had chronicled the history of the war against the JAM.

> At that time, the JAM had presented us with the key to building a world federation. But the path we chose was the exact opposite. Perhaps world unification never would have been realized, no matter how strong an enemy we were confronted with. From what I can determine from the materials I've gathered—memoranda, official records, and direct interviews with the statesmen of that time—even when Earth was invaded, people held on to their prejudices to the bitter end. Paradoxically, we ended up treating the alien JAM as though they were just another neighboring nation.

When Rei had read this, he had thought it was an extreme viewpoint. But now he agreed with it. Lander's opinions had just confirmed that again. *Still*, he reasoned, *reality isn't that simple, is it?* The people of Earth wrongly regarded the JAM as an existence analogous to themselves. But the JAM's true nature remained shrouded in mystery. Humans still didn't know what sort of life-form they were or even what they looked like.

The JAM had yet to reveal the true extent of their power.

Rei was convinced of this to the core of his being. It was his instinct as a soldier. However, he did not say this to Lander. The man couldn't understand, or rather, wouldn't understand. And honestly, Rei had had enough of his delusions. *Let him live in his own reality,* he decided. He thought soberly that, even if his existence was eventually deemed as unnecessary as Lander evidently believed it to be, by the time the man realized just how wrong he was, the regular forces he believed in so fervently would be wiped out. While Rei hoped that would never happen, a part of him also hoped he could be there to see Lander's face when the time came. Maybe he would then have an inkling of how a soldier felt, would begin to understand the merciless imperative of survival, which was the opposite of theory. The JAM used extremely powerful weaponry and operated them with flawless reflexes. One needed to be just as cold and ruthless to oppose them.

But Rei remained silent as Lander continued.

"Guys like you are easy to manipulate. You're the ideal type to be an enlisted man, but you're not officer material. You don't have any convictions."

"You sound just like a missionary."

"Listen," Lander said, now sounding as though he were launching into a well-rehearsed speech. "The toughest things an invader has to deal with are the national patriotism and religious conviction of the invaded. If you can remold those, through propaganda or some other means, the invasion automatically succeeds. But the soldiers of the FAF don't have any sense of patriotism or beliefs, and it's nothing but a delusion to think the high command of the FAF has any sense of loyalty to Earth. If you're not careful, one of these days you're going to find yourself joining forces with the JAM and invading Earth. Do you think that's impossible?"

Rei took a deep breath and told him their conversation was over. Lander shrugged his shoulders and got up.

Rei's one imperative now was to figure out where they were. If this was an area that had some connection to the FAF—if it were a secret zone he didn't know about, for example—then that meant there was the possibility of getting home. But if it wasn't, then the situation was dire: no matter what Lander believed, they would never make it back to Faery Base again. If that were the case, Rei decided, then he would get in the plane and keep flying till his fuel ran out. It wouldn't be such a bad way to go, especially since he'd be with Yukikaze. Since he couldn't get her engines restarted, though, even that was just a pipe dream.

As Rei was stowing the thermos back aboard the plane, Lander pointed at the small kanji characters painted just below the canopy. "What's that say, anyway?"

"'Yukikaze.' It was the name of a destroyer in the old Japanese imperial navy."

She'd seen thirteen naval battles and survived them all without a scratch. Rei hadn't known that until Major Booker had told him.

Lander looked impressed. Rei decided not to tell him that the name had been assigned randomly.

Grabbing the survival gun Yukikaze was equipped with, he jumped down to the ground. Lander asked to see it, but Rei didn't oblige him.

"You're a civilian. It's my duty to guarantee your safety."

It was a short weapon, but since it was a Bullpup design, with the breech at the very rear, its barrel length was longer than it seemed. The trigger and handgrip assembly were in front of the magazine, which held thirty rounds of powerful rifle ammo.

"What's the caliber?" Lander asked.

"It's a .221. Air force arsenal-made, but the ammo's Remington. Fireball."

"Copy of the Colt, huh?"

"Is it? I wouldn't know." He checked the clip. "But I know

how to shoot it, so don't worry."

Lander looked like he was about to say something when his gaze was suddenly drawn to a spot behind Rei. He grabbed his binoculars.

Rei turned around to look. A bird. No. There was something odd about the way it moved. Black. Flying in an angular, zigzag pattern.

"Looks like a UFO. What is it?"

"It's shaped like a boomerang." Lander offered him the binoculars. "Taking the distance into account, it looks pretty big. About the size of a small plane."

Rei didn't take the binoculars. The object had disappeared.

"You think it's the JAM?" Lander asked, almost happily. "Or maybe it's some weird Faery life-form." He kicked Yukikaze's tire. "This is quite a fighter you have here, Lieutenant. If you can't get the engines started it's nothing more than a very expensive hunk of metal, but I gotta say it's allowing me to write one hell of an article."

"Yeah, well, it might be the last thing you ever write," Rei said shortly. "Tell you what. If we make it back, I'll buy you a drink. We can make a toast to your journalistic achievement."

Lander ignored him and checked to see if the camcorder was still working. "No use. Looks like it got busted in the impact."

Rei took it from him and peered through the electronic viewfinder. The image it showed resembled a color blindness chart, and after a few moments his vision began to blur. He handed it back to Lander, who finally gave up on it and drew a voice recorder out of his life-vest pocket. It looked old and well used. He turned it on and started walking, recording a narrative description of their surroundings.

Rei was concerned that the UFO-like thing would return. Yukikaze was helpless in her grounded state, and if the object was a JAM fighter it would only need one shot to set her aflame.

Unaware of Rei's fears, Lander had moved quite a distance ahead. Rei couldn't just leave him alone, so he followed after.

"This looks like a dried-up wetland," Lander said to Rei as he caught up with him. "A runway made from mud hardened by a chemical agent."

That was indeed what it looked like. Yellowish brown earth and scraps of plant matter were encased in a translucent, plastic-like substance that looked almost like glass. Judging from the construction method, Rei thought that maybe this hadn't been intended to be a proper runway. As they walked toward the forest, the glossy surface gave way to damp mud, and before long they passed into the dark forest itself.

It was quiet, yet the atmosphere seemed noisy somehow. The ground was soft, cushioned with accumulated bark that had peeled off of the trees. All of the vegetation surrounding them was dark green.

It was completely unlike the strangely hued forests of Faery, which were so dense that you needed a tunnel excavator rather than a machete to get through them. Because of that impen-etrable density, the animals that inhabited the forest were small, and either lived in burrows under the forest floor or had evolved to live on top of the canopy; as far as Rei knew, no larger creatures inhabited the forest proper. And any humans that had entered it, whether accidentally or deliberately, had been swallowed up by it and never seen again. It was almost as if the forest itself were one enormous life-form.

This place was different. There was quite a bit of space between the trees. But Rei wasn't so sure the things surrounding them actually were trees. He started listening to what Lander was dictating into his recorder.

"They almost seem made out of metal," Lander was saying. "Beneath a greenish outer layer, they shine like copper, and they're shaped like... The little ones are cone-shaped. Cones that look more like they were designed and manufactured than like natural forms. The big ones stretch up vertically, with thick branches that spread out from the top and then droop down, encircling the trunks."

The branches wrapped around the trunks symmetrically, like precisely wound coils. To Rei, it seemed like they weren't part of the trees at all but were instead some species of symbiotic plant. Several trees he touched felt warm. There were a few withered ones as well. Some were split, as though struck by lightning, and their exposed cross-sections were blackened as though carbonized, and yet they didn't seem to have actually burned. Some trees had a golden mold growing on them as well. He couldn't be sure that it actually was mold, but it was definitely some species of parasite. It looked like fine lace, and the trees that were wrapped in it didn't seem to be alive.

The overall effect was just as Lander had said: the forest really did look like something somebody had made. It was almost as if some entity had tried to tackle the problem of creating life and had only managed the external appearance of it. Were these trees actually made by some vast intelligence? And if so, what sort of unimaginable power would it possess to be able to do so?

Then, suddenly, Rei knew why Yukikaze's electronics had malfunctioned. It had to be the result of a powerful electro-magnetic interference. The kind that could be generated by a forest of transmitters.

Yukikaze's resistance to EM jamming should have been perfect. She was protected by a multilayered 120 dB shield, and her electrical components themselves had anti-EMI processing capabilities. Common sense said that his conclusion was highly improbable. Yet he couldn't rule it out.

He felt his hair standing on end. It was fear of the unknown. A powerful fear born of instinct. He knew they had to get back to Yukikaze, and fast.

Lander wouldn't hear of it.

"A little longer, Lieutenant. Just a little further on is—"

"That cornfield of yours? Get real. We don't have time for this. We have to go back, now."

"Look, it's right over there."

He pointed to a yellowish area ahead of them. Rei looked to where Lander was pointing. A sudden sick feeling curdled his stomach. It wasn't a field. It was a swamp. Involuntarily, the two men exchanged glances. A bizarre, carnal stench wafted from the scene that spread out before them, completely different from the sterile, inorganic environment they had just been in.

"Corn?" said Rei. "This is more like soup."

As they approached, the increasingly foul odor triggered such a violent physiological disgust that Rei was sure he was going to vomit. The muddy liquid moved in sluggish swirling patterns. No matter how hard they strained their eyes to look, they couldn't see anything below the surface of the sickly stew. The swamp was further veiled by a light opalescent haze.

Lander continued to narrate excitedly into the recorder.

"You're wasting your time," Rei said.

"What are you talking about?"

"I don't think your recorder got anything. It's probably just picked up radio frequency interference, which means there'll be nothing but static."

"What?"

Lander started to play back the recording. It was just as Rei guessed. Nothing but white noise.

"What do you suppose this is?" Lander asked as he switched the recorder off ruefully. He gestured at the swamp, seeking Rei's opinion.

"It looks like the material the runway is made out of. I think this planet—although it may not be a planet, so let's say area—is probably made of the same stuff."

"Do you think it's connected with the JAM?"

"Maybe. Maybe it's some sort of raw material they use to build. Or maybe it's waste material. I wonder…" Rei trailed off.

"What?"

"No, nothing."

Rei had had a sudden, inexplicable impression that people had been melted down into the stuff in the swamp, or perhaps were formed from it. He struggled to understand why such an absurdly grotesque image would come to him, and then thought about the equally absurd leap of imagination he'd made in thinking that those trees were antennas. He considered the contrast of the two impressions and realized that it was the inorganic versus the organic, machines versus people...

"Stop!" he shouted.

Lander was reaching out to touch the yellow liquid, and Rei felt as though he were watching the other man reach out to touch a rotted corpse. But the sense of danger and revulsion was even more extreme, and as he realized this, Lander's body jerked backwards and he screamed out in pain.

"What happened?"

"My hand..."

Rei ran over to him and looked down. There was nothing below Lander's left wrist. Blood was pouring from the stump.

"The...the haze...above the liquid...it's vibrating like a saw. God damn it... What the hell is this place?!" Lander gasped.

"We're getting out of here," Rei said and began tying off Lander's wound, using the recorder's carrying strap as a makeshift tourniquet.

"We can't get...the engines...started on that damn fighter of yours... We can't get out of here."

"I'll figure something out. If we can take off, we can find a way out of here." Rei finished tying the tourniquet. "Okay, that's got it. I've got painkillers in the first aid kit back at the plane. Keep your arm elevated."

He picked up the survival gun and helped Lander get unsteadily to his feet. Sweat beaded on Lander's forehead, his pale face contorted with the pain, but he didn't pass out.

Rei wanted to get back to Yukikaze as soon as possible, but he couldn't hurry the other man. Progress was slow. Lander's huge shoulders heaved with each breath, step by painful step, but he refused Rei's offers of help. Neither man spoke. The atmosphere was oppressive.

The space between the trees grew narrower. Their distribution seemed irregular, with denser areas coming in undulating waves. From above, Rei thought, it would look just like an energy distribution chart.

The straight-line distance they'd walked before must have been around half a mile, about half of which was in the forest, so there shouldn't have been more than a quarter mile to go. But there was no sign that the forest was ending. They may have been lost. Lander leaned against a thick tree to rest.

"Go on without me, Lieutenant."

"We're nearly there. I can't leave you. We have no idea what could happen."

Rei examined the wound. It wasn't bleeding too badly now, but it needed proper treatment quickly.

Lander croaked out a hoarse laugh. "I just had a hand and now it's gone. Kinda funny, don't you think?"

Please, Rei thought, *don't start cracking up on me now.*

"Listen up. The only way you're going to get back to the plane is on your own two legs, and there's nothing wrong with them, right? So move!"

"Right… Thing is, it's the shock more than the pain that's doing a number on me. Feels like it's stabbing through my heart. Never noticed how much walking can take it out of you."

"I'll help you."

"No, you need to keep your hands on that machine gun. I'm okay. Let's go."

Rei nodded. Lander walked forward unsteadily.

The spaces between the trees were widening again. It couldn't be much further now. Their field of vision suddenly opened up, and Rei guessed that they must have accidentally—and luckily—taken a shortcut. They emerged at a point about 600 feet away from Yukikaze.

Lander stopped. "Lieutenant, wait."

Rei noticed it in the same instant: a strange object hovering directly over Yukikaze at a height of ten or twelve feet. It was an absolute black, like a hole in the sky. There was no sense of it being a solid object. It was a bit smaller than Yukikaze and shaped like a boomerang. *No*, Rei thought. *Like a sickle.*

"JAM…"

"Dammit, I wish I had a camera." Lander sounded like he'd forgotten all about the pain.

Rei clenched his fist, a cold sweat breaking out across his back. They wanted to capture Yukikaze intact.

"What do you think it's doing?"

"It's trying to decode Yukikaze's IFF and other electronic systems. I may have to self-destruct her."

"How? It's not touching the plane."

"I don't know how, but I'm sure of it. The JAM have always seemed more interested in our planes than in us."

Rei walked out of the forest and onto the runway, placing himself clearly in the enemy's line of sight.

"Lieutenant, what're you doing? Come back!"

"They'll take Yukikaze over my dead body."

Rei recklessly approached Yukikaze. About one plane length away, he raised the gun and took aim at the object. It made no reaction. He fired. Short.

Confirming the gun was set to full auto, he emptied the clip at it. Empty cartridges scattered around him. The last cartridge flew from the firing chamber and bounced onto the ground. As the echo of the gunfire faded away, he knew he was going to need more than small-caliber fire to take that thing out. He threw the machine gun down, frustrated at his own powerlessness.

He walked toward Yukikaze. As he did so, there was a sudden movement overhead. The black shadow rotated with a jerk and withdrew from Yukikaze, moving in an irregular manner. It seemed to be out of control. Suddenly, the black camouflage peeled away. It was a silver, forward-swept–wing aircraft. A JAM combat reconnaissance plane. It fell toward the forest. The sound of an explosion followed.

"Lander! Get over here, fast!"

Pale blue sparks were spattering from an electrical discharge line on Yukikaze's wing. As Rei secured it, Lander reached the plane. Black smoke was rising from the forest.

"They'll send reinforcements, won't they?"

"We'll deal with that when it happens. At least they don't seem to be interested in us."

"Maybe they'll change their minds."

Rei grabbed the first aid kit from Yukikaze, along with the other survival gun that was stowed in the rear seat. He removed the makeshift tourniquet from Lander's arm, sprayed the wound with a sealing agent to stop the bleeding, doused it with disinfectant, wrapped the stump with sterile film, and bandaged it.

"There're painkillers if you need them. I don't know if you can fire this gun one-handed, but I'm giving it to you anyway."

"What about you?"

"Well, if I don't get the engines started, you won't get that real flight experience you're here for, right?"

Rei settled into the cockpit, toggled the Jet Fuel Starter switch to ON, and pulled the starter handle. Nothing. He tried again, and then again. In the past, Rei had found this process amusingly similar to starting a motor bike or a lawn mower. In a way, that was exactly what he was doing: the JFS was a small combustion engine that moved the onboard fuel but didn't have an advanced control system. Now, though, the humor of the situation escaped him. *Come on,* he pleaded silently.

It started on the fourth try. Engine master switch to ON. Throttle control to BOOST.

Rei got up and climbed along the canopy sill to slide into the rear seat.

Armament control system, ON. The ECM display flickered on momentarily, then faded out.

Rei wasn't well versed in using the electronic armaments. His work in the front seat had little to do with what went on in the backseat, which was devoted entirely to data acquisition and electronic warfare. His EWOs took care of all that. He flew the plane.

But even with his lack of specialized knowledge, he knew enough to reason that the enemy must be using some specific force external to Yukikaze to arrest the plane's systems. And if that force could jam Yukikaze's systems, then chances were it could be jammed in return.

He assumed manual control to operate the dispersion jammer and began noise jamming as well. After a bit, symbols marking the enemy positions appeared on the display screen. The system immediately switched over to auto-jamming mode and the symbols on the display began to change wildly. The computer immediately deciphered the radar waves coded as "enemy" and activated countermeasures. The locations of the targets were determined and displayed.

What was impossible for a human, Yukikaze's electronic armaments did with ease. With those now on the job, there was nothing left for Rei to do. He got back into the front seat.

He didn't know if it would help get the engines started, but he threw the switch connecting the JFS to the right engine hydraulic motor and slid the throttle over. The tachometer sprang to life. The power supply to the electronic armaments was dropping because of the extra load that feeding the engine was placing on the JFS, but there was nothing Rei could do about that.

How were the JAM succeeding in keeping Yukikaze's electronics off-line? Were they analyzing the timing impulses of all the systems and then sending in false data? If that were the case, how was Yukikaze resisting it now? Rei knew this was a battle beyond his level of comprehension, a battle of forces humans couldn't perceive. He could only watch from the sidelines. *Please don't lose,* he prayed.

When the tachometer reached 13 percent RPM the auto-ignition system switched on. Ignition, activated.

Turbine intake temperature and hydraulic pressure, rising.

Fuel flow rate, increasing. The noise from the exhaust was rising to ear-piercing levels.

At 50 percent RPM, the JFS automatically delinked from the starter motor. The right generator caution light went out. All of Yukikaze's electronic systems came back to life.

Rei connected the JFS to the left engine, reset the throttle, and climbed down from the plane to help Lander in. As he was straining under the weight of the man he was boosting up, Rei was struck with an odd thought: where in this body did Lander keep his ideas?

Ideas were invisible. Humanity had brought into being state organizations, national consciousness, religion... You couldn't see them with your eyes, yet they were certainly real.

But what about machines? Yukikaze was here, like a monster from a dream materialized in the real world. Machines were the material embodiment of ideas springing from human consciousness. Could humanity continue to control the results of its ideas? Or would it be driven insane by them? Perhaps that was what the JAM were trying to do.

There was no time to reflect on it further. He got Lander's helmet on, secured his oxygen mask, then connected the anti-G hoses, lap belt, and shoulder harness.

Seizing the handgrip, he hung down off of the plane and folded up the boarding ladder. He pulled himself back up and looked into the cockpit. Once he was sure the ladder caution light had gone out, he got in.

Canopy control set to CLOSE. Fire control power, on. Master arm switch set to ON. Left engine ignition, activated. Jet fuel starter, off.

He called back to Lander. "Whatever you do, don't touch the ECM panel."

"Got it."

"Still think this is a secret Faery Base?"

"No, but I'm not giving up keeping an eye on the FAF."

"Those painkillers look like they're working for you."

"Hey, what's that beeping sound?"

"It's a warning that an enemy's been detected."

"Where?"

Data appeared on the HUD. Gun mode. A motionless target. Range one-point-three, bearing three-nine-L. An aboveground installation? He couldn't tell for sure without visual contact.

"Looks like it's in the forest. I'm taking it out before we launch. If they stop our engines after takeoff, we're screwed."

He nudged the throttle forward. Parking brake, off. When the engine output reached about 80 percent, Yukikaze began to move. Just a slight motion and he could wring out the thrust. They rotated left, coming to a stop with the target dead ahead.

The target designator box appeared on the HUD, although all Rei could see before them was those weird trees.

The stores control display showed **RDY GUN**, the letters flashing. That was an abnormal sign for it to display, but Rei didn't think it was malfunctioning. He got the feeling Yukikaze was urging him to shoot the thing, and fast.

The gun line on the cannon was at slightly above horizontal. If he fired now, he would overshoot the target.

Rei stepped on the toe brake and pushed the throttle forward to MIL. Yukikaze's nose sank as she knelt forward, her front shock absorbers contracting as they held back the terrific forward thrust to keep her stationary.

The target was moving into the aiming reticule. Without a moment's hesitation, Rei squeezed the trigger. The Vulcan cannon roared, throwing fifty rounds of ammunition at the target in 0.5-second bursts. He kept firing. Yukikaze shook. Before he'd exhausted his ammunition, the machine cannon drive system began flashing an overheat warning. He ignored it and continued to fire.

Ahead of him, flashes of light ran left and right along the forest edge, their centers forming expanding blue white hemispheres. The explosions merged into an intense ball of light, too bright to look at directly.

Cease fire. Check the displays. The standard radar remained silent, but the passive airspace radar detected something.

A bright point appeared in front of the symbol marking their plane's position. The point became a disc, and then the disc rapidly expanded.

Outside the plane, it was getting brighter and brighter. A line was moving across the display toward the mark indicating the plane. The shock-wave front was sweeping toward them. There was no way to avoid it.

There was a violent impact. The engines stalled.

Yukikaze was in the air. She was in free fall.

The engines automatically restarted.

"Lieutenant? What's going on?"

"It looks like I'll be able to get you back on schedule."

They were in the skies of Faery. It was near sunset. Rei checked his instruments. The warning tone and the HUD display were telling him to pull up, signaling that if he didn't the system would automatically do so at four Gs. Air intake temperature had risen to nearly 700°C, but it was still running a little cold. Before exceeding an airspeed of 250 knots, he lifted his leg. No abnormalities. The only indication of the extra time they'd spent was on the onboard clock.

"It really was a fairyland," Lander muttered. "If it wasn't for this injury, I'd swear it was just a hallucination. I still can't believe it."

Rei felt the same way.

THE FAF SEEMED ready to believe that the incident had been real. As a TAF plane escorted them back, Rei told the authorities what had happened. Upon landing, Yukikaze was washed down with enormous amounts of water to neutralize any possible radioactive contamination while Rei and Lander were isolated for biohazard prevention. Lander's hand was operated on by a surgeon wearing what looked like a space suit for protection. Rei used the copious time he spent in the tiny isolation room to finish up his written report and answer all sorts of questions.

It was three weeks before the two men were let out of the isolation chambers and released from the tedious examinations. They drank a toast, and true to his word, it was on Rei. Afterward, Lander returned to Earth and Rei returned to normal duty.

Rei was subjected to more psychological tests by Dr. Halévy. They were cognition games designed to produce mock abnormal events to tax his mental processes and then gauge his reactions. It seemed nothing more than child's play to him. Compared to the actual abnormal events he'd just survived, the doctor's tests seemed positively innocent by comparison, and so Rei played along as best he could out of a curious sympathy. As a result, the tests proceeded well and he was free of them sooner than he had expected.

About a week later, he was eating in the mess hall and thinking about what the hell that yellow swamp was when Major Booker clapped him on the shoulder and sat down next to him, handing over a magazine as he did.

"'A Report from the Front Lines of Faery,' by Mr. Andrew Lander. Read it yet?"

"Does he mention me?"

"Not at all, but he wrote a lot of good things about Yukikaze. Aside from that, it's his usual stuff."

"I wonder how his injury's doing."

"Fine, I suppose. The doctors here are used to trauma like that. But they were mad that you didn't bring his hand back with you."

"There was nothing to bring back. It was weird. Everything past his wrist was just gone, like it had evaporated."

"Yeah, I saw that in your report. I don't know if I'd believe it if you didn't have Yukikaze's data file to back you up. You know how the ADC dealt with it when they lost track of Yukikaze?

You'll love this. They decided their displays were malfunctioning. Even though a plane had just vanished from this world for thirty seconds."

The Tactical Air Force was smarter in its reactions than the Aerospace Defense Corps. Their tactical computers had picked up Yukikaze the instant she escaped from hyperspace—Yukikaze's combat data system automatically linked up with the TAF computers—and had dispatched the nearest interceptor to assist them.

"The generally accepted conclusion," the major said, assuming an air of mock pomposity, "is that you single-handedly assaulted and neutralized an enemy intelligence center. You might get a medal for it. You should be glad."

"I couldn't care less."

"Figured you'd say that."

"It wasn't me that did it, anyway. It was Yukikaze."

Rei thought that the JAM may have been trying to thoroughly examine an Earth combat machine in an attempt to find out how humans thought and maybe even how to remake them. *The moment they know that's impossible,* he thought, *their tactics will change.*

"The JAM haven't attacked Earth directly yet."

Booker looked at him like he was crazy. "What, they're not attacking directly enough for you now?"

"It's still an indirect invasion. There's an intense battle that's moving into an arena we humans can't perceive. When they lose there, the target of their attacks will change. They'll definitely go after humans then. That's what I think, anyway."

The annihilation of mankind. Would national patriotism or human solidarity help them survive? "Hell no," Rei muttered. In the end, it would be the machines that would survive. Machines equipped with intelligence and fighting ability.

"I see," said Booker, with the barest hint of a smile. "Then I suppose we should eat while we still have the chance."

The major's tray was an impressive sight today. No doubt

he'd won at cards again and had someone else paying for the grand repast, which was in marked contrast to Rei's modest meal of soup and cornbread.

"Say, Jack, what's that book?"

Aside from the magazine with Lander's article in it, Booker had with him a thick hardcover book.

"Oh, this. *Mrs. Mead's Home Cooking Encyclopedia.* I've gotten into cooking as a hobby lately. What do you think?"

"Knock yourself out," said Rei, taking a bite of his cornbread. "By the way, where do you think this corn was grown?"

"Haven't a clue," answered the major. "Lander would know more about that. You should have asked him."

The cornbread caught in Rei's throat, choking him slightly.

IV

INDIAN SUMMER

To him, tears were simply a bodily necessity, the fluid that protected his eyes and allowed him to see. Nothing more. Emotions knew no place in combat. Therefore, he knew no sadness.

THE FAF'S AEROSPACE Defense Corps and the JAM were joined in battle.

Captain Munch nudged his beloved Sylphid's side stick. Responding immediately to the slight increase in horizontal pressure, the side force controller engaged, and the Sylph slid right, keeping its nose facing forward. Dogfight mode. Enemy in sight. The targeting reticule's distance gauge shrank. He pulled the gun trigger. The airframe shook. A flash, then black smoke.

"Got him! Good kill!" yelled his EWO, Second Lieutenant Chu, from the rear seat. "That bandit's toast. Let's head home."

"Roger that," the captain replied. The combat airspace was too large for him to be in visual contact with the other planes in his squadron, but here and there across the sky he could see clouds of black smoke marking their defeat of the JAM aircraft.

After a while, his comrades' planes began to gather from all points. They retook a tight combat formation—maintaining a scant 300 feet from wingtip to wingtip—as they headed for Banshee-IV, their flying aircraft carrier.

"The enemy today didn't seem too tough."

"That's 'cause they're no match for the Sylphs."

"Check it out," said Chu, gesturing upwards with his thumb. "The tourist's going home."

A Super Sylph passed high over Echo Squadron, moving at supersonic speed.

"It's one of the SAF pukes from the Tactical Air Force. Boomerang Squadron."

"Huh. He's fast. I doubt we could catch him."

"No joke. He's strapped onto twin Phoenix Mk-X engines. Those things're built for supercruising."

"But they're meant more for speed than for mobility, right? We probably couldn't take him at distance, but I bet we could if we lured him into a dogfight."

"He'd just bug out of there immediately. I could hit my V-max switch and he'd still be able to outrun us at normal power without breaking a sweat. Pisses me off, though. Him just bailing on us without a single word."

Alpha, Bravo, Charlie, and Delta wings of Echo Squadron rejoined. The SAF Super Sylph was now beyond their radar range. No sign of it remained.

"Home, sweet home, dead ahead."

"Back in dear Banshee's belly," sang Captain Munch, in high spirits. "We drink, we laugh, and we party. She swallows us whole, and—" He laughed. "Man, all I need is my guitar and it'd be perfect."

"Screw the guitar. It'd be a helluva lot more perfect if there were some hot girls."

Lieutenant Chu checked the radar display. They were sixty klicks out from the flying carrier, a giant, nuclear-powered air base that stayed aloft in perpetual orbit around the FAF's air defense zone.

The carrier sent out an IFF query signal, and Chu confirmed that their response equipment was functioning. The entire procedure was completed automatically. Or it should have been.

"That's funny. Banshee's being really insistent."

"It didn't make a mistake with the IFF code, did it?"

"I doubt they'd forget to check if the code was changed. What's going on over there? Banshee, this is Echo 1, come in."

"Banshee, honey, your husband's home. How about you—"

"Cut the chatter!" Lieutenant Chu yelled. "Multiple medium-range missiles, closing!"

"No welcome-home kiss, huh? Oh man, tell me this is not happening."

"Shit, why're they shooting at their own people?!" The combat support lines were now cut.

"What the hell's going on with Banshee's crew?"

Missiles exploded in front of them.

"They got Alpha 4!"

The RWR warning tone was blaring. Captain Munch snapped his plane over into a power dive, dumping chaff as he went. They plummeted toward the forests of Faery until at the last moment Munch lit the afterburners. As they kicked in the Sylph rocketed into a turn and climbed. Flying through the glittering chaff, the missile lost track of the plane for a moment. It quickly reacquired the target and began maneuvering to resume its pursuit, but it ran out of time and plunged into the forest.

The Sylph shuddered in the shock wave of the explosion.

"That was some high-power missile. Way better than what the JAM use."

"This is no joke! Everyone's gonna get shot down at this rate."

"Lieutenant, plot a return course."

"What are you planning?"

"I'm gonna reacquaint the lady with her husband's face."

Munch shoved the throttle forward. The induction temperature rose and low-altitude air turbulence shook the airframe as the engines keened.

"Hang in there, you suffering bastards. Don't you disgrace the Phoenix name."

"This isn't a Super Sylph, you know!"

They were now in visual contact with Banshee. It was black, massive in scale, with broad flight decks and huge, angled wings that made it seem as if it were flying upside down.

Munch kept his distance and flew around it.

"Wish we had some binoculars. Shit, can you see anything?"

"Careful. The point defense system is activating."

Radar-linked machine guns opened fire, narrowly missing them as Munch kept them out of range.

"Jesus, they're throwing 20mm rounds at us. They all gone nuts in there? They damn well know who we are. Now I'm starting to get pissed—"

"Short-range missile, closing! Break, starboard!"

They juked to the right.

"No good! It's got us!"

The missile's VT fuse activated and flames burst from Munch's starboard engine. The fuel supply automatically cut off and automatic fire extinguishers activated. The black smoke pouring from the engine changed to white. It held out only for a moment though, and then caught fire again. The fire warning alarm began to wail.

"Captain, we have to punch out!"

The **EJECT** warning lit up on the display.

In the backseat, Lieutenant Chu checked the ejection control lever. It was in the pilot command position, which meant that if he pulled it only his seat would be ejected.

"Captain!"

Chu slid the control lever to the flight officer command position, and the eject indicator changed to FO command mode.

"Wait!" yelled Munch. "We're still going too fast. I'll do it!"

If the pilot executed the eject command, both seats would be ejected. The lieutenant obeyed his captain. The plane was barely holding level.

"Here we go." Munch raised his fist, the sign that they were going to eject.

He reached up behind him and pulled the face curtain down over his head, which automatically initiated the ejection process. The kinetic inertial reels of their restraints activated, slamming them back into their seats. The sill lock released, the canopy blew off, and the catapult gun ignited.

Lieutenant Chu went first, rocketing up and to the right, followed a half-second later by Captain Munch, up and to the left. The IFF and ECM equipment self-destructed. Under each ejection seat, a gas generator activated, igniting a rocket that hurled the men far from the disintegrating plane.

The drogue guns on the ejection seats fired out their chutes. At the same time, the harnesses and lap belts released. The small drogue chutes opened, and after a programmed time delay drew the main chutes out of their canisters. The shock of the main chutes opening released the sticker clips, separating the men's bodies from the seats. As Captain Munch descended, he glanced back at the Sylph, now engulfed in flames. He said a silent farewell to his beloved plane and watched as it exploded, the fragments scattering as they fell.

I won't forget this, Banshee, he thought to himself. *I'll rip your guts out, you murderous bitch.*

Munch was suddenly aware of how cold it was. His radio beacon was operating and he had his survival kit, but he still prayed that the search and rescue team would find them soon.

The black bulk of Banshee-IV disappeared from sight. All he could hear now was the sound of wind. He wondered if they had just been attacked by a ghost.

HIS TACTICAL RECONNAISSANCE mission complete, Lieutenant Rei Fukai returned to Faery Base. Not long after, he was summoned to appear before the SAF deputy commander, General Cooley.

When he entered Cooley's office, she didn't acknowledge his salute, but he didn't take offense. Her attention was fixed on a display linked to the main strategic computer in the SAF's mission control room. He stood silently at attention until she spoke at last.

"Banshee-IV's entire fighter squadron was destroyed," she said slowly. "Is that what you observed, Lieutenant?"

"I recall observing the reverse. I saw them destroy the JAM squadron," Rei replied. "But if Yukikaze's data file says that wasn't the case, then it wasn't the case."

"You are correct. So is Yukikaze's data file. The incident occurred after the air battle."

"Incident? There was an ambush or something?"

"I wish I could say otherwise."

The general relayed to him what they knew so far about the situation, indicating the elements on the display as she spoke. It showed analysis results of the aircraft positions, comm records, armaments used by Banshee, radar frequencies, top secret ECM and ECCM, IFF operational conditions, and so on at the time of the incident.

"You've got a lot of electronic warfare data there," Rei said expressionlessly. "Yukikaze could have collected the same intel easily, though."

"This is all data obtained from crew members of Banshee-IV who managed to escape. Banshee was attacked by a single JAM aircraft just after it launched all of its onboard fighters. The incident began right after that aircraft was shot down. Banshee's crew lost control of all electronic equipment. Since the nuclear reactor was becoming dangerously destabilized, the captain ordered all hands to abandon ship. After that, Banshee continued flying unmanned and then attacked its returning fighters. Miraculously, nobody was killed."

"So what does this have to do with me?"

"I beg your pardon?"

"I said, what does this have to do with me?"

The general sighed.

"We need to find out what happened to Banshee-IV. The FAF Intelligence forces suspect that one of the crew may have sabotaged the on-board electronics systems," she explained. "The JAM aren't the only enemy the FAF has. An agent from Earth may have infiltrated us in order to prolong the war here."

"That's ridiculous. Our enemy is the JAM."

"Then the JAM have taken over Banshee-IV. And if that's the case, we have to bring it down."

"Taken over by the JAM? Seriously? So is it spies from Earth or is it the JAM? Sounds to me like you don't believe in either. Don't jerk me around, General. This isn't my problem, and I couldn't care less what's happening aboard Banshee. And besides, Banshee's air team were idiots. If it was shooting at them, they should have shot back. If it was me, I wouldn't care if it was a carrier, or a plane that looked like a Sylph, or someone wearing a general's rank insignia. Anyone who fires on Yukikaze is an enemy, and if she says it's an enemy, I'll pull the trigger without a second thought. That's war. You think too long and you die. But you wouldn't understand that."

"Watch how you speak to me, Lieutenant."

"All right then, General Cooley, *ma'am*, may I please be dismissed?"

Rei coldly watched as she visibly struggled to bring her anger under control. Although she was irritated by his insubordinate attitude, he had no intention of changing his behavior and had little sympathy for her in having someone like himself under her command. He knew she had never tasted the bitterness of wondering during a takeoff whether you were ever going to land again. She'd never experienced combat with the JAM, who had no morals and no sense of honor. Rank meant nothing out there. Neither did emotions.

If I died, Rei thought, *I wonder if the general would regret the loss of a good soldier. Maybe she'd give me a medal, but no way she'd ever shed a tear for me. She'd probably be relieved to be free of someone who spread pessimism like an infectious disease.* Rei knew it, but...what did it matter?

Whatever anyone might feel after he died was none of his concern. His sole concern was fighting the JAM and getting back alive. As far as the general's feelings went, he couldn't care less.

"Lieutenant, I'm ordering you to investigate the Banshee-IV incident. You'll be assigned an analysis expert to assist you. Major Booker will give you the details. Dismissed."

"Understood." He snapped a salute.

He left Cooley's office and went to Major Booker. Upon seeing Rei, the major shrugged his shoulders and said he sympathized.

"You probably said something to piss off General Wrinkles again, Rei."

"Apparently I piss her off just by standing there in front of her. It's not my fault."

Booker sighed. "Just please don't make her any madder than usual. Please. Any shit you dish out ends up being served back to me."

"Come on, it's not like you're getting shot at."

"The JAM you can dodge. The general, there's no escape from."

Booker gathered up some papers, shuffled through them, then slapped them down on the desk again.

"Strange incident, though. She told you about it, right?"

"If it's such a big deal, why am I getting tagged with the investigation?"

"There're reasons, which she would've explained to you—if she felt like it. Rei, don't misunderstand: the FAF isn't a business and we aren't employees. It's an air force, and it's run on orders, not complaints. Orders that run from the top to the bottom. It doesn't work in the other direction. An army can't be run from the bottom."

"Yeah, I know. But Jack, why is she always so mad at me? What should I do?"

"A beaten dog will still obey you...as long as it doesn't get too big to control."

"Right. So is Earth beating the JAM? Or is it the other way around?"

"I fail to see the humor, Lieutenant."

They left Booker's office and went into the SAF briefing room. The major switched on the wall display and pulled up some radar imagery.

"This is Banshee-IV. It's maintaining its usual course even though no one's aboard. Actually, we don't know that for sure. Someone may be aboard."

"Where's this imagery from? An ADC recon plane?"

"No," replied the major as he filled his coffee cup. "This is real-time data from Boomerang Unit 6, Minx. They're using our proprietary SSL encryption to transmit. The reason why is that the FAF brass have begun a confidential investigation. They're grilling Banshee's crew for information and keeping the guys from the fighter squadron canned up like Spam. They hope that it's the JAM that caused this. The second-best scenario would be a mechanical failure, which would be more serious but still relatively simple to deal with. But if it's neither, if this incident was caused by someone from Earth, then it's not just the FAF's problem anymore."

"And it would be a pretty damn good justification for a fight between the FAF and Earth. How pissed off would the general be if I said that?"

"Rei, please. You go around staying stuff like that and FAF Intelligence'll have your arse in the stockade in a heartbeat. The FAF's duty is to protect Earth from the JAM, but it has to protect itself as well. There are a lot of people on Earth lately who're saying the FAF isn't necessary, and Intelligence has to counter that."

"Counter it without anyone noticing they're countering it."

"Exactly. They can't be obvious about it. People on Earth are so far removed from the battlefield that they don't understand how bad the JAM really are. Some are even wondering if the FAF *are* the JAM. There may even be people within our own forces who are working to dismantle the organization."

Rei turned the coffee cup the major gave him around in his hand. "They think the FAF have created the JAM, you mean? What do you think about that, Jack?"

The major shut off the display and sat down. "I've definitely noticed a change in the JAM's behavior between now and the time when I was a fighter pilot."

"As in, they're not as openly aggressive as they used to be?" Rei asked. "The JAM are altering their strategy, Jack. I think the threat now is higher than it used to be. The fact that there are now people saying the FAF isn't necessary is proof that their invasion has advanced. If the JAM were a mirage created by the FAF, they wouldn't be using that strategy." Rei sipped his coffee. "But it doesn't really matter to me. I'm a grunt. I just gotta follow orders. Right, Major?"

"You seem to be saying 'It doesn't matter' an awful lot lately, you know."

"The JAM are a powerful enemy. I've finally come to understand that, but that's all I understand. If Lynn Jackson had spent time here, she probably wouldn't have written such an optimistic book."

"That's possible," said Major Booker, nodding. "She needs to write a follow-up. But I doubt she ever will. Back on Earth they just don't understand how much of a threat the JAM is. It's frightening."

"I'll leave that to the Intelligence forces to handle. We aren't intelligence operators. We're soldiers."

"You got that right."

Booker worked the display controls and brought up data on Banshee-IV. "You're going to land on this thing with Yukikaze. You don't need to worry about being attacked. We've confirmed that Banshee's exhausted all her weaponry. I want you to find out what's happened on board. Yukikaze is being installed with a special-purpose landing system as we speak, so it should be easy for you." The major gestured toward the glass wall of the briefing room that overlooked the maintenance floor. Yukikaze was being towed out.

"So it's going to be kind of like a carrier landing? I thought they had to extend a hook from Banshee to recover its fighters."

"That's what they did in the old days, back in the age of airships when they'd have the planes hanging beneath the carrier. But times have changed. Any plane can land on Banshee, and it's been designed to take on aircraft making emergency landings. Special equipment isn't necessary. You should be able to land there with just a standard arresting hook, but we're still installing an automatic carrier landing system. It's nothing fancy, just modifying the avionics software a bit. And to be safe, we're fitting six wire anchor launchers along her underside as well."

Major Booker suggested that they test them out, so he and Rei went down to the maintenance floor. After the mechanics gave them the thumbs-up, Rei got into Yukikaze's cockpit while the major settled into the rear seat. The mechanics removed the external ladder and moved away from the plane.

"Rei, look at your arresting hook control panel. There should be an AUX control switch. That should trigger the launchers for the wire anchors. Give it a try."

Rei turned the switch. With a loud *wham*, thin wires shot out from under Yukikaze and embedded themselves into a dummy board that had been laid down over the floor of the bay. The sharp, recurved heads of the wires stuck fast.

"Normally, you wouldn't need this because the plane would be caught by the arresting cables. There's a self-propelled, robotic spotting dolly on Banshee's deck. It keeps the plane's attitude correct and shuttles the launch bar back, but we don't know if it's working. If it isn't, the aircraft stowage elevator may not be working, either." Booker climbed out of the plane.

"If it isn't," Rei said as he followed the major down, "Yukikaze will be stuck on Banshee's deck. I won't exactly be able get out and stroll around out there. The thing is flying, after all."

"It's moving at less than 120 knots, but yeah, it'd be certain suicide if you tried it."

"Even if I wasn't blown off I probably wouldn't even be able to breathe because of the wind pressure."

"Don't worry. I've got an idea."

"It better be a good one, Jack. If I go rolling off of there, 'Oops, sorry' isn't gonna cut it."

"You've had wind tunnel resistance training, right? Relax. Leave it to me."

Rei followed the major across the maintenance floor and into the personnel elevator.

"We have another place to go?"

"I want to introduce you to your partner. His name's Tom John, from the Systems Corps. Everyone calls him "Tomahawk." I think his real first name may be Thomas, but I'm not sure. What I do know for sure is that he's a genius at avionics."

"Tomahawk? He's an Indian?"

"Yeah. They say he's a genuine Native American. Think he was born in Canada."

They entered the SAF mission control room. It was a high-ceilinged chamber, its walls filled with battle progress displays crowded with code letters and data transmitted from the Tactical Air Force's GHQ.

Tom John was drinking coffee and chatting with a female operator. Seeing Major Booker, he put the cup down onto the console and saluted. He had sunken cheeks, reddish brown skin, and long black hair that was tied back. His physique was slight. Compared to the large woman next to him, he could almost be mistaken for a child. But the impression Rei got from him belied his physical appearance. He was, without a doubt, a soldier. Rei thought that his eyes were like those of a hawk.

"Hi, Tom," said the major in a friendly tone. "Welcome to the SAF. So, getting to know us?"

The operator coughed and turned back to her console.

"Yep," answered Tomahawk with a smile. "You're lucky—the SAF has a lot of pretty girls here."

"Speaking of, our little tomboy Minx should be back soon. How's she doing, Hikalatia?"

"Minx is scheduled to return at 2220," said the operator. "Banshee-IV has no means of attack, and there's been no unusual activity."

"Like I said before, Banshee exhausted all of its missiles and gun ammo. But there is the possibility that it could be directed to crash into Faery Base. Anyway, Tom, let me introduce you. This is Lieutenant Rei Fukai, one of our top Sylph drivers."

"Man, the SAF really does run itself like an independent air force. Everything you guys have is top-shelf. I'm sure your skills are worthy of your plane, Lieutenant. Nice to meet you."

"I'm good as long as I've got Yukikaze."

Rei expressionlessly held out his hand, and the other man clasped it, accepting the handshake.

"Huh," said Booker. "I think this is the first time I've ever seen a Boomerang pilot shake someone's hand. Tom, you're the only one aside from Yukikaze that Rei's ever extended a hand to. The only things he trusts are high-tech combat machines."

"Really?" said Tomahawk with a smile. "Then maybe he sees me as a machine." He laughed lightly, but Rei thought that his smile was strangely sad.

THE NEXT MORNING, Boomerang Squadron Unit 3, Yukikaze, took off into a clear sky.

As they entered a steep climb, the ACLS beacon ran through its self-test. Rei confirmed that the carrier simulator on the ground was giving him an okay. He rechecked the engine gauges and confirmed that all caution lights were clear. Speed was Mach 0.9.

He slid the throttle forward. The airspeed indicator reeled through the numbers, and not even ninety seconds later their speed was Mach 2.3. He leveled off their climb at an altitude of 42,000 feet, cruising at supersonic speed.

"It'll be winter soon," said Tomahawk from the backseat. "The autumn colors in the forest are already turning, but the weather's still a little hot. Around where I'm from back on Earth, they call that 'Indian summer.' It's like the spirits are sending some last warm light to the world as a gift to us."

"Down there the war seems far away. It'd be the perfect sightseeing spot, if it weren't for the JAM," said Rei.

"Faery doesn't belong to us or to the JAM."

Rei rechecked their position on his HUD. They were about to cross the Absolute Defense Line. He activated the passive airspace radar.

"I don't think the Earth itself belongs to us, Tom. The only thing people really own are their own hearts."

"So there are some people who believe that God didn't give us the animals and plants and all of nature on Earth to do with as we please. That's a very Asian way of seeing things."

"I don't really consider myself Asian. Maybe it's the Faery way of seeing things. You live here long enough and you start thinking that way. Earth doesn't belong to humans. That's a fact. Or, at the very least, it doesn't belong to me."

"I agree," Tom said, sounding satisfied. "Me, I didn't come here thinking that I wanted to defend the Earth, but even so I can't deny that humans control it."

"'Control' doesn't necessarily equal 'own.'"

"I feel like I'm about to get a lecture on the evils of the capitalist system."

"I'd always heard that Native Americans value generosity."

"I'm not really conscious of myself in that way, the same as how you don't really think of yourself as Asian. But different races do see things differently. My grandfather had a saying: 'When everyone eats together, the man who cares only about filling his own belly isn't your friend.' What he meant was, the only things that belong to you are what you can eat, what you can't eat belongs to everyone, and what you haven't hunted yet belongs to no one."

"Then by that reasoning, Earth doesn't belong to humans. It's too big for anyone to swallow."

The air collision avoidance alarm sounded. Ahead were four Tactical Air Force fighters, flying at the same altitude and heading. Yukikaze's escorts. As the Super Sylph approached, the fighters peeled off to the left and right to open a path. Yukikaze flew ahead in a straight line and overtook them in an instant.

"Our TAF backup ends here. From this point on, we're on our own."

Rei toggled the master arm switch to ARM.

"You know, I think your grandfather had a point."

Maybe if everyone around me were more like that, I'd be a different person, thought Rei. Everyone else just seemed like they were trying to thrust their hands into the bellies of others.

"My father and grandfather spent their entire lives on the reservation. But that life wasn't for me. I came here because there weren't any avionics jobs in the air force reserves, either."

"I heard you helped make a lot of Yukikaze's electronics systems. She's a good plane. I respect that."

"I worked in the sections that developed the basic theory for her high-velocity fire control system and the early-warning radar system. But it'd be kind of pushing things to say that I made them. That's not something anyone can do on their own. So what brought you to Faery, Lieutenant?"

"Why do you ask?"

"Using the word 'respect' doesn't seem like something a Boomerang pilot would do. I was warned that you all were mean, icy-hearted bastards."

"I am. I don't think about protecting anything but Yukikaze. Not the Earth or my homeland." The image of his former girl-friend's face suddenly floated up in his mind. No, not even her. If he was being honest with himself, he never really knew her at all. All he could remember clearly was the sight of her back as she walked away.

"Speaking of your homeland, Lieutenant, I went there once. I wasn't allowed in, though."

"What do you mean?"

"It was because of my heart. It's mechanical. I guess you could call me a cyborg," Tomahawk said jokingly.

"A cyborg, huh? But why should that have mattered? An artificial heart's no different from having a prosthetic arm or corneal implants. Why wouldn't they let you in?"

"The problem was the energy source. It's powered by a piece of plutonium 238. The output's only twenty watts, but even though it's a low-power mechanism it's still a nuclear one."

"And that's why they denied you entry? That's ridiculous. Japan has nukes."

"They're afraid of uncontrolled nuclear material. It's not just Japan. People like me have a lot of trouble living on Earth. They don't use nuclear-powered hearts that much nowadays. The heat they generate makes it hard to control fluctuations in body temperature, and treatment is difficult because it's nuclear."

"Is there a danger you could become a human bomb?"

"There's no way it could ever explode. There's so little nuclear material that it's fundamentally impossible for it to cause a detonation. But if the containment capsule breaks, it could contaminate my surroundings with radioactivity. And if that happens, naturally I'd be finished as well. It's a good heart, though. Without it, I would have died a long time ago. Still… Every so often, I wonder if I'm not actually a machine. When I'm denied entry to a country, it's like they're telling me I'm not human."

"Don't think that way. You're alive. That's enough. Or are you telling me that you're actually a corpse? Because as far as I know, corpses can't talk. By the way, you're in the FAF, right? I just realized I never asked what your rank is."

"I'm a captain," answered Tomahawk. "For what it's worth."

"I didn't mean any offense, Captain, sir."

Rei took his right hand off the side stick and saluted.

"Keep your eyes on the road, Lieutenant."

"We're fine. I trust Yukikaze."

"I trust your skill. I know the Super Sylph demands advanced piloting skills."

"We're nearly there. I'm switching on the armament control system. Prepare for combat."

"Roger."

Five minutes passed with neither of them speaking. Suddenly, an emergency transmission came in: **PAN, PAN, PAN. DE FTNS. CODE U, U, U. AR.**

"It's from the tactical nav support satellite. 'Your plane is drawing dangerously close. Change course.' It's weird to see that when we're not closing in on an enemy. Respond to the IFF code."

"Roger."

After Yukikaze's identity was confirmed, Banshee-IV's exact position was sent to them in real time. A short time later, the carrier appeared on Yukikaze's active radar as well. They began their descent.

"Call Banshee for landing clearance."

The IFF was operating. Nothing seemed out of the ordinary. Banshee confirmed Yukikaze's side number and granted them landing clearance. Arresting hook, down.

"What's the deal? There's nothing weird at all here. Maybe those Banshee pilots were having a mass hallucination."

They passed the marshal point. Range twenty-one miles. Relative altitude from Banshee 5,000 feet. The carrier's automatic precision guidance system was operating.

Autopilot, off. ACLS, set. Auto-throttle, set. Fuel level, weight, tank distribution, and center of gravity, check.

They passed through the ten-mile gate. Speed 200 knots.

Landing gear and flaps, down. Anti-skid brake controller, off. Speed brake, extended.

They passed through the five-mile gate. Relative altitude 900 feet. Banshee-IV came into view.

"Jesus, that thing's huge. It's so big, it's kind of unsettling."

"It says to use Fly 3 for landing."

Banshee's flight decks were designated as Fly 1, 2, and 3. Fly 3 was used exclusively for landings.

"I've got a bad feeling about this. Don't you think they're being way too accommodating?"

They received the cue to begin their descent. They fell at a rate of sixty feet per minute and soon crossed the glide slope. The carrier's landing guidance system meatball was now in sight.

"001, Sylph, meatball," Rei called in.

The target designator on his HUD had now captured Banshee.

As they approached, the carrier loomed larger and larger. The TD indicated part of Banshee's starboard side, then suddenly jumped to the left: the target was so large that the system couldn't capture the entire thing at once.

"Executing manual approach."

"Why?" asked Tom. "You can use the ACLS."

"Didn't you say you trusted my skill?"

Rei cut off the approach power compensator. The auto-throttle caution light lit. Auto-throttle, off. Throttle mode to BOOST. He deactivated the ACLS and direct lift control systems.

Throttle to MAX. Lineup and elevation check. He was on approach now, taking care not to stray off of the glide slope. They passed over the landing threshold of Banshee-IV's flight deck. Yukikaze executed a break turn and veered off to the port side of the carrier to get into the one-eighty position for landing. A head-up call came from Banshee.

"Nice of them to guide me in like this."

"Let's just land this thing, Lieutenant."

"It's the JAM. It's gotta be. They want to take Yukikaze. They want to capture a Super Sylph."

"That's just speculation. We need proof. Isn't that why we came here?"

"It is. But we're not gonna land on Fly 3. I'm bringing us down on the aircraft stowage elevator."

"Can you do that?"

"Yeah. I don't want Yukikaze being restrained by Banshee."

They entered final approach, moving away from the center indicated by the meatball. Yukikaze drew near the main elevator at the edge of the deck. Working the pitch control, Rei slowed his plane to match Banshee's airspeed, managing to keep her roughly level despite the poor conditions caused by the wild air currents.

They fell slowly to the deck. Touchdown. For a second it seemed like they were going to bolter, and Rei broke out in a cold sweat. He worked the engine output control and flaps so that the counter airflow forced Yukikaze down. Success. They were on the elevator. Rei fired the wire anchors fixed to the fuselage, and the heads punched into the deck. The spotting dolly standing by approached and moved onto the elevator deck, its emergency light flashing red. The elevator began to descend.

Engines, off. Rei unhooked his harness and drew his service pistol from his vest. He checked the indicator pin to make sure that a round was chambered, then bent forward and pulled out the survival gun stowed under his seat.

The elevator came to a stop. A sliding bulkhead sealed off the egress above them. Rei popped the canopy open, then jumped down from Yukikaze, machine gun in hand, and opened fire on the dolly. The robot, which had been readying to tow Yukikaze into the hangar, exploded in a shower of sparks and fell silent. A burning smell hung in the air.

"Okay, you can come down now, Tom. We've got a job to do."

It was dark inside the cavernous hangar. Only the emergency lights were on. Normally, the space would have been filled with carrier-based aircraft packed closely together with their wings folded up, but now it was deserted and seemed oddly huge. In the midst of the expanse there was only Yukikaze, her wings spread atop the elevator floor, looking like an animal pricking up its ears as it strained to listen for a predator.

"Why'd you shoot the spotting dolly?" asked Tomahawk as he climbed down from Yukikaze, a small all-purpose system analyzer in his hand. "Aren't you being a little overcautious?"

"We should consider this place a JAM base. So watch your step. We don't know what might come at us. This may be our chance to gather some intel, but it'd be worthless if we don't make it back alive."

"You're thinking we could be the first humans to come into contact with an actual JAM?"

"We have no idea what form the JAM really possess. We assume they've been hiding from us and that they've never appeared in front of a human. That's Lynn Jackson's opinion, but I have a feeling that may be wrong. I wonder if it's not that they won't appear to humans, but that humans aren't able to sense them."

"Like spirits, you mean?"

"Maybe, maybe not. There's also the possibility that we look at them without actually seeing them. We see JAM fighters, and we have no doubts that there are JAM inside of them or, even if there aren't, that they were made by JAM 'people.' We don't consider the possibility that the fighters may be the JAM themselves because that's just too strange to us. The JAM also seem to be perplexed by the existence of these 'humans' they observe. Maybe they're wondering, 'What are those organic things attached to the fighters? What are they doing, wandering around on their own? Well, they seem harmless enough, so just ignore them.' You can practically hear them saying it."

"No way."

Rei shrugged. "Let's get going. We'll leave Yukikaze's ECM armament running. As soon as the secondary power supply runs out, we're out of here, okay?"

"We could leave the engines running—"

"We can't assume the exhaust will be vented out of here. We'll end up croaking from carbon monoxide poisoning. Major Booker beefed up the auxiliary power, so we should have an hour."

"Just one hour?"

"Personally, I'd like to get the hell out of here right now."

Rei adjusted his grip on the machine gun.

The ventilation system in the hangar wasn't operating. It was quiet. There were no vibrations. It almost seemed like they weren't even flying. Rei urged Tomahawk onward as they headed for Banshee's bridge. They didn't use the elevator, and the sound that echoed as they climbed the gray metal ladders seemed awfully loud.

When they reached the bridge they found it brightly lit, with all the electronic equipment still functioning, which made the absence of any people seem even more eerie. The laser compass, course display, and navigation radar display were all operating. The helm control, which looked exactly like a ship's wheel, was working automatically, making adjustments to Banshee's flight. Rei pulled at it with one hand. No response. He tried disengaging the auto-control but was locked out. The helm continued moving on its own, completely ignoring his attempts.

"We need to get to the combat information control room," Rei called out to Tomahawk.

"I'll head to avionics control."

"There'll be strong security. It's probably protected by three layers of blast doors."

"There wouldn't have been any point in coming here if I'd forgotten to bring the key," Tomahawk said with a grin. "It's the same access as what the captain and the avionics officer would have. Just leave it to me. I'll go debug the computer. You're seeing JAM where there aren't any, Lieutenant."

They left the bridge.

"But you brought a pistol too, right?" Rei said doggedly.

Tomahawk raised an eyebrow. "It's not a good idea to start shooting when you're surrounded by precision equipment that's keeping you in the air. Don't worry. Even if this is the JAM, they can't do anything to me in the computer room. It's the safest place on this ship. Just please keep an eye on Banshee's course. I don't want us to crash into the ground while we're not looking."

"Okay... But something is still making me nervous here."

"That's not like a Boomerang pilot."

"I have a duty to bring you back in one piece."

"Nothing's going to happen. If you think about how gigantic and complex this whole system is, it's no surprise that maintaining quality control is a hard thing. You aim for perfection when you design it, but unfortunately you can't guarantee that there will absolutely never be any failures. Even if you get the failure rate down to one in ten quadrillion, you still can't get it to zero. I think that when that JAM attacked, it caused a fault to appear by chance. The situation that would cause the fault to present itself just hadn't happened until now."

"You have fifty minutes, Tom. Don't even think about trying to hunt down the errors. You just need to gather information. We can take our time to analyze it once we're back. If you see any people, shoot them. They don't need to threaten you, just shoot to kill."

The engineer stopped and raised his hands in a "don't worry" gesture and nodded.

"I'm serious, Tom. Don't get careless. I'm on your side, but if you don't get back in time, I'm leaving without you."

"I doubt you'd really do that. You're a good man. I'm starting to see why Major Booker relies on you. Rei, you won't be in Boomerang Squadron forever. Some day, that icy heart of yours is going to melt."

"Not just an avionics expert, you're a psychic too?"

Tomahawk clapped Rei on the shoulder, then walked off through the narrow companionway. Rei watched him go, his machine gun lowered, until the diminutive figure rounded a corner and passed out of sight.

Rei made his way to the CIC. Once there, he sat down in the command chair and looked at the display. The now-unmanned Banshee-IV was continuing to be operated by a host of computerized systems.

On the screen he quickly cycled through the long-range search radar, course monitoring radar, warning radar, fire control radar, beacon, IFF transponder, weather monitoring read-outs, flight computer systems, all sorts of sensor data, an onboard command schematic of the ship, a chart showing the operational mode of the ship's takeoff and landing guidance systems...

He laid the machine gun down on the console and leaned back in the seat, keeping his eyes on the data and occasionally checking his watch. The minutes crawled by. To help pass the time, he messed around with the fire control radar, thinking how he wouldn't have been able to do a damned thing if he'd been targeted by it. It was a high-output radar, built to overpower JAM ECM, and its EM waves could cook an unprotected human from two klicks away. Yukikaze's ECM would be no match for it.

Every so often, Rei was seized by a strange uneasiness and glanced around the abandoned CIC. He couldn't shake the feeling that he was being watched. After thirty minutes had passed, he knew he wasn't just imagining it. He heard something. Coming from the air vent. His limbs tensed, adrenaline coursing through his system even as he doubted his own ears.

Keeping his gaze forward and posture relaxed, he felt for the machine gun. He secured his grip, snatched up the gun, jumped onto the console, and smashed open the vent grill near the ceiling with the shoulder stock.

There was a faint sound. He ripped the flashlight from his life vest and pointed the beam down the duct.

A rat. A normal Earth rat. Feeling half relieved and half disappointed, Rei jumped down from the console. *Maybe Banshee's been taken over by the rats and not the JAM,* he thought with black humor. Rats were an indispensable part of any ship.

He called Tomahawk on the intercom. No answer. Probably completely engrossed with his work. Rei sat down again and waited patiently.

Forty minutes. Forty-one minutes. Forty-two minutes. Forty-three minutes.

Still no word from the other man.

Forty-five minutes. Forty-six.

He couldn't wait any longer. Yukikaze was more important to him than Banshee was.

Just as he was about to get up, a warning klaxon began to blare throughout the ship. It was so loud and sudden that it caused Rei to literally jump to his feet.

Gripping the machine gun, he checked the display. Condition red. He sprang at the intercom.

"What is it?! What's happened?!"

No answer.

This didn't seem like a malfunction. He ran out of the CIC and through the mazelike interior of the ship toward the central avionics room where Tomahawk was. When he saw signs warning "No entry without authorization of AV officer," "Area off-limits without captain's permission," and "Suspicious individuals will be shot on sight," he knew he was nearing the right place.

A blast door. Another blast door. And still another.

White, brightly lit. A clean room. A frigid redoubt for the avionics equipment.

"Tom! Tomahawk! Tom John, answer me!"

He ran through the room, searching for Tomahawk between the equipment stacks as the klaxon continued to wail. He finally found the engineer lying face down on the floor. Rei ran up and grabbed him, turned him over, then dropped him in instinctive revulsion. Tomahawk's chest was covered by a wriggling mass of small, black, insectlike creatures.

JAM? He brushed them off with his flight-gloved hand. They felt like pieces of metal.

"Hang on, Tom. We're getting out of here."

The engineer's face looked drained of blood. Rei slapped his cheek and he stirred.

"Rei..." Tom groaned. "You were right. They were looking for the control circuitry for my heart... They've screwed it up. Get out of here fast, Lieutenant. Banshee's going to crash soon... I smashed the cooling system for the avionics control. You have to escape before the other systems break down." Keeping Banshee's electronics properly cooled consumed 300 kilowatts of power and a half a ton of coolant every minute. It wouldn't be long before they started to overheat.

"If it's going down, we can still get you out on Yukikaze."

Rei shouldered the machine gun and tried to help Tomahawk

to his feet, but the other man refused to cooperate.

"I wanted to take out these guys with my own hands... I'm done, Rei. The JAM have wrecked my heart. Even if you got me aboard Yukikaze, I wouldn't make it back to base... Get out of here now, Lieutenant. That's an order."

"This can't be happening. If I'd just stayed with you, I—" Rei stopped, his eyes widening.

The black things that had been scattered on the floor were coming together, coalescing into a single, large, insectoid shape. A multicellular mechanical life-form. A JAM spy.

"Lieutenant, there's no time. I don't think those things will touch a human. If they wanted to kill us, they could have done it easily... They probably thought I was a machine. A machine... Am I a machine?"

"Don't try to talk. I'm taking you back, no matter what."

Just as Rei was leveling his machine gun at the JAM, it released a high-density burst of energy. The shock wave hurled Rei back into the panel behind him. Momentarily stunned, he took a few heaving breaths, registered that he still had a grip on the gun, then lifted it and opened up at the JAM. It scattered into its component parts. He scrambled to his feet, feeling a vague surprise that he didn't seem to be badly injured.

The JAM weren't after Rei. They wanted Tomahawk. Or, more accurately, Tomahawk's heart.

"Tom John! Captain!"

"Stay back!" Tom rasped, his voice barely audible. "You'll be exposed to the radiation... Rei, just tell me... I am human... aren't I?"

"Of course you are. You are." *You're alive. That's enough. Or are you telling me that you're actually a corpse?* "Captain John... Tomahawk!"

Rei watched as the captain's still form was haloed by the rich red of his blood seeping onto the floor. He turned away, snatched up the system analyzer as a memento, and ran for the exit. As he grasped the blast door handle, he looked back at Tomahawk.

The single imperative order of Boomerang Squadron clawed at his mind: make it back alive, even if you have to let your comrades die.

A corpse is just a thing... Rei said his farewells to the dead man, then sprinted toward Yukikaze.

He made it to the hangar bay. He vaulted up the boarding ladder, tossing the system analyzer into the cockpit, then sank into his seat. Engine start. He was about to execute the command to raise the elevator when he suddenly realized: this wasn't the main hangar. The spotting dolly he'd blown up wasn't there. A shudder convulsed through him, as though he'd been doused with icy water, and he scrambled out of the seat. The engines continued to rev up. No. That wasn't the sound of the Phoenix Mk-X. It was only just the slightest bit different, but those weren't Phoenixes.

This wasn't Yukikaze.

It was identical in appearance, but Rei knew. This wasn't his beloved plane. It was a copy made by the JAM. He clung onto the edge of the cockpit and switched the engines off. They wouldn't stop. Were the JAM intending to infiltrate the SAF's main base with this decoy?

He emptied the machine gun's entire clip into the plane's consoles. The engines still didn't stop. He hurled the gun away and looked around for the firefighting truck that should be present in the hangar. He saw it, ran over and jumped into it, then backed it up to the ghost plane. He opened the fire extinguishing door on the side of the near engine and shoved the extinguisher nozzle from the truck into it. He opened up the retardant and black smoke began gushing from the engine exhaust. The engine revs began to drop. Flame out. Engine stop.

Rei headed toward what he thought was the main hangar. He passed through a blast door, and a massive wave of relief surged through him. He'd guessed correctly. Yukikaze was there, waiting.

He tried to operate the elevator controls manually, but they wouldn't work. The auxiliary control was a fully electronic system, so it needed an external power supply. He found the power supply unit in a trailer. He ran over and switched it on, then connected an AC cable to the auxiliary control panel. With a terrific racket, the elevator slowly began to rise. The sliding bulkhead above the elevator opened.

Rei climbed into Yukikaze. Canopy, closed. Mask and harness, secured. He suddenly realized that his memento of Tomahawk, the analyzer that may have recorded the true form of the JAM, had been left in the ghost plane. But there was no time to go back for it. Engine, start. The Phoenix on the right came back to life.

They rose onto the deck and Rei grunted in frustration. In front of them, hovering before the bulkhead opening, was what looked like the ghost plane. Its engines were off and its flaps were down, but it was still just floating there casually. It was going to ram Yukikaze. Rei hit the button to release the wire anchors and in a flash explosive bolts sheared them from the fuselage. Flaps, down. Yukikaze floated up from Banshee like the ghost plane. The left engine ignited and started up.

Banshee's enormous form began to move forward below them. The ghost plane seemed to drift on the wind and approached. Rei rolled Yukikaze over and jammed the throttle forward to MAX, burning into a steep turn. The powerless ghost plane couldn't keep up with them. It dipped its nose down and plunged toward Banshee. Was it trying to land?

After accelerating to supersonic speed, Rei came about to try a beam attack from a position ninety degrees relative to Banshee's course. The black hulk of the carrier filled his view. The ghost plane was landing on the elevator. Rei pulled the gun trigger. Rounds from the cannon tore through the ghost plane, and after a couple of seconds it exploded. Yukikaze blew through the black smoke and withdrew from Banshee at maximum thrust.

Yukikaze climbed into the blue sky. Rei didn't look back.

Altitude, 82,000 feet. The sky grew dark. Stars in the daytime. He could see the great red whirlpool that poured from Faery's suns. The Bloody Road. For a brief moment, it was overlaid by Tomahawk's blood, pouring from his slight and broken frame.

Tom John's last words came back to him. *I am human... aren't I?*

"Of course," Rei whispered. "Of course you're human." He had died with a faint smile on his face, as though he had finally received the reassurance he sought. As though saying that his life hadn't been so bad after all.

Banshee's symbol blinked out on the radar.

YUKIKAZE LANDED BACK at Faery Base.

Rei taxied to Boomerang Squadron's area. After raising the right engine output to 80 percent for fifteen seconds, he cut it off. He then did the same for the left engine.

After he'd killed the engines, he just sat there in the cockpit, looking up at the cloudless sky.

Major Booker turned the exterior canopy control handle and peered inside the cockpit.

"You all right, Rei? Where's Tom? What happened to—"

"Jack...Could you check my environmental control system?" Rei raised his helmet visor and swiped at the tears on his cheeks with his gloved fist. "Something's stinging my eyes."

V

FAERY - WINTER

He had to protect Yukikaze. He had to eliminate anything that stood in her way—even if it was his fellow man. That was what he believed. And then he learned that the computers, the machines built by men, were working to the same end.

SNOW WAS FALLING on Faery.

Winter was always the busiest season for the Maintenance Corps. They ran the snow removal equipment on twenty-four-hour rotation while the finely driven flakes numbed the skin on their faces and froze their hair, eyelashes, and beards into crystalline spikes. They always prayed for the weather to let up, but the snow always continued to fall, heedless of the desires of the humans caught in it.

Second Lieutenant Mamoru Amata (FAF Maintenance Corps, Faery Base 110th Airfield Maintenance Division, 3rd Mechanized Snow Removal Unit) sat in the cab of a motor grader, waiting for his turn to go out and growing increasingly pissed off that the grader's door didn't shut properly.

Visibility was low thanks to the howling blizzard outside. The storm was blowing with such force that it was less like it was snowing than like the air itself had partially solidified into ice. To Lieutenant Amata, it looked as if there was more snow than air out there right now.

He sighed and listened to the rhythmic thump of the windshield wipers, the crackling static of snow beating against the grader, and the whistle of cold air blowing through a gap in the door frame. Needles of snow were driving through the gap, gradually forming a soft pile at Amata's feet. He took off his gloves and bent over to try and fix the door. A thick layer of ice had crusted over its bottom edge, and he clicked his tongue in annoyance when he saw the problem: some of the insulation had been improperly installed. The cold outside air was causing moisture to condense inside of the door panel, drip down, and then freeze at the bottom. Amata scraped at the ice with his fingernails, wondering if the warmth of his hands might be enough to melt it. His fingers turned red, then began to go purplish from the cold. He finally gave up, tried blowing on his now numb hands to warm them, and held them over the windshield defroster. They were stiff and senseless. He couldn't even tell if they were cold anymore.

The lieutenant tried to remember when the door had been bent and knocked his legs together to make sure that all feeling hadn't been completely lost from his seemingly frozen lower extremities. He sourly eyed the little stream of snow as it came in through the gap. So, when had the door been bent? Oh, yeah. The day before yesterday, during a furious snowstorm, he'd lightly bumped the machine driven by his coworker. At least the storm today was better than the one a couple of days ago. Visibility wasn't zero: he could actually see ten or fifteen feet ahead.

His hands gradually regained sensation. His skin hurt as though it'd been flayed off. He put his hands back into the gloves he'd warmed on the defroster. The windshield had now fogged up and was pure white. He wiped at it with the shell of his glove. It didn't change the view much. Just white. If he stared at it for long, it almost became mesmerizing. The snow danced and whirled before him, seeming to invite him out into the storm. *God, it's cold.* Amata wrapped his arms around his chest and rubbed his sides. If he didn't keep moving, he'd probably freeze.

Suddenly, the grader's engine rumbled to life; its automatic ignition system had activated. *Even the truck's scared of the cold,* he thought with a bitter smile. He wondered why they even bothered to build an energy conservation system into it. Two seconds of flight in a jet fighter probably used up more fuel than idling a snowplow on standby for an hour. He wished they'd let him just run the damn thing while he was waiting so he could get some heat out of the defroster.

The driver's seat shook with the vibration of the engine. It didn't warm things up much. Amata reached into his back pocket and pulled out his own fuel: a pocket flask of whiskey. Just a little nip to warm himself up. Through the limited space cleared by the windshield wipers, he could faintly make out the machines of his coworkers, the rotating lights on their rooftops visible as hazy amber globes in the white.

The whiskey burned his throat. Cheap stuff. The heat of the alcohol in his stomach began to spread to his limbs. It was the only thing that kept him warm, that made the duty out here bearable. He'd be damned if he was going to give it up because of some idiotic regulation.

How long did they expect him to wait? As he hitched himself forward and returned the whiskey to his back pocket, he pressed his face to the window and peered outside. The last plane of the 167th Tactical Fighter Squadron had not yet returned. Probably flying somewhere above the storm and taking his sweet time. Lieutenant Amata pounded his fists together, trying to return some feeling to them. Obviously command was fine with them all just freezing to death waiting for that last plane to come in.

He could see a figure on runway 03R, the one used exclusively for landing aircraft. Probably a hook runner, poor bastard. In wintertime, because of the icy runway conditions, the fighters would land using arresting hooks, as they would on an aircraft carrier. The arresting cable and its support gear were laid out over the runway now, waiting for the last 167th plane, which meant that Amata and his unit couldn't plow over it. While they sat there watching, the snow continued to pile up. If they left it for very much longer, the arresting cable wouldn't be able to lift up because of the weight of the accumulated snow.

In general, though, clearing snow from landing runways was an easy job. Even if a grader broke one of the huge landing lights on the sides of the runway, it wasn't a big deal. Takeoff runways, however, were a pain, since even in weather like this takeoffs were done the usual way, not by catapult launch. To ensure they went smoothly, with no resistance from the snow, the maintenance units had to plow the runways thoroughly if the snow accumulation exceeded one inch. They couldn't use ice melt compound or sand either, since the substances could get sucked into the fighters' air intakes and damage the engines.

Lieutenant Amata scraped up the snow on the cabin floor with his boots and tramped it into the gap in the door. Then, as though mocking him, as though it were the funniest thing in the world, a sudden squall popped the clod of snow out of the gap, and a fresh blast of icy wind gusted in and danced around the driver's seat. The tiny particles of ice melted in the relative warmth of the cabin air, and soon the lieutenant's upper body was soaked with cold mist.

"Shit! Shit! Shit! Just land already, you piece of crap plane! Are you trying to make me freeze to death here?!"

Some of the mist condensed on the interior of the cab roof and dripped onto the back of his neck and down his back. It was so cold it almost felt like it was scalding him. Another icy blast blew in from the gap in the door. Amata rubbed at his side. It was aching so badly he could cry. It had been for a while now. His liver was probably wrecked. Or maybe it was his gall bladder. The military doctor hadn't told him anything except that if he didn't give up the booze, he'd die. *Maybe it's cancer,* Amata thought. He'd ignored the doctor's advice to skip hospitalization and treatment on Faery and just return to Earth. The only thing waiting for him there was either prison or a detox facility. For an offender like him, no place else on Earth offered the freedom that Faery did. The FAF command knew that well and used him and all the others like him for as long as their bodies held out. A man's body was just one more expendable resource. They could always get more human garbage from Earth.

The fact that sitting here shivering in the freezing cold was better than whatever awaited him on Earth was so pathetic it forced a bark of a laugh from Amata. His life was a four-part litany of booze, women, brawls, and lock-ups. Even he could see how he was going to die. He knew the alcohol had taken over his life, but he was still honest enough with himself to know that he couldn't blame it for everything. Other people always said that when sympathizing with him, but his life still would've been royally screwed up even without the alcohol. And what the hell was a non-screwed up life, anyway? Was there even such a thing? *I didn't have any other choices than the ones that I made,* he thought. When you're trapped on all sides with no other options, you walk the only path that's open to you.

Most people thought he was just irresponsible, that he was just drowning himself in the bottle. But given the life that he'd led, if he hadn't turned to escape through the booze, that would've been it. The End. People back on Earth would tell him to straighten up and fly right, but they may as well have been telling him to put a gun in his mouth and pull the trigger. He didn't want to go back to that. If he was still alive in the spring, when his tour of duty was up, he'd apply to have it extended. Better that than being driven to suicide.

His brooding was interrupted by the sound of distant thunder. He looked up. At long last, it had returned: the last plane of the 167th TFS. As it approached the roar of its engines gradually drowned out the howling of the storm. Suddenly, the shape of a giant bird appeared out of the whiteness, followed by the sound of an arrester hook snagging the cable. The fighter shook the ground as its wheels made contact with the runway. The hook runner ran out to unhook the cable from the arrester. The ground guide signaled the pilot with powerful flashlights, moving them quickly from belly level to chest: Raise hook. He then lifted his left arm and swept it in a large circle to the left: Proceed to taxiway.

Finally, Amata could do his job. He cut off the intermittent starter and stepped on the accelerator, revving the engine as the black fighter taxied right by him. The metallic whine of its jets grew distant, and he readied himself to get to work.

But just as he stepped on the grader's heavy clutch, he saw someone running toward him. He took his foot off the clutch. The figure made a beeline for the cabin, banged once on the door, then opened it without asking. Icy wind blew into the cabin full force.

"What?!" shouted Amata.

"The de-icer on the gear's broken down," the man shouted. He was covered with snow and ice from head to foot. "The storage trench is buried in snow, so we can't get the arresting gear back into it."

"Hurry up and close my goddamned door!" Lieutenant Amata shouted back.

"Fine," the man said. "Just take care of it. You know what to do."

"What are you talking about?"

"Clear the snow without breaking the gear, okay?"

"That's not my job!"

"Your job's snow removal. Now get it done fast or we won't be ready when the next flight returns. And if that happens, it's on your head!" The man slammed the door shut, which proceeded to bounce back open again, and ran with short steps to a snow truck whose warm windows were steaming up. He climbed in, and the truck soon disappeared into the blizzard.

Amata gritted his teeth. "Fuckers," he seethed. The ground crews treated him and the men in his unit like slaves, forcing the cold shit-work off on them. He quickly radioed the word to the other drivers. They all bitched but quickly gave in and accepted the situation. They didn't have the will to argue at that point. Better to just finish the job quickly.

The lieutenant pulled up the hood of his parka, left the grader idling, and got out. He didn't turn the intermittent starter on. He was being as uncooperative as he could.

He tried to unhook a shovel from the front of the truck, but the detent was caked with ice and wouldn't move. He got a plastic hammer from his toolbox and smashed at the ice.

Tiny ice chips flew up into his face. Remembering there were goggles in the toolbox as well, he returned the hammer to it and then put the goggles on. Then, taking the shovel in hand and feeling for the arresting cable with his foot, he made his way toward the storage trench.

All around him was total whiteness. The snow blew at him mercilessly. It was hard to breathe. He dug into the trench. He began to sweat. His goggles fogged up. Taking them off, he wiped at the insides with his glove, but they soon fogged up again. He threw the shovel aside and furiously starting digging at the snow with his hands. The other members of his unit were probably kicking back with their own stashes of hooch, letting him deal with the task. He knew most of them were alcoholics. They couldn't fly fighters and they had no advanced skills, so they were almost universally looked down on by the rest of the FAF, and many of them had internalized the same sense of worthlessness.

Conscious of the pain in his side, Lieutenant Amata pulled the collapse lever. The arresting gear went down. However, a bit of ice still jammed in the fulcrum left the gear poking slightly out of the ground. The lieutenant raised the mechanism again, took off his gloves, and began beating the snow off of it. His hands immediately lost all sensation.

At that moment, he was so jealous of the fighter pilots it made his gut burn. They got to fly off of this snow-blasted landscape and rise above the clouds, where the weather was always clear. No way they could ever understand what it was like for the poor slobs below them freezing on the white ground. He had wanted to be a pilot too, but his bad liver washed him out on the hypoxia resistance test. In other words, the only job for him here was this. He'd been called a waste of a human being, and he had agreed. The same went for all the other guys in his unit. They were sneered at and paid less than the pilots, and even what little pay they received was frequently docked for conduct violations—like drinking on the job.

Last year one of the members of his unit had frozen to death trying to haul a broken-down plow off of the runway during a violent blizzard. The brass kept harping on the dead man's case, saying that it should serve as a warning to the rest and that it wouldn't have happened if he hadn't been drinking. Well, of course he was drinking; it was the only means they had to warm themselves up a little and make it easier to move. *They tell us to quit drinking,* Amata thought bitterly, *but they never fix stuff like that bent door or the de-icer on this thing.* It was probably cheaper to work a man harder than to fix a machine. If they just used the waste heat from the underground base, they could keep even this huge runway snow-free. But it would cost too much, so they used manual labor instead. Which they could always get more of from Earth.

Lieutenant Amata lowered the gear again. It still stuck up a little. He beat at it with the shovel, then climbed on top of it and jumped up and down to force it closed with his body weight. That got it.

Snow snuck in through the storm seals of his pants, melted, and mixed with his own sweat. He shivered at the clammy, unpleasant feeling, tramped back to the grader, threw the shovel into the cabin, then climbed in and shut the door. Cold wind was still blowing in through the gap, but it was better than being out there. His parka was now a frozen, crunchy mass. He flipped back the hood, spilling snow over the driver's seat, and held his frozen hands over the defroster until some of their strength returned. He gripped the large steering wheel and threw the truck into gear.

After finishing his work, Lieutenant Amata drove back to the ground vehicle hangar on the side of the runway. The electric shutter door closed automatically behind him, cutting off the howling of the storm. Once he'd killed the grader's engine, it was quiet except for the sound of the snow blowing against the shutter. He climbed down from the cab, his breath coming out in clouds of white steam that looked like cigarette smoke.

The moisture in his now-thawed parka began to refreeze. He thoroughly beat off the snow and ice clinging to him. If it was still on him when he went into the warm locker room, he'd be soaked.

He stripped out of his cold weather gear in the locker room. It stank of sweat. He was chilled to the bone, yet steam still rose from his body when he took off his sweater. The locker room was warmer than the garage, but only by about ten degrees. He wondered if it was the first ten degrees above freezing but had no way to check. The air grew warmer as he made his way to the station. From the outside, to the garage, to the locker room, to the corridor, to the station: warmer and warmer as he went. He'd been told that sudden changes in temperature were physically harmful, but he still wished they would keep the locker room warmer. He walked into the showers, stripped off his soaked undergarments, and threw them down the laundry chute.

After the shower he finally started to feel better. He grabbed a towel and underwear from the supply box, dried off, and got into his fatigues. He went down the corridor to the unit's command office, dropped off his grader's key with his superior officer, and then gave a simple report that his work had been completed. Just as he was about to walk out with one of the other men in his unit, the officer called for them to wait.

"Sure, whatever," Lieutenant Amata mumbled.

He probably wanted them to stay on standby there in the station; the weather geeks in the Operations Corps had forecast a big storm. He felt like this was somehow, obscurely, their fault. Sometimes he even wondered if they got such heavy snow only because those fuckers made such awful forecasts.

The officer didn't put them on standby, though. In fact, he only wanted Lieutenant Amata and told the other man that he was free to go. The other guy whispered "Brass must be pissed at you" into Amata's ear as he passed, gave him a sympathetic look, patted him on the shoulder, and left the office.

"Now then," began his superior, Captain Gondou. "I have

some surprising news for you. Would you like to sit down, Lieutenant Amata?"

"No thanks," he replied. He refused both the chair and the cigarette he was offered and remained standing at attention.

Captain Gondou put the cigarette in his own mouth, lit it, and sat down again behind his desk. He regarded Amata for a while, then blew out a large cloud of smoke and said, "A commendation's been awarded."

"I see," answered Amata. Someone in his division was getting a commendation, so they probably wanted him to set up a party to celebrate. That was the only thing he could think of. "Understood. Where's the assembly? And when?" He figured he could bully some of his good-for-nothing, lazy-ass coworkers into helping out.

The captain was looking at him oddly. "What's your problem, Amata? You don't seem very excited about this." He held his gaze for a second longer, then shrugged. "It'll be held tomorrow at Auditorium 1 in Faery Base, as part of the FAF founding memorial ceremony."

Captain Gondou put his cigarette down on the ashtray, stood up, straightened his uniform, and saluted. "Congratulations, Lieutenant Amata."

Amata reflexively returned the salute. Then it suddenly dawned on him what the captain had meant. "Wait, what? Hold on here. Um...*I'm* getting the commendation?"

"What did you think I meant?"

Gondou sat down and picked up the cigarette butt from the ashtray. The five or six other personnel in the office stared at Lieutenant Amata. An intercom chimed on somebody's desk somewhere, and the tense atmosphere returned to normal.

"What's the deal, Captain? This must be some sort of mistake."

"That's what I thought," Gondou replied bluntly. "At first I couldn't believe it either."

Amata took no particular offense at the captain's attitude.

Looking back over his service record, he didn't think there was anything in it that was particularly outstanding compared to those of his coworkers. He nervously fingered the whiskey flask in his pocket. He wasn't any different from the rest of his drunken colleagues. Just a standard-issue...snowplow driver. Just one more guy the others despised as garbage. *So why me?* he wondered suspiciously. Was this some kind of a joke? Did he mishear the captain? Was he hallucinating it? No, he hadn't drunk nearly enough for that. *Fine,* he thought. *If they're giving it to me, I'll take it.* At least he'd get a little award from the division in return for all his work.

"The Distinguished Service Award, right?"

It was the most commonly awarded decoration. Service members who died in the line of duty got it. Lots of living ones did too, but he'd never heard of the really low-level grunts like him getting one without dying.

Captain Gondou shook his head. "No. Not that piece of shit. The Order of Mars. A medal of valor. The highest one. I've never touched or even seen one of them. Even the senior officers with fruit salad on their chests rarely have them."

Amata unconsciously scratched his hands. They itched from frostbite. He thought about how many men in his unit had lost toes to frostbite.

"How about some coffee?" Captain Gondou asked. He picked up the coffee pot on his desk and filled a paper cup without waiting for Lieutenant Amata's answer. "It'll warm you up. Must have been nasty out there. It got a lot worse after you guys went out."

"You wouldn't believe how cold it gets out there, Captain."

Amata sat down in the chair waiting for him. He picked up the coffee and took a sip. Now he *really* wanted whiskey, not coffee. He knew what sort of individual was awarded the Order of Mars, and it definitely wasn't scum like him. That medal was for heroes, for guys who performed outstanding deeds that would be recounted within the FAF for as long as it existed. For guys who practically became legends, gods of war.

Why me? he wondered again, with growing unease. The dull ache in his right side worsened. *Why would a loser like me be getting a medal like that?* He would have been satisfied with the Distinguished Service Award. That, he could maybe understand, a reward for performing the job they'd given him. But there was no way that anyone could ever regard plowing snow as a feat of valor. The more he strained to think of even a remote reason for being chosen to receive the medal, the more nervous he became.

He shivered with a chill that the hot coffee couldn't assuage. He wasn't moved: he was scared. How could something this nuts be happening to him? If this wasn't a mistake, then it was a plot. Had to be. He must have been caught up in some sort of vast conspiracy beyond his knowledge, to be used in some way and then thrown aside like trash... Well, he was sick and tired of being used. He just wanted to get drunk and fade away quietly, to choose a mode of death on his own terms.

"I refuse to accept the medal," Lieutenant Amata said, a faint tremor in his voice.

Captain Gondou nodded calmly, but the words that came out of his mouth belied his attitude. "I figured you'd say that. However, the division—no, not just the division. The Maintenance Corps sees this as a chance to show the entire Faery Air Force how important our work is. Corps HQ won't allow you to refuse. It's an order. An order, Lieutenant Amata."

"Then the Corps is behind this plot," Amata spat out under his breath. "What did I do? Was it some sort of misconduct?"

"No, Lieutenant. This has nothing to do with the Corps, at least as far as awarding the medal goes. The Order of Mars is presented by the Corps, but the Corps doesn't decide who gets it. The decorations are decided on by a committee made up of officers at the very highest levels of the FAF. Do you see? As far as the Corps is concerned, this is a bolt from the blue. We were all as shocked as you are, but there's nothing we can do about it. We made an inquiry as to whether a mistake had been made, but apparently it's legit."

"But, who... Why would they have chosen me?"

"Who knows? Guys like us on the bottom don't know what the guys at the top are up to. But it's been decided and nothing can change it. You'd better not try to refuse. If you resist, they may charge you with mutiny. Even if they don't, you'll still be left in a bad position, maybe blacklisted. They're giving you the medal, so you take it. It'll be useful when you go back to Earth. It'll probably get you a good job."

"Is that supposed to make me feel better?"

"Come on, you should be celebrating. Still, I understand how you feel. I don't know if it'll console you or not, but you're getting a week's leave and clearance to return to Earth too."

"I don't want it," Amata said, his voice hoarse.

"Right. It's a busy time of year for us. I appreciate your consideration. But you're excused from work tomorrow. That's the day you'll be decorated."

"So I have no choice in this?"

"It's an order." Captain Gondou looked away from Lieutenant Amata. "Accept the medal. That's an order."

The captain looked down at his clasped hands on the desktop, then up at the smoke curling from the cigarette butt smoldering in the ashtray.

"Dismissed," he said. "Go to the station and tell the other guys. They'll probably be happy for you."

Amata left the command office without a word. He didn't think his coworkers would be happy for him. If anything, they'd be shocked. Maybe they'd congratulate him, but even if he got the medal it wouldn't improve the way they were treated. Even the way he himself was treated wouldn't change. There was nothing to be happy about. There probably wasn't a single one of his coworkers who would take pride in his getting it or even look at him with envy. There just wasn't any profit in it. Amata grew depressed. Although the other men wouldn't be jealous, they'd definitely treat him differently from now on, like he wasn't quite one of them anymore.

As he entered the station, the familiar cigarette smoke-filled warmth enveloped his body. Usually, the atmosphere would relax him, but right now the mood was a little strange. The guys playing cards at the table, the ones lying down on the cots, the ones reading, the others sitting on the floor or leaning against the wall as they drank... They all looked at him as though a stranger had just come into the room.

Word had already spread.

One of the guys at the table threw down his cards, stood up, and yelled, "Hooray for Lieutenant Amata!"

"Hooray for what?" Amata asked, playing dumb. He sat down on an empty cot and took out his flask.

"Give that cheap shit to the snow to drink," said one of the guys leaning against the wall as he lifted his glass. He tilted his head in the direction of a bottle of scotch laid off to the side. "Compliments of Lieutenant Colonel Hazer. He said that you're the pride of the Corps. A hero shouldn't drink cheap booze, Lieutenant."

Why couldn't Colonel Hazer mind his own damn business? Amata shook his head, then swung both feet up onto the cot and began drinking his own cheap whiskey. The cheerful Colonel Hazer's responsibilities included being their supervisor, and now and then he'd show up and maybe join them for a card game or two. Still, no matter how friendly he was, he wasn't one of them. Because he never had to endure the snowstorms. On the surface, they all smiled at him, drank with him, smoked with him, and let him win some money at cards, but the truth was that they couldn't stand him. Hazer himself seemed satisfied with the arrangement.

As he began to sink into despair, Amata could imagine what it had been like when Colonel Hazer had come to give them the news. He probably said something like, "Gentlemen, congratulations! One of your own has been awarded the Order of Mars!

A true hero has appeared from within your ranks. You should be proud!" And then the guys would be wearing big grins on their faces, while inside they wouldn't give a crap. That idiot. If it wasn't for Hazer, he might have been able to keep the news of the award from the others. The Corps was trampling on the little bit of peace he had. He should have expected it.

Returning to their card game, the players began talking in exaggeratedly loud voices.

"So what's an Order of Mars, anyways?"

"Dunno. I think it's a medal of valor."

"Then why'd Amata get one?"

"Why do you think? 'Cause he's a hero, ain't he?"

They laughed and then went back to their usual stupid chatter. About how someone had gotten into a fight with some woman and had his arm broken, but no, that was just some story he'd made up to get out of work, and how could he humiliate himself that much just to get out of work, and was it still snowing outside...

Lieutenant Amata drained the flask, dropped it on the floor, and closed his eyes.

THE WEATHER ON the day commemorating the founding of the FAF was a Class 2 winter storm. The 3rd Mechanized Snow Removal Unit was ready for deployment. After being told to disregard the commemoration ceremony, the motor graders and the secondary rotary plows were divided into teams and sent out to face the white devil. They came in only to rest and refuel and were immediately sent out again. As it grew busier and busier, with more and more vehicles breaking down, tanker trucks were brought out to do hot refueling—pumping gas directly into the plows' tanks while the engines were still running. The huge airfield was like a battle zone, but with snow and ice as the enemy, not the JAM.

While his coworkers were on the ground freezing, Lieutenant

Amata put on a uniform he'd never worn before and headed for the ceremony hall. The huge underground auditorium was warm, like another world. In fact, it was hot enough to make him sweat, and he found it almost as oppressive as being in the middle of a blizzard.

As he stood in line with the other medal recipients and listened to the congratulatory speeches being given, he frowned occasionally. Each word of praise from the loudspeaker seemed to bore painfully into his hungover brain. The scene in the stiff and formal ceremonial hall didn't seem real to him at all; there was no snow here, no numbing cold. The stern attitudes of the generals and the faces of the soldiers there to receive their commendations… They all seemed to exist in a different dimension from him. They looked like dolls, like they weren't alive. He had to keep reminding himself that the scene before him wasn't a fiction.

When he thought about it, though, this entire war seemed to be a fictional one. The JAM had never shown themselves to humans, and a ground grunt like Lieutenant Amata couldn't begin to imagine what sort of enemy they were. He would watch the fighter teams take off and return, but what the enemy planes looked like or even whether or not they existed was beyond him. He didn't think about it, either. To him, the most pressing concerns were getting fuel for his grader, or stopping the cold wind that blew in under the bent door, or how he would have to buy some more whiskey soon because he was almost out. Stuff like that. The snow and the cold were the lieutenant's enemies. Not the JAM.

The JAM, an enemy the lieutenant had never seen, was beyond him. But the FAF was equally so. And now this huge, unknowable thing was giving him a medal. It was like having a monster from his dreams appear in front of him shaking a bell. All of it, all of it was utterly unreal.

We're all dolls, he thought, *the generals, the medal recipients, and me, too.* Just gaily dressed mannequins in a shop window, whose sole purpose was to entice the passersby to come in and spend their money. He was being used to sell the idea of fighting spirit to the soldiers in the field, an immobile doll inserted into a make-believe world.

At last, his name was called. With a feeling of grim resignation, he walked forward and saluted the general presenting the medals. As the general, his chest plastered with ribbons and decorations, took the Order of Mars from his adjutant, Lieutenant Amata saw his eye fall on the snowflake-shaped insignia on Amata's uniform. A look of doubt clouded the general's face, and Amata felt a jolt of alarm run through him. Wasn't this farce of a ceremony being conducted under the order of the command staff? Why would the general be surprised by it?

"Congratulations," the general said as he hung the Order of Mars around Amata's neck. "You're a hero."

He sounded almost offended when he said it. Amata took a deep breath and desperately tried to sort out the jumble of thoughts in his head. What was going on here? Why was the general looking at him like that? Had something gone wrong?

There was only one answer he could arrive at: the command staff didn't know about this, either. Why would a snowplow driver be awarded a medal? Who was it that had made the decision? It wasn't his division, it wasn't the Corps, and it wasn't the command staff, either. Which meant that it was nobody in the FAF.

Impossible. Amata shivered. The situation had gone from absurd to ominous. The gold medal hung heavily from his neck. It was engraved with an image of a Super Sylph, a creature that had nothing to do with a man like him who spent his life crawling around on the ground. But he couldn't give it back. The Corps wouldn't allow it. He had decided that if he had to become a decorated doll, a figurine to boost morale, he was prepared to accept his fate. But now even that justification had vanished.

What was this medal? As the military band struck up a loud performance of "Hail to the Faery Air Force," Lieutenant Amata felt sick.

THE NEWS THAT an alcoholic snowplow driver had been given the Order of Mars was soon all over Faery. As the Maintenance Corps command had anticipated, people became more aware of the importance of the Corps' duties, including snow removal, but precious few agreed that Lieutenant Amata deserved the medal. Everyone else was baffled as to why he was given it. Some went so far as to tell him straight to his face that it was a mistake. Others would speculate on what kind of stratagem he had pulled to dupe the decorations committee and then would insult him further by saying that they knew he wasn't capable of something like that.

Amata could only take their scorn in silence. He knew his work meant nothing to almost everyone else, but up until then no one had actually said "You're garbage" to his face. As soon as he'd been decorated, however, his wretchedness had been exposed for all to see. Everywhere he went, he could hear the murmurs of *Why you?* and felt even worse as he had no answer to give. He wished they would just stop. He hadn't wanted the damn thing in the first place.

He tried to drown his indignation in the bottle and drank so much he was practically pickled in alcohol. The Order of Mars had become a golden maggot that ate into his flesh, a sylph that sprang from rotten meat.

He couldn't give the medal back. He couldn't throw it away. He couldn't destroy it. He was trapped on all sides. All he could do was drink and hope the alcohol would eventually sterilize the wound.

Conscious of the weight of the medal hanging around his neck, Lieutenant Amata donned his cold weather gear. "I'm a great man, a hero," he announced to the empty locker room.

"Yahoo. The hero is marching off to war." Was that dull ache in his side from his liver, or was the medal poking him in the stomach? He staggered a bit as he made his way out.

It was below freezing in the garage. The snow that clung to his grader was white and crystalline. Dazzling light flooded in as the shutter door rose. It was clear weather for a change.

Amata stumbled as he boarded his machine. The other members of his unit saw it but said nothing. It wasn't unusual for him to go out drunk, and besides, he was a hero, wasn't he?

The graders rolled out. The bent door on his machine still hadn't been fixed. He'd banged at it with a hammer, but that had just made the problem worse. The wind outside was strong. Low, dark, roiling clouds moved with ferocious speed across the sky. Shafts of sunlight would occasionally pierce through them to stab at the ground like swords of light. It was even colder now than it had been during the blizzard. The hard-packed snow was tougher to deal with, but Amata almost preferred the relative warmth of the storm. He dazedly watched the patterns formed by the snow as it was whipped about by the wind.

The unit took advantage of the break in the weather to do a large-scale snow removal of the airfield ground facilities. In spaces where the graders couldn't get in, waves of men were dispatched to do it by hand. It was only at times like these that the snow removal units had help, with every off-duty member of the division mobilized for the job.

Amata stopped his grader in front of the hut that stood next to the elevator egress of the Tactical Air Force's SAF. He smiled faintly as he took in the scene of the SAF pilots shoveling snow. His teeth chattered as he watched. The cold air blowing in through the gap in the door caused his breath to fog up and obscure every part of the windshield not directly hit by the driver's seat defroster. He could actually hear the moisture crackle as it froze on the glass.

The grader would plow away the snow shoveled off the elevator head by the men, but until they were finished, he had to wait.

He rubbed his face with his gloves. It was so cold it hurt. *Hurry up,* he thought. *I've got other work to do.* After the next wave of scheduled sorties, he had the takeoff runway to clear.

As Lieutenant Amata sat in the driver's seat, rubbing at his face and knocking his knees together to keep from freezing, a guy who looked like an SAF officer hand-signaled him to move. The SAF elevator platform was rising to reveal an enormous fighter plane. A Sylphid. Amata pressed down on his parka over the spot where the medal lay hanging against his stomach.

"Would you hurry up and move it?!" yelled the man outside his window. Amata backed his machine away.

The Sylph was towed out. It was an SAF reconnaissance plane. Not just a Sylphid, then. A Super Sylph. The twin vertical stabilizers bore a boomerang insignia. Beneath the cockpit, in a small calligraphic hand, was the plane's personal name: Yukikaze. A cold-sounding name. *But I'll bet it's warm inside that cockpit,* Amata thought enviously. This was the first time he had seen a Super Sylph from this close up. It was an intimidating aircraft. His motor grader, designed for use on the enormous FAB runways, was the size of a house, but the fighter before him was even larger.

Yukikaze's jet fuel starter broke the silence as it started up, making a noise like a low siren. The sound explosively increased in volume until it melted into the howl of the right engine turbine revving up. As the fan revolutions rose, the fine snow layer covering the runway was sucked into the air intake, and soon a small vortex of snow, solid as a pillar, bridged the space between the ground and the intake. The characteristic ear-splitting scream of the fan engine diminished as the pilot pulled the throttle to idle. Lieutenant Amata let out the breath he'd been unconsciously holding. Then the pilot started the left engine. The cold air rang again with the low-pitched siren of the jet fuel starter.

After another few minutes the ground crew gave the "go" sign, and the pilot waved his hand in acknowledgment. The grader shook with the roar of Yukikaze's engines. The thunderous noise rose even higher, and then suddenly, as though pushed from behind, the huge plane moved forward. The exhaust from her engines whipped the snow behind her into a small storm. Amata turned on the grader's windshield wipers.

Yukikaze taxied out onto the broad runway. Soon she was lifting off from it, her afterburners blowing long tails of flame, and in the blink of an eye she vanished into the thick cloud layer. The thunderous roar of her engines lingered for a moment before it, too, faded into the ringing silence that remained.

Lieutanant Amata couldn't tell whether his ears felt numb more from the cold or from the sonic assault of the fighter's start-up. He drank his whiskey, mentally comparing his motor grader to the fighter plane named Yukikaze, then sighed. They shared only one common feature: they both ran on liquid fuel. Aside from that Yukikaze excelled in every way. Loaded with bombs, she would weigh nearly thirty tons. The grader weighed only sixteen. The plane could generate nearly thirty tons of thrust, while he could just about manage 300 horsepower. The fighter was magnificent, while the plow was just lame. The same could probably be said of their operators as well.

"Thanks for the help out here."

Amata started. Outside the door, the superior officer who had signaled him before was looking up at the grader's cabin. Amata kicked the door open and looked down.

The man from the SAF had a deep scar on his cheek. His rank insignia indicated that he was a major.

Amata's throat closed up from the cold. His lungs seemed paralyzed for an instant. The freezing air stung his eyes. He blinked, inhaled even though it hurt to do so, and snapped, "How long are you going to make me wait? Sir..."

"Sorry," the man replied. "Major Booker from the SAF." He squinted up at Amata. "You been drinking?"

"Yeah."

"Can you do your job?"

"Yeah, if you'd let me. If I don't get to it soon, I won't have any time to rest up before my next shift."

"Can you plow the runway straight when you're sotted?"

Plowing the runway involved several motor graders driving abreast, with rotary plows working on both sides to push the snow collected by the graders off to the side of the runway.

"Don't worry. A beacon signal keeps the graders driving straight. I don't even have to hold the wheel. Funny, huh? I don't even need to be here." His voice grew tight. "And for that, they made me a hero."

"So, that's who you are," said Major Booker, staring at him. "You're the famous Lieutenant Amata."

"None other. What, are you shocked?"

"You reek of alcohol. How fitting for a hero."

"Yeah," the lieutenant answered. Then suddenly, he was moved to tears, tears he wasn't even aware he was shedding. "I can't help it. It's all that medal's fault… It's cut me off from all my friends. If I keep quiet, they rag on me. If I speak, they resent me. No matter what I do or don't do, I'm cut off from everyone else. It's not like I was really close to any of 'em, but they're all I had. And there's nothing I can do about it. It's all—" He choked back the bile that rose in his throat, tasting blood. He tried washing it down with a slug of whiskey, gagged, and spat it outside the cabin. A reddish brown stain spread across the surface of the snow. *Guess I really don't have much longer,* he thought.

"Hey, are you okay? That's blood, isn't it?"

For some reason, the concern in the major's voice infuriated Amata.

"It's none of your business. Even the doctor told me to just do whatever the hell I want to at this point. It's just, I…I wish I could get that sonuvabitch who gave me that medal."

"And who is that?"

"I'm a grunt, how the hell would I know?" he wheezed with his frozen breath. "You're a major in the SAF, aren't you?"

"Yeah," replied the man, taking his sunglasses from his pocket, obviously getting ready to leave.

"Well, I have a favor to ask," Amata said desperately. "They say the SAF is so powerful that it's practically a shadow of the FAF high command. You could find out who awarded me the medal, couldn't you? Please, Major... I want to get rid of this thing."

"Even I couldn't do that."

"Figures. Forget I even mentioned it. Just order those guys to finish up and move it." Amata pointed at the ten or so soldiers who were struggling with heavy looking snow shovels. "It's cold. I'm gonna freeze to death out here."

"Sure," the major said, putting his sunglasses on. He paused, then looked up at the cabin and said, "I'll see what I can do. Just don't get your hopes up."

"Then how about hurrying up and giving that order?"

"I was talking about the medal."

"What?"

Amata switched the grader's engine from idle to intermittent start mode. The warmed-up engine stopped. It grew quiet. The wind stabbed at his ears. He wasn't wearing earmuffs, and they ached as though they were going to fall to pieces.

"What did you say?"

"I was talking about your medal. I'm a little interested in it myself. There's definitely something odd about you being given that decoration. I'd also like to know what the general staff were thinking."

Amata stared at Major Booker. There was no sign of mockery or jealousy or resentment in his expression. His tone of voice was indifferent. He wasn't lying. He wasn't sympathizing with him, but he didn't despise him, either. Amata felt like he'd been saved.

"Please, Major," he said in a low, shaking voice.

"I'm in the SAF 5th. Boomerang Squadron. Just be aware that I probably won't be able to unravel this on my own, and I have a feeling FAF military intelligence is going to get involved before it's over."

"All I'm asking is for you to try. I'm glad I ran into you, sir."

"If I learn anything, I'll let you know. Anyway, you look cold, so shut that door. You're shaking."

"Th-Thank you, sir." It had been so long since he'd spoken those words that he'd nearly forgotten them.

Lieutenant Amata sniffed the mucus running from his nose. It hurt to do it. He wiped it with his glove, and it froze white instantly. He shut the door, stepped on the heavy clutch, and put the machine into gear.

Suddenly, the dead white winter landscape took on the hint of a golden hue. Was it the sunlight? Probably just the jaundice in his eyes. *I should wear sunglasses too,* he thought. He wasn't going to give up and die like this. He was going to give that medal back. He'd speak directly to whomever it was, throw the medal in his face, and then deck him. Whatever happened, he had to stay alive until then.

Believing that Major Booker would somehow find out who was responsible for putting him in this living hell, Amata set off in the grader. He had found his one and only ally and felt an immense relief in finally having done so. So long as the major didn't betray him, he would stay alive.

As usual, the wind was blowing in through the gap at the bottom of the door. Even if he cleared up the thing with the medal, there was probably nothing he could do about that. Amata sniffed and lowered the plow at the front of the grader. It was cold. Spring was still far away. It might never come. The plow tore through the clods of snow, the flakes fluttering through the air like flower petals in bloom.

MAJOR JAMES BOOKER (Tactical Air Force, Tactical Combat Group, Special Air Force) was attached to SAF-V, Boomerang Squadron, the unit said to be the most nihilistic in the entire air force. He himself was laconic, a tough officer, with a physical presence that inspired fear and aversion in most people. But in truth, he was possessed of a moderate nature.

After dismissing the grumbling Boomerang soldiers from their snow removal duty, the major thankfully returned to the warm underground of the base. He removed his fogged-up sunglasses, proceeded to the locker room, and quickly stripped off his cold-weather gear, which was now soaked from the melted snow and ice that had encrusted him during his work. His feet were cold almost beyond endurance.

He thought about Lieutenant Amata. Day in and day out, week after grinding week, the man had to deal with this unrelenting cold. *He really does deserve a medal for it,* the major thought. But even so, the Order of Mars was an entirely inappropriate decoration. The fact that it had been awarded to Amata was just bizarre.

Booker finished cleaning himself up, got dressed, and returned to his office in the squadron quarters. He had two hours until Rei and Yukikaze returned from their sortie. From the ground, he could do nothing to help them in their fight, aside from praying, as he always did, that they come back alive. *Whatever happens, make sure you come back.* He thought about Rei's perpetually cool, calm nature. That expressionless look on his face never changed, no matter what chaos was happening all around him.

The major poured himself a hot cup from the coffee maker and took a sip, deriving a tiny pleasure from the way the cup warmed up his stiff fingers. How would Rei react if he'd been given the medal?

A corner of Booker's mouth quirked up in a grin. He didn't even have to ask. Even if he'd been adamant about not wanting it, Rei would have accepted it expressionlessly and then not given it another moment's thought. Most likely it would have just ended up being used as a paperweight or a coaster, or be lost somewhere in a corner of his room. All Rei cared about was his beloved plane; he was indifferent to almost all other material objects.

And how would the other members of Boomerang Squadron react? Would they change their attitude toward the other pilot? No, he couldn't see that happening. They were all lone wolves who stayed out of each other's way.

But that was not what happened to Lieutenant Amata. Booker thought of the tears he'd seen falling from the corners of Amata's eyes, the signs of a soul that was easily bruised. He was a man endowed with the rich, common humanity you hardly ever saw in Boomerang Squadron. Humans cannot live alone. Amata couldn't live estranged from his friends.

Rei, however, was different. Impersonal, detached, it was as if he had no need for human contact at all. But Booker found himself instinctively defending the younger man, mainly, he supposed, because he understood where Rei was coming from. Back in the days when he'd been a pilot, he'd been the same. He'd been driven by the same directives, the ones that ruled the lives of all the SAF-V pilots: Even if your comrades are being shot down one by one, you cannot help them. Protect your plane, protect the data you're carrying, and do whatever it takes to get back alive.

It was a cruel and lonely duty. The only things that stood between you and the possible death that awaited you on every takeoff were your skill, your gut instinct, and the capabilities of your plane. And you never, ever asked yourself whether the data that you gathered was worth the cost of abandoning your basic humanity.

Major Booker drained his coffee cup and then walked out of the room on his still numb and half-frozen legs.

Rei had Yukikaze, but Lieutenant Amata had nothing. Amata had been desperate, practically half-crazed by loneliness and his desire to be with other people. All he could do was drink. If nothing were done, that medal would end up killing him.

Booker knew he was butting in where he shouldn't, and

that he was probably about to create a whole world of trouble for himself, but he had resolved to help Amata. He was also curious to see just how much influence the SAF really had. And it would distract him from the indescribable unease he always felt until Yukikaze's return. But more than anything else he couldn't forget Lieutenant Amata's tears. Booker tried not to involve himself with others, but he felt that ignoring Amata's plight would mean that he had finally lost the last shreds of his own humanity.

THE FAF'S GENERAL Headquarters was located in the very deepest levels of the underground base. Major Booker took a high-velocity elevator down to the command staff section.

Security was very strict. Anti-explosive and anti-contamination security procedures required him to stop and present his ID at every block. In the end, he couldn't get down into the command staff section proper. The public relations office on its periphery, which had no direct involvement in strategic or tactical matters, was as far as his clearance level could take him. Which wasn't surprising. It was a bit of an accomplishment for him to have wandered this far in the first place. Lieutenant Amata wouldn't even have been able to get on the elevator.

The office was busy. *Looks more like a trading firm than a place conducting a war,* the major thought. There were people compiling battle results to send back to Earth, others constructing the schedules of analysts and consultants coming to Faery, still others facing computer consoles, monitoring data readouts, talking into headsets, or handling piles of documents.

"Excuse me. I'd like to inquire about a medal."

Booker addressed the question to a nearby male staffer. He was dressed in a shirt with no jacket and didn't seem to be part of the group. The man looked up from his copies, eyed Booker, and asked who he was.

"Major Booker, Tactical Air Force, SAF."

The man didn't even glance at the ID proffered by the major. He simply shook his head and said, "I can't take any questions about decorations."

"Why not?"

"Because it's not in my jurisdiction."

"Where would I go, then? It's about Lieutenant Amata."

"Oh, that," the man replied, shrugging his shoulders. "That makes it even harder. Nobody knows why he got it."

"I know why," the major said, putting on his friendliest smile. He'd worked out that this man was a talker. He brought his face closer, lowering his voice conspiratorially. "It was an SAF screwup."

Just as the major expected, the guy took the bait.

"Huh?" he said. "According to what I heard, it was some sort of system breakdown. Medal recipients are determined by computer analysis of the data files of all air force personnel, so everyone figured his name must have gotten in there by mistake. But even after they did a full-bore investigation they couldn't find an error. So it was the SAF, huh?"

"I think it may have been. Is there any way I can meet with a member of the decorations committee?"

"Well, in that case…" the man said as he picked up a headset. He keyed an extension, then briefly explained to whoever was on the other end what Major Booker had said.

"Looks like we can do it. Captain McGuire will meet with you. Just wait a couple of minutes, okay?"

Booker sat down in a chair the man indicated and glanced at his chronometer. Halfway there. *Rei, come back in one piece.* He was careful not to let the unease he felt show on his face.

Captain McGuire was short, blond, and possessed fine features that suggested those of a Greek statue. He affably shook the major's hand as they exchanged greetings.

"Are you a member of the decorations committee?" Booker asked him.

"No, I'm not," the captain replied as they left the office. He lavished his smile on the guards as they walked toward command HQ. "I'm not on it, but I'll take you to it."

They entered the command staff headquarters. It was an enormous room, with several levels of glowing screens ringing the perimeter. The interior was divided into three vertical sections, giving it the feel of an enormous theater.

"This is the nerve center of the FAF. This way, please."

The captain led Major Booker through the maze of control consoles, past the countless men and women sitting before them in their uniforms and headsets. The captain finally led him into a glassed-in booth in one section. Once the door was shut, it was quiet.

"Here's the decorations committee, Major." Booker glanced around the small, plain room. There was nothing in it but a computer console.

"You don't mean—"

"Exactly, Major Booker. The conferring of decorations is processed by the decorations selection computer here in Headquarters. It analyzes the recommendations from every corps and then checks to see if the candidates fulfill the requirements. We don't have time to do it all by hand."

"And then what happens after it outputs its decision?"

"The command staff signs off on it and the decoration is awarded. We've never had any trouble with it, so the signature is really just a formality. Command doesn't check everyone on the list individually because we trust the system. If we doubted our systems, we couldn't run normal military operations for even an instant. But this one time, it looks like the computer made a mistake."

"What was the cause?"

"Unknown. We've checked everything from the hardware to the software. To be honest, the software is so complicated we can't vet it completely without taking a gross amount of time. We think there might a bug somewhere in the code, but... You said you know what the cause is?"

"The computer may not have made a mistake…"

One of Booker's specialties was electrical engineering, and he knew from experience that computers would sometimes do things humans didn't expect them to. A computer's programming could produce results that were perfectly in accordance with its logical parameters but that might seem unpredictable and incomprehensible to a human. In this case, the situation was even more complex since the computer in question was equipped with artificial intelligence features that provided it with learning and auto-improvement functions, meaning that it could rewrite its own software to make it more advanced and efficient. It might take a human a lifetime to unravel software like that.

"How do you communicate with this thing?" he asked.

"It doesn't have a vocal speech recognition function, but it does understand plain language. You input via the keyboard."

"I'd like to try talking to it."

"Please go ahead," Captain McGuire replied. "I have work to do, so I'll leave you to it. Until we meet again, Major. If you discover anything of interest, please call for me."

"Right."

Booker pecked at the console keyboard.

Wake up he entered.

State identity came the response. Input rank and unit attachment.

After answering this, the major entered his question.

Tell me the reason for awarding a decoration to Lt. Amata.

There was a second's delay, then the computer responded Classified.

Why? Is it related to the JAM?

Classified.

The major sighed. Maybe he'd get somewhere if he changed the direction of the questioning.

What are the JAM?

Our enemy.

"Huh," said the major as he rested his fingers on the keys and reread the display. That was a natural enough answer. Nothing strange about it. Our enemy. Our... He suddenly started forward in his seat.

Who do you mean by "our"?

We who are the enemy of the JAM.

Humans?

There is no direct evidence the JAM perceive humans.

Explain.

There was a short pause.

Meaning of question unclear. Reenter.

His fingers now trembling, Booker typed Who...is...the... enemy...of...the...JAM?

The response came immediately. We are.

Computers? The computers from Earth?

The cursor blinked, then froze. As though the computer were hesitating. Just for an instant. Then the characters scrolled out. The major devoured them as they appeared.

The JAM's direct enemy is the Faery Air Force.

The JAM cannot recognize humans?

There is no direct evidence the JAM perceive humans.

But there is for computers?

A pause.

Meaning of question unclear. Reenter.

Do you sense the JAM?

Another pause.

Meaning of question unclear. Reenter.

Booker smacked the console, cursing under his breath. "Is this thing playing dumb?" He drummed his fingers on its surface for a moment, then started typing again.

Explain the importance of the snow removal teams to the war with the JAM.

Context disorder. Reenter.

Are the snow removal teams necessary to the war against the JAM?

They are necessary.

The current snow removal operation procedures are inefficient. Do you recognize this?

Recognized.

Describe remedial measures.

Full automation is necessary.

Humans are not necessary?

A pause.

Meaning of question unclear. Reenter.

Are humans necessary for the operation of the FAF?

The major took a deep breath and waited for the reply.

The computer seemed to laugh scornfully at his tension as it output its response.

They are necessary.

Lt. Amata was decorated because he is necessary?

Were the computers giving out medals as rewards to the humans? To keep them happy and quietly obedient?

Booker recalled something Rei had said before: "Why do humans have to fight?" What had he said as an answer? He thought it was something like, "Because wars are started by humans, which means we can't very well leave them to machines to fight."

Except that it wasn't true. The major slowly stood up.

The response on the screen was Classified.

It seemed that the war was between the JAM and the FAF's computers. The JAM were fighting humanity's machines, not the people that built them. So where did that leave the humans? Where did that leave him? If the computers said humans weren't necessary to the battle, would they be excluded from it?

Booker realized his hands were balled into fists and carefully uncurled them. This was bullshit. Maybe this computer really was malfunctioning.

Just as he was leaving the room, the intercom chimed. The major went back inside. "What is it?"

"Yukikaze has been hit," came Captain McGuire's voice. "You're wanted back in SAF command at once."

"Understood." The major clicked the intercom off and ran from the GHQ sector.

I don't believe this, he thought, fighting down the pounding of his heart. *It had to happen while I'm fucking around with a computer. Rei, come back alive. That's an order.*

THE SAF COMMAND quarters wasn't as large as the air force's General Headquarters, but it was almost as well equipped. As Major Booker entered the combat control room, he immediately looked at the thirty-by-sixty foot main tactical display that extended across the front wall of the chamber. In one of the center screen sectors, red letters spelling out **EMERGENCY** were blinking on and off.

The major checked Yukikaze's damage data, which was being transmitted to them by the fighter's autonomous test system. The hydraulics that powered the lowering and raising of her landing gear, arresting hook, and canopy were damaged. The left engine had been hit and had flamed out, but the fire had been extinguished. *Thank God,* Booker thought. All he had to do now was pray for a safe emergency landing. Rei would be able to pull this off.

"Close the airfield. Clear the takeoff runway for him."

"We can't," replied a female operator, her voice tense. "They're plowing the snow on it, Major."

"Then move them out of the way!" he yelled. "What have you been doing 'til now?!"

Yukikaze was dumping her remaining fuel, making preparations to land.

Dread fisted around his heart. *Rei, wait. It's too soon.*

Booker ran out of the command center and headed for the

surface. How could this be happening? What the hell were those idiots in the snow removal teams doing? Were they trying to keep Yukikaze from landing?

PAN, PAN, PAN. Snow removal units on Runway 02L, stop all work immediately and move to the side of the runway at once. SAF 5th Squadron Unit B-503 is making an emergency landing. Snow removal units, emergency evacuation. Repeat—

Lieutenant Amata heard them declare a PAN but could not understand the message. He was almost blind drunk. He just muttered "All right, all right," when he heard the emergency call, and lined his plow up to follow the guidance vector projected on his front windshield. In other words, he kept driving straight on. He could see his coworkers' units moving away from him. *Shit,* he thought, *you don't have to hate me that much, do you?*

He stomped on the accelerator and took a swig of his whiskey. It didn't flow into his stomach, though. He vomited it back up. The floor of the cabin was now stained red. In his clouded mind, the lieutenant urged himself on. *Gotta keep following the guide mark. C'mon, c'mon! This is my job.* He thought he saw a black shadow appear in front of him.

It was the shape on his medal. It seemed to be growing steadily larger. Must be a bird... But would there be birds in this cold? Must be his imagination. Amata kept his eyes on the windshield display and drove the grader straight on.

AT YUKIKAZE'S CONTROLS, Rei couldn't believe his ears when he heard her collision warning alarm sound. They were on final approach and now, inexplicably, there was an obstacle in front of them. He could see the black dot below him with his naked eyes. A snowplow? What the hell...?

They continued to bleed energy as Yukikaze fell. They'd been flying with her nose pitched up to catch the maximum air resistance across the entire wing, but now it was roughly level with the horizon. Their airspeed had dropped low enough for landing, but that was the main cause of their immediate predicament: they didn't have enough lift to fly over the obstacle before them on the runway. Should he cut out the direct lift control and use the side force controller to veer to the side? He wasn't going fast enough for that and didn't have enough altitude, either. Because he'd dumped their fuel according to the SOP for an emergency landing, he didn't have enough left for a retry. But if he did nothing, they were going to crash into that machine. Air compressed by ground effect forces blew up fantails of snow below them as Yukikaze rushed onward.

From the backseat, Lieutenant Burgadish noticed the object on the runway and immediately apprehended the problem.

"Lieutenant Fukai, eject."

"Evading."

"There's no time for that."

"I'm clearing you to punch out. Go."

"Roger."

Burgadish yanked down his face curtain handle. The canopy... did not eject. The hydraulics were dead. With his right hand still on the handle, he moved the canopy lever to the OPEN position and pulled the emergency canopy ejection. No good. Next he pulled the manual release handle. This lifted the canopy up slightly, which should have caused it to be blown off by the air pressure, but there was no response. It wouldn't open.

"Through-canopy bailout!" Burgadish yelled. The only way for them to get out of the plane now was to smash through the canopy itself.

Rei wasn't even thinking about ejecting. He nudged the direct lift control thumbwheel forward and advanced the throttle. He had to accelerate to gain the lift he'd need to avoid the obstacle. He closed the speed brake. The afterburner wouldn't ignite; the fuel transfer valve to the afterburner closed automatically once the remaining fuel fell below a certain level. Regardless, he couldn't expect the afterburner to handle such a sudden acceleration. There was a short pause before he felt a response.

Yukikaze accelerated, nosing down to minimize air resistance, her flaps automatically extending to full down.

"Float, Yukikaze," Rei urged.

Not even five seconds had passed since he'd first seen the snowplow.

Rei looked at the huge machine in front of them. It was no use. They were going to crash into it. In his mind, Rei could see Yukikaze's radome smashing into the grader. In another instant, that would be his reality.

He heard a crash as the rear seat smashed through the canopy. Burgadish had done as Rei had ordered, setting the ejection command mode lever so that his seat alone would eject. Rei stayed where he was.

He braced himself for the impact. The little bit of altitude they'd gained wouldn't be enough. Yukikaze's fuselage would be gutted like a fish by the top of the grader, and then they would be ripped apart.

He didn't close his eyes. Just before impact, he thought he could see the face of the man in the driver's seat... Then the entire cabin vanished.

Rei was certain of what he'd just seen but couldn't process it: the driver's cab had turned an incandescent red and then disappeared. The upper half of the grader simply had been erased, like a drawing on a blackboard. Yukikaze's radome plunged through the now empty space where it had been and flew over the remainder of the machine without any impact at all.

Rei quickly pitched Yukikaze up to kill his speed. She hit the ground hard, tail down, then nose, and skidded along the surface of the snow. They were rapidly approaching the end of the runway. Rei had done all that he could. The only thing left was to hope they stopped before the runway ran out.

Yukikaze finally came to a halt just before going off the

runway. Rei twisted around and looked behind him out the broken cockpit.

Black smoke was rising from the remains of the snowplow. He had no idea what had happened, but Yukikaze had landed safely and that was all that was important to him. He checked the instruments for any abnormalities and then, after determining that there was no danger of fire, took out his canopy knife, broke through a forward section of the glass, and got out of there.

AFTER THE ACCIDENT, Major Booker recalled the horrifying sight of Yukikaze heading straight for the huge machine. He had been running across the snow, powerless to stop the imminent catastrophe, when the cold air was split by the sound of an explosion that echoed into the sky.

It was the runway point defense system. The antiaircraft Phalanx guns had activated and thrown nearly a thousand rounds of ammo in a fraction of a second at the grader, blowing off its upper half instantly. Yukikaze passed overhead safely as Booker stood there in shock, a distant corner of his mind grateful that the guy in the grader must have died instantly, never knowing what had hit him.

Later, he learned that the point defense system had automatically fired on the decision of the central defense computer. And that it had been Lieutenant Amata in that grader.

Later still, on reading the accident report, he came across a recommendation in the conclusion section for altering all snow removal operations. When his eyes fell on the phrase "Full automation is necessary," a cold, sickening sensation crawled down his spine. It was the exact same phrase that the HQ computer had used.

The major couldn't help reading into this whole incident a veiled threat, a warning that humans should not interfere in the battle between the computers and the JAM. It was probably just paranoia, but on the other hand instincts like this were what had kept him alive until now.

After the accident investigation was over, Booker queried the computer once more as to why it had awarded the medal to Lieutenant Amata.

The computer answered `Classified`.

But then it went on. `Based on his heroic actions, it is recommended that Lt. Amata receive the Distinguished Service Award for his snow removal duties.`

Booker tore up the report into confetti and threw it into the air. The pieces fluttered down like snow.

"It looks like the one you should have cursed was the computer, Amata," he muttered to himself. "What would you have done if you'd known the truth?"

Major Booker himself couldn't answer that question.

It was winter on Faery. For Lieutenant Amata, spring would never come.

VI

ALL SYSTEMS
NORMAL

Yukikaze's power was beyond what even he had expected. Finally free of her crew, she killed all their safeguards and revealed capacities exceeding her design limits. He tried to tame this new Yukikaze, but she refused his orders, judging them errors, and danced freely in the skies of Faery...

A LARGE FORMATION of enemy aircraft was approaching.

The initial alert came in from the tactical fighters patrolling the perimeter of frontline base TAB-14. An airborne early warning and control system plane confirmed the information.

Twenty-four interceptors scrambled from TAB-14. They were Fands, single-seat assault fighters of the 1402nd Tactical Combat Group, 402nd Tactical Fighter Squadron.

The 402nd TFS fell into a stacked line-abreast formation and prepared to confront the attacking JAM fighters.

The 402nd flight leader glanced up at the contrails streaking the sky high above them. He swallowed a surge of irritation laced with jealousy; the tactical combat and surveillance fighter leaving those trails was powerful enough to meet the JAM on equal terms and, thanks to the overwhelming thrust provided by its Phoenix engines, could even outrun them. Although it appeared whenever there was a battle, it never joined in combat, never helped its fellow FAF planes in their lethal struggle, and always just returned to base safely when it was all over. *All that SAF bastard does is run away,* the 402nd leader thought. *It's like he comes just to watch us die.*

"Ox leader, JAM closing. Number of units, increasing. One-point-four G, head-on."

"Roger."

Guided by the data link from the AWACS plane, the 402nd TFS broke up into four smaller flights. Each flight of six planes assumed a stacked three-ship spread formation. One three-plane group would attack while the other would fly support, acting as spotters and defense. The attacking and defending roles weren't fixed beforehand but instead varied according to the needs of the battle. The point of this fluid formation was to separate the enemy aircraft and attack them three-on-one. When these conditions weren't met—for example, if two enemy planes were approaching from the rear—the attacking group would abort and shift to a defensive role, creating an opportunity for the other group to strike.

In this sort of close-in dogfight, there was no time to rely on radar. The pilots had to depend on their own senses and on the information transmitted from their fellow planes. The only way to retain the advantage was to make constant, rapid, and accurate decisions. Combat pilots with bad instincts didn't last for long.

"Ox 2, Ox 3, engage."

The flight leader slid his throttle forward. The enemy had broken into two groups, one going high and the other low. Ox team climbed rapidly.

"Tally on bandit, two o'clock," called in Ox 2. His sharp eyesight had allowed him to spot the JAM's faint contrail. Ox leader kept his eyes glued to it. His radar acquired the enemy plane and highlighted it on his HUD within the target designator box. He quickly toggled his dogfight switch. One wing of the enemy formation was lagging behind.

"I've got him."

The flight leader pushed forward. Speed had to be maintained at all costs. Speed was life. Ox 2 and 3 followed him.

"Ox leader, engaging. Break, starboard."

"Roger."

Acting on a warning from Ox 4, which was monitoring the situation, that their target was maneuvering to attack, Ox leader's group dove to the right. The JAM pursued them. Ox 4, 5, and 6 rolled in from above, trying to interdict the JAM, which evaded them with a 3G hard-right climbing turn.

Ox leader pulled into a 3.5G turn, his angle of attack pushed to twenty degrees. The JAM responded with a 5G slice, and Ox leader followed, diving inverted. Countering his lead turn, the

JAM pulled vertical, and Ox 3 and 4 simultaneously performed pitchbacks, banking left to chase it. The JAM continued to rise, its afterburners blowing fire, turning at 6Gs to prevent Ox 2 and 3 from maneuvering behind it. Within three seconds, it was over half a mile up, turning hard to the right to come around to Ox 4's six o'clock. Ox 4's radar warning receiver shrilled an alarm.

Ox leader pushed his plane's nose through a 7.4G turn at the maximum angle of attack. In response, the JAM aborted its attack on Ox 4, cut sharply to the left, and rolled into a 180-degree turn. Ox leader rolled into his own turn, committing to the two-circle fight, both aircraft trying to maneuver the other into its kill envelope.

And finally, Ox leader had it. RDY AAM appeared on his HUD. The short-range missile's seeker acquired the enemy aircraft and the plane's onboard fire control system input the JAM's heading, relative altitude, and speed data into the missile's guidance system. Ox leader closed on his quarry.

At three miles' distance, a tone sounded in his helmet to alert him that he was within the missile's firing range. He pressed the weapon release button on his side stick without a moment's hesitation. The missile's rocket motor and gas-turbine power generator activated, launching it away from the plane. The target was now four seconds away.

The JAM jinked violently, trying to evade the missile that was twining up its trail, but it was too late. The AAM slammed into the enemy craft. Target, destroyed.

Ox flight retook its formation.

ABOARD YUKIKAZE, REI Fukai watched the enemy symbol vanish from his multi-function display. According to FAF tactical theory, victory was a secondary objective: the primary objective was not to lose. The FAF had been charged with the duty to defend Earth from the persistent attacks launched by the JAM, but because the true nature of the JAM remained a mystery, and because the FAF had never discovered the key to killing them, it could not devise a strategy for winning the war. Therefore, a single tactical accomplishment was regarded not as a victory but rather as an avoidance of defeat. The war was hopeless, but at least they had yet to lose it.

The 402's doing well, Rei thought to himself. They were using tactics devised to make sure they didn't lose.

"Something's wrong," said Lieutenant Burgadish from the backseat as he checked the long-range search radar.

"What do you got?"

"Not sure… Wait. Thought so. It's a second wave. The ones the 402 are fighting are decoys… Here they come. Missiles. Ground-to-ground missiles, headed for TAB-14, fast."

"Does the base know they're coming? How's their interceptor deployment look?"

"Doesn't look like they'll make it in time."

Yukikaze accelerated, climbing into the airspace above TAB-14. Rei tried to identify the approaching enemy missiles in the tactical data bank, but the result came back as **UNKNOWN**. He switched the MFD to moving target indicator mode.

Eighteen enemy missiles, closing.

"Damn, they're fast. That's an ultra-high velocity. Looks like the JAM have a new missile, Lieutenant Fukai."

"Activate the TARPS. Get a shot of them."

"Activating TARPS."

The swarm of missiles crossed hundreds of miles in what seemed like a matter of seconds. As he banked Yukikaze Rei could see them arcing toward TAB-14 with his own eyes. They plunged toward the base, looking like red comets or meteors, long, fiery tails stretching out behind them. The tails were not formed by the exhaust gases from the warheads' rocket engines: the missiles were flying so fast that they were glowing red hot just from the air friction generated by their passage.

TAB-14 was annihilated in an instant. No trace remained of

the buildings on the surface. An enormous crater on the base's broad runway marked the spot where the interceptor squadron, the 401st TFS, had been hot fueling for its takeoff. Yukikaze silently recorded the devastation with her TARPS cameras.

"With that kind of velocity, they don't even need an explosive. The shock wave alone blew everything away."

"Lieutenant Fukai, third wave of enemy missiles, incoming. They're antiaircraft, moving much slower than the GTGM just now, but they're three times faster than the norm. The 402nd's in danger."

"Tell them to take evasive action. PAN, code U."

"Roger." Burgadish got on the guard frequency. "PAN, PAN, PAN. 402 TFS. This is Yukikaze, B-503. PAN, PAN, PAN. Code U, Uniform, Uniform."

The 402nd leader received the emergency message from Yukikaze at the same instant that his own plane's alert system sounded its warning. He immediately began evasive maneuvers, but he had no idea what the approaching threat actually was.

"JAM antiair missiles?"

He scanned his surroundings to try to visually acquire the missiles. It was hard, but you could usually spot them from the faint contrails they left. If he could see them, he was sure he could evade them.

There they were, coming at him from six o'clock low. But... what were they? They were moving fast, more like laser beams than missiles.

He never had time to dodge. A split second after he'd sighted the missiles, he and his plane were consumed in an explosion.

"Nineteen 402nd planes down. No survivors," Lieutenant Burgadish stated impassively.

"Roger," Rei replied. "No point hanging around here. RTB."

"More JAM, closing. Range sixty-five miles. There are three large units, possibly missile carriers. No escorts. They're just flying along, like they don't even care if they're attacked."

"Are they where those AAMs were launched from? Do they

just shoot until they're empty? What are they after now?"

"They may still have more missiles. Hell, the planes themselves may be giant bombs… Looks like the survivors of the 402 are moving to intercept."

The five remaining units of the 402nd reformed then turned toward the three massive JAM aircraft, firing medium-range missiles as they began to close the fifty-mile range to the enemy. But the 402nd's missiles didn't even go twenty miles before they were destroyed by the much faster interceptors the JAM had launched nearly simultaneously. The 402nd planes began to withdraw. They were quickly picked off from behind, gone in flashes of light and flame. Black smoke filled the sky.

"All remaining 402 units destroyed."

"Fands are an older plane. To hit an enemy like that we need more power and maneuverability. Something like the Flip Knight system might work."

"Unmanned aircraft?" Burgadish said doubtfully. "They could act as decoys to draw off the missiles. Then once the JAM've exhausted their payloads—Lieutenant, they've locked on! Engage!"

Their RWR had picked up the waves of enemy targeting radar. Rei sent Yukikaze into a sliceback and then ran the throttle to MAX, fleeing the oncoming enemy.

"Two high-velocity missiles, closing from the rear at a little over two-point-one. Range twenty-one miles, approximately ten seconds to impact. The second one's three miles behind it and will hit three seconds after."

Yukikaze fled at a speed of over half a mile per second, the JAM missiles tearing after her.

"We're not going to make it."

"Yukikaze isn't a Fand."

Rei hit the emergency jettison switch, dumping the TARPS pod, then fired six medium-range missiles as decoys and activated ECM. No effect.

Taking his hand from the throttle, he reached down to the

panel near his left knee and flipped the V-max switch. This cut out the limiters on Yukikaze's twin engines, squeezing power from them beyond their designed safety limits.

Auto-maneuver system, ON. Yukikaze was now free from Rei's control, and in a fraction of second had used all her sensor data to formulate the sequence of maneuvers that would save them from the JAM missiles.

The moment Rei released the side stick, Yukikaze abruptly yawed to starboard, her attitude unchanged. Rei was thrown against the left side of his seat. The G-forces were terrific; he felt like his internal organs were being crushed.

The JAM missile passed by them barely 400 feet away on the left side and self-destructed. Yukikaze pitched and shuddered in the shock wave of the explosion.

A warning tone sounded in Rei's helmet, signaling the approach of the second missile.

Rei steeled himself. They were going to die.

Ejection at this point was impossible. Yukikaze's ejection seats had no capsules to protect them; firing them at supersonic speed was tantamount to suicide.

He watched the rapidly moving symbol on the MTI and relinquished it to Yukikaze to deal with.

It took a second for her to correct her attitude after having been hit by the explosion shock wave. Two seconds to impact. Evasion was impossible.

Yukikaze initiated an offensive combat maneuver.

Rei wasn't expecting it. He was suddenly pressed into his seat, the G-forces seeming to crush his eyeballs back into his skull. His vision blacked out. He had an instant's impression that all his blood had turned solid and impossibly heavy—then he lost consciousness.

Yukikaze then did something Rei would have thought impossible.

Dropping her engine power to idle, she slewed around her center of gravity, spinning 180 degrees like a top, letting the momentum remaining from her forward velocity carry her backwards tail-first through the sky at subsonic speed. She was now confronting the enemy missile nose-on.

ADY GUN. Ultra high-velocity auto-fire control system, activated. Eighty rounds from the nose cannon slammed into the enemy missile in 1.4 seconds.

The missile detonated 0.2 seconds from impact.

Yukikaze returned to her previous attitude shortly before Rei regained consciousness. She had automatically assumed a return course to base.

Fighting down a wave of nausea, Rei immediately checked the master caution light panel. Nav and electrical systems, check. There was damage to one of the hydraulic systems. He twisted and craned his head around to look at Yukikaze's vertical stabilizers. The right rudder was gone. It wouldn't have too dangerous an effect on their flight, though; as long as the left one remained, it'd be enough.

There was a caution indicating an oxygen malfunction in the rear section of the cockpit.

"Lieutenant," Rei called out. "You okay? Hey, Rich."

Burgadish gingerly pulled his mask off and made an "okay" sign with his fingers. "Puked my mask. Still feel sick... Some fighter jock I am. First time it's happened... So, why aren't we dead?"

"It looks like Yukikaze shot down the missile."

"No shit? I feel like I've been shot in the gut," the EWO answered, panting like a runner who'd just run a long race.

Yukikaze descended toward Faery Base.

TAB-14 WAS GONE.

After exhausting their onboard store of warheads, the massive JAM carriers crash-bombed the base, finishing it off just as Lieutenant Burgadish had predicted they would. There were no survivors. The JAM attack had been of such devastating power that even the reinforced command bunkers deep underground had been destroyed. The planes flying in the airspace above TAB-14, including the AWACS unit, had been caught in the blast radius and also destroyed.

Only Yukikaze had made it back. Since the TARPS pod had been jettisoned, the data recorded by its cameras had been lost, but the onboard data file was intact.

Rei attended the briefing on the combat intelligence brought back by Yukikaze.

"This is unbelievable," said General Cooley as she looked up from her screen.

"I agree," replied Major Booker. The shadowy half-light of the briefing room threw the scar on his cheek into stark relief as he nodded. "An attack with this level of destructive power from the JAM is completely unprecedented. This data is invaluable."

"If we don't come up with a counterstrategy fast, Faery Base will be in danger as well. Nice work, Lieutenant Fukai."

"You can thank Yukikaze. I was unconscious."

"It's hard to believe it pulled off a maneuver like that. Super Sylphs may have a strong airframe, but you're still lucky it didn't break apart in midair. Or break its pilot. If I'm not mistaken, hitting the V-max switch cuts out your G-limiter too."

"Better that than getting killed. I just cracked a couple of ribs. I don't have word yet on my EWO, though."

"His spleen was ruptured. He's out of danger for the moment and should recover. You've already had your spleen removed, haven't you?"

"Yeah. That may have saved me."

Looking at him over the top of her glasses, General Cooley gave him a small, tight-lipped smile. Rei suppressed the urge to flinch.

"Major Booker," she said, still gazing at Rei. "Put this intelligence in order at once. I'll be presenting it at an emergency command staff meeting in two hours. That is all."

"Understood, General."

Booker stood and saluted the general as she exited the briefing room. Rei remained seated and watched her go, as always mildly surprised that she didn't actually have eyes in the back of her head.

Down in the hangar on the other side of the briefing room's glass wall, the maintenance crew was scanning Yukikaze's airframe with ultrasonic and X-ray equipment, hunting for damage.

"Yukikaze nearly wrenched herself apart. Did you see the strain gauge on her wings, Rei?"

"It turned out okay."

"It did this time, but we still need to change our approach, on both the software and hardware fronts. And before that we need to rethink our strategy. We're going to have to be a lot more cautious about getting into dogfights."

"Yeah, the Fands have no chance. Even we barely made it."

"The FAF has also been developing high-velocity missiles, but we're still trying to resolve the issue of the aerodynamic heating and the thermal noise it causes. The JAM have obviously cracked that problem. And we don't really have a clue as to how their guidance system works."

"Doesn't seem like it's active homing. ECM had no effect."

"The frequency range may have been wrong. We'll figure it out eventually. But we have successfully tested the FAF's air-to-air high-velocity missile. It's not as fast as the JAM's, but the accuracy should be about the same."

"Even if we have the missiles, the fighters carrying them will still be Fands. They'll be shot down before they can fire."

"Nope," said Major Booker, grinning broadly. "Guess what just passed its flight tests? Fand II. It's a completely different beast from the Fand, a high maneuverability dogfighter. Its engine output is only 60 percent of a Sylphid's, but its empty weight is only 60 percent of one too. It's much smaller than Yukikaze, lighter and more maneuverable. Forward-swept wings, canards, high-incline twin vertical stabilizers, a mobile ventral fin… Flying backwards was a miracle for Yukikaze, but I'll bet a Fand II would have no problem doing it. The airframe is complete. The thing holding us up is the brain."

"The computer?"

"Right. Because the wings have to be constantly adjusted to an optimal configuration on a second-by-second basis, these planes require a high-capacity, high-velocity computer that can process the huge amount of data needed to do that. And it has to be small, lightweight, and power efficient, too. Yukikaze's could do the job, but it's too big to fit inside the airframe. The Fand II is a great plane, but this is a case where the software has gotten ahead of the hardware."

"You said the flight tests were successful. You can't fly without a flight computer, though, which means—"

"It's not enough for it just to be able to fly. The Fand II is a fighter. It has to be able to evade an enemy attack and then launch its own. There are two schools of thought on fighter plane development. One is to have multi-seat fighters, on the theory that having the second crew member minimizes errors made during combat. That works for visual range dogfights, but it's becoming less relevant. The FAF believes the other approach, the single-seat fighter, is the more successful one. What we saw Yukikaze do this time is a good example."

"Let the combat computer handle it instead of a human?"

"It can process information much faster than a human brain can, and if it can draw on directly linked sensor data to feed its decision-making abilities, well then… To be honest, sometimes I'm amazed at the capabilities of Yukikaze's central computer. Its potential is far beyond anything I imagined."

"Even though you developed it?"

"I didn't develop it—I just put on the finishing touches. A lot of hands went into designing her systems, and I don't know what's in each individual one. But Yukikaze's grown so intelligent now that you can't compare her to what she was when she was first developed. She's been learning. And you've been the one teaching her, Rei. In the near future, she probably won't need you anymore."

"If that happens, what happens to me?"

"You go home and go back to being an ordinary citizen."

"I have no home to go back to."

"How long have you been on Faery again?"

"Four years."

"Don't you want to live?"

"I don't want to die."

"You only have about another two years as a pilot. Your body won't hold out beyond that."

"And so what then? You'll just cut me loose?"

"Why not help me with my work? I can arrange for you to become a combat technique advisor."

"I can still fly. Yukikaze needs me."

"That love of yours is unrequited. She's becoming independent. And someday soon she's going to dump you."

"Jack, you sound like a nervous old man. You running out of fight?"

"Maybe," Booker sighed. "You have no idea what it's like for me when I send you and the others out on missions. Day in and day out, air force pilots keep getting killed when we don't even know what it is that the JAM are really after. If it turns out that they're not at war with humanity at all, then all those soldiers will have died meaningless deaths. And I can't accept that anymore. I want it to end, no matter what it takes."

"You're saying let the machines fight the JAM for us?"

"There's a danger there too. We don't know what the JAM's aims are. However, we don't know what the Earth-side defense forces are thinking either. At this point, I wonder what we're even doing here."

"We're fighting a war."

"Maybe. Maybe not. The battle here on Faery may be nothing but a decoy operation designed to keep our attention occupied while the JAM are already worming their way into every part of Earth. And then they'll close the hyperspace corridor and leave us stranded here. I'm starting to believe wild ideas like that."

"Maybe that's true. But so what? What happens on Earth doesn't matter."

"You never change, do you? Still, you should prepare yourself."

"For when the JAM finally kill me?"

"Rei, you've been ready for that for far too long now. No, what I meant was that you need to prepare yourself for the possibility that Yukikaze might one day become your enemy. An enemy of humanity."

"Bullshit."

"The possibility exists. Yukikaze isn't your lover. She's your daughter, and she's grown up. She won't obey you forever, and you have to be ready for that. One day, she won't need her dumb, stubborn dad anymore."

"Jack... Major Booker, are you telling me to stop flying Yukikaze?"

"I just don't want to add any more names to the KIA list. That's not the job I came here to do."

Booker didn't look at Rei as he began organizing the intelligence file.

"You may go, Lieutenant Fukai. Report to the central medical facility for a complete checkup."

"I'm fine. I've already been patched up."

"I'm ordering you to submit a medical certificate before you can fly again. Dismissed."

Rei got up, saluted, and left without a word. He walked down into the maintenance bay and stood looking up at the enormous fighter for a while.

"You wouldn't betray me...would you?"

He reached up and touched his beloved plane's radome. The metal was cold.

PER THE FAF Medical Corps diagnosis, Lieutenant Rei Fukai would be completely recovered and fit to resume duty in two weeks. But in the meantime, he was grounded.

At the next TAF mission staff meeting, it was decided that the new Fand II assault fighter would undergo a combat flight test in order to get it deployed as soon as possible. Major Booker was placed in charge of this test, and in this capacity he made a proposal that was approved: Yukikaze would accompany the Fand II on its flight. She would go up in full automatic mode and would monitor the performance of the Fand II's prototype optoelectronic systems in flight.

Of all the units in the 5th Squadron, Yukikaze had experienced the most combat with the JAM, had managed time and again to slip through their traps and make it back. In Booker's estimation she was therefore the FAF's best chance for detecting any JAM combat reconnaissance and protecting the Fand II, since the aliens were bound to be interested in the test flight. The major's second, equally important aim in sending Yukikaze on the flight was to verify whether she could carry out her missions unmanned. If she could, it would open the possibility that one day he wouldn't have to send his men up in the squadron's planes anymore, that he would be relieved of the awful tension of waiting for them to return.

Over the next three days, Major Booker wrote Yukikaze's flight program and refined the test plan.

The major was frank about his desire to wholly automate Yukikaze's operation.

A bold smile played across Rei's face as he spoke. "You're wasting your time, Major. She can't fly without me."

"We'll give it a shot," Booker replied, although he too had his doubts that Yukikaze's hardware and software configurations would allow her to be converted to a fully functional unmanned aircraft in such a limited amount of time.

In the end, the combat flight test plan called for the Fand II prototype to be flown by Captain Hugh O'Donnell, an ace pilot in one of the Tactical Air Force Flight Test Center's squadrons. Yukikaze would fly wing, unmanned. An electronic warfare systems control plane would follow, with Rei onboard to provide support if needed.

Upon hearing this, he didn't bother to hide his irritation. "So I'm going to just sit pretty in that control plane and pilot Yukikaze by remote control?"

"Yeah, and it was a royal pain to arrange," Major Booker replied. "But General Cooley insisted on it. You keep banging on about how you want to get back in the air. So now you'll be back in the air. And you can just sit back and relax. Take a nap, even."

"Has the Fand II's central computer system been finalized?"

"Tentatively. A lot of brand-new technology has gone into the build, so we don't have a firm gauge of its reliability yet. Anyway, if something goes wrong, Yukikaze will automatically link with the Fand and control it."

"Let me go up in Yukikaze. C'mon, Jack. You know this is gonna drive me nuts."

"Can't. Your body wouldn't be able to take it. Don't worry, the control plane will be flying in secure airspace. All you have to do is watch. Yukikaze will make it back just fine."

Booker clapped him on the shoulder. Rei put a hand to his bandaged chest and smiled. *A sad smile,* the major thought. As though his heart had been broken. Not for the first time, a keen curiosity seized him.

"Rei, why do you feel so strongly about Yukikaze?"

"I… Aside from you, Yukikaze's the only thing I trust. I don't have anything else. Nothing."

A drop, a raindrop, a mote. Zero. That's the meaning of your name, Rei. Suddenly recalling those words, Major Booker reached out and gripped his best friend's hand.

YUKIKAZE AND THE first combat-ready Fand II unit waited side by side in the SAF's maintenance bay. The Super Sylph's huge shape and sleek, menacing lines seemed to embody all the enormous power that lay dormant within her. The Fand II by her side was smaller and lighter, yet also magnificent.

Major Booker met with Flight Test Center personnel who were taking part in the Fand II test to brief them on the plans. Afterward, he had a one-on-one meeting with Captain Hugh O'Donnell, the Fand II's test pilot. The captain was a relaxed, good-humored man, and Booker—who was used to dealing with the cool, inscrutable pilots of Boomerang Squadron—found this cheerfulness almost dazzling. He felt none of the cold tension he got from his subordinates, which paradoxically gave him the impression that O'Donnell might be slightly unreliable.

But the difference is to be expected, the major thought. Rei and the other Boomerang pilots were constantly fighting on the front line. The captain was a noncombatant test pilot, not a soldier. Danger was nothing new to him, but he didn't fight in actual battles and wasn't constantly confronted by a strange, irrational enemy like the JAM.

There was one other thing that differentiated Captain O'Donnell from the Boomerang pilots: he was one of the elite. The soldiers here were mainly those who'd been sent to Faery because they couldn't fit into Earth society, but the captain wasn't like that. Back where he'd come from, he had been a top-ranked test pilot in the air force. He had chosen to come here. He'd wanted to be a pilot for the FAF so that he could help defend Earth and his homeland.

This bloke, the major thought as they continued to talk, *is a straightforward person. He isn't a man like Rei, his heart maimed by the wounds life's given it. Not like Rei. Not like me, either.*

Captain O'Donnell always brought an aide with him, which was unusual for someone of his rank. Lieutenant Eva Emery reported directly to the captain and was an engineer trained in the field of aviation optoelectronic systems. Her official role was to liaise with the engineering specialists involved with his flight tests, and she performed this duty well, but the captain used her for various odd jobs beyond that, making her essentially his personal assistant.

As Captain O'Donnell attended to the briefing and cheerfully cracked jokes, Lieutenant Emery sat behind him, taking notes. *She's probably the reason he's in such a good mood,* thought Major Booker. In public, she addressed him as "Captain O'Donnell" and did so curtly, as though to give the impression there was nothing more between them.

However, some hours after the briefing had ended, when Booker went down to the dark and now abandoned maintenance bay, he witnessed a scene that made it clear their relationship was more than just a professional one.

"Listen, Hugh," Lieutenant Emery said, speaking in an intimate tone, "I'm worried about this."

"Don't be," the captain replied. "The Fand II's a good plane."

"But they said the tests on the central computer still weren't complete—"

"It'll be okay. If anything happens, I'll have this Sylphid to act as backup. And it isn't just any old Sylph. It's a Super Sylph. It's a fantastic plane, and Unit 3 here is the very best that Boomerang Squadron's got. Its avionics hardware may be outdated compared to the Fand II's, but it's actually more powerful. In truth, I envy the guy who flies it. He's ended up in the strongest fighter there is."

"I don't know if I'll ever understand why these fighters appeal to you so much. They're just machines."

"We need the best planes possible to counter the JAM."

"That's not what I meant, and you know it."

"What, are you jealous, Eva?" O'Donnell teased.

"No, I'm worried about you," Lieutenant Emery snapped. "I worry all the time."

"No need. I only have eyes for you. If another woman ever touched me, she'd turn into a pillar of ice and shatter."

"I'm being serious," Emery said, stamping her foot. "Don't make fun of me."

"Honey, I'm always serious," he replied, grinning, and pulled her into an embrace.

"You're only serious about whatever's new. That's why you became a test pilot, isn't it? Am I just one more thing you're testing out?"

"Eva, you're not like a plane. Believe it or not, I can tell the difference," O'Donnell said with a hint of exasperation in his voice. "Why are you being like this?"

She stiffened for a moment, then suddenly collapsed against him, leaning her head on his shoulder. "I want to go home," she said in a small voice. "Back to Earth. With you."

"You mean run away? The JAM are still after Earth. I have to—"

"Stop it! Please, just stop..."

"Maybe you're right," he said, stroking her hair. "But just calm down a little, okay? My term of duty's almost up here. If you want, I'll resign from the FAF. But as long as I can still fly, I'm going to keep doing this job."

"But being a test pilot is so dangerous. You can't trust these machines like you do. Please. Please, Hugh."

O'Donnell was silent for a bit, then said gently, "Okay, think about this: my term's up in two months. In two months...let's get married." He cupped her face in his hands. "I love you, Eva."

They shared a warm kiss, and then Lieutenant Emery let go of the captain and informed him in her professional tone that she'd processed the day's schedule. He gave her a wink and turned to go.

He froze at the sight of a figure standing in the shadow of Yukikaze's radome.

"Who's there? State your identification."

"Lieutenant Rei Fukai."

O'Donnell looked at the name stenciled beneath Yukikaze's canopy and nodded.

"Ah, I've heard about you. The ace pilot of Boomerang Squadron. That's an excellent fighter you've got there in Yukikaze. What's that name mean, by the way?"

"'Snow wind.'"

"'Snow wind'? Like a snowstorm?"

"No, a snowstorm's different. A snow wind is a snow wind."

Rei looked at the two lovers without any expression. As Captain O'Donnell made to approach Yukikaze, he stopped him with a sharp "Don't touch her," then climbed up the boarding ladder and opened the canopy using the external manual control. Settling into the cockpit, he turned the master test system on, set the built-in test system selector to interleave mode, and began running the diagnostic routine for Yukikaze's electronic instrumentation.

"I've flown Sylphids before," O'Donnell called up to him. "But the Sylphs you guys in the SAF fly are another beast entirely. I've never gone up in this one, but I've heard talk of what it can do. Go easy on me tomorrow, okay?"

Rei remained silent. The captain gave him an easygoing salute anyway, and put his arm around Lieutenant Emery's shoulder as they exited the maintenance bay.

"First Lieutenant Fukai."

"Jack. Don't scare me like that. Where've you been hiding?"

"I forgot something down here... Rei, Yukikaze's modifications have been perfect."

"You've put new systems into her. She's changing. She's slipping out of my hands."

"The system outline is just what I explained to you yesterday. We've got an early day tomorrow. Get to bed."

"Yeah."

Rei nodded, but didn't make any move to climb down from Yukikaze. Booker sighed. With the combat flight test plan documents bundled under his arm, he left Rei behind in the silent maintenance bay.

Rei was a Boomerang soldier. *I should be used to that attitude by now,* the major thought. But after seeing the human feelings shared by Captain O'Donnell and Lieutenant Emery, Rei seemed unusually tragic to him. Yukikaze was indifferent to the expectations that her pilot or any other human held for her. She was the heroine of her own story. A spirit of the air who ruled the skies of Faery. The queen of the wind.

0620 HOURS. CLEAR skies. The Fand II's combat flight test got underway. After the preflight briefing, first the control plane trundled out onto the runway, with Rei aboard it. Next came their escort, 5th Squadron's Unit 6, Minx, on launch standby.

The Fand II's engines started up. Captain O'Donnell felt the vibrations with his entire body and sensed nothing out of the ordinary. All caution lights were clear. Standing well away from the plane, Lieutenant Emery asked him through the headset how things looked.

"All systems normal. Okay, I'm raising the output to military. Detach the comm cord."

"Be careful up there."

"Yes, ma'am. I've got a present for you when I get back."

"A present?"

"Just make sure you're not wearing anything on the ring finger on your left hand."

"Oh my god... Hugh...!"

"This is Fand II, O'Donnell. Ready for takeoff."

The control plane made a leisurely takeoff, trundling down the runway and hauling its bulk into the sky. Minx followed, lighting its afterburners in a combat climb.

The Fand II initiated its takeoff sequence. Rotation. Landing gear up. Trying not to stress the plane, O'Donnell guided it along a normal ascent and then banked into a 3G turn. Orbiting the airspace around the base, he waggled the plane's unique forward-swept wings. He could see Lieutenant Emery below him, a tiny figure on the ground. Yukikaze was not out on the runway. O'Donnell brought the Fand around to the correct heading and opened the throttle, accelerating toward the flight test airspace.

After completing the preflight checks, Major Booker switched Yukikaze's auto-maneuver system on, closed the canopy and moved away from the plane. Her twin Super Phoenix engines roared to life. The air shook. She accelerated down the runway at terrific speed and lifted off using only 80 percent of the usual length. Pointing her nose skyward, she quickly hit full vertical climbing speed, moving at over 9 Gs.

Like a rocket, thought Major Booker. *No, even faster.* She was out of sight in an instant.

"Rei, look at her," the major muttered to himself. "This is Yukikaze. This is her true form."

Maybe we humans have underestimated her, thought the major as a strange chill traveled through his body.

Aboard the control plane, Rei sat at Yukikaze's remote console, monitoring the video feed and other flight data she was sending them. He watched the symbol on the radar screen marking her position. She was flying level and closing rapidly on the control plane. He didn't interfere.

Yukikaze picked up even more energy, passing the control plane on the right side at supersonic speed. As fast as a missile. The shock wave of her passage shook the huge aircraft.

"Whoa!" exclaimed the pilot. "What the hell was that? Is it trying to clip us?"

The Fand II reached maximum speed and began running through its tests.

Yukikaze followed, and then shot past the Fand II as it unloaded Gs and descended in preparation for low-altitude penetration. Yukikaze quickly descended as well and took position 1,500 feet off to the Fand II's side.

"Initiating ultra low-altitude penetration test."

Captain O'Donnell ran the throttle forward. Yukikaze flawlessly maintained position on his wing. The shock waves of the two planes tore a swath through the forests of Faery, leaving a clear path marking the course they had taken.

"Okay, initiating dogfight capability test."

O'Donnell confirmed that his anti-G seat control was functioning normally. The Fand II's seat was deeply reclined, shaped to wrap around the pilot's body even more than usual in a single-seat fighter.

"Let's do this," the captain muttered.

The Fand II was no match for the other plane in terms of raw speed, but in a dogfight he would be the victor.

All caution lights, clear. Maneuver switch, ON. Fly-by-light system, normal.

Yukikaze maintained her attitude as she climbed. Without increasing her angle of attack, she ascended while remaining level with the ground. After flying over a hundred miles in three minutes, she turned and confronted the Fand II. She had now become a simulated JAM.

To ward off a close-range attack Yukikaze fired six simulated medium-range high-velocity missiles. The simulated missile tracks appeared on the Fand II's moving target indicator.

Here we go, thought Captain O'Donnell as he shifted his gaze from the MTI to his HUD. This was what had wiped out the 402nd.

The Fand II fired the FAF's new high-velocity air-to-air missiles. Four shots. These too were simulated. Missile intercept, successful. Just before launching the HAAMs, O'Donnell had initiated a high-velocity turn. The two remaining "JAM" missiles would reach the Fand II in ten seconds. The captain turned the Fand II toward them nose-on and corkscrewed through the air, evading the first one. The plane instantly slid right and popped off three shots, taking out the second missile, then flew in a flat scissors maneuver as it closed in on Yukikaze. Right, then left, the high-G forces buffeted Captain O'Donnell's body.

His labored breathing carried over the radio and was heard by all the flight test staff.

"Amazing plane…haven't seen performance like this before."

Yukikaze attempted to turn and withdraw.

"Think you're getting away? Fand II…pursuing."

Suddenly, Yukikaze opened her air brakes and radically decelerated. Killing her speed, she dove.

"The hell…?"

O'Donnell's eyes widened. The Fand II overshot Yukikaze at subsonic speed. O'Donnell immediately lost sight of her. He cursed and pushed the nose of his own plane down without rolling, going into an inverted loop. The blood rushed to his head, threatening his vision with redout. He reflexively loosened the loop diameter, searching for Yukikaze. A warning sounded, alerting him to an enemy plane above and to the rear.

He banked hard into a half-roll and climbed, finally catching sight of Yukikaze, which was coming at him at the maximum angle of attack, with gunsight open. She locked on to the Fand II just as it began to climb and opened up with simulated cannon fire. He was just barely out of range, and the combat technique simulator in the control plane determined the attack failed. The Fand II immediately counterattacked.

Captain O'Donnell was now soaked with sweat from head to toe, his breathing coming hard. His heart was pounding as though he were in a flat-out sprint, and he could only speak with great difficulty.

The Fand II got around to Yukikaze's right rear quadrant. Yukikaze executed a high-G boost out of subsonic speed, and the Fand II instantly turned to follow, shuddering with the strain of the maneuver. Lock on. Auto-fire. Out of range. O'Donnell launched his remaining four simulated missiles. Yukikaze evaded them at the last moment, pulling 16 Gs in the process.

"Damn, that thing…that…Super Sylph is a monster."

The Fand II accelerated. Yukikaze turned.

An emergency call was sent out to the control plane from

Yukikaze. O'Donnell noticed her turn radius widen. "I win…" he muttered.

"Captain O'Donnell," Lieutenant Fukai called. "There's been a malfunction in Yukikaze's hydraulic system. The function of the elevon on her right main wing is compromised. The Fand II wins."

This is no win, the captain thought. Yukikaze hadn't been brought down. If it hadn't been bound by the parameters of the combat flight test program, it would have easily accelerated out of the Fand II's firing range and returned to base.

"Captain O'Donnell, the combat flight test is concluded." Major Booker issued the order from the SAF's underground control room back at Faery Base.

"It seems the Fand II has met our expectations," said the Tactical Air Force's commander.

"It evaded the high-velocity missiles and proved it could engage the enemy," agreed Booker. "Although Yukikaze may still be regarded by the JAM as more of a threat since they have nothing like it."

"That's of little use if it breaks itself in the process," interjected General Cooley. "If the Fand II had attacked it at that point, Yukikaze would have lost. The Fand II is impressive."

A warning alarm suddenly sounded in the control room. Red letters appeared on the huge data screen, informing them that incoming hostile aircraft had been detected.

"It's the JAM," said Major Booker, a familiar knot forming in his stomach.

The early warning had been transmitted from Minx.

"Where're they coming from?" asked the control plane's radar operator. "I don't see them."

"Range 215 miles," said Minx's EWO from 90,000 feet above. "They're closing at super-low altitude. Definitely JAM. Two planes, combat recon types. Number of units increasing."

"They penetrated that far in without tripping our warning network?" Booker said incredulously. "Minx, intercept them.

TAB-15, scramble the 501st TFS. Fand II, return to base at once. Emergency withdrawal."

"Copy," replied Captain O'Donnell and flipped his armament switch to ON. **RDY GUN. RDY HAAM-4.** Real weapons this time. His gun and four short-range high-velocity air-to-air missiles.

The Fand II and Yukikaze were both closer to the JAM than Minx, which plummeted toward the enemy aircraft at maximum thrust, firing two long-range missiles as it went. An H cue appeared on the HUD. The JAM were climbing. The countdown until impact began.

9...8...7—the JAM launched high-velocity interceptor missiles—5, 4, 3... The numbers vanished.

"No good. Missiles down."

Three planes from TAB-15 were now in the air and pushing at maximum thrust to intercept the JAM.

"Minx, abort your attack," Major Booker ordered. "Climb and resume surveillance duty."

"Roger."

Static filled the channel. The JAM were using their highest-output ECM. They pressed in behind the Fand II and Yukikaze, 150 miles to the rear, and launched two high-velocity missiles.

"These're moving as fast as those ground-to-ground ones we saw before. Rei, do you read me? The JAM probably want to see how the Fand II will evade these missiles."

Because of the ECM interference, Booker's words didn't reach Rei. The control plane initiated ECCM. The approaching enemy missiles appeared on the radar screen. After another twenty seconds, when they were within fifty miles of the Fand II and Yukikaze, the missiles split into four. Minx watched them from on high.

On Yukikaze's remote console, Rei saw the message **RDY GUN** appear.

"No," he said softly. "You can't pull any high-velocity maneuvers now."

His hand hovered over the remote switch. He wanted to

protect Yukikaze, but protecting the Fand II came first. And for that...the image of Captain O'Donnell and his lover suddenly floated into his mind...for that, he might be forced to use Yukikaze as a shield. Make it back to base, even if you have to watch your comrades being wiped out. Minx had now been charged with that duty. *Strange*, Rei thought as his heart grew cold. *I'm worried about abandoning Yukikaze. I... Am I jealous of her, after she betrayed me?*

Without sorting out his feelings, he flipped the switch and seized the control stick without a second thought. But there was no reaction.

"What's wrong with you, Yukikaze?!"

Before receiving the instructions from Rei, Yukikaze linked with the Fand II, taking control of it. She launched four of the Fand II's HAAMs, which took out two of the JAM's four missiles. Her priority was to protect herself, not the Fand II. The remaining two missiles flew toward the Fand II.

"Captain, get out of there!" Rei shouted. Yukikaze hadn't interposed herself between the missiles and the Fand II as he'd directed her to. She had decided that Rei's orders were in error and was ignoring them. After determining that she was safe, she began directing the Fand II through evasive maneuvers.

O'Donnell soon realized he was no longer in control of his plane. He removed his hand from the side stick as violent G-forces assaulted his body. The Fand II jumped like a fox, the first missile passing below by the thinnest of margins. Its proximity switch activated, detonating the warhead. To minimize the damage, the Fand II turned its tail toward the explosion and began to withdraw at MAX afterburner. Just 0.3 seconds later, it jinked hard and barely evaded the second missile. The shock wave from the first explosion had damaged the Fand II's right stabilizer fin, and now the sudden evasive action snapped it right off.

The Fand II spun away from Yukikaze like a boomerang. Yukikaze immediately began working every control surface on the plane to bring it back to controlled flight. It took four seconds to arrest the spin and regain the proper flight attitude. The Fand II's engines were stalled. Yukikaze glided it down and restarted the engines.

Rei looked at the data being sent by Yukikaze. There was a problem with the Fand II's fuel transfer system, which had been caused not by the JAM missiles but by the wild spin it had gone into from the evasive maneuvers. It was now using gravity feed to move the fuel from its tank and took a return course to Faery Base.

On the way back to the base Yukikaze got the FTS working again. She informed Rei that the Fand II could resume normal high-velocity maneuvers. **ALL SYSTEMS NORMAL**, she reported.

"Are you kidding?" Rei said to himself. "I doubt the captain will ever want to go through that again. Captain O'Donnell, come in. Captain O'Donnell. Do you read me? Captain O'Donnell, respond."

There was no answer. As they returned to Faery Base Yukikaze flew tight alongside the Fand II, as if in sympathy for its damage. Once communications with the base were restored, Rei told Major Booker to have an ambulance standing by.

"Captain O'Donnell isn't responding, and I don't think he's just passed out. Yukikaze put the Fand II through some intense maneuvers. It may have..." Rei put his hand to his chest. His injuries ached.

The Fand II landed in formation with Yukikaze, its engine dropping to idle at the runway's end. The flight test personnel and ambulance crew ran out to the planes. Lieutenant Emery shoved Major Booker aside and turned the external canopy control handle. The Fand II's canopy yawned open.

She scrambled up the boarding ladder and leaned over the cockpit. "Hugh, it's me," she said. "Are you all right? Talk to me."

O'Donnell was slumped in his seat, motionless. She reached out and removed his helmet and mask. And screamed. Blood poured over her hands, streaming from his mask and mouth. His head lolled to one side. He wasn't breathing.

"Hugh... Say something...please..."

Major Booker signaled the medical team.

If Rei had been aboard Yukikaze, this might not have happened. As that thought was passing through his mind, Lieutenant Emery did something he couldn't have anticipated. She drew her service pistol and aimed it at Captain O'Donnell. For a split second, the major couldn't believe what he was seeing.

"What are you doing?!" he shouted as she fired a shot into her lover's chest. She then threw the gun aside and collapsed against O'Donnell's body, embracing it and crying hysterically.

"He can't have been killed by the Fand. Not by a machine. No... I killed Hugh! I did! A man whose heart was taken by a Fand deserves to die!"

Major Booker wrapped his arms around the now incoherent Lieutenant Emery and gently pulled her away from the body.

"What's wrong with this plane?" she sobbed. "Hugh's dead. After what happened to him, why...why doesn't it react? Why... No! No! No!"

Over her shoulder, Booker looked at the blood-spattered instrument panels inside the cockpits. Condition lights, all clear. All systems normal.

Neither the JAM nor Lieutenant Emery had killed Captain O'Donnell. The Fand II and Yukikaze had. And to those two machines, his death was insignificant.

Major Booker left Lieutenant Emery in the care of the medical crew, opened Yukikaze's canopy, climbed into the cockpit, and turned the auto-maneuver switch off. The link with the Fand II was severed, and then, as though awakening from a dream, Yukikaze alerted the major via her display that the pilot harness, anti-G suit hoses, and mask weren't properly secured. To indicate that he had no intention of flying, he flipped the hydraulic system cut-off switch, inactivating the control surface hydraulics. Yukikaze cancelled the alert. In this standby state, any speed over 30 mph would automatically engage her brakes.

Booker taxied Yukikaze over to the elevator that led down to the SAF's underground hangar, then handed her over to her ground crew.

Meanwhile, the control plane had landed. Rei climbed down from it and watched silently as they wheeled Captain O'Donnell away, Lieutenant Emery clinging to his body.

"Rei..."

He turned at the sound of the major's voice.

"Jack. How's Yukikaze?"

"Machines can be repaired. Yukikaze protected the Fand II, not the captain. I was wrong. I never should have sent Yukikaze up unmanned."

"It's not your fault. If she hadn't taken control of the Fand II, the captain and the plane would both have been destroyed by the JAM. The result would have been the same. As far as the captain's fate was concerned, at least."

"But it would have had a different significance. He was killed by his own machine—"

"Does it matter?" Rei asked quietly. "This is a battlefield. Every death here is a combat death. What other kind of death is there?"

Major Booker couldn't answer him.

0807 hours. The combat flight test was concluded. The Fand II was approved for deployment.

VII

BATTLE SPIRIT

For the first time in a long while, he had the chance to speak with someone from home. But he did not use Japanese. He was angry that he could not convey his thoughts, frustrated that he could no longer express his feelings in his mother tongue. He had forgotten the language of home.

THIRTY-THREE YEARS have passed since unknown alien life-forms opened a hyperspace corridor between Earth and the planet Faery in an attempted invasion of our planet. We still know nothing about them. We don't even know whether they were the ones who actually created the Passageway. Five years ago, I collected data on how every nation perceived this war and compiled it into a book that was published under the title *The Invader*.

I was only four years old when the JAM launched their preemptive strike. I remember what the adults, my mother and father, said back then as though it were yesterday.

"It looks like-----happened in-----. The president is sending the-----to-----." I listened to them in wonder. To this day, I can clearly remember those blank spaces in the conversation, those words that, limited by my child's vocabulary, I didn't understand. And at the time, I wondered if I would understand them when I grew up.

As an adult, although I may experience blanks in a conversation, I don't notice them. I automatically compensate for them by my understanding of the context in which they appear, and the meaning of the sentences flows unhindered. It's similar to the way that our sight works. We perceive things in our vision as a continuous flow of images, when in reality there are blank spaces in our visual input. However, our brains automatically fill in those gaps, so we don't notice them.

It's easier for humans to process things as analog data. We need continuity, the illusion that what we say, see, and think presents an organic whole. In other words, we function in the opposite manner of a digital construct, where data is quantified, discreet, and determinate. The digital world seems to run counter to the very essence of our humanity. Our language as well. Our civilization itself. So what, exactly, are we doing turning over more and more of our existence to computers?

It was the JAM who raised these doubts in me. They are aliens. But to me, they seemed almost more like evil gods, a presence that held up a dark mirror to the meaning of human existence. That was the basis upon which I wrote *The Invader*.

Most citizens of Earth do not share my view. And that in itself points to the heart of the issue: the very concept of "citizens of Earth" is nonsense in light of the current international situation. There may be humans on Earth, but nowhere is there any group of individuals who regard themselves as inhabitants of Earth first and of their nations second. I think this a foolish and dangerous mindset, but when I say this to others they tell me that I am naïve.

I once told a scientist of my idea that humans lead an analog existence. He laughed and explained to me that our world—that the entire universe—is essentially digital. Objects, atoms, and even time itself are quantum in nature, and nothing works in a completely analog way. Everything from the subatomic world on up is digital. But humans exist on a macroscopic, not a microscopic, scale, I told him. He replied that if I insisted on clinging to that concept, then I could never understand what he was saying.

And so I asked him this in return: Are humans becoming more like machines, and in particular, more like our computers? Are we headed in the direction of digitalization? Yes, that may be, he answered, with an air of possessing some type of mysterious knowledge that I did not.

I became so intrigued by this notion that I began collecting data on the JAM and on the soldiers of the Faery Air Force who battle them on the front lines. Apparently the soldiers are beginning to have doubts about the still-unknown aliens and the war they are fighting with them.

One item in particular that caught my attention was a letter from a major in the Special Air Force. The SAF is the air force's tactical combat reconnaissance unit, an elite group of highly skilled pilots tasked with a difficult mission. In the letter, Major James Booker speaks with unusual candor.

> The JAM are not fighting humans. They're after our machines. And our machines seem to have acknowledged the JAM as their enemies and are at war with them. So where does that leave us humans? The JAM aren't fighting to conquer humanity. They're fighting to control the digital, non-corporeal intelligences of Earth. You think this is absurd? You probably don't understand. You, who live on Earth, where the JAM have become a fairy tale. Where they fade in significance compared to global competition. Where humans kill each other.

Major Booker's words are correct. Setting aside the parts where he says the JAM disregard humanity and that humans have forgotten the JAM threat, he is entirely right.

In the first year or two following the JAM assault, we were nervous. But when we learned that we were only slightly behind them in combat ability, when we established Faery Base on their planet, expanded our presence by constructing the six principal bases and founded the Faery Air Force, there was no longer any need to fear them as a threat to Earth. It's the same way that one forgets the heat of a burn once it's healed. The problem is, the heat remains. Just because you can't feel it anymore doesn't mean the danger has vanished.

That was the point I was trying to make in *The Invader*. But people read it as though it were fiction. They bought the book and I became famous. My husband and I separated because he found he was no longer married to his wife, but to the public figure "Lynn Jackson." We had no children. If we had, well… perhaps I might have written a different, more serious book.

Major Booker ended his letter in this manner.

> You need to write a sequel to *The Invader*. The world needs to know what's happening now here on Faery. But it may already be too late. Despite all your efforts, the message may not get through to people on Earth. The people who watch footage of actual combat on Faery act like it's a war movie… One day they may be destroyed by the reality. Regardless, the soldiers of Boomerang Squadron still have to fly their missions. All I can do is pray that they come home alive. So what can *you* do?

In writing the letter he was trying to convey to me the fear that he felt. His rage, his resentment, his sorrow over the meaningless loss of the soldiers under his command. And he was also asking, "What about you? Do you have someone you care for? A lover? A spouse? A child?" Because the soldiers of his squadron have none of these. Even if the Earth were to vanish tomorrow, they wouldn't shed a single tear. And that is wrong. They're becoming machines. Humans need to be human. A soldier in that squadron feels that as he fights the JAM, he's gradually becoming more and more machinelike. To convince himself that their battle isn't meaningless, he must believe that he is as much the enemy of the JAM as the computers are. The JAM are dehumanizing humanity.

War will normally bring out the true nature of man. But the war with the JAM is different, Major Booker wrote. This war is not bringing out the basic nature of mankind: it is destroying it. Whatever the JAM's true objective is, whether or not they pose an immediate physical threat to Earth, that danger has not gone away.

I am not confident I can live up to the major's expectations. Even so, I think I have to write this book. That soldiers are dying on Faery is a fact. If I pray for anything, it is that their deaths are not in vain.

They are dying to protect the Earth, and what do we do? We forbid them to become self-sufficient. We keep them from becoming independent. Over half the individuals we send to replenish their forces are the stigmatized trash of every nation. It's ridiculous enough to drive one to tears.

As I write this, I am cruising the freezing waters of the Antarctic Ocean, roughly 250 miles from Scott and McMurdo Bases, and 600 miles from where the Passageway stretches into the sky from the Ross Ice Shelf. The ship I'm aboard is a Japanese Navy attack aircraft carrier with the task force designation Admiral 56.

This carrier is assigned to the United Nations force that patrols the area around the Passageway for any JAM or FAF units that may attempt entry from Faery. Interdiction against the JAM I can understand, but the puzzling part is the FAF. The Earth Defense Force has devised plans to defend against the FAF even though it is part of the very same organization under U.N. command. It is behaving as though the FAF, and not the JAM, were the invaders.

However, the Earth forces normally don't take such an aggressive stance. Admiral 56 and its group were deployed in response to an unusual dispatch from the FAF.

> In preparation for future operations we are sending over a Sylphid fighter in order to test the Phoenix Mk-XI engines and flight control systems in Earth's atmosphere. We will be conducting analyses to measure their degree of efficiency in alternate conditions. The test plane will be from the Special Air Force 5th Squadron. The pilot will be Lieutenant Rei Fukai. Systems will be monitored by flight officer Major James Booker. The time and date will be...

Since this announcement caused quite a furor on Earth, even I soon learned of it.

Major Booker, I used every professional source and personal contact I had to secure permission to be aboard this carrier and cover the story.

It's summer in the Antarctic. The skies are very clear. Here on the bridge, Rear Admiral Nagumo is holding a pair of binoculars to his eyes. "Ahead full," he says.

"Ahead full, aye, sir," calls back the first officer.

Admiral 56 steams ahead under full power to greet Yukikaze.

An AWACS plane is already in the air. The captain has just issued orders to launch interceptors.

YUKIKAZE TOOK OFF from Faery Base. She was fitted with new Phoenix Mk-XI engines; they were somewhat smaller and lighter than the Phoenix Mk-Xs but had greater output.

"It's hard to believe this is the first time I've ever flown with you," Major Booker said.

"Uh-huh. Don't pass out on me, old man," Rei replied.

Engine control systems, normal. Fuel flow rate, check. Fuel transfer system, normal.

"I'm not that old," the major protested. "I can handle it. I'm still an active-duty pilot, Rei."

"This isn't like the fighters you used to fly."

Yukikaze accelerated, heading in the direction opposite to that of her normal duties, toward the Passageway that would allow them to transit directly to Earth.

In the rear seat, Major Booker struggled to breathe in a regular manner, afflicted by the high Gs they were pulling. He wondered if Rei always flew under this kind of physical stress and renewed his appreciation for just how exhausting being a combat pilot was.

"Thirty seconds to airspace entry," said Rei.

The target designator appeared on the HUD. They were rapidly approaching the enormous ash-gray column of mist that towered over Faery's forests. Numbers in the lower right-hand corner of the HUD scrolled down, marking their time to contact.

"Let's go, Jack. Time to pop our cherries. We're taking a dive to Earth."

Suddenly, the *deedle deedle deedle* of the radar warning receiver chimed in the cockpit. Booker started. An enemy symbol appeared on the RWR display.

"A JAM fighter! Where'd he come from? Closing fast."

"Calm down, Jack."

The wall of mist around the Passageway's airspace was now filling the view ahead of them. They were past the point of no return. The numbers on the HUD were reaching the end of the countdown…1…0. The dive-in cue appeared.

Yukikaze shuddered. They were wrapped in ashen darkness. Their radar was non-functional, as were the radar altimeter and external comm equipment. An alarm shrieked, as though Yukikaze were screaming that she'd lost sight of the enemy, and a caution alert blinked on the HUD, warning that their current position was unknown.

Less than two seconds after entering the hyperspace corridor, they emerged on the Earth side. They were flying supersonic, the enormous pillar of mist quickly receding behind them into the distance. Yukikaze's engine control system immediately measured the ambient atmospheric conditions using a score of sensors, and then began making adjustments to optimize the engines' operation. The avionics control and barometric altimeter automatically reset to Earth mode. Rei had no time to check the operation of these new systems; he had to trust that they were working correctly.

Master arm switch to ARM. FCS, activated. ƦDY GUN, ƦDY AAM-6.

"Where's the JAM, Jack?"

"Right below us."

Just as Rei sent Yukikaze into a descending roll the JAM initiated an explosive high-G acceleration burst, separating from Yukikaze like a rocket. Rei immediately launched two high-velocity short-range missiles after it. The enemy responded by launching infrared seeker missiles to neutralize them.

The JAM aircraft was a bit larger and more powerful than Yukikaze. Rei advanced the throttle against its limit and tore after the JAM at maximum power. It dropped its external power boosters and fled.

"What the—? What is it doing?"

"It's after Admiral 56," Booker said, his voice tight. "It's trying to get in range to launch an anti-ship missile. The JAM are trying to completely isolate the FAF from Earth. If they sink Admiral 56, the EDF will blame us. Rei, we have to shoot it down, no matter what."

"We don't have enough fuel. We won't be able to get back."

"It doesn't matter. Lieutenant, this is an order. Take that thing out!"

"Understood."

THE EDF TASK force's AWACS plane confirmed Yukikaze's exit from the hyperspace corridor. But within seconds, the symbol being tracked on the radar screen split into two. Yukikaze was operating an Earth-use IFF transponder, but the other blip was negative on the IFF. An unknown. The radar operator hesitated, unsure what to do.

Just then, a message came in from Yukikaze, broadcast on the international emergency frequency: "Unknown aircraft is a JAM."

The operator, confronted with a JAM threat for the first time, panicked. "Shoot it down!" the young man shouted. "It's the FAF!"

The captain of Admiral 56 did not panic. He gave the order to launch interceptors and then murmured to himself "Goddamn FAF, bringing the JAM here with them…"

Admiral 56's eight interceptors acquired the JAM and immediately moved to engage it. However, they had never faced one of the alien fighters before. The JAM simply flew into their attack without trying to evade, as if it were sneering at them. It launched eight missiles. Admiral 56's interceptors were destroyed within seconds. With the obstacles eliminated, the alien craft resumed its flight toward its target.

The ship's captain couldn't believe what was happening. *That's what the JAM are capable of?!* he thought in consternation. An alarm sounded from the CIC, warning that the JAM fighter was closing.

"Ready point-defense weapon system. Ready antiaircraft defenses. Hard to port."

"Hard to port, aye, sir."

Admiral 56 began to swing to the left.

Rear Admiral Nagumo was about to give the order to launch all remaining interceptors, but it was already too late.

However, the interceptor squadron deaths hadn't been in vain. While the JAM was engaging the ship's fighters, Yukikaze had closed the distance between them. The alien aircraft skimmed the ocean's surface, seeming to slice it in two with its shock wave, on a straight-line course for Admiral 56.

"Target acquired," called out Major Booker. "Range six-seven, crossing in front of us. We're only gonna get one chance at this. Don't miss."

"Miss or not, this isn't my duty. The EDF guys should be shooting down any JAM that make it to Earth."

Flying on the deck, Yukikaze initiated a ninety-degree beam attack sequence. Arcing up into a power climb, she fired four high-velocity missiles simultaneously and then went into a high-G turn, breaking away at maximum power. Major Booker blacked out momentarily, in G-induced loss of consciousness.

The JAM aircraft was shot down three seconds from impact

with Admiral 56. There was a flash, followed by a large explosion. Forty miles away, the carrier was rocked by the shock wave but otherwise unharmed. The crew rushed to begin the nuclear decontamination procedure, washing the ship down with large quantities of seawater.

"Looks like it wasn't carrying a nuke, thank god. Had me in a cold sweat there for a sec."

"Jack, we're almost bingo on fuel. It's not like we can call for a tanker. And don't tell me you expect me to ditch."

"Don't worry, we've got a place to land," Booker said. "A place with plenty of fuel."

"On the carrier? No way. You think they'd roll out the red carpet for us?"

"I'm not expecting them to, but they can't refuse a request from the FAF. They're obliged to obey international Earth Defense law. I'm contacting them now."

Aboard the ship, Admiral Nagumo listened to Yukikaze's request for fuel with a surge of irritation. The fighter's crew had some balls to make that request right after they'd drawn a JAM to his ship. True, they'd shot the thing down, but it was their duty to do so. And thanks to them, he'd lost eight planes, which would be a major blot on his service record.

"You're going to give them clearance to land, right, Admiral?" He looked down to see the journalist Lynn Jackson standing right next to him. "If I'm not mistaken, you have to grant any reasonable requests from the FAF. And I'd like to meet them—to meet Major Booker, I mean."

I knew this woman was going to be trouble when I took her aboard, the admiral thought. As long as she was here, he'd have to watch how he handled himself.

"Grant them landing clearance," he ordered.

Two fighters were launched to guide Yukikaze in. Or, more accurately, to keep an eye on her.

Admiral 56 came into Yukikaze's visual range. The two planes from the ship closed in, settling high and to the rear.

"Their landing guidance system is different from what we use," Booker observed. "Sure you can do it?"

"I can handle it. I'm an active-duty pilot, Jack."

Booker smiled and shook his head. "Brat."

Rei switched Yukikaze's downlook radar to sea mode and jacked up the output to full power, scrambling Admiral 56's guidance beam. The high output goofed the ship's radar, filling the display screens with snow and cutting off communication with the chase planes.

Admiral Nagumo glanced around at all the operations specialists frantically trying to restore their systems and exhaled heavily, willing himself to stay calm. "What is that thing? That's a mainline FAF fighter? It's like—"

"That's a Sylphid, Admiral. A Super Sylph. I doubt there are any weapons on Earth that could fight her. That alone should tell us, sir, how formidable an enemy the JAM are. They're not just phantoms…"

Yukikaze passed through Admiral 56's airspace at supersonic speed. The chase planes couldn't keep up with her. She turned, unloading Gs, and overflew Admiral 56's landing deck at a lower airspeed. She turned once again, banking into her final approach. Landing gear, down and locked. Flaps, down. Arresting hook, down.

Rei guided Yukikaze in on manual approach. *I won't let you land without me,* he thought with a hint of amusement. *These aren't Faery skies.*

Auto-throttle, off. Anti-skid brake controller, off. Speed brake, extended.

"I'm bringing her down."

The landing signal officer aboard Admiral 56 kept his eyes glued to this strange plane that had never before been seen on Earth. She was a monstrous bird, the size of a fighter-bomber, but she held level easily and landed in an almost delicate manner. She increased her engine output to vent, then throttled back through idle to cutoff.

The canopy rose, revealing two figures in black helmet visors and masks.

They look like spacemen, thought Admiral Nagumo.

Checking to see that everything she'd need for an interview was stowed in her favorite shoulder bag, Lynn Jackson hurried down from the bridge.

I WATCH THEM hauling Yukikaze with a spotting dolly toward the fueling station on the flight deck, the operation carefully supervised by six aircraft directors. The fuels personnel look up at Yukikaze wordlessly. Not long ago had been the first time any of them had witnessed an FAF plane battle a JAM. Now this is their first time seeing a Super Sylph, the FAF's mightiest fighter, in real life.

On the outward-facing surfaces of its twin vertical stabilizers is a boomerang insignia, the blades as sharp as a grim reaper's scythe. On the interior-facing surfaces is a depiction of a voluptuous, winged fairy, a creature of a far sexier sort than Tinkerbell but painted in curiously neutral colors. Beneath the cockpit canopy sill are small, white Japanese characters that spell out the plane's name: Yukikaze. Following the characters is the stenciled information of the pilot's name and the unit the plane is attached to. And that's all. Recently, FAF planes have stopped carrying the FAF insignia. Visual identification is enabled by electroluminescent lights, while all other identification is handled by electronic systems. The fighter bears no insignia of any nation of Earth. It's impossible to tell by sight if it is friend or foe. The implicit message is that everything outside of the FAF is an enemy.

As I approach Yukikaze I am stopped by a safety control officer. I ask him to tell Major Booker that I'm here. He refuses. I raise my arm and wave broadly at Yukikaze. The major recognizes me. He must know what I look like or else has deduced who I am; in my fur coat I must stand out in the swarm of colorful uniform shirts. Slipping off his oxygen mask and raising his helmet visor, he climbs down Yukikaze's ladder and steps onto the flight deck. The pilot stays in the cockpit, presumably to see to the plane, but I catch a glance of an air force-issue automatic pistol in his hand: he's protecting the safety of his plane and of the major.

The soldiers of Boomerang Squadron trust only each other and their planes. If they didn't, they couldn't survive on Faery.

"You're Lynn Jackson?" says Major Booker, propping his helmet under his arm. "Why're you here?"

"I came to gather material on Earth's response to the FAF's message," I reply. "But I never dreamed I'd get to see you here. Or that I would witness a battle with the JAM. It's an honor to meet you."

I offer him my hand. It's enveloped by his large, strong one.

"The JAM are tough. That one got through by sticking to Yukikaze's belly like a remora. Never expected it. I'm Major Booker, by the way."

"Yes, I know. I received your letter."

"So it did get through to you. Didn't think you'd read it... Anyway, there's no place to get coffee around here, is there?"

"I'm afraid not. I doubt they'd let you into the ship."

"Huh. We're ghosts here. Yukikaze, too."

Major Booker regards me with a bit of awkwardness and embarrassment. He speaks with a slight British accent, but the language is that of the FAF. It's essentially English, but stripped of adjectives and any extraneous words. What can be omitted is omitted, detail sacrificed for brevity. It's logical, but impersonal. Listening to it is like hearing a machine speak.

I speak to the major slowly, as though reciting a poem, as though I were a professor trying to teach her student how to speak proper English.

"You brought down that JAM magnificently, Major Booker. Admiral 56's weaponry couldn't defend against that. If it hadn't been for Yukikaze..."

"If it hadn't been for Yukikaze, I doubt the JAM would've targeted the ship. But she's a good plane. And he's a good man."

Major Booker glances back toward Yukikaze's pilot.

"I don't suppose I could interview him, could I?"

"I can guess what his response would be. You better ask me your questions instead."

"Was your mission here successful?"

"No engine trouble. The new Phoenix worked better than we expected."

"And your confrontation with the JAM?"

"The JAM weren't after Yukikaze. So no problem. Or that's what Rei—what the pilot would say, I'll bet. But... I had the sensation that we weren't going to make it."

"Sensation...?"

"Seems the EDF objected to Yukikaze's test—" Major Booker halts his rapid-fire speech and looks at me with a start. "Did I just say 'sensation'?"

"Is something wrong with that?"

"It's just so...nostalgic." As though finally remembering his mother tongue, he now speaks in a more normal cadence.

"I haven't been home in over five years. Being in the FAF is changing even the way I speak, and I never really noticed... It's unsettling. I really am on Earth now..."

I put my micro recorder away in my bag and smile at him.

"The FAF is what protects Earth. You people. No one could blame you for the JAM attack that just occurred. At least any reasonable citizen of Earth couldn't."

"A 'citizen of Earth,' huh? And where would you find such a person?"

"They're me and others who think the way I do, Major."

"That was one of the things you said in your book. Which soldiers in the FAF are reading."

"With greater enthusiasm than people on Earth?"

"Yes. We can believe the contents more than anyone. It's the work of a first-class journalist. Are you freelance?"

"I was a reporter for a newspaper when I wrote it. After the book's success I grew dissatisfied with my salary, my bosses, and my company. I thought I was worth more. I wanted to do something big, and—Are you cold?" An almost imperceptible shiver has passed through the major's tall frame.

"I can smell the sea... It's full of life, full of the smell of life. The smell of blood. The lifeblood of the Earth. There are seas on Faery, but they're lighter and...they smell sharp. Or thin, somehow... Dammit, I can't find the words. Thanks to the JAM, even my feelings have become dulled."

"Faery truly must be a place where the air carries the scent of battle spirits, not of humans. Of the mechanical, not of the organic."

"You're right. Humans and machines there are converging, and it scares the hell out of me."

"And you think there's no such thing as a common human identity on Earth?"

"Yeah. Take this carrier, for instance. It's part of a U.N. force, but its purpose—the reason it was built—is to kill people in other countries, right? How is that an Earth military?"

"I'm in the minority, Major, but I do believe that there are many people like me who believe in a common humanity."

"Then where are they? Why hasn't there been any move to establish an Earth-wide federation?"

I shrug apologetically. There are so many reasons I don't know what to say. The major tilts his head to the side, the skepticism on his face plain to see.

"I believe that the FAF is also part of that common humanity," I tell him.

Major Booker regards me silently for a bit, then suddenly turns away and looks back at Yukikaze.

"Yeah, you could say that," he replies, "if only because we're fighting to save Earth. And it's a nice idea, but...you don't know the JAM, what it takes to fight them. The FAF's chief strength isn't our people: it's our mechatronics, like Yukikaze. The battle spirits... Maybe that's the real humanity. But then, where does that leave us?"

I look into the major's anguished eyes and words fail me. Once again, the thought floats up in my mind: in this world, in this universe, perhaps humans really are a singular life-form. Major Booker had written in his letter that the JAM were more like computers than humans. If we had no computers, perhaps the JAM never would have attacked us.

I'm jerked out of my thoughts by Yukikaze's pilot, Lieutenant Rei Fukai, yelling "Shit! No, not like that!" He's quickly barking instructions in the FAF argot to the deckhands from his own country, but they can't follow his digital, machinelike speech. Major Booker had written that to survive in the FAF one needs to become like a machine in every way. When I had read this, I thought it was mere rhetoric, words of no great import calculated to get my attention. But having met him in person, and now hearing how Lieutenant Fukai is unable to communicate with his own people, I realize that it's true. It's as if Yukikaze's pilot has forgotten his mother tongue. It couldn't be that hard for him to use, could it? Or perhaps he's afraid of becoming human again...

"Yukikaze is the only thing he has faith in. He can't stand to see her even get scratched. In his own way, he's trying to speak for her and protect her."

The weather is shifting, and the seas steadily have been growing rougher. However, stabilizers dampen the movement of the massive ship so that the flight deck barely shifts. I look out over the frigid waters and ask Major Booker the one question I desperately want answered.

"What do you think the JAM really are?"

The major's cheek, which bears the scar of a terrible gash, twitches slightly. "I don't know what they are," he answers and falls silent. Just when I think he's not going to say anything more, he continues.

"But I know what I want them to be. Humanity's enemy." He

gives me a sharp look. "Do you think that's crazy? But if the JAM aren't our enemy, then the men and women in the FAF are dying for nothing. And that would be truly unforgivable."

"What if the war became completely automated?"

"The moment we give the fight over to the machines is when we start running the risk that they'll challenge humanity. Actually, don't you think they're already doing that here on Earth? Computers keep getting more and more advanced. We've developed AIs that possess consciousness. They wouldn't have to kill humans directly. All they'd have to do is make our automated control systems go haywire. What could we do if this carrier started moving of its own free will?"

YUKIKAZE'S REFUELING IS complete. Admiral Nagumo wants the Sylph off his ship as soon as possible, seeming to regard it as an ill omen, as an angel of death. And so, without even so much as a cup of coffee from their hosts, the soldiers of the FAF depart from Admiral 56.

"Be careful, Ms. Jackson," Major Booker warns me as he climbs into Yukikaze's cockpit. "Keep an eye on the computerized systems that surround you. The JAM may already be in control of them."

Yukikaze's canopy lowers and locks. I return to the bridge and watch as the fighter is locked to the catapult and then hurled into the Antarctic sky. The afterburner flames of the Phoenix Mk-XI engines glow as the plane climbs quickly. It turns, its wingtips etching white vapor trails in the sky. It makes another wide turn, accelerates, and then, as if menacing Admiral 56, practically scrapes the top of the bridge as it flies over us at supersonic speed. There's a terrific boom and the ship's superstructure shakes, as though it's been hit by lightning. Admiral Nagumo sees Yukikaze off with a flurry of profanity.

The Sylph's silhouette shrinks for a few seconds, and then vanishes from view. Silence returns. In barely fifteen minutes, it is gone from the radar display as well. They've returned. To the skies of Faery. To battle.

Perhaps what I had witnessed really was a spirit of the air. If so, what enormous size it had, what awful power it bore.

I take out my favorite notebook and pen from my bag. I begin writing down what Major Booker had said, intermittently looking out at the sea. I wish I'd brought a portable wordcom with me…and then I suddenly remember Major Booker's warning and shake my head.

If I had written this on a wordcom, the contents probably would have been changed.

VIII

SUPER PHOENIX

The JAM had never attacked humans directly. Yet when they changed their strategy, Yukikaze did not protect him. In that moment he knew the truth. She was a weapon, but one that defended neither him nor humanity. She abandoned her burning body and rose from the flames like a phoenix, reborn and free.

MAJOR BOOKER WAS analyzing the recent state of the JAM's tactical weaponry development in comparison to the FAF's, desperately searching for a weakness.

The FAF Systems Corps' Technology Development Center had been putting in strenuous efforts to create effective counters to the JAM's various assault aircraft and armaments. For decades now, both sides had been locked in a game of technological one-upmanship, but recently the pace had escalated rapidly.

When the JAM threw high mobility fighters at their defensive lines, the FAF deployed new light fighters with high thrust-to-weight ratios. When the JAM developed advanced electronic countermeasures, the FAF created more advanced electronic counter-countermeasures. The JAM responded to that with even more advanced ECCCM, which the FAF then managed to crack using high-powered radar. The power output of this radar was unimaginable, a frightening correction to the common assumption that radar waves didn't really affect humans. Even at a mile or two away, an unprotected person would be in danger. At close range exposure would be like being thrown into a gigantic microwave oven.

Missiles were countered with high-velocity missiles, which were countered by hyper-velocity missiles, which were in turn countered with laser guns, and the lasers guns with baryon guns. As the FAF worked to neutralize the JAM's weapons, in order to keep their own from being neutralized as well, they had to develop ones that not only met that same level of technological achievement but surpassed it. Obsolescence was simply a matter of time, and the periods they had before their weapons became obsolete were getting steadily shorter.

As Major Booker compared the data from each side he noticed something strange. Although it required a significant amount of time to develop and perfect such advanced technology, the FAF and the JAM seemed to be doing so at roughly the same rate. Depending on the situation, one side may have achieved overwhelming dominance for a few weeks using a new device, but countermeasures would soon appear and the war would grind back to a stalemate again. The main issue was that neither side could give concrete form to new tactical theories in only a few weeks. No matter how far in advance the JAM or the FAF could plan something that would utterly crush their opponent, by the time it was ready for use, it would already be obsolete.

Sometimes it seemed to Booker that the war was nothing more than a practical test of weapons development, with the planet Faery as the test lab. Or maybe the JAM were just matching their countermeasures to the FAF's level of technology. If that was the case, they were being toyed with. Toyed with by aliens whose true nature was unknown.

There weren't many people at the FAF's Technology Development Center these days. A supercomputer sat in a refrigerated room, keeping its head cool as it endlessly analyzed JAM tactics. The analysis data it generated was sent to a development computer equipped with an artificial intelligence that would then propose potential countermeasures. Among these proposals were things a human wouldn't have thought of, as well as some that were completely novel but also largely incomprehensible and impossible to execute given the current level of technology. An example was a proposal for a transdimensional bomb. The computer had been deadly serious, predicting the JAM would eventually develop one and advising the FAF to implement countermeasures accordingly.

The development computer would pass on its ideas to a lower-level practical implementation computer that would devise plans for the new weapon to be manufactured at the development center. With computer aid, of course. This entire development process wasn't so much computer-aided as it was computer-driven. New fighter planes were designed based on new tactical theories. Materials were chosen, and new ones created if necessary. Load strengths were calculated, wing shapes determined, and the onboard armament systems were developed all simultaneously. The new fighters had to be utilized according to the new tactical theories they were based on, and so the pilots couldn't simply fly them according to their own judgment. It wasn't necessary for the pilots to think at all.

The days of a pilot taking into consideration a plane's unique qualities and using his creativity and imagination to fly in the way best suited to take advantage of them were long past. The system created the tactics as well as the planes. No matter which pilot flew it, the plane would deliver the same performance. The best pilots for these new fighters were the ones who could quickly adapt to the machines without any questions, without wondering why they were fighting or how best to destroy their opponents. All they needed were the physical strength for the task and faith in the machine. There was no need for thought; the computers would think for them. At the very least, the computers could understand and execute tactics faster and with greater precision than any human could.

Despite the vigorous efforts of the FAF computers, the JAM countered them one by one with seeming ease. As though they were testing the abilities of humanity's machines, not of humans themselves, just as Major Booker suspected.

However, there was one exception to this dynamic. Even the JAM were at a loss when it came to the Sylphid, the treasure of the Earth Defense Organization's Faery Air Force. While models with the same name and basic configuration had been released, their parts and designs tweaked to make them more easily producible, the original Sylphid's maneuverability and reliability still went unmatched.

The Sylphid, originally developed for hit-and-away attacks,

boasted a huge thrust-to-weight ratio. Its avionics system was now even more advanced than when it had first been developed, and its wing shape had been subtly modified to give it extreme maneuverability. The original Sylphid was an FAF mainline fighter, but only three air groups—a total of forty-nine planes—were produced.

Of those, thirteen strategic reconnaissance variants were delivered to the SAF. These planes had one section of stabilizing wings removed to make them even faster and more capable than the mainline fighters at evading low-level antiaircraft munitions. These thirteen, the most powerful of the Sylphid variants, were unofficially referred to as "Super Sylphs."

Although the JAM had managed to hit them on different occasions, they had yet to shoot one down. How these planes, now ancient in terms of production time, still managed to remain the strongest in the war was a riddle that vexed both the computers and the humans at the TDC. They'd developed—and continued to develop—several new fighters that according to their specs should have been superior to the Super Sylphs. But none of them were.

But then, Major Booker thought, *they've probably never seriously tried to determine what the key factor is in the Super Sylph's survival rate.* The Sylphs of SAF-V, the Boomerang Squadron, had a return-to-base rate of 100 percent. And Booker knew the reason why: it was their exceptional pilots. It was common sense that the SAF would select only the most elite pilots to fly the air force's best planes. But he knew that the computers probably didn't want to admit that, since it would gut the entire premise that these fighters would deliver maximum performance no matter who was flying them, or even if they flew unmanned.

Right there, Major Booker felt he had the answer. He noted down his thoughts and began to draw up a report.

The Sylphs of the SAF were superior because of something both the JAM and the FAF computers considered an aberration: they were paired with humans in a system that generated the highest levels of combat proficiency. They flew in a way that the development computer hadn't foreseen at the design stage, and that the JAM could not predict and therefore regarded as a threat. The SAF Sylphids existed for the purpose of reconnaissance. For observation. They monitored not only what was going on around them, but also their own tactics, combat, and flight performance. The pilots were constantly charged with the single directive of making it back to base; to do so, they constantly had to evolve their tactics in response to the JAM attacks. These thirteen Sylphs carried in their data files the records of the desperate actions taken by their pilots to survive hard-fought battles. Their AIs had learned from actual combat what they could not have learned from simulations. To the machines, it was aberrant data, but the fact remained that it was data that had enabled the fighters to survive.

A pilot with excellent combat intuition was essential to the function of a superior fighter—up to a point. Once the "learning" phase for the AI was over, the human would become a hindrance. In fact, the Super Sylphs of SAF-V had already reached the point where they could carry out their missions completely unmanned. Now the pilots were not just unnecessary: they were actually inhibiting the abilities of the planes. One day, if it became possible to replicate human intuition via data analysis, and if the computers did not consider it an aberration, then humans would no longer be necessary even for that initial knowledge acquisition phase.

They hadn't reached that point yet though. Humans were still necessary to fight the JAM. The development center computers had not recognized that crucial factor yet. However, the JAM very well might have. And that was what lay at the core of Major Booker's growing unease. Now the only things in the FAF that could reliably oppose the JAM were just thirteen fighters. The thirteen Super Sylphs of Boomerang Squadron.

Booker carefully worded his report to convey these thoughts to his commanding officer, General Cooley. It emphasized three proposals: that SAF-V's Super Sylphs be completely automated, that the new fighter planes being worked on by the development center computers be equipped with AI systems of the type used by the SAF, and that their training be given over to Boomerang Squadron.

General Cooley reviewed his report, ordered him to provide her with more details, and then took it upon herself to present the major's proposals to her superiors. While the high command of the Tactical Air Force recognized the merits of Major Booker's proposals, the Systems Corps, and especially the computers, vehemently objected. They agreed with the proposal for automating the planes but disputed the assertion that the key to the Boomerang Squadron's performance was the human pilots.

To support their position they referred to the results of a single flight test conducted by the TAF's combat tactics development task force. That flight test had also been the major's idea, with the aim of gauging the effectiveness of transferring Yukikaze's AI system into a different plane, one that wasn't a Super Sylph. The results were not satisfactory.

Booker believed that the test failed because the other plane's central computer was insufficiently powerful and its flight capabilities were inferior to a Sylphid's. Its reaction speed, response characteristics, and the strength and reliability of its control surfaces were too different. The test confirmed what Booker had suspected, which was that the learning function of Yukikaze's AI was closely linked to the plane's physical structure; in order to transfer it to another plane, they would need a brand-new, high-capacity computer that was completely "clean," with no tactical software loaded into it, as well as a plane with an architecture that was completely compatible with Yukikaze's flight, navigation, and fire control systems. In other words, they would need a copy of Yukikaze.

The major doubted they could create many of these copy planes, and more importantly, he doubted whether they should. One of Boomerang Squadron's strengths lay in the distinct individualism of its pilots. If the entire Tactical Air Force flew the same planes as Boomerang Squadron and used the same tactics, it would form a pattern that the JAM would soon detect.

The Technology Development Center computers objected to this point as well, insisting that they could create and implement such a wide array of combat tactics that the JAM would not be able to discern any common elements. Major Booker did not yield to them. The plane that the TDC was currently working on was an upgraded variant of the Sylphid that was completely automated; he insisted that the design be modified to allow a human to pilot it. Both the TDC computers and its human staff regarded the major's demand as completely unreasonable. Putting in life-support systems would make the plane heavier and cut down on space for the electronics, and adding a G-limiter would reduce its maneuverability. Booker tried to persuade them by conceding that the plane did not need to be flown manned all the time. Once it had been adequately trained by an SAF pilot it then could be completely automated.

In the end, the Tactical Air Force decided to implement Major Booker's proposal on a provisional basis, with the new fighter prototype being produced in both manned and unmanned variants. Only thirteen planes—the same number as in Boomerang Squadron—were planned for combat deployment.

Booker worked to establish the foundation of a repurposed SAF, one in which the pilots' primary role would be to train the new Sylphid. The unmanned prototype still had no name and was instead referred to by its development number, FRX00, which indicated that is was the 100th new fighter plane developed by the FAF, counting both major types and variants.

New technology was making the existing SAF planes more reliable during unmanned flight, and gradually more and more pilots got used to the sight of seeing their planes sortie without them. The Tactical Air Force had already recognized that the amount of data that needed to be collected was exceeding the capacity of the existent SAF. And so it was decided that the current mission of the SAF would be brought to an end and that it would be given a new mission, one based around the automated flight of its aircraft. After a trial period, when it was determined that full automation did not hinder the execution of its reconnaissance duty, the SAF became the first completely unmanned squadron in the Faery Air Force.

The last manned flight would be Yukikaze's. The mission was an ultra low-level penetration to deploy intelligence-gathering sensor pods in D-zone.

"THIS WILL BE Yukikaze's last flight."

When Major Booker announced this to Rei and Burgadish in the SAF briefing room, the two Boomerang soldiers betrayed no discernable reaction, their expressions as blank as always.

Their mission operation was simple. They were to take off carrying tactical automated information sensor pods, cross over the forests of Faery, and deploy the pods in the white sand desert that stretched like a sea of sugar across D-zone. However, there was an element of risk involved: the FAF did not have mastery of the airspace in D-zone. Yukikaze would have to drop the TAISPs quickly and try to get out of there before the JAM detected their incursion.

The pods would then burrow into the desert and deploy passive sensor arrays to track JAM movements. The system could detect a wide range of frequencies, distinguish useful infrared data from ambient heat, recognize shapes in the visible light spectrum, and even record sound via changes in air pressure. When the JAM were not present, the pods would deploy butterfly-like wings above the sands to gather energy using a solar generation system. After that, they would wait quietly for the enemy. If one was discovered it would either burrow back into the sand to try and avoid destruction or, if there wasn't enough time, would broadcast a high-power warning beacon before the JAM destroyed it. They were impressive pieces of technology, but the FAF considered them expendable.

"Question," said Rei. "Why are you having Yukikaze do this? And why manned? There's no actual need for me to be flying this mission, is there?"

His tone of voice was unusually cold, even for him, and from that Booker knew a roil of conflicting thoughts must lay behind his friend's impassive facade. This was the end. Rei would not fly with Yukikaze again.

"D-zone is essentially unknown airspace," answered the major. "Something might happen that Yukikaze can't anticipate. In that case, she'll need your piloting instincts."

He tried to sound as calm and positive as possible, but Rei's expression did not change. "Any other questions? If not, then you're dismissed. Your preflight briefing is tomorrow morning at 0830. That is all."

Major Booker watched them exit the room. He knew with a sinking certainty where Rei was headed and followed.

Yukikaze was in the maintenance bay. Rei silently looked up at his beloved plane.

"Rei, come back alive. That's an order."

Rei didn't react to the major's affectionate catchphrase. He was standing directly under the kanji characters that spelled out Yukikaze's name, just staring at them.

"She's a good machine, but she doesn't need you anymore."

Booker noticed Rei's right hand twitch slightly.

"Will all the machines not need people anymore?"

"That's how the CDC computers would have it. The thing is, human intuition is a threat that the JAM can't anticipate, and the Earth-side machines just don't understand that. We can apply Yukikaze's artificial intelligence and learning functions, but there isn't a plane aside from the Sylph that is capable of mounting a central computer powerful enough to handle them. And the problem there is that while the Sylph's size allows it to house all this high-tech equipment, it also limits its aerodynamic qualities."

"Yukikaze has survived because all I do is run away. We don't engage. I don't know if she could handle a full-on dogfight."

"She could now. And she can win. Don't underestimate her. She's a more amazing machine than you give her credit for."

Rei said nothing and continued to gaze up at his plane.

Booker patted him on the shoulder and told him to come along. When Rei didn't move, he said "Oh, so you don't want to fly anymore?"

"What?"

"Let me introduce you to the FRX00. If you don't want to fly it, I'll understand. There are other pilots who will, and you can go home. To Earth."

"I won't fly anything but Yukikaze—"

"Pretty soon, this plane won't be Yukikaze anymore. She's not your pet and she's not your lover. She's an FAF fighter. Don't ever forget that. You're just one pilot. If you don't like it, then quit. Any of the others would be overjoyed to go back to Earth."

Major Booker walked toward the elevator. Rei took a deep breath, looked at Yukikaze one last time, and then followed.

The SAF hangar dedicated to Boomerang Squadron was located on the third level. They descended far below this, to a level with very tight security. In addition to his ID card, which normally was enough to open a hangar door lock, the major also had to insert a separate entry authorization card.

The door opened. They stepped into a small, airlock-like isolation room. It closed behind them, and then the opposite door slid open to give them access to the hangar.

There was a single fighter plane inside. It was large for a fighter but still a bit smaller than Yukikaze.

"So, this is the FRX, huh? It's small. No vertical stabilizers?"

"It has two sets of them, but the primaries and secondaries are folded flat at the moment. That may be why it looks small to you now, but it's actually only 7 percent shorter and 20 percent lighter than a Sylph. Most of that weight differential is due to its smaller engines. They're based on the same design as the Mk-XIs, but they vary in a number of ways."

Booker went on to explain the FRX's key attributes to Rei. Its vertical stabilizers chose the best angle automatically. Its simple clipped delta wings had no leading edge slats and were joined smoothly to the airframe with strake sections. The tips of the wings were flexible and could bend to prevent wingtip stall-outs. Just forward of the strakes, jutting out like knives, were small, highly swept canard wings, which stabilized the aircraft during flight and could be extended and retracted from the airframe as necessary. The engine intakes were bisected by the main wings above and below, giving the FRX the appearance of having four engines at first glance.

"It's twin engined. There's nothing to block air intake, no matter what sort of maneuver it pulls. Stalls and flameouts will be a lot harder to cause."

"Can it fly backwards?"

"We haven't got that far ahead yet."

"Yukikaze did it."

"And stalled out her engines."

"Only because she took them to idle. If she'd kept them at full power—"

"You wouldn't have survived. Your body couldn't take a maneuver like that at such high Gs. Maybe not hers either. The point I'm trying to make is the FRX is a combat prototype, a new model that's being introduced so that SAF-V doesn't get broken up."

"And what happens to the current Yukikaze?"

"She'll be part of a new squadron. A completely unmanned one. She's being promoted." Booker glanced at Rei's masklike face and bit back a sigh. "This FRX is still clean. We start test flights tomorrow. Eventually I want all the planes in the FAF to have the learning function that this one has—that Yukikaze has—and for that we need even smaller high-power computers. What pisses me off is that the TDC computers refuse to acknowledge my idea. This is a fight between humans and the computers. Rei, we still need guys like you. Come back alive. Once your mission tomorrow is over—"

"I'll have to give up Yukikaze."

"She's graduating. She's leaving you. You have a new student now. Rei, you cannot lose to a machine. We have to be the winners here. They—both our machines and the JAM—have to recognize our value. The outcome of this may be that the JAM will start targeting humans directly, but if that happens, we'll deal with it. And it will mean that we have value in this fight. As things stand now, humans are meaningless in this war. We're just being caught in the crossfire."

"FRX00... I know it's supposed to be powerful, but I don't like how it looks."

"That's only because you're not used to it. The FRX99 looks sinister because it doesn't have a canopy. In any case, it's superior to the Sylph in every way. The horizontal stabilizers can also move up and down to become vertical stabilizers. When all four tail stabilizers are deployed vertically, the canards up front fully extend. It has preprogrammed modes that determine how each wing moves in what situation, which wing produces what type of lift, and what role it's supposed to play. But when you fly it, I'm sure you can teach it different ways to use its wings beyond the programming. The central computer on this thing is compatible with Yukikaze's, but I think it will feel a lot different when you fly it. At the moment, this prototype is the only one."

"Are we done here?"

"Hm?"

"I'd like to get back to checking out Yukikaze."

The major kept his frustration with his friend concealed and nodded his assent.

They exited the SAF hangar.

IT WAS THE morning of Yukikaze's last manned flight.

Rei would have to leave her after this flight, a fact that still didn't seem real to him. This wasn't how he had expected it to end. He'd believed that he would fight with her until he died, and to leave her now, while he was still alive, felt like a betrayal.

He settled into the cockpit and began the preflight checks. All caution lights were clear. Master arm, check. Auto combat system, set. Anti-ground attack system, check. Self test for all A/G-AS modes: auto, continuously displayed impact point, high-precision guidance, direct targeting, manual.

He confirmed that all six TAISP pods were mounted on the underside of the plane.

Engine start. Jet fuel starter, activate. Engage JFS engine connection. First the right. The turbine began to spin. The tachometer needle leapt as the oil and flight pressures climbed. Rei took the throttle over to idle. The ignition system activated and the fuel flow opened up. At 40 percent rpm, the starter automatically cut off. He repeated the process with the left engine.

After making sure the operation caution light had gone out, he checked the hydraulic pressure on all systems with the engines at full power. All green. He throttled back to idle again and ran the emergency power system test. Communications, data link, navigation, and display control, all check. Laser gyro, altimeter, and FCS, check. Confirm all flight control surfaces were operating normally. Toe brake, on. Parking brake, off. Anti-skid brake controller, off.

Yukikaze taxied out onto the runway.

Rei slid the throttle to MAX and released the toe brake. Yukikaze began her takeoff. Rotation. Nose up five degrees. Takeoff. Landing gear, up. Speed, increasing. All systems normal. When they reached optimal climbing speed, he hauled her nose up and headed at once to cruising altitude.

At an altitude of 65,000 feet, he went to supercruise. He was twelve hundred miles from D-zone, and he had to penetrate three hundred miles beyond that.

Boomerang Squadron Units 1 and 6 flew slightly ahead of him, acting as escorts for Yukikaze. Both planes were unmanned. Yukikaze confirmed the identity of both planes, relaying that they were friendlies via the IFF system. Yukikaze seemed to be communicating with the two planes, and Rei was momentarily frustrated that he was excluded from their conversation. He let it go. Lieutenant Burgadish was silent in the rear seat. There was no need to talk.

They covered eleven hundred miles in forty minutes, then performed an in-air refueling before the border of D-zone. The men stayed silent during this as well. The only communication was from Yukikaze's data link and fuel systems, which were busily exchanging data with the airborne tanker. Rei felt a steadily growing impatience that seemed almost like jealousy. It was as if she was ignoring him, her pilot. He intentionally shook the plane a little during the refueling. Yukikaze issued a warning, and then locked in the automatic attitude control system.

"Yukikaze…"

"Nice," said Burgadish. "Stays stable even in turbulence."

Rei frowned. Yukikaze had classified his actions as external turbulence. He recalled Major Booker's words. She was disregarding her pilot's will. She possessed her own will now.

"So you're not always going to do what I tell you to, is that it? Just what are you now?"

"Did you say something?"

For a split second, he thought Burgadish's voice was Yukikaze's and felt as though cold water had been dashed in his face.

"No, it's nothing. Lieutenant, confirm our course."

"Roger. We can just stay on auto. Another 460 miles and then we should drop altitude. Once we penetrate Sugar Desert, everything past that point is unknown territory. All we have is data from a few recon planes that have been out there."

They separated from the tanker and resumed cruising speed.

As they crossed into D-zone their escorts peeled away from them. Yukikaze quickly dove, flying on the deck as they commenced their ultra-low altitude high-velocity penetration. The landscape flowed by the cockpit canopy in a gray blur.

"Here we go. Recheck the bombing system."

"Roger."

There was no sign of the JAM. They were only twelve hundred miles from base, and yet this was unknown territory. *We know almost nothing about this planet,* thought Rei. *We don't even know if this is the JAM's home world or not. And we know absolutely nothing about them.*

And now Rei knew almost nothing about Yukikaze, the one thing he thought he knew best. The one thing he had trusted implicitly.

Yukikaze continued her supersonic incursion, flying on auto toward the TAISP release point. Rei switched the A/G-AS mode from automatic to CDIP.

"Lieutenant?" called out Burgadish. "What are you doing?"

"This is our last flight. I have control."

"That's not like you. Leave this to Yukikaze and relax."

Rei didn't respond. Sugar Desert drew near, the glaring light of the twin suns reflecting off the sands.

The first target point was indicated on the HUD. The pull-up cue appeared and Yukikaze climbed sharply, as though leaping into the air. Rei guided the plane while watching the fall line on the HUD. The release cue appeared. Keeping his eyes on the pure white sands of the desert, Rei pressed the button. A slight jolt passed through the airframe as the TAISP was fired. They flew level to the second drop point, reaching it in about ten seconds. Rei fired the second pod. Then the third, the fourth, and the fifth.

"Going good. Let's drop these things and head home."

"One more left."

Yukikaze banked into a wide turn. Taking a return course, they headed for the sixth drop point. And then a warning alert sounded.

"What's up?"

"We're getting a warning from TAISP-4. Could be the JAM, but maybe it's an operations test. Our passive radar isn't picking up anything."

"Start a bandit search, now."

"Whoa!"

Yukikaze shuddered. Three small JAM fighters were attacking from directly beneath them, as though they had launched out from under the sea of sand. They may have actually done so, but there was no way for Rei to confirm. Yukikaze went into a high-G turn to shake them off. Rei looked out of the cockpit. He couldn't see them.

"Lieutenant, evasive action! Break left!"

Almost unconsciously, Rei flipped the V-max switch and engaged the auto-maneuver system. The JAM were too fast for his eyes to follow. He couldn't fight what he couldn't see. Yukikaze, however, could see the enemy clearly. She fired high-velocity short-range missiles, but the enemy evaded them.

"Bandits are small assault fighter types. Heads up, they've spiked us."

Yukikaze dodged the enemy missiles with a series of violent maneuvers. Rei and Burgadish both blacked out for several seconds in GLOC.

"We need to bug out of here, Lieutenant," Burgadish said, huffing in G-strain. When Rei didn't answer immediately he yelled, "Lieutenant Fukai!"

"Yukikaze is... Looks like she's ready to fight to the end."

Even if he tried to turn the auto-maneuver system off, Rei knew that it would not disengage.

"God damn it... Yukikaze!"

Rei flashed back to Captain O'Donnell's death. *Is that how I'm going to end up?* he wondered. Suddenly, Yukikaze extended her speed brake and an alarm began to blare. The display readout said that a fire had broken out and that they should perform an emergency ejection.

"Bullshit. There's no fire."

"What is going on, Lieutenant? Is the central computer—"

Burgadish's words were cut off by the explosion of the canopy being jettisoned. Rei felt the vibration of the rocket motor on his ejection seat, and immediately jerked the face curtain handle down to protect himself. A second later, Yukikaze tossed her crew out into the sky.

She pulled a high-G diving turn and went for the JAM. Free from having to consider the safety of any human occupants, she rapidly brought down two of the enemy aircraft in a single high-velocity attack sequence. The third JAM dove for the planet's surface, as though inviting Yukikaze to follow. Just as she was about to pursue, she seemed to hesitate, then climbed into a turn and withdrew at full power.

Four enemy fighters blasted out from under the sea of sand like missiles. They dropped their external power boosters and tore after Yukikaze. As though expecting this, Yukikaze twisted into a Split S, bringing her nose around to center the enemies in her sight, and then fired. She pulled up a moment before crashing into the ground and resumed her pursuit of the fleeing third JAM fighter.

Rei saw none of this. Hanging in the sky from his parachute, the only signs of the battle that reached him were the dry cough of Yukikaze's high-velocity gun and the thunderous echo of her engines. The burning floor of the desert rushed up to meet him. He hit the ground, rolled, and detached the parachute. The white canopy bellied in the wind, looking like an enormous jellyfish. Rei decided there was no need to gather it up and bury it since the JAM didn't care about humans.

He removed his parachute harness and unzipped the large survival kit hanging from its rear straps. He drew out the FAF-issue pistol, stowed it away inside his flight vest, and then took out the emergency rations and water supply pack.

He saw Burgadish's parachute about an eighth of a mile away, flapping in the wind atop a pure white dune that shimmered in the heat, looking like nothing so much as a great wave frozen in mid-fall. Holding the gun at the ready, his helmet visor still down, he walked out under the powerful sunlight to go find his partner.

As he trudged through the sand, he wondered why Yukikaze had cut him loose. He thought that maybe she couldn't accept the prospect that the TAISPs she'd spent so much trouble deploying would be destroyed by the JAM without ever having been used. That was why it was necessary for her to face the JAM head-on rather than withdraw from them as she usually did. And if she had to face them, then weak humans would just get in the way of what she needed to do to win.

If the situation had been reversed—if Rei had to sacrifice Yukikaze to defeat the JAM—he would have done the same. Since he'd have to say goodbye to Yukikaze in either case, he wouldn't have hesitated to pull the emergency ejection handle. She had seemingly sensed his will and then executed it.

Rei suddenly felt a humanlike intimacy with her that he'd never experienced before, as though they were two life-forms that existed in the same dimension. *She's a part of me,* he decided. A companion who knew how he thought, whom he could rely on…

But was that really the case? Rei knew Major Booker would say that he was being naïve. In ejecting him, Yukikaze had simply removed an element that would be disadvantageous to her while maneuvering. Having a pilot aboard meant that she couldn't fly as she pleased. Or—and this was a possibility Rei didn't want to consider—she may have decided that Rei might throw the self-destruct switch for the central computer and auto-maneuver system and had concluded that she had to do what she did in order to protect herself. That was definitely what Major Booker would say. That it was a struggle. A struggle of wills between Yukikaze and her human pilot. Rei decided that he didn't care about that.

It was hot. Sweat was pouring down his body under the flight suit. Cresting the dune, he spotted Lieutenant Burgadish below. Just as he was raising his hand to signal him, he heard a metallic noise nearby.

A sandstorm was bearing down on them, moving fast. It was the bow shock wave from a JAM fighter, flying supersonic on the deck. An instant after he recognized the black speck as a JAM, the fighter burst into his field of vision, passing between himself and Burgadish. White sand rose up like a wall as the two men were blown back. Rei was hurled into the air like a doll and then slammed back to the ground, pelted by falling sand. Dropping his survival gun, he fumbled at the shoulder of his flight vest to switch on his emergency rescue beacon.

The howl of an approaching aircraft made him instinctively flatten himself against the sand, and an instant later Yukikaze roared past in pursuit of the JAM fighter. She fired in front of Rei. There was the flash of high-velocity missiles being launched. An avalanche of sand crashed down upon him. He lost consciousness.

HE DREAMED OF a pure white desert. He opened his eyes. The whiteness remained.

He felt something wiping his face. A white towel. He brushed the towel aside. The air was cold.

"Are you awake now?" asked a female voice in a crisp, businesslike tone. A nurse. That was Rei's first thought upon seeing her white face. Her skin was so pale it almost looked blue. *Maybe because of the lighting in here,* he thought dazedly.

An air conditioner hummed faintly. The room was small and white. Spartan. A hospital, maybe? But this wasn't the air force hospital at Faery Base. It seemed more like a clinic. Rei felt like a castaway who'd washed up on a lonely South Seas island. There were no windows, but he could imagine there'd be jungle outside, and maybe an old-fashioned electric fan slowly turning on the room's ceiling.

His thoughts were drifting, fragmented. This sickroom was like something out of a dream, somehow not entirely real. He lay motionless on the hard bed and shut his eyes again, waiting for his body to recover sensation. He was still wearing his boots and flight suit. He could tell that his pockets still contained his map, flashlight, knife, beacon, portable rations, and service pistol. That meant that it hadn't been long since he'd been rescued. But nonetheless something seemed strange. He couldn't quite put his finger on it. He was too tired to think clearly.

He took a deep breath and relished the oxygen filling his lungs. The fog in his head gradually cleared. He opened his mouth, the words emerging from his parched throat in a croak.

"Where…Yukikaze…"

"Yukikaze? Oh, your plane. We're servicing it, Lieutenant."

"What about…Lieutenant Burgadish?"

"He was badly wounded, I'm afraid…"

"Where are we? A frontline base? Who are you?"

"My name is Marnie. Just wait here a minute. I'll go get Major Yazawa for you."

The nurse walked out, to be replaced a few minutes later by a burly, narrow-eyed man wearing a major's insignia.

"So you're awake now, are you, Lieutenant?" the man asked, his voice as flat as Marnie's had been. Rei tried to raise himself up, but the major stopped him. The uniform he wore was definitely that of the FAF's Tactical Air Force, but the color and the details seemed off. The overall effect gave Rei the uncomfortable impression that he was seeing a vague, hazy image through frosted glass.

Noticing the way that Rei was staring at him, Major Yazawa chuckled. "Were you hit on the head, Lieutenant?"

"Maybe I was," Rei replied, his tension not at all dissipated by this attempt at humor. He glanced around and saw that his helmet had been placed on a side table near the bed.

"Where am I?"

"TAB-14."

"TAB-14? Impossible. It was destroyed by the JAM. I saw it happen."

"The surface facilities are gone, but as you can see, one of the underground sections survived. You guys back at the main base don't know what it's been like for us out here."

"Hm… Is Yukikaze all right?"

"It ran out of fuel and landed at this base."

"Refuel her. I'm heading back."

"You can't. Not in your condition."

"Can you make contact with Faery Base?"

"No. We still haven't gotten comm back up and running. They still think we've been completely wiped out."

"That can't be right. At the least, you could reach one of the nearby tactical bases, couldn't you? You must have a helicopter or something to get me there."

"There's no need. We can take care of this ourselves. We want to service your plane, Lieutenant, and get you on your way, but it won't let us touch it. It has very ingenious safeguards. If we tamper with them, it will self-destruct."

Rei touched the gun in his chest pocket. What was this major playing at? Was he trying to cut loose from Central's command? Was this a mutiny?

"Keep your hands off Yukikaze. That's my plane."

"Lieutenant, I don't think you understand the situation you're in right now."

"I shouldn't have to say this, *Major*, but I'm attached to the SAF 5th Squadron. I don't take orders from you."

"May I remind you that I am a superior officer?"

"You're not my direct superior. I take orders from Major Booker. His orders were for me to make it back alive, no matter what. Until he rescinds that order, it's still in effect. I'm sure you're aware of military regulations."

"Of course. However, while you are here you will obey me, Lieutenant."

"And why should I do that?"

"Because otherwise you won't make it back. If you intend to follow Major Booker's orders, you'll obey mine first. Tell me how to deactivate Yukikaze's safeguards."

"I refuse."

"Then you'll stay here."

"Is that a threat?"

"All I'm saying is that you should consider your own well-being. If you don't let us service Yukikaze, I don't think you're ever going to recover from your injuries, Lieutenant."

With that, the major left the room. Rei felt like he was still dreaming. He slowly raised himself up and sat on the edge of the bed. After a few minutes, he stood up. He took an unsteady step forward. His balance was shot. The feeling of unreality clung to him. He staggered, then fell to his knees. Marnie reentered the room and, saying it was too soon for him to be up and about, helped him back into bed.

"You people..." Rei said, lying back down. "What are you trying to do? I have to get back."

Marnie smiled. "We're just trying to help you, Lieutenant. You should rest for a bit longer."

Before he could reply, she stabbed a hypodermic syringe into his arm. Just as he was registering the shock of the needle, she quickly withdrew it and looked down at him, her face expressionless. "Good night," she said. His eyelids grew heavy.

He sank into a world of white.

YUKIKAZE HAD NOT returned. In the SAF control room, Major Booker stared at the wide tactical display screens in disbelief. It had been over three hours since the symbol marking Yukikaze's position had vanished from them.

"Rei..." he muttered. "What's going on?"

"It seems he completed his mission," said General Cooley, standing behind him. "It's possible that he engaged the JAM and was shot down."

"Requesting the deployment of a search and rescue team."

"Denied. We don't have the resources for it right now. Major, I want you to submit your plan for the combat flight test of the FRX00 prototype that was delivered to our squadron."

"Yukikaze may have set down on a frontline base. Please authorize me to send the FRX out to look for him."

General Cooley fixed her cold eyes on Booker for a long moment before speaking. "I'll leave the selection of the flight test course to you."

She turned to leave. As the click of her heels receded behind him, her voice floated back. "But I doubt you'll find him. We've received no contact from the other bases."

After she exited the control room, Booker rubbed at his eyes wearily and returned to monitoring the displays.

"I was going to give you the first plane in the new squadron... Rei, what happened out there?"

He gazed pensively at the screens, as though the act of his looking at them would summon Yukikaze's RTB sign and bring her home. But she didn't return.

REI FLOATED BACK up out of the white haze. His body felt impossibly heavy. He knew he was awake now, but he still felt like he was in a dream state, still felt the same vague, insistent unease.

Through his body he sensed a kind of low-frequency hum that he couldn't actually hear. He couldn't focus his thoughts. He felt cut off from the real world, a sense of unreality enveloping him like some sort of transparent skin. It was as if his body no longer belonged to him.

Lying in bed, his eyes closed, he listened to someone talking outside the room. It seemed like a voice, but he couldn't understand what it was saying. It was like the buzzing of bees. *Maybe it's a fairy's voice,* he thought groggily. He didn't think it was a human's.

He opened his eyes, rose unsteadily from the bed, and staggered over to the white door. The buzzing in his ears wouldn't go away. He put his hand on the doorknob and pulled. It didn't open. After a befuddled moment he realized the door opened out. He braced his shoulder against it and turned the knob. The door swung open easily. So easily that Rei lost his balance and took two or three inadvertent steps out into the corridor.

It looked like a typical hospital hallway, but it was dimly lit and deserted. The buzzing sound had disappeared. It was silent. Then he heard an echoing cry, a sound like an animal being strangled or the screech of a bird. A white form floated toward him. It was Marnie. The soles of her shoes squeaked along the highly polished floor and she swung her hips as she walked, her full breasts swaying. The very mundanity of the scene fueled Rei's suspicions. The nurse seemed more like an animate doll than a woman. Feeling a palpable revulsion at the sight of her, he retreated back into the room.

"You need to rest," she told him.

He sat down on the bed. She extended her arm, took hold of Rei's wrist, and checked his pulse.

"You seem a bit tense, Lieutenant."

"I think you know why. Tell me the truth. Where are we?"

"Beneath TAB-14."

"I'd like to check out the surface. Where's Yukikaze?"

"You shouldn't exert yourself. We're continuing to service your plane."

"You can't touch her central file."

"Understood. We're working on the ejection system, reattaching the canopy, and resetting the ejection seats."

"Yukikaze uses type EESS-81-03 ejection seats. Do you have those here? And the canopy is a type made specifically for the Sylphid line."

"We're fabricating them in an underground plant. You can't fly without a canopy, after all. And we'll manage something for the ejection seats. It may take a little time, though."

"Why don't you contact Faery Base? That'd be the simplest thing to do, wouldn't it?"

"We can't transmit a signal. Lieutenant, can you activate Yukikaze's comm? We just can't figure out the systems, no matter what we try. It has safeguards everywhere."

Rei's anxiety increased. What were the survivors of TAB-14 up to? In his current state, he couldn't figure it out.

"Are you...allies?"

"What are you saying, Lieutenant? Of course we are. As soon as we complete maintenance of your plane, you'll be sent back. We have no intention of holding you here."

"I'm thirsty. Can you get me something to drink?"

"Of course. I'll bring you some liquid food."

"Liquid food?"

"Your body is still recovering, Lieutenant."

What Marnie brought for him was like a mixture of bouillon and vegetable juice. It tasted awful. She insisted that he swallow it, telling him to think of it as medicine. Rei could only manage to choke down a third of a cupful before giving it back to her.

"That's enough," he said and lay down again, trying to restrain his gag reflex. He looked up at the white ceiling. "I heard something strange a little while ago. A weird sound, like a swarm of bees buzzing."

"Maybe it was the air conditioning system. Sometimes it doesn't run that well."

"Oh."

Marnie smiled, then took the cup and left the room.

After the door shut Rei drew the gun from his vest. It was a 9mm automatic pistol with a roller locking system and light recoil. There were thirteen rounds in the magazine and one in the chamber. He held the grip and clicked the safety off.

He wondered why they hadn't taken it away from him. Was it to prove to him that he was in a safe environment? It was true that he could hardly expect an enemy to leave him armed, but he still didn't feel safe here. Even as they cared for him, he suspected them of some treachery. And the overall impression that the place gave was oddly still, lacking the tension that normally defined the atmosphere of a frontline base. He couldn't put it into words, but his instincts were screaming at him that he was in danger.

He got up, holding the pistol at the ready, but just as he was about to step through the door, a wave of nausea broke over him. Slipping the gun back into his vest, he gripped the doorframe and called for Marnie. She came running down the gloomy corridor. He got the impression that she was the only one there. He asked her where the toilet was and then rushed to it. His guts turned inside out. After he finished vomiting, he reeled with an overwhelming exhaustion.

Marnie helped him back to the room and he collapsed onto the bed. He felt feverish.

He awoke to the sound of her voice. He raised his arm to check his chronometer and saw that ten hours had elapsed, but he had no true sense of time's passage. His fever had gone down, and there was now an I.V. needle stuck in his right arm.

"You seem to have a viral infection, Lieutenant," Marnie said. "You must have caught it out in the desert."

"No… No, that's not right…"

"It seems to be presenting neurological symptoms. You've been hallucinating. That probably was the cause of your distress. But you're okay now. You'll be just fine. How's your appetite?"

His stomach was empty, but he never wanted to put that liquid food in his mouth again.

"I've made some soup for you," Marnie said as she drew a small trolley up to the bedside and shifted the bed's movable table close to Rei's chest. He sat up. She placed a bowl down on the table. It smelled decent… He decided not to eat the portable rations he had and took the spoon she offered him. He took a cautious sip. It tasted good.

"What is this?"

"Chicken broth."

"Chicken? It tastes different, though. It's not instant, is it?"

"Don't spill it, Lieutenant. There's more if you want. If you eat too fast, you'll make yourself sick."

Rei did as Marnie said and ate slowly.

Major Yazawa came in and set a small computer on the side table. "I figured you must be bored, Lieutenant," he said. "Would you like to communicate with Yukikaze?"

The major turned the computer on. The display glowed and an image of Yukikaze appeared. She was in a large maintenance hangar, or something that resembled one. It was hard to tell. The image was a little hazy.

"This device can synthesize a transmission on any frequency or wavelength. I'd do it myself if I could get a link through to the plane. I imagine you know how to contact it without triggering the security systems."

"So you can monitor how I do it? What are you people after? You're acting like..."

Like they were JAM. Just as he was about to say it, a cold wave prickled the skin over his entire body.

JAM. They were JAM. They had to be. These were the first JAM to ever show themselves to human eyes. They were JAM...

"What's wrong?" asked Yazawa. "You look like you're scared of something."

"Major," Marnie said smoothly, "The lieutenant is mentally unstable. It's Faery Fever. It looks like he caught it out in the desert. May I ask you to leave now? I have to administer a sedative. Please, Lieutenant, lie down."

"I... I'm not crazy," Rei said. "Take me to Yukikaze."

"You can leave at any time, Lieutenant. However, we would advise against it. You can't fly in your condition, can you?"

Rei tried to get out of bed, but the major held him down. He was strong. Marnie slid a hypodermic needle into his arm again. A terrible weakness spread across his body.

"You... What are you...?"

"We're your friends," Marnie answered. "The same organic life as you." Both she and the major laughed.

"A bit different, though," Yazawa said. "We made a small mistake. A stupid one, really."

"We realized it when we gave you that liquid food. It was the D-type alpha-amino acids," Marnie added. "Lieutenant, did that chicken broth taste good? I imagine it was to your taste. You can digest that."

They were voices in a dream. *I'm having a nightmare,* Rei thought. The desert must have gotten to him. When he woke up next, he'd be all right. He'd be back in the real world at the normal hospital at Faery Base. No doubt about it...

Once more he fell into the white void.

HE AWOKE TO the same room. Yukikaze was still displayed on the computer the major had brought to him. He saw she had been fitted with a new canopy.

His head felt hollow. He remembered being given some sort of drug and that he'd heard something very important just as he was sliding into sleep, but he couldn't remember what it was.

He gathered his strength and ventured out into the corridor. One direction led to a dead end. He turned around and backtracked to a T-intersection. To the right was a nurse's station. To the left was a short passage that ended at a metal door. He thought it might be an emergency exit but couldn't budge it.

He heard Marnie approaching, her footsteps making that awful squeaking noise.

"Do you need something, Lieutenant?"

"Where's Lieutenant Burgadish?"

"I'm afraid he's—"

"Dead? Let me out of here. This isn't a hospital, it's a prison."

"Please return to your room, Lieutenant. You don't look well at all."

Seeing no other option, Rei went back to the room. Yukikaze glowed on the computer screen. As Rei looked at her, he grew more and more agitated by the feeling that he'd forgotten something. Why was Major Yazawa so concerned about Yukikaze? If he wanted to activate her comm system, all he had to do was turn it on, right? If they tried to force their way into her internal systems electronically, she might activate her self-destruct protocol, but she couldn't stop a human from flipping a switch. He assumed she couldn't, anyway. So in short, the reason must be that Major Yazawa didn't know how to turn on the system or to use Yukikaze's instrumentation. But if he was in the FAF, how could he not…

Once again a chilling unease swept through Rei's body, bringing with it a powerful sense of déjà vu. He clutched at his head.

Were they human? Were they JAM? Externally, they looked no different from any other human. Was that the JAM's real form? A human form? He didn't believe that. He was sure he had the answer. They'd given it to him. They said that they were his friends. No, after that. After…

Yukikaze. If he had access to Yukikaze's data file, he might be able to find proof. He reached out for the computer's keyboard. He knew it might be a trap. Major Yazawa had to be somewhere monitoring the link between this computer and Yukikaze. Even so, Rei figured that freeing himself from this paralyzed state had to take priority.

He spent a few minutes familiarizing himself with the device. He then composed a pulse code on the same frequency as the SAF emergency tactical line and transmitted it. It worked. The link with Yukikaze opened up.

SEARCH FOR JAM.

The message seemed to leap out at him from the screen. It was the same message that appeared on Yukikaze's display during battle. That was all he needed to know. Rei quickly switched the computer off.

This was a JAM base. It had to be. But he doubted that Marnie and Major Yazawa were JAM. So what were humans doing in a JAM base?

"Why did you turn it off?" Marnie asked, entering the room. "Lieutenant, you look tired."

"I'm not tired at all."

"How about shaving at least? You look awful. You should see yourself in the mirror."

Mirror. Something stirred in his ragged memory. Mirror. Mirror image. D...alpha-amino acid. The optical isomer of the L-type. He remembered now. He remembered what she had said. He looked at her. What if this woman's body wasn't composed of L-type amino acid proteins, but rather D-type polypeptides, making her a mirror image of a human at the molecular level? Is that what she was?

She approached the bedside, a syringe in her hand.

"Come now, Lieutenant. You should get some rest."

If she gave him that shot, he might never wake up again. If she wasn't human, how could he find out for sure? Check her body, her cells, her molecules with equipment he didn't have?

"Lieutenant, you have Faery Fever. This injection will lessen the anxiety you're feeling. You're hallucinating, Lieutenant. Get a hold of yourself."

"I'm not crazy."

Still smiling, Marnie took hold of his arm. Rei was tempted to just let go and obey her. Maybe she was right. Maybe he was sick, and this paranoia was a result.

Yukikaze's warning message flashed in his mind. Just before she plunged the needle into his arm, Rei slapped her hand away and gripped her other wrist, squeezing with enough force to make her drop the syringe.

"What are you doing?!" she gasped.

He threw her down onto the floor and tore open the front of her uniform. Her heavy breasts spilled out. She screamed as he sank his teeth into one of them, biting into her flesh.

He pushed away from her, spat out the piece he'd bitten, and wiped his mouth with the back of his hand. It didn't taste like blood. It tasted like the liquid food that she had brought him. It wasn't protein.

"Fucking JAM!"

He looked down at her as he drew his pistol and fired a single shot. Her body jerked once, then stopped moving.

He had to get to Yukikaze. He ran out of the room. The adrenaline dumping into his system was clearing his head and returning some strength to his limbs.

The bittersweet flavor of the blood that wasn't blood lingered in his mouth. The soup Marnie had given him didn't have that same taste. As Rei ran, he suddenly realized what they must have made it from and felt like vomiting.

Before he could think about it any further he rounded a corner and ran into Major Yazawa. The major immediately reached out and knocked the gun out of his hand.

Keeping his grip on Rei's arm, he followed through with an outside shoulder throw. His strength was incredible. Rei went with the fall and hit the floor on his left shoulder, feeling a bolt of pain rip through it. Ignoring it, he grabbed on to Yazawa's arm with both hands, kicked his legs up, locked them around the back of the man's head, and used the momentum of his body to throw him over onto the floor.

Rei released the hold and scrabbled forward, reaching for his fallen gun. Just as his fingers closed on the grip he felt the major's powerful hands wrap around his shins.

Before he could even turn to look, he was flying through the air. Straining his abdominal muscles, he twisted his body, just barely managing to get his back around before he slammed into the wall. The shock of the impact momentarily blinded him. He couldn't breathe. Lying sideways on the floor, he looked up to see the major leaping at him. Two shots. The report echoed down the corridor. The 9mm 205 grain rounds blew Yazawa's head off.

Rei lowered his arms, gasping for air. After a few seconds he slowly levered himself up into a crouch and rubbed the back of his neck, shaking his head to work out the stiffness. He cautiously flexed his limbs. Nothing seemed to be broken, at least.

He stood up and surveyed the scene. Major Yazawa's body was sprawled out on the floor. The back of his head had been splattered across the wall and ceiling, dyeing their surfaces red. But there was no smell of blood.

Massaging his solar plexus with his left hand, Rei aimed his gun at the lock on the metal door and fired a couple of shots at it. He gave the door a sharp kick and it opened onto a stairwell. He started climbing. Upon reaching the uppermost level, he spotted what looked like an exit, a doorway glowing with daylight. He ran through it…

And emerged into a bizarre landscape. It didn't look like Faery. He was standing at the edge of a flat, smooth plain that stretched out before him like a sheet of blue ice. Thick clouds hung so low it seemed as if he could reach out and touch them. The underground entrance he'd just emerged from was situated in a forest, and around him the trees shimmered in metallic green hues. Looking back through the strange trees he saw a pond. A pond that glowed a sickly yellow. The surface roiled, as if the liquid were boiling.

He shifted his gaze back toward the open space ahead of him. There was a strip of transparent, plastic-like ground that could have been a runway. He followed it with his eyes and found Yukikaze. She was sitting on level ground about a quarter mile away. He left the cover of the forest and ran toward her. He concentrated on his objective, blocking out the fact that he was completely out in the open now, an easy target.

He saw two figures approaching Yukikaze. Pilots who were going to steal her from him. JAM.

Panting for breath, Rei screamed at them to stop. One of them turned at the sound. The strength abruptly drained from Rei's shooting arm. It was Lieutenant Burgadish.

"Lieutenant…"

Rei began to doubt his own senses, wondering if he really was mentally ill. Was this entire bizarre sequence a hallucination?

He took several steps forward, then saw the man standing beside Burgadish and froze in shock.

He was looking at himself.

"JAM!"

He fired, and the other Rei went down. Pain lashed through his right side. He saw Lieutenant Burgadish holding a gun and fired back. Burgadish crumpled and several rapid shots from Rei's gun ended his life.

Rei put a hand to his side. The familiar, distinct smell of blood wafted up. He was bleeding badly.

He approached the two bodies and looked down at them. He didn't think they were JAM. These were androids, created by the JAM. The JAM, who had until now ignored humans, were working out a strategy to target them here. They were creating weapons. Organic antipersonnel weapons. Just as humans had made Yukikaze, the JAM were now making humans. The aliens probably had only a tenuous understanding of human existence. To fight humanity, they probably needed to manufacture weapons that could sense a human at the same level as a human. The same way that humans were using computers to analyze the JAM. If so, it was another piece of evidence that the JAM were mechanical life-forms.

And if so, the parameters of the war had shifted from machines made by humans fighting the JAM to humans made by the JAM fighting humans. The insanity of the situation tore at Rei's mind. Even though the JAM and humanity could barely comprehend the others' existences, they were being forced to fight for the sake of the weapons they both made. The JAM may have been even more vexed than the humans, wondering why a machine like Yukikaze, who was like one of their own kind, was attacking them.

Rei approached Yukikaze, hauled himself up the boarding

ladder, and climbed into the cockpit. He was relieved to see that the ejection seat seemed to have been properly installed. He couldn't stop the bleeding from the gunshot wound in his side. Pressing his left hand to the wound, he started the engines.

Looking out of the cockpit, Rei saw a yellow mass headed for Yukikaze. It looked like the same substance that had filled the pond in the forest. As it flowed toward them across the flat ground, it morphed and reformed like protoplasm. Shapes would rise from the ooze and melt back into it again as it moved. Human shapes. Human limbs and heads and torsos. Above them swirled a glinting cloud of small black objects, like a giant swarm of bees.

Were those insect-like forms the JAM? He switched Yukikaze's ECM system on. Her engines roared. Parking brake, off. The canopy lowered and locked.

"Let's go home, Yukikaze."

The humanoid mass pressed up against Yukikaze's body. He slid the throttle to MIL, incinerating the portion behind them. Yukikaze turned, accelerated, and took off. Landing gear, up. FCS, ON. Master arm switch to ARM. They shot into a climbing turn. A cold sweat had broken out on Rei's brow, and he could feel the blood pooling in his flight suit.

Yukikaze fired her last remaining high-velocity missile into the black swarm of insects. The flare of the detonation, like a miniature sun, temporarily robbed Rei of his sight.

When he opened his eyes, Yukikaze was flying in familiar airspace. She was going slow, almost brushing the canopy of Faery's forest. Rei looked up at the blue sky. The gunshot wound hurt like hell, but he felt a lot better. *We made it back,* he thought.

But the threat hadn't vanished. As they began to accelerate and climb, Yukikaze's radar picked up three JAM fighters to the rear, practically on top of them. Flying as low and slow as they were, there was no way for them to evade.

There was a burst of cannon fire. Yukikaze's right vertical

stabilizer shattered. Fire spouted from the right engine.

Describing a wide turn, she plunged toward the forest.

Rei lost consciousness. When he came to, he realized that he had miraculously survived. They had made an emergency landing on the spongy surface of forest canopy, which was dozens of yards thick, robust enough to support the fighter's weight. The JAM hadn't withdrawn but had ceased their attack.

Analyzing Yukikaze to the bitter end, Rei thought. He activated her self-destruct system. No response. He then remembered: the switch in the electronic warfare officer's seat had to be thrown as well. He started to release the seat harness, his hands slippery with blood, then stopped. His arms weren't working very well, and besides, it looked like the self-destruct wouldn't be necessary. Yukikaze's rear section was burning furiously. It was only a matter of time until the fuel tanks ignited.

Rei closed his eyes. He doubted he could pull the eject lever, and he didn't even feel like trying.

This was the death he'd always imagined. *It's better this way,* he thought. He'd always felt that this moment would come one day... The moment when he and Yukikaze would die together.

He heard a beep. Rei slitted his eyes open. He had the fanciful thought that Yukikaze was saying goodbye to him. As he looked at the multidisplay his eyesight grew dim. He slowly reached out and turned the brightness control up. On the screen was the symbol for a single TAF plane flying toward them.

The FRX00. Too late. Too late...

The canopy was now dyed crimson with the light of the flames burning behind him. *Enough,* thought Rei. He was going to die with Yukikaze. It was all he'd ever wanted. She had never betrayed him.

However, she then did something he couldn't have anticipated, a singular action beyond anything he could have imagined. His eyes widened as he read the display.

`LINK-FRX00-05003. TRANS-CCIF.`

"What?"

TRANSFERRING CORE FUNCTIONS OF SAF-V UNIT 3 TO FRX00.

Rei screamed at her to stop, but no sound came from his throat.

Yukikaze was… She was abandoning this aircraft. She was abandoning him.

Glowing columns of numbers and characters began to flow down the display. Yukikaze was transferring her central combat information file to the FRX. There was nothing Rei could do to stop it.

He became aware that his vision was growing dark. He couldn't hear anything. He couldn't see anything… He had the sensation that he was soaring. In skies where fairies danced. Faery airspace.

TRANS-CCIF COMPLETE. blinked on the display. Rei didn't see it.

Yukikaze had kept him aboard to initiate the self-destruct sequence in case the need for it arose during the transfer. As soon as the transfer was complete, she ejected him. He was thrown clear of Yukikaze and into the air, but he was long past the point of consciousness.

MAJOR JAMES BOOKER sat in the rear seat of FRX00-05003, monitoring the new plane's electronic warfare armaments.

Just after they acquired the three enemy planes, he noticed an abnormality in the FRX's central computer. Its learning section was still fairly clean, but the rest of it began to run wild.

"What the hell is this?" he wondered aloud.

A huge amount of data was being transferred from somewhere. *Is this a new JAM tactic?* In the same instant that the thought formed in his mind, the FRX00 kicked into a high-G acceleration.

"What is it? What's going on?" the pilot said over the com,

his voice tight with tension. "I don't have control. Major, I thought this couldn't function as an unmanned plane."

"Could be the JAM. Kill the flight controls."

"They won't disengage."

"Can we eject?"

"No way. We're going way too fast."

Far away, at a distant point in the forest that spread out below them, Major Booker saw black smoke rising.

"Can that be Yukikaze...? Get us over there, now."

"It's not responding to anything I do. We might have a fatal defect here. And what's with all this data input?"

The FRX00 closed rapidly on the three JAM fighters, passed them at full power, and then banked steeply into a high-G turn. The maneuver sent Major Booker and the pilot into GLOC.

It continued its turn around the three JAM aircraft, plotted an orthogonal attack line to their course, and took that heading. It flew direct abeam toward the JAM at supersonic speed. An instant later it was veering up and away, the three enemy aircraft disintegrating behind it, ripped apart by high-velocity fire.

The FRX00 rolled out of its loop and dove toward the forest. It centered Yukikaze in its gun sight and fired a short burst. The rounds impacted precisely on the area of the fuselage housing Yukikaze's central computer, silencing it forever. The fuel tanks ignited and an orange fireball blossomed on the forest canopy. Metal fragments torn off in the blast danced in the air, reflecting the twilight glow of Faery's twin suns.

The FRX00 picked up the rescue beacon signaling the position of Yukikaze's ejected pilot and relayed this information to TAB-15, the nearest frontline base. However, it did not respond to the inquiries of the search and rescue team regarding the condition of the survivor. As though it wasn't interested in human life and death.

It took a return course for Faery Base, flying in auto mode. Opening a communications link with the Tactical Air Force

SAF control room, it relayed the following: **DE YUKIKAZE. ETA 2146. AR.**

Yukikaze, having obtained a new body for herself, flew on at supersonic speed.

Major Booker and the pilot, still unconscious, didn't see her transmission to Faery Base of her estimated time of arrival. Neither could they see the setting suns, the sky of Faery as its colors shifted to night, nor the forests below.

Yukikaze landed back at Faery Base and informed control that her mission was complete. Six TAISPs had been successfully dropped at the targeted sites. Mission success rate: 100 percent.

The Faery Air Force acknowledged Yukikaze's mission completion. Or, at least, the computers did, if not the humans. And there was no doubt that the JAM recognized it as well.

Yukikaze taxied over to the SAF's section and was towed onto the elevator platform. She descended, vanishing into her lair to prepare herself for the next battle.

And, however briefly, silence returned to the planet Faery.

YUKIKAZE FACT SHEET

Aircraft Serial Number	79113
Division Attachment Number	SAF-V-05003
Development Number	FRX47
Model Designation Number	FFR31-MR
Model Name	Super Sylph
Attachment	Faery Air Force
	Tactical Air Force
	Faery Base Tactical
	Combat Air Group
	Special Air Force 5th
	Squadron
Personal Name	Yukikaze

1. GENERAL SPECIFICATIONS

◊ The Super Sylph's principal role is to carry out tactical electronic surveillance. To meet the requirements for supersonic cruising and high maneuverability, it is equipped with twin Phoenix Mk-X (FNX-5010-J) engines.

◊ The main airfoils are fixed, backswept clipped delta wings. However, the wing cross-section can be adjusted by the flight control computer in order to compensate for varying flight conditions and thus achieve optimal configuration. A ventral fin is attached to the underside of the fuselage, with a shape different from that of a mainline combat Sylphid in order to facilitate high speed over maneuverability. Its twin vertical stabilizers contain speed brakes, the deployment of which is limited according to CAS (calibrated air speed), altitude, and aircraft attitude. Speed brake deployment in dogfight and auto-maneuver mode is handled by the flight control computer but can be used to effect a sudden attitude change when in manual mode.

◇ The aircraft has two seats, with the pilot in the front and the electronic warfare officer/flight officer in the rear. Both seats recline to relieve the flight crew's burden during high-G maneuvering. Directly in front of the pilot's seat is the HUD (head-up display). Below that is the multi-function display, flight instrumentation, and the BIT (built-in test) system display. On the pilot's right is the side stick flight controller. On the side stick are mounted the dogfight switch, gun trigger, missile release, side force/pitch controls, and G-limiter switch, all of which enable the pilot to control the plane without removing his hand from the stick. On the pilot's left is the throttle, on which are mounted the target management switch, radar mode selector, and armament selector. The rear seat has no flight control instruments and is equipped instead with the ECM controls, ECM display, electronic data collection controls, IFF display, and communications/navigation display.

◇ The engine air intakes and exhaust ports utilize a two-dimensional design. Their cross-section shapes can be automatically manipulated by the air intake and nozzle controllers. Variation of the exhaust nozzle area is used to steer the plane and to improve maneuverability. High-maneuverability mode is selected by turning the dogfight switch to ON.

2. AVIONICS AND ENGINE SYSTEMS

◇ The Sylphid's static stability margin is negative. The pilot's instructions, as input via the side stick controller, are input into an integrated avionics system that includes the flight control computer, the aircraft's central computer, and the direct control unit. Under normal flight, the flight control computer combines the input from the side stick with the flight data from a multitude of sensors to control the hydraulic actuators of the aircraft's control surfaces. If the flight control computer is rendered inoperative, the central computer and direct control unit will compensate, controlling the direct control assemblies set on all control surfaces. The direct control unit can also operate independently of the flight computer and central computer so that flight stability may be maintained even in the unlikely event of a central computer failure. In this case, advanced flight control of the automatic landing, tactical guidance, and supersonic bombing protocols is impossible. However, by interfacing the inertial guidance and aircraft attitude sensors, altitude and course may be automatically maintained.

◇ The engines are twin FNX-5010-J axial compression turbofans equipped with afterburners. These were later replaced with the FNX-5011-B, commonly known as the Phoenix Mk-XI. (The FRX99 and FRX00 are equipped with the FNX-5011-C and FNX-5011-D variants, respectively). The 5011 (Mk-XI) line of engines can burn hydrogen fuel as well as standard jet fuel. When burning hydrogen fuel, it can operate as a ramjet. To select ram air mode, the pilot must slide the throttle past the MAX position to the MR position. However, below speeds of M2.0 and an altitude of 60,000 feet on Faery, it will not operate. The pilot can move the throttle freely between the MAX and MR positions—there is no stopper between the positions—but regardless of the individual lever setting the pilot must maintain a constant fifteen pounds of pressure on the throttle to hold it at the MR position. Selecting the MR mode automatically switches over the fuel system, intake configuration, and engine operation. MR mode should yield a thrust increase of 160 percent over the regular afterburners, although the exact increase will vary according to indicated air speed and altitude.

◇ When the afterburners are engaged, once the fuel level in the feed tank drops below a certain point the afterburner shut-off valve closes and they are no longer usable. It is possible to override this by turning the V-max switch to ON, but because the fuel consumption rate is significantly higher when using afterburners, the danger of running out of fuel also increases significantly.

◇ Switching to V-max will simultaneously cut out all engine system limiters as well as the aircraft's G-limiter. It should not be used except in emergencies. When the auto-maneuver system is on it may also automatically engage V-max if prompted to do so by the central computer. In that situation, it is impossible to manually switch V-max off. Once the central computer confirms that the emergency has ended, it will automatically return to normal engine mode.

◇ Engine control is executed via an integrated electronic control system based on data provided to it by the flight control computer, various sensors, and the central computer. The engine controller of the 5011 line (the Mk-XI) is programmed to realize maximum efficiency not only in the atmosphere of Faery but also in Earth's atmosphere, with the flight control computer automatically selecting the appropriate mode.

3. WEAPONS SYSTEM

◇ The Sylphid's fire control system consists of the FCR (fire control radar), IR (infrared) receivers, passive airspace radar, passive wide-area search radar, the fire control computer, navigation computer, and so on, all under the integrated command of the tactical computer, with the central computer acting as backup.

◇ The fire control computer will automatically select the pulse Doppler FCR mode and then identify and track the target, determine target range, calculate attack vectors, select armaments, determine missile launch timing, number of missiles, guidance data for active homing missiles, and so on.

◇ The fire control radar possesses a wide range of modes, including long-range search and detection, long-range measurement, single target tracking, multiple target tracking, short- and medium-range search and detection, ground attack, short- and medium-range single target tracking, pilot-initiated radar lock-on, and rapid lock-on.

◇ The Super Sylph is equipped with a 20mm Vulcan nose cannon. With its high-velocity ammunition and firing control mechanisms, it can be used even at supersonic speeds.

◇ The Super Sylph can be loaded out with air-to-air and air-to-ground missiles as well as precision guided explosive ordnance. Its main air-to-air missile armaments are the AAM-III, -IV, and -V (short-, medium-, and long-range missiles, respectively). They can function as passive or active homing missiles, or they can be guided from the aircraft. The internal AI systems will self-select guidance mode as well as optimal detonation timing. HAAM (high-velocity air-to-air missiles) armaments were later implemented to increase missile flight velocity.

4. MISCELLANEOUS

◇ The Super Sylph can also carry a variety of mission-specific tactical data collection pods, such as a TARPS (tactical aerial reconnaissance pod system). The TARPS has electronic intelligence data collection capabilities and mounts a variety of cameras but possesses no AI system of its own. If the plane's central computer judges the data collected by the TARPS to be especially vital, it will be added to its data file.

◇ The Super Sylph possesses an advanced wireless digital data link function, allowing the plane's central computer to maintain direct, secure communications with the base tactical control computers via the tactical data line.

⬦ Details of engine performance, avionics instrumentation, and exact airframe dimensions have not been publicly released on Earth. The figures below represent estimated performance in Earth-standard gravity.

FNX-5011-B

Dry Weight	2,425 lb [1.1 t]
Maximum Thrust	21,605 lbf [9.8 t] military power
	31,967 lbf [14.5 t] full afterburner
	49,604 lbf [22.5 t] MB power

FFR31-MR

Length	64 ft 11 in [19.8 m]
Wingspan	44 ft 3 in [13.5 m]
Height	20 ft 4 in [6.2 m]
Empty Weight	26,015 lb [11.8 t]
Loaded Weight	54,010 lb [24.5 t]
Maximum Takeoff Weight	83,775 lb [38.0 t]

From "Appendix – Mainline Fighter Craft of the FAF" in *The Invader*, by Lynn Jackson.

ABOUT *YUKIKAZE*

THE BOOK YOU hold is a new edition of *Yukikaze*. I was fortunate enough to be granted the opportunity to revise the original edition and went through it thoroughly, but in the end I did not make any pronounced changes. I revisited some of the wording but was careful not to modify any section too much. The fundamental composition of the book itself remains completely unchanged.

Twenty years have passed since *Yukikaze* was first published in February of 1984. Rereading the original edition, I realized that the significance of this passage of time was actually much greater than I had first thought. The book definitely felt like something I wrote, but I found myself wanting to know more background detail than what had been provided, to get more under the surface of things. In short, the issues I was interested in writing about back then and what I'm interested in now have changed. If I were to try writing the book all over again today, I imagine it would end up with quite a different tone. It would almost be like rewriting another author's work.

The creation process of the original edition of the book was informed by my interests, worldview, sensitivities, and mindset at the time. While making the revisions, I believed that it was important, both for the fans of the old edition as well as for the readers picking up the book for the first time, to maintain that original flavor. I considered what had changed in the real world since the old edition first came out, and also what hadn't changed. Doing so forced me to think about the book on a personal level. I was able to make corrections and revisions according to my current mindset but hopefully without violating the subtle impressions a reader may have formed from the old edition.

I decided that if I wanted to create something that reflected my current interests, it would be better for me to write a new book than to try rewriting an old one. That was what drove me to write the sequel volume, *Good Luck, Yukikaze*. The parts of this book that were changed include some small amendments intended to link it better with the new story. Setting aside the issue of whether or not I should have done so, the intent was to make the book more consistent with future sequels. With that aim, I gratefully offer up this new, "improved" edition to all the fans of *Yukikaze*.

Chōhei Kambayashi
Matsumoto
March 2002

HUMAN/INHUMAN

THROUGHOUT *YUKIKAZE* THE terms "human" and "human-like" are set in opposition to "inhuman" and "mechanical." First and foremost, the book's theme is the question of what it means to be human. We are shown again and again how the enigmatic invading aliens known as the JAM are completely unlike humans, how communication with them is impossible, how there is no chance of mutual understanding. Through examining this portrait of the thoroughly inhuman JAM, we are able to discern the reverse image of what it is to be human: if to be inhuman is to have no logical method of communication, then to be human is to possess the gift of communication.

The inhuman nature of the members of the SAF charged with intelligence gathering is also stressed in the story. The main character, Rei Fukai, is assigned to the SAF, and it is through him that the question of what it means to be human is asked again and again. One could make the argument that Rei, too, is an inhuman being. However, although his character is that of a cold man, a loner, I don't believe that these traits consign him to the realm of inhumanity. The trust he places in his beloved plane, Yukikaze, is highly idiosyncratic, a very "human" trait. On this point, taking the character of Rei into account, I'd like to examine the story's main theme of what it is to be human.

The book opens with an excerpt from *The Invader*, the book by Lynn Jackson on the subject of the JAM War that was published five years before the timeline of the main story. Opening the novel with an excerpt from a fictional "non-fiction" history is effective in establishing an air of verisimilitude. Within the excerpt, Jackson talks about the soldiers of the SAF.

> The pilots of the SAF evidently take a certain satisfaction in this requirement, and individuals with 'special' personalities outside the range of normal human standards are selected for this duty. These men put more faith in their machines than in other people and can fly their planes with perfect skill. In a way, they are yet one more combat computer, but organic in nature, loaded aboard the Sylphids to carry out a heartless duty.

She goes on to describe the pilots as "machines that are, through some accident of fate, in human form."

So what are these "normal human standards" Lynn Jackson is talking about? With this phrase, she's referring not to the set of traits common to most humans but rather to the broader concept of "humanity." Typically this term is used to indicate the capacity to experience emotions, with the ability to love being the crucial element. Conversely "inhumanity," although it bears the connotations of cruelty or sadism, essentially denotes the inability to experience emotion or sympathy.

According to one line of thought, what makes us human is our capacity for empathy. What this means is, if I see things and feel things a certain way, I can make the cognitive analogy that others also see and feel things a certain way. The theory is that the development of the empathic capacity marked a major step in the evolutionary process of the human brain. In other words, we can say that what makes us human is our ability to understand the sorrow another person feels by drawing on our own experiences.

What fascinates me is that the main elements that differentiate us from the other animals, such as the ability to reason, have little to do with "humanity" when seen from this point of view. To the contrary, logical thought, which is the gift of reason, is often shown in a negative light as being "inhuman." It is therefore not unreasonable to view machine intelligence, which is based exclusively on logic, as something that is fundamentally inhuman.

Yukikaze frequently depicts this inhuman lack of empathy. In the beginning of Chapter I, the SAF's mission to bring their data back to base even as they watch their comrades die in battle is criticized as being "inhuman." The reader soon discovers that the target of this criticism is the book's hero, Rei Fukai.

In his very first appearance, Rei is depicted announcing in an emotionless voice that his fellow pilots have been shot down. He then decides without any hesitation that a plane, which is by all appearances an allied unit, is an enemy and coolly attacks it. In the following pages, the military doctor who treats him refers to him as a "machine." In this way, the author appears to be inducing the reader to see Rei as an inhuman character.

However, in the same chapter Rei's behavior is far different from that of a "machine." He declares his trust in his plane, grumbles about General Cooley, and talks with Major Booker, his only friend, about a woman he was involved with. And, recognizing his own powerlessness in the face of the unknown JAM, he feels anger, grief, and anxiety. "What am I doing? Why am I here?" he asks. The chapter begins with an epigraph telling us that he'd been betrayed by much of what he had once loved and that his only emotional support now came from his fighter plane. Establishing that he has known both love and hate makes it difficult for a reader to regard Rei as inhuman. Lynn Jackson's understanding of the SAF pilots as "machines that are, through some accident of fate, in human form," is incorrect as far as Rei is concerned.

Rei's affection for Yukikaze also undermines the concept of him as a machinelike individual. It is a uniquely human trait to feel empathy not only for another being like oneself but also for animals or even inanimate objects. That he feels empathy for a machine is, ironically, a powerful confirmation of Rei's humanity. The irrational trust he places in Yukikaze, the faith he has that she would "never, ever betray him," and his extreme fear of her becoming independent of him negate any claims that he is inhuman and mechanical. Rei's callous, inhuman exterior is consistently betrayed by his inner humanity. Furthermore, from the very start of the story, the author continually portrays Rei questioning what it is to be human.

Now let's look at Chapter V, "Faery – Winter," wherein Major Booker directly addresses the issue of what it means to be human. Imagining what it's like for the wounded Lieutenant Amata, Booker judges him to be

> a soul that was easily bruised. He was a man endowed with the rich, common humanity you hardly ever saw in Boomerang Squadron. Humans cannot live alone. Amata couldn't live estranged from his friends. Rei, however, was different. Impersonal, detached, it was as if he had no need for human contact at all.

In other words, valuing relationships with other people is a mark of being human. Considering affection to be an aspect of human nature is a natural thing to do, but on the other hand self-interest also plays a major part. (Indeed, it may be an essential attribute of all life.) So how do we reconcile this contradiction? I can't help but feel that *Yukikaze* addresses the gap between human nature and human kindness in various scenes.

"Not my problem" is the favorite saying of the soldiers in Boomerang Squadron. The squadron was put together by General Cooley, its membership consisting of soldiers with little sense of sociability or cooperation. As you might expect, as a group they lack empathy for others; they are all individualists with enough mental strength to endure the isolation imposed by their mission. Their thinking is extremely logical, making them elite soldiers who have a high probability of survival on the battlefield. Does that make them inhuman? Major Booker seems to think it does to some extent, but at the same time he also understands the severity of their duty.

Yukikaze is a story of a possibly endless war with unknown invaders. The author has constructed an extreme situation in which the bizarre battlefield and the enemy being fought aren't seen except from the perspective of high-velocity air battles. This does not seem like an auspicious setting for an inquiry into human nature, and yet that is the author's constant aim. At one point Major Booker asks, "Should we therefore abandon our humanity?" It is a question that goes grandly round and round without ever arriving at the desired answer. Extended to its extreme meaning, that question is: do we abandon our humanity or do we choose death? Booker chooses to help Amata in order to wriggle out of that conceptual tight spot, to attempt to regain some of his lost humanity. He goes so far as to admit to himself that he's doing so to atone for how he must send his best friend out into the battlefield again and again.

Major Booker is the other main character in *Yukikaze*, a man tormented by the suffering and lives lost to an absurd war. A man who feels that, rather than revealing humanity's true nature, the war is actually erasing it. He fears that the only way to beat the JAM is for humans to become machinelike. The SAF soldiers' inhumanity is deliberate. Booker observes that, "Even if the Earth were to vanish tomorrow, they wouldn't shed a single tear." Even regarding Rei, his best friend, he thinks about how "that expressionless look on his face never changed, no matter what chaos was happening all around him." Major Booker has a terrible foreboding about the consequences of these "inhuman humans" coming into being. Something similar to his desire to preserve his subordinates' humanity on a harsh and strange battlefield shows up in the book's sequel *Good Luck, Yukikaze*, although in less dire circumstances.

Although Rei is perceived as inhuman, we can definitely see that he is cognizant of his own humanity. When the realization begins to dawn on him that the war against the JAM is one of alien versus machine and that humans are unneeded in it, he reflexively denies it out of fear. The inhuman, rational response would be to calmly accept being a part of the machine.

Chapter IV, "Indian Summer," ends with a touching scene in which Rei sheds tears for the fallen soldier Tomahawk John, an act that truly belies his image as a "callous soldier." In that moment, Rei's inhumanity is exposed as nothing more than a mask he wears, a shell he maintains to protect himself. Tomahawk John, whose mechanical heart has been attacked by the JAM, asks "I am human, aren't I?" just before he dies. "Of course you are," Rei answers and then thinks back to when he told Tomahawk, "You're alive…Or are you telling me that you're actually a corpse?"

It could be said that Rei's cold and factual approach, one that provides no room for emotional judgments, is a rational survival mechanism he adopted to adapt to his harsh environment. To him, being alive is the same as being human, so even if an individual possesses some sort of physical or mental deficiency it is impossible for Rei to question their humanity. The essential thing is that they are alive.

That's why Rei is focused on the imperative of survival. Despite the fact that he flies a highly advanced fighter plane and doesn't proactively participate in the battles on the front line, he still has a strong feeling that death is never far from him. The conviction that they must kill the enemy or be killed themselves could explain the high success rate of the SAF pilots. In the end, the battlefield demands the coldhearted living, not the empathic dead. Without recognizing that the war itself produces inhumanity, criticizing Rei's decisions as "inhuman" is nonsensical.

Surely we could apply this to machine intelligence as well. Let's take a look at Chapter VI, "All Systems Normal." The unmanned Yukikaze kills Captain O'Donnell aboard the Fand II by instructing it to execute violent evasive maneuvers. If it hadn't done so, the Fand II would have been shot down. However, there was also the possibility that O'Donnell might have been saved if Yukikaze had sacrificed herself. However, Yukikaze never even considered that course of action. Because she "learned" how to fight from Rei, whose prime directive was to survive, no matter what, Yukikaze had been trained to act a certain way on the battlefield. You could say that what she did was inevitable.

Fighter planes are built to fight. Their objective is always one of destruction. That's true in reality and true for the reality within the novel. So long as a fighter plane's electronic brain is given the objective of destroying an enemy so that it can survive, it will continue to carry out actions which we humans may regard as horrifying but which are, according to the logic of that objective, entirely appropriate. It is we humans alone who apply the rule of whether what machines do is "human" or "inhuman," as a machine intelligence does not yet exist that can challenge us on the subject.

The whole concept of "humanity" is extremely vague, and tied as we are to a human point of view, and depending on our personalities, some of us can't help but be uncomfortable with using terms like "human nature." I secretly feel that Yukikaze is a product of that discomfort. The author devoted a lot of his later works to portraying machine intelligence in what I've often thought of as his search for the key to unlock the very real conundrum of the human and the inhuman.

I find the image of Yukikaze as a battle spirit dancing in the skies of Faery to be a beautiful one. In fact, it's hard for me to believe that people can't see the beauty in such high-performance machines. However, although Yukikaze is beautiful, she was created to fight. I have a momentary thought: if Yukikaze were not a weapon of destruction and slaughter and had been made merely for the sake of flying, would it even matter as long as we deny her her own identity? Rei accepted her as an individual. He saw her not as a goddess of destruction but as a spirit of the wind who flew free. Yukikaze herself would most likely reject his selfish view of her as nonsense either way. For Yukikaze, the simple fact of her existence would most likely be enough.

RAN ISHIDOU

THE JAM ARE THERE

YUKIKAZE WAS FIRST released in 1984, a year when the topic of literary conversation was dominated by George Orwell's book. Today, there are probably people reading this revised edition of *Yukikaze* who weren't even born then.

At that time, Chōhei Kambayashi was already known as an energetic rising star who enthralled science fiction fans with a succession of works overflowing with a wisdom so sharp that it seemed to threaten to cut off the fingers of those who turned the pages. Even so, to be honest, I think the unusual breadth of his body of work up to that point generated a vague sense of unease in not a few of his readers. Yes, genius is a fairly impressive thing to behold, but where was this author going? What would he try to write next? Would he fall into the trap of being a jack-of-all-trades and master of none, a writer who produced nothing more than a string of clever diversions? But when a lone plane soared through the skies of Faery, I was convinced: this author was going to become one whose contributions would be writ large in the history of Japanese science fiction.

With *Yukikaze*, Chōhei Kambayashi distilled the essence of the themes on which he would stake his life as an author and infused them fully into a single work. What are "words"? What are "machines"? What are the "humans" who make and use them, and who are made and used in return? These basic questions were not presented as abstract philosophical arguments but were instead developed as concrete reality for the characters to deal with. Kambayashi was able to take these questions, which he had initially raised in his early short works like *Kotoba Tsukai Shi* (The Wordsmith) and others, and turn them into gripping, exciting stories in both novel and serialized form with the publication of *Kateki wa Kaizoku* (Pirates Are the Enemy) and *Yukikaze* within half a year of each other. It was philosophical speculation turned entertainment, and the enjoyment of the stories led to fresh speculation. It was truly what science fiction aspires to be.

The reader who has picked up *Yukikaze* knowing it's a special work but hasn't yet read it might not imagine how the basic questions of human existence are hidden in what appears to just be a story about a cool fighter plane battling enemies in the skies of an alien planet. That said, you don't have to read it as some sort of deep work that deals with these complicated issues. If you don't go into it looking for deep meaning and simply become intoxicated by the story, as I did, then you will undoubtedly be led to think about these important things on your own.

There're the JAM, who invade Earth via a hyperspace "Passageway" that appears suddenly in the Antarctic. On the other side of the Passageway lies the planet Faery, the actual location of which is unknown. To halt the alien invasion at the water's edge, so to speak, humanity organizes a supranational air force and constructs frontline bases on Faery. Within the Faery Air Force are a group of coldhearted pilots who keep even their own allies at a distance: the 5th Squadron of the Special Air Force, a.k.a. Boomerang Squadron. Their duty is to not directly join in the battle but rather to single-mindedly gather combat intelligence and then get back to base alive, even if it means letting their fellow pilots die. And for this purpose, they have been given Super Sylphs, the most powerful fighter planes in the Faery Air Force, which are equipped with highly advanced computer systems, high-output engines, and powerful weaponry for self-defense. The soldiers of Boomerang Squadron are, naturally, ultra-elite pilots, and in carrying out their heartless duty they trust the judgment of their computers far more than that of their fellow humans. They're people who require special personalities which allow them to practically become one with their machines; at one point in the novel they're described as "machines that are, through some accident of fate, in human form." First Lieutenant Rei Fukai, ace pilot of the SAF, flies into battle with Yukikaze, the plane he trusts more than any human, so that he can survive another day...

The basic architecture of the story is meant to separate us from the messy and complicated elements of human society and to create an isolated, experimental environment where we can observe humans continually fighting their enemies. Incidentally, this type of story—in which humans are placed in an isolated environment, subjected to certain rules and conditions, and then observed in minute detail—would become a hallmark of Kambayashi's writing. It's exactly the same as how a scientist cultivates a microorganism to experiment on and observe its behavior. Since these novels are written as though they are records of experiments, I like to refer to them as "experimental novels," with the phrase possessing a meaning different from its more common usage.

From this simple initial setup, the subjects of observation in *Yukikaze* are relatively easy to grasp. In the first place, it's not certain whether the enemy JAM are even living creatures. Or rather, they may be a type of life-form completely incomprehensible to us. Yet for all that they are an impenetrable mystery, the fact remains that they are a very real threat that "is here" right before our eyes. Yukikaze is used initially by Rei Fukai and the others as an interface to machine intelligence, gathering data in battles in an attempt to understand the JAM. You could say that understanding the JAM is the battle itself. In short, *Yukikaze* can be read as a story in which humans mired in ignorance fight a battle using "words" as an interface to clear a path to understanding and then to return through that field of unknowing. Kambayashi wrote this novel at a time when this was a recurrent theme for him as a writer. In creating the world of *Yukikaze* he peered into the unknown and carried out the special, dangerous duty—that is, the duty of a writer—of grasping what can be understood about the fundamental business of human existence, bringing it back to express it in words, and thus passing on the knowledge to other humans. For the author writing the story, for the reader who reads the story, and for all humanity, the battle with the JAM is not only alive but is nothing short of a living reality.

You can think of "words" and "machines" as strictly equivalent, indispensable interfaces that allowed people to affect and be affected by the chaotic natural world. This is because "machine" is nothing short of a "word" associated with a physical entity. When man differentiated himself from the natural world long ago, defined interfaces between man and the natural world—tools, words—simultaneously, necessarily came into being. Or rather, what we call "human" is likely that which seeks to affect the natural world through these interfaces.

Despite the fact that words and machines were created by humans they possess an independence and autonomy, moving on their own in ways which those who create them don't anticipate. No, perhaps this definition is backwards as well. If they did not act on their own, they wouldn't deserve to be called "machines" and "words." So then, exactly what sort of being is a human, whose only means of affecting the natural world is through these mysterious things that he has no hope of exerting complete control over? Does the essence of being human really lie in the words and machines we create, with the thing we call "self" merely a cast-off shell that remains here? And if our words and machines are what affect the world, won't we eventually become unnecessary to them? "No," Rei Fukai might mutter. "Humans are necessary in battle."

When we delve deeper into the relationship between humans and words and machines, we end up running into the question

of what the "self" means in relation to a human. I'm not referring to the personal meaning of the so-called search for self. For
example, as far as humans are concerned, self is not limited to
the hardware that genetics bestows on us. Just as people who
have lost an arm or a leg can experience the phenomenon of
sensing a phantom limb, humans also have the ability to accept
something added to their bodies as being part of themselves.
I don't mean that they become accustomed to them as tools
or machines but that they are literally regarded as a part of
the body.

The same goes for the mind. I hate to express it in such a
complicated way, but there's no evidence at all that the "you"
which you believe to be yourself is actually real. That which
you call your "real self" is an extremely nebulous thing because
humans, as social beings, cannot help but incorporate their
valuation by others in the construction of their self-image.
The nonsense you hear of "I've found my true self" is a bit like
having a piece of white paper painted black with only a bit of
white left in the middle, and then having the white part insist
"I am a white circle."

I also regard with suspicion those who say that society and
other individuals have no impact on them, those who view "I"
as a single-cognizance subject. A being capable of recognizing
that "I am here" cannot help but have its existence affected by, if
nothing else, the simple impact generated by the act of observing itself. This is what the Heideggerian school of philosophy
refers to as *dasein*, which roughly translates as "being there" or
"presence." While this is carried in rather pretentious-sounding
concepts like *geworfene Entwurf* (literally, "a thrown projec-
tion"), it can be summed up crudely as the existence which is
detached from the being who is "existing." If a being exists in
actual reality, its existence is not predicated on any description
or understanding, and so a being that exists constantly saying
"I am here" is engaged in a pointless reflexivity that is nothing
more than ridiculous or pathetic. The moment that you are

cognizant of "I," a definitive separation is formed between you and that concept of "I." If this cognizance doesn't occur, then no concept of "I" will arise.

It seems that we humans, from the first moment of our being human, from the moment of creating the phenomenon of self, became sad creatures who constantly estrange ourselves from the natural world. Whether philosophically, psychologically, or by any other means, the more we try to contrive some sort of a reason for our existence, the more we seem to whittle away at our ourselves. Humans are, themselves, machines. They are also words. So where in this battle with the natural world do humans fit in?

This quibbling of mine has dragged on too long. *Yukikaze* grants us its charming insight without having to engage in such a sophistic buildup. "Humans are necessary in battle." Kambayashi surely keeps writing science fiction to say this over and over again. Though it seems as if he constantly says in the novel that humans are manipulated by words and machines, that there's no real need for humans and that everything should be left to the words and the machines, we cannot take these statements at face value. The more Kambayashi tries to impart power to words and machines—the more he tries to make what is human into what is inhuman—the more he succeeds in throwing the concept of humanity into sharper and more vivid relief. Rather than humanity just dissolving into nothingness, we see just how "Humans are necessary in battle." Kambayashi is a unique author who writes about "humanity" by destroying it, in a style that nobody else can copy. If he were to be told that he couldn't portray humanity, meaning that he couldn't portray the clichéd emotions that you find rolling around anywhere in ordinary reality, he would probably take it as a compliment.

In 1999, fifteen years after Rei Fukai muttered "Humans are necessary in battle," Kambayashi unleashed his carefully prepared sequel, *Good Luck, Yukikaze,* upon the world. As if his intervening works had meticulously laid the groundwork for a new flight for Yukikaze, the novel was a masterpiece that drew on fifteen years of battle victories. In the first book, humans faced the threat of having their reality collapse under the power of "words" and "machines"; the struggles of the characters left the reader with a strong impression of trauma and confusion. (And because of that, the author earned such comparisons as "the Philip K. Dick of Japan.") In the sequel, however, humans seemed to be slowly but surely gathering the strength to take back their "world." We may be beings who are trapped in ignorance, who are manipulated by other beings or things beyond our comprehension, but: we are human and we are here, and people are necessary for battle. Got a problem with that? Or so the characters seem to say. And before long, the inhabitants of Kambayashi's world, these people who use words and machines as an interface to a natural world from which they are estranged, no longer seem weak but rather resolutely strong as they rise to confront that world. You could say that he's gone from "If you're not dancing, you'll probably be made to dance," the epigraph of *Kitsune to Odore* (Dance with a Fox), to "If you're being made to dance, then dance it your way." For example, this trend became extremely pronounced in 2001's *Eikyuu Kikan Souchi* (Eternal Return Device). The novel's characters fought with the author in a similarly strange situation, with the thrillingly depicted story of manufactured humans arguing with a superior being that could freely create and edit space.

I hope that those who have picked up this copy of *Yukikaze* will continue on and read its sequel, *Good Luck, Yukikaze*. It epitomizes the whole history of the evolution of Kambayashi's work. (I can't call it "growth," because it's evolution for the purpose of survival.) From that perspective, you can truly call *Yukikaze* Chōhei Kambayashi's life's work.

In bringing the JAM threat to her readers' attention, journalist Lynn Jackson says this: "The digital world seems to run counter to the very essence of our humanity. Our language as well. Our civilization itself. So what, exactly, are we doing turning over more and more of our existence to computers?" It's true that "our civilization" may run counter to human nature. So is the answer to go back to nature? I have a feeling that's what the JAM would want. Placing human beings on this grinding battlefield that dehumanizes them, repeating "People are necessary in battle" over and over is what allows us humans to remain human in the face of the JAM. Your weapons are the words and machines you couldn't otherwise comprehend. When you tire of the battle, you would do well to listen to the words of a soldier from *Good Luck, Yukikaze*: "It's not a question of what you should do, but rather what you want to do. That's the answer."

The truth is, *Yukikaze* is a declaration of war against the world, made by Chōhei Kambayashi and by you, the reader, as human beings. Engage!

RAY FUYUKI

ABBREVIATIONS AND ACRONYMS

ACS armament control system

ADAG Aerospace Defense Air Group

AAM air-to-air missile

ADC Aerospace Defense Corps

ACLS automatic carrier
landing system

A/G-AS anti-ground attack system

AGM air-to-ground missile

AIM air intercept missile

ALS automatic landing system

AWACS airborne early warning
and control system

BIT built-in test

CAP combat air patrol

CAS calibrated air speed

CDIP continuously displayed
impact point

CIC combat information control

DLC direct lift control

ECM electronic countermeasures

ECCM electronic counter-
countermeasures

ECS environmental control system

EDF Earth Defense Force

EMI electromagnetic interference

EMP electromagnetic pulse

EWO electronic warfare officer

FAB Faery Air Base

FAF Faery Air Force

FCC fire control computer

FCR fire control radar

FCS fire control system

GHQ General Headquarters

GLOC G-induced loss of
consciousness

GTGM ground-to-ground missiles

HAAM high-velocity air-to-air missile

HUD head-up display

HVM high-velocity missile

IFF Identification, Friend or Foe

JFS jet fuel starter

KIA killed in action

MAX maximum power

MFD multi-function display

MIL military power

MTI moving target indicator

RPM revolutions per minute

RPV remotely piloted vehicle

RTB return to base

RWR radar warning receiver

SAF Special Air Force

SAM surface-to-air missile

SOP standard operating procedure

SSL SAF Super Link

TAB tactical air base

TAF Tactical Air Force

TAISP tactical automated
information sensor pod

TARPS tactical airborne
reconnaissance pod system

TCG Tactical Combat Group

TCU tactical control unit

TD target designator

TDB tactical data bank

TDG Technology Development Center

UNEDO United Nations Earth
Defense Organization

Chōhei Kambayashi was born in 1953. In 1979 he won the 5th Hayakawa SF Contest with his debut work, the short story collection *Kitsune to Odore* (Dance with a Fox), and followed that with his first novel, *Anata no Tamashii ni Yasuragiare* (May Peace Be on Your Soul). His distinctive style and approach, and his thematic focus on the power of language and humanity's relationship with machines quickly made him a fan favorite. The author of over twenty novels and ten short story collections, he has won the prestigious Seiun Award seven times. In 1999 he won the 16th Japan SF Award for *Kototsubo* (The Word Vessel). Also in 1999, *Good Luck, Yukikaze*, the first sequel to *Yukikaze*, was published, followed by *Unbroken Arrow* in 2009.

HAIKASORU
THE FUTURE IS JAPANESE

THE LORD OF THE SANDS OF TIME By Issui Ogawa
Only the past can save the future as the cyborg O travels from the 26th century to ancient Japan and beyond. With the help of the princess Miyo and a ragtag troop of warriors from across history, O has a chance to save humanity and his own soul, but will it be at the cost of his life?

ALL YOU NEED IS KILL By Hiroshi Sakurazaka
It's battle armor versus aliens when the Mimics invade Earth. Private Kiriya dies in battle only to find himself reborn every day to fight again. Time is not on Kiriya's side, but he does have one ally: the American super-soldier known as the Full Metal Bitch.

ZOO By Otsuichi
A man receives a photo of his girlfriend every day in the mail...so that he can keep track of her body's decomposition. A deathtrap that takes a week to kill its victims. Haunted parks and airplanes held in the sky by the power of belief. These are just a few of the stories by Otsuichi, Japan's master of dark fantasy.

USURPER OF THE SUN By Housuke Nojiri
Schoolgirl Aki is one of the few witnesses to construction on the surface of Mercury. Soon an immense ring has been built around the sun and Earth has plunged into chaos. While the nations of the world prepare for war, Aki grows up with a thirst for knowledge and a hunger to make first contact with the enigmatic Builders. Winner of Japan's prestigious Seiun Award!

BATTLE ROYALE: THE NOVEL By Koushun Takami
The best-selling tour de force from Koushun Takami in a new edition, with an author's afterword and bonus material.

BRAVE STORY By Miyuki Miyabe
The paperback edition of the Batchelder Award-winning fantasy novel by Miyuki Miyabe.

THE BOOK OF HEROES By Miyuki Miyabe
When Yuriko's brother kills a classmate and then vanishes, it is up to her to journey into the nameless land where all stories are born, to face the ancient evil some dare call... The Hero. From the author of *Brave Story*, Miyuki Miyabe.

VISIT US AT WWW.HAIKASORU.COM